Imogen stopped and turned to face him, a soft, warm glow lighting up her eyes.

Looking down at her eager expression, Beresford felt his heart seem to skip a number of beats, and it occurred to him that, at this moment, there was nothing in the world that he would not do to keep that ardent look on her face. He was then obliged to remind himself of the vow he had made less than twenty-four hours previously, and as he did so he felt a sudden lowering of spirits—for it was now becoming quite obvious to him that every minute he spent in Imogen's company was going to place him in serious danger of breaking that vow, and it was absolutely imperative that he should not do so.

To become involved in a casual affair with Imogen Priestley was totally out of the question, and any suggestion of a more lasting attachment, highly compelling though that thought might be, was even more impossible to contemplate.

Dorothy Elbury lives in a quiet Lincolnshire village, an ideal atmosphere for writing her historical novels. She has been married to her husband (it was love at first sight, of course!) for forty-five years, and they have three children and four grandchildren. Her hobbies include visiting museums and historic houses, and handicrafts of various kinds.

Recent titles by the same author:

A HASTY BETROTHAL
THE VISCOUNT'S SECRET

THE OFFICER AND THE LADY

Dorothy Elbury

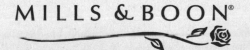

MILLS & BOON®

First published in Great Britain 2005
Paperback edition 2006
Harlequin Mills & Boon Limited,
Eton House, 18-24 Paradise Road, Richmond, Surrey TW9 1SR

© Dorothy Elbury 2005

ISBN 0 263 84633 4

Set in Times Roman 10¼ on 12 pt.
04-0206-90175

Printed and bound in Spain
by Litografia Rosés S.A., Barcelona

THE OFFICER AND THE LADY

Chapter One

August 1816

As the two carriages reached the brow of the hill, the driver of the first, having heard a sharp rap from within, brought his team swiftly to a halt and cocked his ear to await further instructions from his passengers.

'Well, here it is, David,' said Matt Beresford, as he lowered the window and, with a broad sweep of his hand, indicated to his companion the extent of his late father's property. 'Thornfield—I suppose you might call it my "ancestral home"—for what it is worth!'

David Seymour gave a wry smile. His friend's sarcastic tone had not failed to register.

'Still not really made up your mind, have you?' he observed.

Beresford shrugged. 'As I recollect, I hardly seem to have been given a great deal of choice in the matter.'

Leaning forward, he opened the door, leapt lightly out of the carriage and motioned to the driver. 'Wait here for about ten minutes, then carry on—my guess is that you will find the house gates about half a mile further up the road.'

Turning to Seymour once more, he said, 'I noticed a door

in the wall further back—I have a mind to try and get into the park and see what sort of state it's in. You go on and I will meet you at the front of the house.'

With a resigned sigh, his companion watched him striding back down the lane. He had been acquainted with Beresford for some nine years now, ever since they had both set sail for India under the aegis of Seymour's father who had, at that time, been a Resident District Commissioner with the British East India Trading Company. With Colonel Seymour's help and support both young men had carved out very successful careers for themselves within the company and might possibly have remained in Hyderabad for the foreseeable future had it not been for the urgent and totally unexpected summons that Beresford had received from his estranged father's solicitor some six months earlier.

Over the years, Seymour had managed, partly from the occasional conversation with his friend, but mostly from local gossip, to glean a good deal of Beresford's early history. He was aware that Matt's father, Sir Matthew Beresford, who at that time had held the office of Governor of Madras, had been so racked with grief at the death in childbirth of his beloved young wife, that he had instantly rejected his newborn son, having chosen to lay the full blame for the unfortunate lady's demise upon the infant's innocent head.

Accompanied only by a returning Company junior and a hastily acquired wetnurse, the child had been bundled on to the first available East Indiaman to sail for the home country, where he had been abandoned into the care of his maternal grandparents. Although Sir Matthew had, through legal channels, arranged adequate financial provision for his son's upkeep and education, these ageing relatives had been obliged, forthwith, to entrust their grandson's welfare to the hands of a succession of nursery maids and colourless governesses. Consequently, the young Beresford might have led a cheerless and somewhat prosaic upbringing had not an acquaintance of his grandfather chanced to recommend the services of an excellent, if rather avant-garde, tutor, one Thomas Hopkirk.

In addition to making sure that his young pupil was furnished with a wide and varied education, this highly enlightened academic had taken it upon himself to see that the boy was equipped with all the necessary sporting skills that a gentleman of his station might be likely to require. The very fact that Beresford had straightway knuckled down and made such a success of his mandatory career in India was, without doubt, due mainly to Hopkirk's years of devoted teaching.

'But, did you never attempt to contact your father?' Seymour had asked in amazement, when hearing his friend's history for the first time.

'My grandparents tried on several occasions to win him over,' Beresford told him. 'However, as he seemed bent on continuing to ignore all of our communications, Grandfather finally gave up trying.'

'But, when you yourself were older?'

'You may be sure I did,' said Beresford, with an emphatic nod. 'As soon as I had completed my time at Oxford and had gained my majority, I made it my business to seek him out but, since his solicitor refused to divulge his current address, this was not at all easy. However, I eventually managed to track him down to his club in St James's and screwed up the courage to confront him.'

His bright blue eyes clouded over in remembrance of that fateful meeting. 'At the time, I was desperate to join my college friends in the Peninsula and I petitioned him to use his influence to recommend me for a commission.' He laughed, almost awkwardly. 'I seem to recall I fancied myself as a lieutenant in the Rifle Brigade!'

'Well, you always were a damned fine shot!' laughed his friend, then his face at once grew serious. 'But your father still refused to acknowledge you? After twenty-one years he must surely have recovered from his earlier resentment?'

Beresford shook his head. 'Apparently not. Certainly, my turning up had the most curious effect upon him. He took one look at me, his face went as white as a sheet and he then became quite abusive—accusing me of downright effrontery and so on. I was somewhat taken aback by his manner but, seeing that as soon as I finished my time at Oxford, he had chosen to withdraw his financial support, I felt that I had no alternative but to persevere with my request. He then insisted that he had no contacts with the military—I later discovered that to be quite untrue, of course.'

'But he did find you a position with the Company?' persisted Seymour, finding his friend's father's attitude hard to fathom, always having had the benefit of a close and harmonious relationship with his own parent.

'Yes, he did,' admitted Beresford. 'Although, that came about in a rather odd way, too. He had all but dismissed me—I had, in fact, turned to go—when he suddenly called me back and offered to fund my passage on the East Indiaman that was about to set sail for the sub-continent. He then called for some writing materials and straight away scribbled out the letter of introduction to your father—and the rest, of course, you know.'

Seymour nodded. 'Sir Matthew was my father's mentor when *he* joined the Company back in '82—I heard he made a mint in his heyday. A regular "nabob"—or so I have been told.'

'Pretty much consistent with the type of man he seems to have been,' Beresford replied, his tone unemotional.

Seymour was chagrined. 'Sorry, old man. I meant no insult—it was just a phrase they used at the time when one of the Company chaps got back home with a huge fortune—no disrespect to your sire.'

Beresford grinned at his friend, giving him a playful punch in the shoulder. 'Forget it, David. We both know that most of our predecessors made their piles by underhand and far from scrupulous deals in the opium trade. I hold no brief for my father—I never even knew the man. Although, to be fair, it is thanks to him that I met you, and a truer and better friend a man would be hard pressed to come by.'

Since his father had made it clear that he intended to offer his son no further financial support, Beresford had reluctantly found himself more or less obliged to take up Sir Matthew's offer, and had forthwith presented himself at the Company's Head Office in Leadenhall Street, from where he was directed to David Seymour's lodgings, just prior to that young man's own embarkation to join his father.

Almost nine years had passed since that fateful day, during which time neither Seymour nor Beresford had had occasion to return to England. Seymour had never hankered after his homeland, as both of his parents were permanently domiciled in Mysore, and Beresford had had no reason to do so. His grandparents were no longer living and, as far as he was aware, he had no other relatives apart from his father, who had, in any event, ignored all of his early letters from India. It seemed that all communication between the two of them had ended with that abrupt meeting in St James's and it was, therefore, with considerable surprise that, in the January of this present year, Matt Beresford had opened the letter from his father's solicitor to be informed, somewhat bluntly, of Sir Matthew's death. To his even greater astonishment the writer had then informed him that, due to an anomaly in the wording of his father's will, there was the distinct possibility that, since he appeared to be Sir Matthew's heir, he must return to England as soon as possible, in order to untangle the complications of his father's bequests.

Beresford had been inclined to ignore the summons, but his friend Seymour had eventually persuaded him that they were long overdue a trip to their native land and, now that the war in Europe had ended, to be present at the prospective celebrations in London might prove to be quite exciting.

'And just think of the scores of lovely young ladies we shall meet!' Seymour had declared, his hazel eyes gleaming in anticipation. 'The only females we come across here are either taken or well past it!'

'Oh? I rather thought that you seemed to be doing pretty well with Mrs Ledger the last time I looked!' observed his friend, laughing. 'You were both certainly taking your time looking for her gloves in the shrubbery last week.'

'Oh, Susan Ledger!' shrugged Seymour carelessly. 'I have moved on since then—matter of fact, I chanced upon a rather pretty little ayah in Strickland's nursery on Saturday after the polo match—what about you?'

Beresford shook his head. 'Had a bit of a fling with Lillian Ashton before she went off to marry old Bunter in Madras last month,' he said briefly, 'but you are quite right, women are pretty thin on the ground this year.'

'And only the blessed monsoons to look forward to,' Seymour reminded him. 'Good time to get away, if you ask me—just for a few months, anyway. What do you say? You can sort out your pa's legal tangles, whatever they are, and then we can have some fun in dear old London Town!'

Unfortunately, Sir Matthew's legal tangles had turned out to be something of a nightmare since it appeared that, unbeknown to his son, he had remarried some nineteen years previously and had produced a second family, comprising a wife and two children. However, although it had clearly been his intention to leave them well provided for, not one of his bequests could be fulfilled until it was resolved which of his sons was the rightful heir.

When he had instructed his solicitor to draw up his will, he had bequeathed the bulk of his estate to his 'son', obviously intending that his property should go to the now sixteen-year-old

Nicholas, having either conveniently dismissed the existence of his firstborn or, as Matt was inclined to suspect, had presumed that, being as fair-skinned as his late mother, the boy must surely have succumbed to the rigours of the unforgiving Asian climate.

When Beresford learned of his father's duplicity, he had coldly instructed the solicitor to carry out what he felt must have been Sir Matthew's true intentions. Through his own hard work and diligent application to duty, he himself had accumulated more than enough wealth to last him a lifetime and he wanted no further part in his father's affairs.

'Unfortunately, sir,' Mr Robbins had sternly informed him, 'due to the continuous lack of funding since your father's death last year, the estate is now in a somewhat parlous condition and Lady Beresford who, if I might be so bold as to point out, is your stepmother, is, as such, entitled to expect your support!'

Further protestations had proved futile, with Mr Robbins constantly reminding Beresford of his duty to his family.

'I will do my best to sort out the title at this end,' he assured the exasperated Beresford, 'but you really must go up to Lincolnshire and see Thornfield for yourself. The family has been without proper funds for almost a year now—it has taken me almost as long to establish your whereabouts. Your family is clearly in dire need of the help and guidance of someone who has had as much experience in land management as you have had, sir.'

'But surely you could have released the female portions?' retorted Beresford angrily. 'And, if I relinquish any claim to this—Nicholas's—inheritance, then surely they have some sort of estate manager who can deal with the other matters?'

'Best go and see for yourself, sir,' the solicitor advised him. 'Then you may return home with a clear conscience.'

Chapter Two

Beresford approached the wooden door in Thornfield's perimeter wall with slight trepidation. He was by no means a man of nervous disposition, but the idea of coming face to face with an entirely new and unwanted set of relatives—however tenuous their connection—was not one towards which he could bring himself to feel the slightest spark of enthusiasm.

To his surprise, he found the gate unlocked. He frowned as he entered the park, carefully securing the door behind him. This was certainly not good practice and, as he cast his eyes around the copse through which the path towards the house ran, he was quick to register a good many signs of neglect: fallen saplings, uncut brambles and a profusion of weeds, the extent of which threatened to overtake the path itself.

He walked on, dismally reminding himself that he might well have to use his own money to put these matters to rights, if they were to be attended to before winter set in, and his irritation grew as his mind dwelt on the vexing imposition with which he had been saddled.

As he rounded a bend in the path, he became aware of the sound of raised voices in the copse some short distance ahead. His curiosity raised, he began to tread more carefully and sidled quietly towards the clearing from where the altercation seemed to be emanating.

Peering through the bushes, he managed to make out the figures of a man and a young woman, apparently engaged in a heated argument. The man had the dark, almost swarthy look of a gypsy about him and seemed to be threatening the girl in some way. She had her back towards Beresford but, the minute he saw the man appearing to raise his fist at her, he cast aside the bushes and immediately leapt to her defence.

The man staggered back in astonishment at Beresford's sudden arrival and, as Beresford's hand reached out to grab his collar, one arm came up in self-defence and the other, holding a shotgun, swung wildly in Beresford's direction.

'Who the hell are you?' he spluttered, 'And what are you doing on private property?'

By this time he had his gun under control with both hands and aimed squarely at Beresford's chest. His dark eyes glittered as he took in the interloper's appearance, which, judging by the immaculate superfine breeches and made-to-measure jacket, was clearly not that of a tramp or vagabond. He hesitated, momentarily unsure of his ground until the sound of barely smothered laughter caused him to swing round angrily to confront the young woman behind him.

'What's so funny?' he demanded. 'You know this man?'

Unable to stifle her amusement, the girl, who had been watching the by-play between the two men with unconcealed interest, shook her head and delved into her pocket for a handkerchief to mop her streaming eyes.

'It has to be Matthew Beresford,' she choked, still trying to control her mirth. 'Thornfield's new master, Mr Wentworth—we were told he would be arriving shortly—and now, it seems, here he is!'

Wentworth's eyes swivelled back to Beresford, who was

presently engaged in removing the leaves and twigs that had attached themselves to his clothing during his headstrong dash.

'You're Matthew Beresford?' he asked truculently. 'How d'ye come to be up here in the copse then?'

'I take it that you are a member of my staff, my good man,' replied Beresford coldly, casually inspecting his cuffs. 'I presume that you wish to keep your position, whatever it is?'

The man blanched as the girl quickly interposed on his behalf. 'This is Philip Wentworth, sir—he is—has been in charge of the estate since Sir Matthew died.'

Beresford gave her a brief glance; a strikingly pretty girl, with soft brown hair and wide grey eyes, wearing a faded blue cotton print gown, a rather battered chipstraw bonnet and carrying what looked to be a basket of wild strawberries. Probably one of the upper maids or some such. He concluded that he had probably interrupted a lovers' quarrel.

'And you are?' he queried.

Her amusement disappeared in an instant. A slight flush crept into her cheeks and she straightened her shoulders. She recognised a put-down when she heard one. 'I am Imogen Priestley,' she replied in an even voice, meeting his gaze squarely.

Beresford merely nodded and proceeded to walk back to the path.

'Perhaps you would see that the wall gate is kept locked in future,' he threw at the now sullen Wentworth as he passed him.

A slight exclamation from the girl halted him and he turned to find her at his elbow.

'I am afraid that was me,' she blurted out, her hand to her mouth. 'I went across the lane to see if there were more berries under the hedge and—I must have forgotten to lock the gate when I came back. Wentworth is not to blame—on this occasion.'

Intrigued, Beresford studied her more carefully. Something about her bearing, or perhaps it was the lilting timbre of her voice, caused him to reappraise his first impression of her. Not a servant, certainly, perhaps a governess?

'You are returning to the house?' he asked.

She nodded. 'I would be happy to show you the way, although, to be perfectly truthful, you can hardly get lost as the path goes straight down to the front driveway.'

He smiled. 'I had an idea that it might.'

Imogen, hurrying to keep pace with Beresford's long strides, found a great deal to admire in his appearance as they wended their way through the copse together. Tall and undeniably handsome, she could see that his complexion, even after the long passage home, still held the healthy glow of the fading remnants of the tropical suntan that he had acquired from his years on the Indian continent, emphasising the startling blueness of his eyes and the guinea-gold brightness of his hair.

Slightly discomfited by the searching glances that were being cast in his direction, Beresford walked on in silence for a few moments then, 'How did you guess who I am?' he asked curiously. 'Wentworth was right in his assumption that I could have been anyone.'

Imogen laughed. 'Not so, sir. I have seen your mother's portrait. You are as like as a man can be to a woman—same golden locks, same blue eyes…' She stopped in confusion as Beresford gripped her arm and swung her towards him.

'My mother's portrait?' he demanded. 'Where have you seen my mother's portrait?'

She tried to pull away. 'You are hurting me, sir,' she protested.

He loosened his grip immediately, but kept hold of her nevertheless. 'I beg your pardon. It was not my intention to startle you. You say you have seen a portrait of my mother?'

'Well, yes,' she averred, 'although it was some years ago, when I was younger. It used to be kept in one of the attics where we were wont to play hide-and-seek and I often wondered who the lady could be, but when I asked about it Sir Matthew got very angry and forbade us all to go up there again, so it could well have been removed by now.'

She stared pointedly at his hand. 'You may let go of my arm now, if you please, sir.'

He dropped his hand as though it had been stung and pondered over her words. Then a thought struck him.

'You say you have lived at Thornfield since you were a child?'

'All my life, practically.'

At the questioning look on his face she smiled. 'Lady Beresford took me in when I was six years old,' she said patiently. 'Jessica was barely two at the time…'

'Jessica?'

'Your half-sister.' She looked at him quizzically for a moment. 'You do not seem to know a great deal about us, if I may say so.'

'Nothing at all, as it happens,' he said bluntly. 'I was totally unaware of your presence until two weeks ago. You have the upper hand here, it seems.'

'How do you mean?'

He thrust his hands into his pockets and strode purposefully on.

'Well, you all presumably know everything there is to know about me, I dare say.'

She hurried after him. 'No such thing!' she protested. 'None of us were even aware of your existence until a few months ago. Lady Beresford has barely recovered from the shock. Apparently, Mr Robbins was the only one in whom Sir Matthew confided and even he thought that you might well be—oh, dear, I did not mean to say that!'

Beresford let out a hollow laugh. 'I have long suspected that my father hoped I was—dead, that is. I am almost certain that was his intention when he sent me out to India. Robbins intimated that it had taken several months to track me down. Personally, I wish he had not gone to so much trouble!'

'Oh, no! Please do not say such things! I, for one, am very glad that he found you!' came her incredulous rejoinder.

Intrigued at her somewhat vehement response, he swivelled his eyes in her direction and was startled to register the very animated expression that had suddenly appeared on her face. What was even more curious, however, was that her eyes, which he had previously thought to be an indeterminate shade of grey, now appeared to be a much more vibrant colour and streaked with the most amazing flashes of silver. For a moment he stared down at her lovely features in a fascinated confusion then, hurriedly collecting himself, he blinked and shook his head.

'Well, now that I am here, I will certainly endeavour to do what I can to sort out the mess Sir Matthew left you in,' he heard himself saying and then cursed himself for uttering such an insensitive remark.

Imogen, however, seemed to have taken no offence at either his protracted stare or his lack of tact. 'Yes, I was perfectly certain that you would,' she acknowledged. 'As soon as I set eyes on you I could see that you were not a man to be trifled with and I must tell you that I've been having such problems! Wentworth has been proving most uncooperative and the books are in such a state. It will be a relief to be able to go through them properly at last!'

Beresford frowned. 'I think you may leave all that sort of thing safely in my hands from now on,' he said. 'Is that what you and Wentworth were arguing about back there?'

She hesitated. 'Well—no—not exactly. It was quite another matter—it will keep—anyway, here we are at the house at last!'

She sounded relieved and Beresford found himself wondering if his first supposition about her and Wentworth had been correct after all and was startled to find that the thought of such a liaison was quite distasteful to him.

The wooded pathway had taken them down to the gravelled driveway at the front of the house and, as he got his first glimpse of the building, Beresford felt bound to concede that Thornfield was certainly a fine-looking mansion house, its graceful neo-classical architecture highly reminiscent of the Senior Resident's house back home in Calcutta. Standing three storeys high, with more than twenty elegantly pedimented windows visible on its east-facing cream-stuccoed Palladian façade alone, it boasted a columned *porte-cochère,* which not only covered the impressive-looking flight of steps that led up to the front door, but a goodly portion of the front drive as well.

Motioning him in the direction of the steps, Imogen made for the archway that led to the north wing of the house. 'I need to get these strawberries to Cook.' She smiled. 'Otherwise we shall have no dessert with our dinner!' And with that, she whisked away through the archway.

Looking slightly bemused, Beresford watched her until she vanished from his sight then, suddenly conscious of the fact that the two carriages were already standing within the *porte-cochère* and that his friend Seymour seemed to be having some difficulty directing the disparate group of rather hapless-looking servants in the business of unloading the baggage, he groaned and hurried forward to take control of the situation. Having been used to the well-run, orderly life of a hill-station for so long, it seemed to him that the entire household looked to be in a total shambles.

When all of the trunks and boxes had finally been carried into the rather dust-ridden but magnificently appointed great hall, he looked about him, expecting to see some sort of welcoming (or otherwise) committee, but, apart from one elderly manservant who was shuffling uncomfortably at his elbow, there was no one else in sight.

'Remarkably shy lot, it seems, your new family,' grinned Seymour, unbuttoning his topcoat and handing it, along with his hat and gloves, to the servant.

Beresford frowned at him and looked down at the man.

'Where might I find Lady Beresford?' he enquired. 'She will be expecting me, I imagine. Kindly take me to her at once.'

The old man shook his head. 'Her ladyship will be indisposed, sir—that is to say, she never rises before noon and it is more than my life's worth to have Mamselle disturb her before then.'

Beresford's brows knitted together in exasperation and he bit back an angry retort, cautioning himself that it would not do to lose his temper at this stage. Taking a deep breath, he walked towards one of the rooms that led out of the hall, which, judging from the shelves of books that he had glimpsed through its open doorway, appeared to be either the library or an office of some sort.

'Very well, my man,' he said curtly. 'You may bring me a decanter of brandy. Mr Seymour and I will take a little refreshment while we wait upon her ladyship's convenience.'

'Yes, sir. I will see what I can do, sir.' The man bowed and scurried away.

The room was, in fact, a large and very well-stocked library, but, to Beresford's dismay, it was dominated by a huge portrait of the late Sir Matthew that hung above the fireplace. Wearing the most forbidding expression, his late father seemed to be glowering down at them with arrant disapproval. Taking one horrified look at it, Beresford shuddered and swung one of the leather armchairs round to face away from the fireplace before taking his seat.

'What an extraordinary welcome!' commented Seymour, following his friend's example. 'It certainly looks as though you are going to have your work cut out here, Matt—not a friendly face in the place, as far as I can see.'

For no apparent reason, the image of a pair of laughing grey eyes shot into Beresford's mind. He shrugged it off, saying, 'We could certainly do with old Jimi and his houseboys here, David. A more slapdash set of servants I have yet to come across. It is clear that they need to be taken in hand—and so few of them—did you notice? One would have thought, in such a large establishment—'

His comments were interrupted by the arrival of the elderly manservant, who entered the room bearing a silver tray upon which rested a half-empty decanter and a pair of glasses.

'Best I could do, sir,' panted the man, laying down his burden on the drum table at Beresford's elbow. 'Mr Wentworth keeps the keys to the cellar, sir, and I cannot seem to locate him just at the moment.'

'Who do you suppose this Mr Wentworth is?' Seymour asked curiously, after the man had departed and closed the door behind him.

'Oh, I have already had the dubious pleasure of making that fellow's acquaintance,' returned Beresford. 'Met him up in the copse—apparently my father's estate manager—a pretty shady sort of cove, if you want my opinion. Doubt if I will keep him on, but I suppose I shall have to make use of him to begin with. Or, at least until I get the feel of the place. Difficult to see why he should have the keys to the cellar, though. More the butler's province, I should have thought.'

The two men drank their brandy in companionable silence, each mulling over the strange events of the morning.

All at once, the door to the library burst open and a very young woman rushed headlong into the room, her eyes alight with excitement.

'It is really true!' she exclaimed, clapping her hands. 'You have arrived, at last!'

Beresford and Seymour scrambled hastily to their feet in some confusion, their discomposure due partly to her sudden arrival but, more probably, because she was without doubt the loveliest creature that either of them had ever set eyes on. Ash-blonde hair, falling in entrancing ringlets to her shoulders, huge emerald green eyes, framed by long, sooty lashes and soft, rose-petal lips that were smiling the most captivating smile a man could ever wish to see. And, if that were not enough, beneath her simple white muslin gown, the girl clearly had the figure of an angel.

Both men held their breath as the vision looked from one to the other with a perplexed frown.

'But *one* of you has to be my new brother!' she said, with a small pout. 'I was sure of it—but neither of you resembles Papa in the slightest!'

Beresford let out a sigh and strode forward with his hand extended. 'I am Matthew Beresford,' he conceded. 'You must be—Jessica?'

She nodded swiftly and, reaching forward, took his hand in both of hers and proceeded to drag him towards the nearby sofa.

Highly amused, he offered no resistance and, at her command, sat down on the sofa beside her. She gave him a little flutter of her lashes before bestowing him with the full benefit of her extraordinarily bewitching eyes.

'You have been *so* long in coming,' she said plaintively, holding his hand in hers and stroking it gently.

The little minx, thought Beresford, grinning inwardly. Barely eighteen years of age and already well on the way to becoming a highly accomplished flirt! He would be prepared to wager that she had broken quite a few hearts amongst the local swains. He turned his head, in order to catch Seymour's eye in a conspiratorial wink, but blinked in despair as he registered the look on his friend's face. Oh, Lord, he sighed, here we go again! It was clear that there would be no support from that quarter!

'England is rather a long way from India,' was his apologetic reply to his new sister.

She nibbled at her lower lip in the most provocative way. 'I have been wanting you to come so dreadfully. Everything has been so horrid since Papa died. I have not had a single new gown for over a year—and we missed all of the Victory celebrations in London! I did so want to see the Prince Regent in all his finery!'

Beresford hid the smile that was forming. 'Well, as you can see, I am here now,' he said soothingly as he patted her hand. 'And I am sure we can sort out all your troubles very soon.'

'And I may have my allowance again?' Her wide eyes were fixed upon his once more and she clasped her hands together in pleading entreaty.

'I dare say that can be arranged without a great deal of difficulty,' he assured her laughingly, as he rose to his feet. 'But I really do need to speak to your mama without delay—your butler tells me that she is indisposed?'

'Oh, Mama is *always* indisposed,' she retorted, with a careless toss of her silver curls. 'She will come down soon, I should think, but only to take her nuncheon in the little salon and then she will spend the afternoon resting on the *chaise-longue* in there.'

'But she knows I have arrived, surely?' he asked, perplexed.

Jessica pondered over this, then nodded. 'I should imagine so,' she said. 'Imo will have told her.'

'Imo?'

Jessica jumped up. 'Cousin Imo—you know. She is probably the one you will need to talk to, anyway. Mama *never* concerns herself with household affairs. Imo deals with all that sort of thing.' She flashed him another of her dazzling smiles. 'I will go and fetch her for you, if you like,' she offered, as she darted like quicksilver out of the room.

Beresford gazed after her in despair. What sort of a household had he inherited? A reluctant staff, an inefficient manager, a sister who was, clearly, far more proficient in the art of flirtation than she should be, a sickly stepmother and now, it appeared, some sort of dependant spinster cousin. He grimaced, wondering what on earth the boy, Nicholas, might prove to have amiss with him.

A heavy sigh from Seymour caught his attention and he turned to see his friend gazing soulfully into the far distance.

'What an absolute beauty!' his colleague gasped, as he caught Beresford's enquiring glance. 'Did you see those eyes?'

'Stow it, David,' replied Beresford, somewhat tetchily. 'I trust that I do not have to remind you that the child is my sister.'

'Hardly a child, old man,' Seymour was quick to point out. 'But I take your meaning—she will come to no harm at my hands, I promise you.'

'I never thought otherwise,' said Beresford absently, his mind on more important matters. 'And now, it would seem that we have no option but to wait here for this Imo woman, who-ever she is.'

Chapter Three

Imogen had barely had time to change out of her working garb into a more respectable morning gown when she was summoned by her aunt. Quickly pinning her soft brown curls into a careless twist at the back of her head, she hurried to her aunt's bedchamber.

'Oh, Imogen,' wailed Lady Beresford, wringing her hands. 'He has come! I feel sure that he will turn us all out! What is to become of us?'

Blanche Beresford was a plumper and more faded replica of her daughter, reluctantly owning to some thirty-eight summers. Sir Matthew had married her at the height of her first Season when she, too, had been an acclaimed beauty. But, unlike Jessica, she had always been of a rather retiring, delicate nature, which, living with the stern and autocratic Sir Matthew, along with the several miscarriages that she had suffered during her marriage, had gradually turned her into a nervous shadow of her former self. Privately she had regarded her husband's sudden death as something of a welcome reprieve from her marital duties, but the complications of the subsequent legal revelations, followed by the increasing privation, had had the effect of reducing her to a clinging neurotic.

'Hush, Aunt,' Imogen soothed her. 'I am certain that he will do no such thing. He seemed quite a reasonable sort of gentleman.'

'You promise me that you will not leave Thornfield until we know what the man's intentions are?'

'I have no intention of going anywhere until I see that you are perfectly comfortable, Aunt Blanche. Widdy is quite prepared to travel to Kendal without me and I shall join her as soon as it is convenient. Please do not distress yourself any further.'

'But how I shall ever manage without you I cannot begin to contemplate,' moaned Lady Beresford, clutching at her niece's hand.

Imogen gently extracted herself from her aunt's grip.

'Now, dearest, you promised me that you would not continue to repine about my leaving. We have discussed the matter many times and you must see that I cannot remain here. Mr Beresford is not my relative and, if he is to be the new master of Thornfield, I have no claim upon his generosity.' She gave a little grimace. 'Apart from which, I do not care for the idea that he might easily believe me to be dependent upon him.'

Aghast, her aunt stared at up her. 'Then you have already judged him to be the tyrant I supposed him?'

Imogen laughed and bent to kiss the other woman's pale cheek. 'I hardly had time to form any real opinion of him,' she said. 'But I did get the impression that he was not—how shall I put it—unapproachable.'

'Unlike your uncle,' exclaimed Lady Beresford bitterly then, closing her eyes, she lay back against her pillows. 'I have another of my headaches coming on, dearest. I believe I shall remain in my room today. If you could send Francine to me…?'

Sighing with exasperation, Imogen quietly closed the door of Lady Beresford's bedchamber behind her and walked to the head of the long, curving staircase and stood for some moments with her hand on the balustrade, wondering how she was ever going to persuade her aunt to venture out of her bedchamber long enough to be introduced to her new step-son.

Suddenly, her brow furrowed in a despairing frown as, from her vantage point above the hallway, she was dismayed to observe Jessica dashing headlong out of the library. Her cousin then proceeded to hurl herself up the stairs two at a time, in a most unladylike manner.

'Oh, there you are, Imo,' she panted, as Imogen put out her hands to prevent the girl falling at her feet. 'Why ever did you fail to mention that the man was an absolute Corinthian! Just like one of those Greek gods you see in the paintings and both he and his gentleman friend are so adorably bronzed!'

Imogen shook her head. 'I do wish you would try for a little more decorum, Jess. All this rushing about is not at all seemly at your age, you know. If Widdy were to have seen you…'

Jessica made a little moue and tried to flatten her disarranged curls. 'Sorry, Imo. I was *so* excited. I am to have my allowance as soon as Matthew—' She stopped and a questioning frown appeared on her face. 'I suppose I may call him Matthew?' she asked.

'I should imagine so,' laughed Imogen. 'He is your brother, after all—although you had, perhaps, better check with him first. It is possible that he may prefer some other form of address.'

Jessica considered this. 'Well, he is not *Sir* Matthew,' she reasoned. 'Papa was awarded his knighthood for his commercial success in India and it was not hereditary, was it?'

'Very true,' nodded Imogen, as she turned to leave. 'Your brother is plain Mr Beresford.'

'Hardly plain!' chuckled her cousin saucily, then gave a little gasp. 'Oh, but I almost forgot! I am come to fetch you to him—he is waiting for you in the library with the other gentleman.'

'Waiting for me?' Imogen was puzzled. 'Why should he be waiting for me?'

Jessica wriggled uncomfortably. 'Well, I sort of told him that you ran the household!' she said, with an apologetic blush.

'Oh, Jess, you really are the limit!' began Imogen crossly, then paused as she realised the intrinsic truth of her young cousin's remark. It *was* true; for the past twelve months or so, at any rate, the entire day-to-day running of the household had devolved upon her and it was she, along with the Beresfords' stalwart governess, Miss Jane Widdecombe, who had striven to keep all their heads above water. Using her own quite generous allowance, which had been left to her by her parents, she had succeeded in eking out a fairly basic living for the family when the estate funds had eventually dried up. By careful budgeting she had even managed to pay some of the servants parts of their wages, although the majority of the staff, having seen how matters were turning out, had gradually drifted away to seek other employment. Matthew Beresford had arrived not a moment too soon, as far as she was concerned, and as soon as she had acquainted him with the bones of the various problems that were besetting her, she and Widdy would be on their way to the Lake District to join Miss Widdecombe's friend Margery Knox in running the little school that she had recently set up.

She smoothed the folds of her blue-sprigged muslin gown into place, tucked back a wayward tendril that was threatening to escape its confinement and, tentatively tapping on the library door, entered the room.

Beresford, who was sitting in the window embrasure on the far side of the room dismally contemplating the park's neglected state, failed to register her knock and it was Seymour who was first made aware of her presence.

Leaping to his feet, he walked forward to meet her. 'How do you do?' he said eagerly, his hand outstretched in welcome. 'David Seymour, at your service, ma'am—friend of Matt's.' He gave her a wide smile, his candid hazel-coloured eyes lighting up at this fresh onslaught on his rather susceptible senses.

The slight tension Imogen had been feeling evaporated as she returned his smile. She perceived that he was not as tall as Beresford, his tan was slightly deeper and he was of a stockier build, with short, dark brown hair. He, too, was dressed immaculately although, as Beresford approached, she found herself observing that Seymour's kidskin breeches and superfine jacket did not seem to sit nearly so well on him as did his colleague's. She turned to greet the newcomer.

'You asked to see me, I believe?'

Momentarily taken aback at Imogen's altered appearance, Beresford looked perplexed. Good heavens! Surely this attractive young woman could not be Cousin Imo? Now that he was able to study her more closely he saw that she was really quite lovely, her oval face blessed not only with a smooth, creamy complexion, but also a neat, straight little nose and wide, well-shaped lips. Barely a head shorter than his own more than six foot height, she had a very fine figure, 'nicely rounded in all the right places', as Seymour would say. He cleared his throat.

'Ah! Cousin Imo!' he exclaimed, taking her hand in his.

Their eyes met and, once again, he noticed those tiny flashes of silver.

'I believe I have already informed you that my name is Imogen Priestley,' she said, in a level voice. 'And you are mistaken about our kinship, Mr Beresford. Lady Beresford is my aunt—my father was her brother. Her ladyship was good enough to take me in when both of my parents perished in a carriage accident.'

'I beg your pardon,' he replied, bending over her hand. 'It seems that I still have a great deal to learn. Please forgive my ignorance.'

She looked at him suspiciously. She could have sworn that his lips were twitching. Surely the man was not laughing at her? She swiftly withdrew her hand and moved towards the sofa. Taking her seat gracefully, she adjusted her skirts with studied nonchalance before saying, 'Jessica said that you wished to speak to me. If there is anything I can help you with, I am at your service. As I mentioned earlier, I, too, have one or two matters that I should like to bring to your attention.'

She looked pointedly at Seymour, then turned once more to Beresford. 'Perhaps your colleague would care to be shown his room?' she suggested. 'Shall I ring for Allardyce? I am sure that your luggage will have been taken upstairs by now.'

'No need, ma'am,' cut in Seymour, as he made for the door. 'I'm perfectly happy to seek out the old fellow myself—give me a chance to get my bearings.'

'There does seem to be the most incredible shortage of staff,' remarked Beresford, taking his seat again as soon as his friend had departed. 'I should have thought a place this size would have warranted a good deal more help.'

Imogen pursed her lips. 'Most of our workforce left within three months of Sir Matthew's death,' she replied. 'There were insufficient funds to pay them all on the first quarter day and those of them who had families to support were bound to seek other employment. We have managed to persuade the remainder to stay on by giving them parts of their wages whenever we could afford to do so—and by promising to make the rest up to them as soon as the will is ratified. The few who have stayed are the older members of staff who have been here for a good many years, of course,' she added, her bright eyes clouding over. 'Most of whom were due to be pensioned off and have nowhere else to go until they receive their promised annuities.'

Beresford was silent for a moment, then, 'I shall speak to Wentworth as soon as possible,' he said, his voice quite firm, although his heart was beginning to sink once more at the thought of all the problems that were mounting up. 'No doubt he will have a list of all outstanding items. You must not concern yourself. I shall deal with the matter immediately.'

'There is a slight difficulty,' stammered Imogen, her cheeks

colouring. 'That is—I am not perfectly certain—it is merely a
suspicion on my part…' Her voice trailed away.

At her continued hesitation, Beresford frowned. 'If you have
something to tell me, Miss Priestley,' he said briskly, 'and, especially if it has anything to do with my putting the estate to
rights, I suggest that you stop all this shilly-shallying and come
straight out with whatever it is!'

Imogen was mortified. She had been perfectly prepared to
confront Beresford with all her growing worries and supposi-
tions, but somehow, now that she was actually sitting here in
front of him and the man's infuriatingly discerning eyes were
fixed upon her, waiting impatiently for her to explain herself,
she began to wonder if her suspicions about Wentworth were
flawed. Could she have overreacted? Her cheeks took on a
deeper hue and she struggled to control her breathing.

'It is simply that I cannot understand what has happened to
all the revenue,' she began, then, to her horror, the words seemed
to trip over themselves in their efforts to be heard. 'There should
have been more than enough to get us through the year—and
there are the rents—I have barely managed to get a peep at the
books, but what I did see simply made no sense to me—and I
could swear that some of the stock has disappeared…'

'Now, now, my dear Miss Priestley—' Beresford raised his
hand and, in a calm, soothing voice, interrupted her incoherent
monologue '—estate management is a very complicated business and hardly one for a young lady to be bothering her head
about. You really had best leave it all to me. I shall sort it all
out in no time at all, I assure you.'

Imogen sprang to her feet in consternation. 'No, no—you
do not understand—there is so much that you do not know…'

His face darkened as he, too, rose to his feet. 'I do not need
your constant reminders of my unfamiliarity with the situation
here, Miss Priestley,' he said coldly. 'I intend to remedy that de-
ficiency as soon as I may. In the meantime, I would really ap-

preciate it if you would do me the honour of allowing me to go about it in my own way. Let me assure you that I have a great deal of experience in these matters. And now, with your permission?' He turned from her and started towards the doorway, adding curtly, 'If you could, perhaps, arrange some refreshment? I was given to understand that that is your province?'

In a mounting fury, Imogen stared after his departing back. She could hardly believe what had happened. He had treated her like a child—or worse—more like some sort of feather-brained nincompoop! *She* who, for years, had sat at Chadwick's right hand, mastering the fascinating intricacies of estate management, even riding with the elderly manager on rent collection days and doling out the servants' wages while he marked them off in his book. In fact, so adept was her understanding of how the estate functioned that she had gained even the uncompromising Sir Matthew's grudging respect.

Her whole body seemed to be trembling uncontrollably and she was forced to sit down rather abruptly. As she subsided on to the sofa, her mind was filled with a whirling mass of conflicting emotions.

Very gradually, as her anger dissipated, she began to review Beresford's manner. She could leave the arrogant beast to his own devices and hope that he would discover Wentworth's scheming for himself—if, indeed, it *did* transpire that it was Wentworth who was at the bottom of all the inconsistencies, she hastily reminded herself!

She had wanted desperately to share her suspicions about the man with Matthew Beresford, but had clearly made the mistake of expecting him to listen seriously to what she had to tell him. She had also assumed that the two of them would sit down together and discuss the problem rationally and, hopefully, reach some sort of agreement as to how best to deal with it. She had never at any time considered the man's contemptuous dismissal, not only of her, admittedly, rather clumsy attempts to furnish him with the truth behind the estate's unanticipated impoverishment but, seemingly, of herself as well!

At this point, it seemed to her that she might as well leave Thornfield without further ado, just as she and Widdy had planned to do last year, had not the complications of her uncle's will prevented their departure.

As if prompted by Imogen's thoughts, Jane Widdecombe appeared in the doorway.

'Oh, there you are, my dear,' she smiled, advancing into the room. 'Jessica said that I would find you here. But—Mr Beresford? I thought he would still be here with you.'

A plump, neat dab of a woman, Miss Widdecombe had been the mainstay of the Beresford family since shortly after Imogen's own arrival at Thornfield. In addition to having guided all three children through their academic studies, she had been, without doubt, the principal shaper of their manners and moral codes, Lady Beresford having involved herself very little in their upbringing.

Still undecided as to what would be the best course of action for the two of them, Imogen shook her head.

'I believe he went to look for his friend,' she replied with a dismissive shrug.

Peering over the top of her glasses at her one-time charge, Miss Widdecombe frowned.

'Is there something wrong, my dear?' she asked in concern. 'You seem a little put out.'

Imogen gritted her teeth. 'Honestly, Widdy! The man is so dreadfully arrogant! He refused to listen to a single word I said! He dismissed me as though I were not so much as a boot-boy!'

Miss Widdecombe considered this statement. 'Perhaps he was tired after his long journey,' she suggested.

'Long journey!' scoffed Imogen. 'They stayed the night down in Kirton Priors—Cook recognised the driver of the chaise they hired from The Wheatsheaf.'

'Well then, my dear, you must try again. He certainly needs to know what has been going on in his absence.'

Imogen jumped up. 'Then he must discover it for himself! I have decided that we shall leave for Kendal as soon as possible, Widdy!' she pronounced.

'But, my dear!' Miss Widdecombe stared at her in distress. 'We do not have the wherewithal to travel until the will is settled. I cannot imagine that it will take very long now that Mr Beresford has finally arrived. Surely we should wait until he has had time to familiarise himself with the situation?'

Apart from the pension Sir Matthew had arranged for the governess to receive at her retirement, there was also the matter of the small personal sum that he had bequeathed to her, which she intended to use to buy her own share in the little school in Westmorland.

'It is but four weeks until the twenty fifth of September,' declared Imogen stoutly. 'Then I shall have the whole of my next quarter's allowance. That will be more than enough for both of us to hire a chaise to Kendal and to purchase our shares. You can reimburse me when you are in funds—it is really of no importance, I promise you.'

'The idea is very tempting,' admitted Miss Widdecombe. 'Margery has been waiting for us to join her for almost a year now and, in the normal way, I would be more than happy to acquiesce.' Pausing, she slowly shook her head. 'However, Imogen, I am afraid that it will not serve. We cannot leave Lady Beresford to deal with this monster, if he is as overbearing as you say he is. She simply has not the resources to cope, as you are perfectly well aware.'

Imogen gave a little grimace. 'I know, Widdy,' she said. 'And I did promise her that I would stay until she was settled. But, when I first met Beresford, he did not seem at all like Sir Matthew—although,' she recollected, 'it is true that he did fly up in the boughs when I mentioned his mother's portrait.'

Miss Widdecombe regarded her with interest. 'Sir Matthew's first wife,' she acknowledged with a sigh. 'I fear that she has, unwittingly, been the cause of so much grief in this family—your uncle was forever holding her up to Lady Beresford as the paragon of all that was good and clever but, no matter how hard she tried, our poor lady was never going to be able to live up to her dead predecessor's alleged faultlessness.'

'Presumably because my uncle was still obsessed with her memory,' suggested Imogen thoughtfully. 'As a matter of fact, I have often wondered why it is that anyone who has had the misfortune to die before their due time seems to be forever imbued with some sort of unlikely perfection.'

'That does often seem to be the case,' agreed the governess, 'although I am inclined to believe that it is often merely because one prefers to dismiss the bad memories and remember only the good. No human being could possibly have been as unflawed as the first Lady Beresford was depicted as having been. I am told that, at one time, your uncle was used to creep into the attics at night and sit staring at her portrait until the early hours!'

'That presumably explains why he was in such a dark mood on so many occasions!' Imogen remarked drily.

'I dare say,' nodded the governess. 'Although, sadly, it seemed that many things in life were wont to irritate him. Jessica was the only one of us who had no difficulty in reviving his spirits.'

Imogen laughed. 'I'd like to meet the man who holds himself impervious to that little baggage's wiles! I really do not know what will become of her!'

'She is a worry,' Miss Widdecombe acknowledged with a smile. 'Had her father not died, she might have had her London Season and could well have been safely married off by now.' Her faded blue eyes suddenly lit up. 'Do you know, my dear, I believe that I have had the most wonderful idea!' She tugged at Imogen's hand and pulled her down on the sofa beside her. 'Do you suppose that we could persuade Mr Beresford to sponsor his sister's come-out?'

'I cannot imagine anyone persuading Mr Beresford to do anything he did not want to,' declared Imogen, with a disdainful sniff.

'Nonsense! We simply need to do some little thing to make him grateful to us!'

'Oh, Widdy, really! What in the world would make *him* grateful to *us*? I doubt if we shall even be able to provide the pair of them with a decent nuncheon—oh, bother, I clean forgot!' She scrambled to her feet and smoothed down her gown. 'I shall have to go, Widdy! I was supposed to be organising refreshments for them and it's almost two o'clock!' She gave the governess a swift hug. 'We will work something out, dear. There is no need for you to worry unduly, I promise you.'

Chapter Four

Beresford had been allotted his father's suite of rooms and he was far from pleased about it. The heavy, dark furniture in the bedchamber was not at all to his liking and the plum-coloured velvet curtains and bed-hangings were highly oppressive. There was, moreover, a sickly cloying scent that pervaded the whole atmosphere.

He glanced at Babcock, his late father's elderly valet, who was shuffling nervously in the doorway, awaiting instructions.

'Are these the only rooms you have available?' he demanded.

The man flinched. 'This has always been the master's suite, sir,' he stammered. 'Mr Allardyce thought it would be the right thing to do.'

'Well, you may tell Mr Allardyce that I'm not at all happy with it!'

He strode over to one of the bedroom windows and thrust it wide open, then proceeded to do likewise with its fellow.

'You can get someone to remove those ludicrous bed-hangings for a start—and what the devil is that infernal smell?'

'Smell, sir?' The man's nose wrinkled as he sniffed the air. 'Do you mean Sir Matthew's pomade?' He walked across to the dressing room and, picking up one of the many jars that stood on the dressing table, held it out for Beresford's perusal.

Beresford backed away in disgust. 'Take it away, man—take them all away and burn them!'

'All pretty depressing, ain't it, old man?' came a familiar voice from the doorway.

Beresford spun round, a look of relief on his face.

'God, David, it is all far worse than I expected! The sooner we can sort out this damned mess the better! I cannot wait to get away from this place.'

'Learnt nothing helpful from the lovely Imo, then, I take it?'

'Not a bit of it. She was rambling on about the books being in a mess—although how the devil she knows anything about estate matters escapes me. Women have no business messing about in men's affairs, in my opinion!'

'Steady on, old chap!' laughed his friend. 'My father used to say that Mother was better than his own right hand when it came to checking the tax revenues in the province.'

Beresford gave a rueful grimace. 'Perhaps I was a touch short with the girl,' he admitted. 'Probably that damned picture of him in there glowering at me for having the effrontery to survive him—that will certainly have to come down before I am prepared to use that room again!'

'When are you going to cross swords with this Wentworth chap, then?'

'After we've had a bite to eat, I thought—if that unlikely event ever takes place,' said Beresford. 'Seems that this Imogen female is in charge of all the domestic matters—as well as poking her fingers into estate management!' he added, with a grin. 'Hope she knows a bit more about feeding her guests than she appears to know about accountancy!'

At that moment the strident clanging of the gong was heard and Beresford turned to Babcock, who was busily shovelling his late master's collection of toiletries into a valise.

'You may go and have your meal, too, Babcock, but, when you return, I want you to clear all Sir Matthew's belongings out of these rooms—everything, you understand? Empty all the closets, drawers, whatever! I do not want to see a single possession of his when I return. Understood?'

The man, wide-eyed with trepidation, nodded, picked up the bulging valise and scurried from the room.

Seymour shook his head. 'Becoming quite the little martinet, aren't you?' he said, with a slight frown. 'It don't sit well on you, Matt. You ain't usually this boorish with people.'

Beresford hunched his shoulders. 'Must be this infernal place, old chum. It is almost as though *he* is here—watching me—I simply cannot seem to shake it off.' He smiled apologetically to his friend. 'Need some sustenance, I suppose—better go and see what delights our young hostess has arranged to tempt our appetites!'

Allardyce conducted the two men into what, to Beresford's surprise, appeared to be the breakfast room, where he saw that places had been set for six at one end of a large mahogany table and a meal, of sorts, had been laid out. Imogen and Jessica were already in attendance, along with a dumpy grey-haired lady of indeterminate age and a slim, pale-faced bespectacled youth, whom Beresford took to be his half-brother Nicholas.

At the men's entrance, the boy rose from his seat and came forward to greet them, tentatively holding out his hand.

At once, Beresford reached out and clasped the boy's hand firmly in his own. He had seen the look of apprehension in the boy's eyes and was, in turns, angry and full of remorse. Angry that the youth should be so obviously afraid of him before they had even met and full of remorse that his sixteen-year-old sibling should have been allowed to grow up to exhibit so little self-confidence. Yet another indictment to lay at his father's door, he thought darkly.

'You must be Nicholas,' he said, smiling warmly. 'How very pleased I am to meet you at last!'

'And I you, sir,' answered the boy warily.

'Matt, if you please, young man—if we are to be friends—and I hope that we are?'

'Y-yes, of course, sir—that is—I mean—M-Matt, sir,' came Nicholas's shaky reply.

'This is my friend David Seymour,' said Beresford, nodding towards his colleague. He could see that it was not going to be at all easy to gain the lad's confidence. 'Miss Priestley and your sister we have already met. Do be a good fellow and introduce us to your other lady guest and then we may all sit down and eat. I, for one, am famished!'

At Seymour's grin and hearty handshake, a slight smile appeared on the boy's lips and he went quickly to Miss Widdecombe's side and, taking her arm, brought her to Beresford and nervously performed the necessary introductions.

'I must explain that we have lately taken to having all our meals in this room, Mr Beresford,' said Imogen when, at last, they were all seated at the table. 'With so few servants we found that it proved a more sensible size than the dining room.' His surprisingly gentle treatment of her young cousin had not escaped her notice and she was determined that he would find nothing in her own manner that could cause him displeasure. 'Although, I fear that our refreshments may seem rather niggardly to you. Cook was able to manage only part of a raised pie and some fruit and cheese, but you have my word that she is hoping to conjure up something a little more substantial for your dinner.'

'Pray, do not apologise, Miss Priestley,' he replied, helping himself to a generous slice of the rabbit pie before passing the dish to Nicholas, who was seated on his left. 'I am sure it all looks most appetising.'

Silence reigned for several minutes as they all got down to

the serious business of doing justice to Cook's hastily prepared offerings, although Beresford could not help noticing that both Imogen and the governess took very little.

'That was delicious!' he said, finally laying down his knife and fork. 'And, please allow me to take this opportunity to say how truly sorry I am that you have all been placed in this dreadfully awkward position.'

'Oh, it has all been absolutely beastly!' Jessica blurted out, ignoring Miss Widdecombe's admonishing frown. 'You have no idea! Rabbit stew or pigeon pie every single day—whatever Nicky manages to shoot—and hardly any desserts at all, lately! You *will* get us all back to normal very soon, won't you, *darling* Matt?'

'Jessica!'

Deeply shocked at her cousin's outrageous behaviour, Imogen was about to remonstrate with the girl when she felt Miss Widdecombe's hand gently squeezing her knee beneath the table. She hesitated, not entirely sure what the governess intended.

'Poor dear Jessica misses her little treats,' interposed the governess, nodding in Beresford's direction. 'It has all been rather difficult for her to understand. A young lady of her age, as you must be aware, should really be concerning herself with assemblies and balls and other such entertainments as her contemporaries enjoy.' Smiling at him in, what seemed to Beresford, an almost conspiratorial manner, she went on, 'Still, we have no doubt at all that, now that you *are* here, you will be more than happy to take charge of your new sister's début, will you not, Mr Beresford?'

He cleared his throat. 'I'm afraid there are a good many matters to deal with before we can think of that sort of thing, Miss Widdecombe,' he managed, sensing rather than seeing the pout of disappointment that appeared on Jessica's face. 'But I have no doubt that something can be arranged for next year.'

Privately, he was determined to have dealt with all the

problems with which he was presently beset well before spring came round. David Seymour, however, seemed to have other ideas.

'Now, please do not fret yourself, Miss Beresford!' he cajoled, crinkling up his merry eyes at her woebegone expression. 'You have my word that there is very little going on in London at this time of year—most of the celebrations are over and nobody of note stays in the capital during the warmer months. However, I am quite certain that there must be local entertainments not too far afield that you may be allowed to attend— even before you are fully "out". Is that not so, Miss Priestley?'

He looked questioningly at Imogen, who felt obliged to smile and nod her head, although she too was planning her imminent escape from Thornfield.

'There you are then!' exclaimed Seymour, leaning back in his chair in satisfaction. 'You see, Miss Beresford! You have an excellent chaperon in your cousin and I, myself, would deem it a great honour if you would allow me to act as your escort to any local rout or assembly.'

Jessica's face immediately lit up and she began fluttering her lashes at Seymour in what seemed to Beresford to be the most irritatingly obvious manner.

'I should think that Miss Priestley is rather too young to be placed in a role of such responsibility, David,' he remarked drily, glancing across the table to Imogen.

A soft blush appeared on her cheeks. 'I believe I am perfectly capable of ensuring that my cousin conducts herself as she should in any public gathering, Mr Beresford,' she said, defensively.

'You have a good deal of experience in these matters then, I take it?'

She was momentarily confused as she registered the unmistakable trace of sarcasm in his voice.

'I was often wont to attend the local assemblies when my uncle was alive,' she replied, unable to tear her eyes away from his intent gaze. 'You may be surprised to learn that I am not quite as green as you apparently take me to be, sir.'

His deep laugh rang out across the room as he rose and pushed back his chair.

'Clearly not, Miss Priestley! However, if you will excuse me, I believe I shall leave the matter of Jessica's launch into society until some other time. There are other, more pressing matters to deal with today. Where do you suppose I might find Mr Wentworth?'

At this, Nicholas got to his feet. 'I can take you to him, if you like,' he offered shyly. 'He is normally in the office at this time of day. We can go through from the hall—if the door isn't locked.'

Beresford was puzzled. 'Why should the door be locked on the house side?' he asked the boy.

Nicholas flushed. 'It always is these days, sir. Wentworth does not care for any of us poking about in there—not that I would ever do so,' he added quickly. 'I am pretty useless when it comes to stuff like corn yields and livestock sales—Father always used to get rather angry with me over my lack of understanding of estate matters.'

'It will all be yours one day, Nicholas,' Beresford reminded him. 'I would not like you to think that I have come here to steal your inheritance from you. I merely want to sort out the most urgent problems as quickly as possible and leave you to it.'

A look of alarm appeared in the boy's eyes. 'Oh, I wish you would not, sir! I really do not wish to keep the property—and nor does Mama—apart from her jointure, of course. I, myself, will be perfectly content with the allowance he left me.'

Frowning, Beresford regarded his brother intently. 'You are not interested in taking over Thornfield when you come of age?'

Nicholas shook his head vehemently. 'Never! I was as glad as I could be when I heard that you were to succeed. I intend to go into the Church—it is what I have always wanted. And, if you do not intend to stay, I shall sell the place as soon as I am able!'

A breathless silence filled the room as Beresford, in perplexed dismay, struggled to come to terms with this new and unexpected development.

Seymour got to his feet. 'The estate still has to be put back to rights, old chap,' he pointed out. 'Whether it is to be kept or sold makes very little difference at this stage. The debts have to be cleared and, judging by what I could see from the lane as we passed, there are at least two fields well past their best for cutting. You simply cannot pull out now, Matt.'

Beresford's face darkened. 'I had not intended to,' he said shortly. 'But this does pose an entirely different problem.'

'I am awfully sorry, sir.' Nicholas's voice was shaking. 'I had not meant to cause you any more worry.'

Imogen rose and came to her cousin's side. 'It is probably just as well that Mr Beresford knows your intentions, Nicky,' she said firmly. 'There are certain aspects of your father's temperament of which he cannot possibly be aware.'

'I believe I had the pleasure of discovering several of Sir Matthew's delightful idiosyncrasies some years ago,' was Beresford's terse rejoinder.

She coloured. 'Yes, of course. I do beg your pardon.'

He suddenly found himself musing over the extraordinary colour of her eyes. One minute they were a bright, clear grey and then, before you knew where you were, they had changed to the colour of a thundercloud! And that, he noted, was when those fascinating little sparks of silver were at their most obvious. A useful warning sign for future reference, he thought, turning away with an appreciative grin.

Somewhat flustered over his intense examination of her features, Imogen's thoughts became erratic, her pulse began to race and she found herself obliged to sit down quickly. At first, the idea that Beresford might find her amusing filled her with a cold fury and yet—there had been something else in his penetrating gaze, she could swear—something she could not identify. And, whatever that something was, it had caused her to experience a momentary flutter of a feeling somewhat akin to panic!

Chapter Five

Beresford followed Nicholas out of the room and into the hall, from where the boy led him down a side passage and indicated a doorway at the end.

'This is the office,' he said, trying the handle. To his surprise, the door appeared not to be locked. 'I suppose Wentworth must have known you were bound to want to look around,' he grinned, as he pushed it open.

It seemed that Wentworth had indeed been expecting them, for he was sitting at the big mahogany desk leafing through a pile of papers. He stood up as they entered and held out his hand.

'Mr Beresford,' he said, his voice fawningly apologetic. 'So sorry we got off on the wrong foot this morning, sir—I thought you were an interloper at first—a natural mistake in the circumstances, as I feel sure you'll agree.'

His lips twisted into an insincere smile. 'You'll no doubt be wanting to take a peek at the books—I think you'll find everything in order, sir.'

As far as Beresford was able to judge, Philip Wentworth appeared to be one or two years older than himself. With piercing black eyes and crisp, dark curls falling about his temples, he was not unhandsome in a raffish sort of way. In addition, he had a brash, self-confident air about him. Beresford quickly decided that he had been quite correct in his first impression of the man and liked him no better on second contact.

'I will look at them later, perhaps,' he replied. 'At the moment I believe we need to deal with the staff shortage. How many outside hands do you have?'

'No one permanent, really—not unless you count old Chadwick and his son.'

'And they are?'

'Chadwick was the estate manager before I came,' explained Wentworth. 'Sir Matthew brought me in to replace him—said the old man was getting senile, and that's a fact! Still potters around doing stuff about the place—can't keep him away, seeing as he still lives up at the farm—seems Sir Matthew gifted the house to him for life several years ago, which means that I have to make do with a measly gamekeeper's cottage.'

Choosing to ignore the man's somewhat petulant grievance, Beresford paused momentarily before asking, 'And the son?'

'Ben—got his foot shot off at Waterloo—came back late last year—no use to anyone, if you want my opinion.'

'Hold hard, Wentworth!' Nicholas cut in heatedly. 'That is pretty shabby of you! Ben Chadwick was a fine soldier and a brave man—he was injured fighting for King and Country!'

'More fool him, then, is what I say. Should have stayed at home like the rest of us did and kept out of trouble,' sniffed Wentworth.

Seeing that the scarlet-faced Nicholas was about to round on the manager once more, Beresford put his hand on the boy's shoulder.

'Leave it, Nicky,' he said gently. 'Mr Wentworth is entitled to his opinion, however unenlightened it may be.' Ignoring the flicker of animosity that appeared on the man's face, he went on. 'Our immediate concern is the speedy acquisition of a good many more hands—you have a hiring fair hereabouts, I imagine?'

The man shook his head. 'The annual fair isn't until Michael-mas—although these days you can usually be sure to find quite a few chaps looking for work at the weekly market in Ashby—tomorrow, that'll be.'

'Tomorrow? Excellent! There should be no shortage of suit-able men available, given the current high level of unemploy-ment. About a dozen to start with, I should imagine. We will, presumably, be able to accommodate at least that many in the estate cottages that have been vacated—and we will need house staff, too—although, upon reflection, perhaps it would be pref-erable to leave that side of things to Miss Priestley?'

'Might as well. She'll be sure to want to have her say any-way. Always poking her nose in—' He stopped, having caught sight of Beresford's stony expression. 'Well, *women*—you know,' he finished self-consciously, with a half-hearted attempt at a careless laugh.

Beresford studied him in contemptuous silence for a few mo-ments then, as his eyes alighted on the bunch of keys that lay on the desk, he said, 'I have been given to understand that you have the keys to the cellars in your keeping. Why is that, pray?'

Wentworth warily shifted his stance. 'Thought I ought to stop anyone making free with the master's—that is—Sir Matthew's wines. Quite an expensive collection, I understand. Wouldn't do to have any of it go missing, now, would it?'

Beresford picked up the keys. 'These will remain in my possession for the time being,' he said curtly. 'And now, since I imagine that you have plenty to attend to, you may continue with your outside activities. I will send for you should I require your services.'

For a moment Wentworth looked as though he were about to protest at Beresford's summary dismissal of him then, with a nonchalant shrug, he turned and swaggered out of the room into the stable yard, giving Nicholas a mocking grin as he passed him.

'Hateful man!' muttered Nicholas, slamming the door shut. 'Shouldn't be at all surprised if Imo ain't in the right about him.'

Beresford looked up from the papers he was reading. 'In what respect?'

The boy coloured and looked down at his feet. 'No—it's nothing, really. I should not have said that.'

'Come clean, Nicky,' Beresford advised him. He had suddenly recalled Imogen's disjointed words. 'If there is anything in the least bit havey-cavey going on, I really think I ought to be told about it, do you not think so, old chap?'

Nicholas shuffled uncomfortably. 'Imo said that she tried to tell you in the library, but you refused to listen to her,' he blurted out. 'You really should hear her out, sir! She has been running the place almost single-handedly since Father died and it is only because she has been using her own money that we have managed to survive this far!'

'Miss Priestley has her own finances?' asked Beresford in surprise.

'Oodles. Her father was filthy rich and both her parents left everything they had to her. She only gets it as a quarterly allowance until she's twenty-five, though, but she has managed to eke that out in the most fantastic way over this last year. Chadwick is always saying...' He hesitated and an expression of shame appeared on his face. 'It really is pretty bad form to be discussing Imo like this, you know.'

Beresford drew in his breath. 'You are quite right, Nicky. Tell me about her suspicions instead. What has she told you?'

'Not a lot, really. Fact is, incomes and revenues and so on are a total mystery to me, but Imo seems to think that the books have been tampered with. She is convinced that there should have been more than enough money available to run the estate properly for at least a year, without any cutbacks at all!'

'Does your cousin have some understanding of accountancy methods, then?' enquired Beresford, incredulously.

'Lord, yes!' nodded the boy. 'Chadwick says she is an absolute genius with figures! She has been doing the books with him for years—she knows as much about this estate as Wentworth does—probably more, I dare say!'

Beresford sat in dismayed silence. A fine fool he'd turned out to be, he thought with a shudder, remembering his unwarranted rebuff of Imogen's tentative attempts to caution him. Small wonder that she had been treating him with such disdain. He got to his feet and began to pace up and down, cudgelling his brain for some way to put matters right, having discovered that he really didn't much care to be in Miss Priestley's black books.

Nicholas watched him, a perplexed frown on his face.

'H-have I said something to upset you, sir?' he asked anxiously.

'Not at all, Nicky,' Beresford hastened to reassure him. 'It is merely that I have just realised what an absolute idiot I have been! I really should have listened to her!' He gave his brother a rueful grin. 'Hardly the most auspicious start to a budding friendship, would you say?'

The boy's face cleared. 'No need to worry about that, sir. Imo has never been the sort to bear a grudge, I promise you.'

'Thank God for that,' exclaimed Beresford. 'For I intend to try and remedy the matter without further ado.' He paused, weighing up the possibilities of an idea that had just come to him. 'Would you mind popping back to the other room and asking your cousin if she would be willing to spare me a few minutes of her time—and Mr Seymour, too, if he is still about?'

Nicholas nodded and at once made for the house door.

'Oh—and one other thing, Nicky!' called Beresford, just as the boy was about to leave. 'Do stop calling me "sir"! Matt is my name—understood?'

'Understood—er, Matt!' shot Nicholas over his shoulder, as he sped up the passageway to carry out his errand.

Beresford laughed and returned to the desk where he began to take a more serious interest in the pile of papers that Wentworth had left behind. He had barely begun this task, however, when he was interrupted by the sound of a man's teasing laughter, interspersed with a breathless giggling, which he had no difficulty in recognising as his sister Jessica's.

He got up at once and peered curiously out of the window into the stable yard. A sudden fury overcame him as he surveyed the scene.

Philip Wentworth was leaning over the top of the stable's half-door, casually chatting to Jessica Beresford. His manner, insofar as Beresford could determine from this distance, seemed highly impertinent and over-familiar. His sister, in return, was behaving in what Beresford could only describe as the most 'hoydenish' way imaginable, tossing her curls and flirting abominably with the grinning Wentworth.

With an angry, forbidding expression on his face, he flung open the office door and strode over to the couple.

'Go to your room this instant, Jessica,' he ground out forcibly.

At his sudden intervention the girl's giggles subsided into a squeak of dismay.

'Oh, honestly, Matt, we were only—' she started to protest but then, having correctly interpreted the warning light in Beresford's eye, she clamped her lips together and, without a backward glance at her co-conspirator, flounced off in the direction of the kitchen.

'Don't be so hard on the lass—she's entitled to a bit of fun!'

Wentworth, apparently unperturbed at Beresford's sudden arrival, had turned back to his work and was nonchalantly coiling a leading-rein. Beresford leaned over the stable door and beckoned to him.

'A word, Wentworth, if you please,' he said, in a voice that brooked no argument.

Somewhat warily Wentworth approached the door, his lips parted in a tentative smile. 'Now then, Mr Beresford, you surely aren't going to fly off the handle about a bit of harmless teasing,' he challenged his new master. 'Jess and I often have a bit of a chat when she's in the yard.'

Beresford gritted his teeth. 'I do not care for your attitude, Wentworth. In future you will oblige me by referring to all members of the family in the correct manner and, if I have any more of your insolence, I shall have no hesitation in dismissing you. It has become increasingly clear to me that you have taken to acting well above your station since Sir Matthew's death. Allow me to inform you, my man, I have no intention of putting up with it!'

Without waiting for a reply, he turned on his heel and strode back to the office, where he perceived that Imogen and Seymour, having witnessed the final moments of the conflict, were standing in the doorway, anxiously awaiting his return.

'God's teeth, Matt!' muttered Seymour, as he stepped aside to allow his friend to enter. 'You have certainly made an enemy there! You should have seen the man's face! What the devil did he do to get you so riled?'

Still inwardly fuming, Beresford described the events that had led to the confrontation. 'I shall have to get rid of the fellow as soon as possible,' he said. 'Unfortunately, we will have to keep him on until we get some more hands, but I doubt if he will cause any more trouble—not if he values his position!'

Privately, Imogen was not at all sure that Wentworth would take his public chastisement quite so meekly, but she was glad that Beresford had warned him off Jessica and was happy to tell him so, adding, 'I must admit that I was getting quite worried about the way she hung around the stables whenever he was there. Miss Widdecombe and I have both spoken to her about it on several occasions and when I challenged him about the matter in the copse earlier he lost his temper and told me to mind my own business.'

Much as I did myself, Beresford was thinking and, determined to clear up the matter without further ado, he cleared his throat and said, 'I believe I owe you an apology for my own crass behaviour this morning, Miss Priestley.'

'I am inclined to think that we should put that regrettable episode behind us, Mr Beresford,' replied Imogen, endeavouring to keep her tone light, for she had not totally forgiven him for his previously dismissive attitude towards her. 'I am sure that it was merely an unfortunate misunderstanding on your part. You had no reason to suppose that I would know anything about estate matters. I understand that Nicholas has informed you that I used to help Mr Chadwick with the accounts before Wentworth took them over?'

'It *is* somewhat unusual in one of your sex,' he pointed out, with a smile that suddenly caused Imogen to experience the most extraordinary palpitations.

With an effort, she forced herself to tear her eyes away from his and, somewhat flustered, began to fumble clumsily with the sets of accounts books that were situated in a cabinet behind the desk.

'Yes, so I believe,' she managed somewhat breathlessly, at the same time selecting and preparing to take down two of the heavy volumes. She found herself forestalled by Beresford who, realising her intention, had promptly reached out to relieve her of her burden while Seymour, who had been watching the highly charged interchange between the pair with unconcealed interest, swept aside the piles of papers on the desktop to make space for the books.

'Your cousin tells me that you suspect some irregularities in the figures,' said Beresford, as he motioned Imogen into the big leather chair behind the desk. 'Do you think you could show us what you have found?'

'You will need to look at the two previous years' accounts first,' she replied, already thumbing her way through the pages of one of the volumes. Having managed to still the disquieting sensations that had threatened to overcome her resolve, her voice was now perfectly calm. Now that she finally had the opportunity to vindicate her suspicions, she was determined not to allow anything to distract her from that task.

'This first one is for 1813—it will give you some idea of the rents we normally received from the tenant farmers and the revenue from the corn yield. Corn prices, as you must be aware, have increased quite dramatically throughout the war years but, when you look at last year's figures,' she said, indicating the relevant column in the second ledger, 'you will see that the corn revenue for the year appears to be considerably lower than one would have expected it to be.'

Beresford and Seymour studied the figures she had indicated and both men agreed that there was certainly a surprising difference.

'Perhaps last year was not as good a harvest,' suggested Seymour. 'I understand that the weather here was pretty poor during the summer months.'

'Yes, that is perfectly true,' admitted Imogen. 'But, as a result of the war, corn prices have almost doubled since 1813 and now—if one of you gentlemen would be so kind as to pass me 1814...?'

Beresford again sprang to carry out her request and laid the book at her elbow, watching her with interest as she riffled through the pages.

'Yes, here it is,' she eventually announced, her face alight with satisfaction. 'If you look carefully, you will see that some of the figures have been altered—someone has scratched parts of the eights out to make them look like threes, sevens have been turned into fours—and here...' She jabbed her finger on place after place in the neat columns of figures. 'Sixes to noughts—all giving the impression that the revenue was much lower than it actually was—and that, gentlemen, is by no means all.' She flicked over the pages, searching for more anomalies to show them. 'See here, on the debit side, threes and fives have been altered to the figure eight and the number one has become either a four or a seven and, sometimes, even a nine!'

'They certainly look like alterations,' agreed Beresford, with a puzzled frown. 'But there is no way of knowing whether they have been tampered with recently or were merely corrections made at the time of entry—even the best accountants have been known to commit errors!'

Dismayed at his negative reaction to the quite considerable research that she had managed to carry out under very difficult circumstances, Imogen heaved a sigh. 'There is a perfectly simple way to prove my point, Mr Beresford,' she said wearily. 'In the first place, if you tot up the columns you will see that the altered totals do not agree. Secondly, I know that the figures have been altered, because they are in my own handwriting!'

She looked up at him with a triumphant smile, having assumed that he would now be highly impressed with her discoveries, only to find herself confronted with the beginnings of a cynical smile hovering on his lips.

He raised one eyebrow, and the mocking note in his voice was unmistakable. 'And you, Miss Priestley, never make mistakes, of course,' he drawled.

Imogen's self-confidence collapsed in an instant and all of the original hostility she had felt towards him came rushing back. Resolutely squaring her shoulders, she drew in a deep breath. 'It was always Mr Chadwick's practice to set out his figures in pencil,' she informed him, her voice even. 'My contribution was to double-check the entries and agree his arithmetic—he believed that it was the best way of learning the system and—since his own hand was getting a little shaky in later years—only then would he allow me to ink in the final figures. So you see, Mr Beresford, there is simply no way that any of these rather numerous alterations could have occurred.'

In the silence that followed her words, Beresford almost groaned out loud at the ill-thought-out foolhardiness of his remark. He had not missed the sudden darkening of her eyes, nor those entrancing little silver flashes that had emanated from them. You utter fool, he apostrophised. Hoist by your own petard yet again!

Throughout Imogen's halting evidence of her findings, Seymour had been continuing to peruse the three ledgers, comparing the figures one with another and closely inspecting the suspect alterations. He straightened up and shook his head at Beresford.

'Well, old man, it seems perfectly obvious to me that Miss Priestley was quite right to voice her suspicions. There is absolutely no doubt that somebody has been messing about with the figures in these books.'

At the look of concern in his friend's eyes, Beresford's face grew grim.

'And I think we all know who that person is likely to be,' he said shortly. 'Yet another reason to dispense with his services, it appears!'

Then, still conscious of the undercurrent of tension that had, once again, developed between Imogen and himself, he turned to her and executed a little bow.

'I appear to have excelled myself today, Miss Priestley,' he confessed. 'I fear I owe you yet another apology. My remark was totally unwarranted—please tell me that I am forgiven for exhibiting such appalling bad manners.'

This time Imogen, who could not rid herself of the feeling that he was merely trying to humour her, was careful to keep her eyes averted from his face.

'It is of no moment, I assure you, Mr Beresford,' she replied, rising from her seat. 'And, now that I have delivered the problem into your hands, you will please excuse me, for I must go and try to persuade my aunt to join us for dinner.'

Seymour grinned appreciatively as he watched her departing figure.

'Two enemies in one day, Matt!' he chortled. 'Must be something of a record!'

'Stow it, David!' grunted Beresford sourly, as he picked up the three ledgers and thrust them back on to their shelf. 'I am not in the mood!'

With a speculative gleam in his eye, Seymour regarded his friend silently for a few moments before making his way to the house door, saying, 'So it appears! Well then, old boy, if you have no objection, I think I will just cut along after the lovely Imogen and see if we can't arrange for some decent fodder to be sent up from the village—what do you say?'

'Good idea,' returned Beresford, mentally kicking himself for not having given any thought to that equally pressing matter. 'I suppose I had better go and find this Chadwick fellow and get his version of events.'

After a cursory perusal of the papers on the desk, the majority of which proved to be demands for immediate settlements of outstanding accounts, he left the office and walked out into the stable yard, carefully locking both doors behind him. Wentworth was nowhere to be seen but, recalling what the man had told him about Chadwick's place of residence, he made his way around the stable-block into a little back lane where he found a neat little row of cottages, all twenty of which were clearly uninhabited.

At the far end of the lane, situated next to a cluster of farm buildings, was a slightly larger, more dignified-looking property that must, he assumed, be the ex-manager's residence. Seated on a bench in the front garden of this house was a well-built young man, who Beresford took to be the injured ex-soldier, Ben Chadwick.

At first glance there appeared to be nothing amiss with either of his legs, since they were both encased in the strapped knee-high leather boots that were common wear among countrymen. In fact, it was not until the sound of Beresford's approaching footsteps caused the young man to hurriedly lay aside the coach lamp he had been polishing and scramble awkwardly to his feet that Beresford realised that he was having to support his weight with a stick.

He motioned the young Chadwick to return to his seat, ignoring the discomfited flush that covered his face. Both men were well aware that it was normal practice for an employee to remain standing in his master's presence but, in this instance, Beresford was disposed to do away with protocol and, catching sight of the wooden bench beside Chadwick's chair, sat himself next to the young man.

'My name is Beresford,' he announced, somewhat unnecessarily, since his identity was hardly in question. 'May I take it that you are Ben Chadwick?'

'At your service, Mr Beresford,' the young man faltered. 'Was it my father you were seeking?'

'In a moment, Ben,' said Beresford pleasantly. 'I thought I would have a few words with you first, if I may?'

Ben nodded in surprise. 'What can I do for you, sir?'

'I could not help but notice that, although you are fully booted, you are not able to bear your weight on your right leg. I imagine your injury still causes you a great deal of discomfort?'

'It is improving daily, sir,' came Ben's flustered reply. 'I pack the boot with clean rags but, after a while, there is a certain amount of friction which makes long-distance walking impossible at the moment—I try to make myself useful in other ways though,' he added, defensively. 'I do the milking and keep all the tools and tackle in order.'

'Pray do no think that I am criticising you, Ben—far from it,' Beresford assured him. 'I merely wanted to assure myself that you had received the full benefit of all available medical treatment—I understand that it is possible to have special surgical footwear fitted, for instance.'

'Somewhat costly for a man in my position, sir,' said the

young man with a grim smile. 'I dare say that that sort of treatment is probably considered to be standard procedure for the
likes of Lord Uxbridge and his ilk, but, seeing as it takes Father all his time to cater for our basic necessities, I think the last
thing he needs is me badgering him for fripperies of that sort!'

Beresford regarded him seriously for a moment or two. 'I
understand that you were a lieutenant with the 7th Light? Can
you still mount a horse?'

'Aye, that I can do, sir,' affirmed Ben, adding bitterly. 'Not
that I get much chance to ride these days, if Wentworth has anything to do with it.'

'Well, I am happy to inform you that you need no longer
concern yourself with that particular problem,' Beresford replied, rising to his feet. 'In fact, that is mainly what I wanted
to speak to your father about—is he within?'

Ben directed him to the rear of the farmhouse where he
found Chadwick senior tending vegetables in the kitchen garden. Eyeing the displaced manager's activities with considerable interest, Beresford was surprised to see that Ben's father
was far more agile than Wentworth had given him to suppose.

At Beresford's approach, the elderly man straightened up,
took a kerchief from his pocket and wiped his hands.

'Welcome to Thornfield, Mr Beresford. Miss Priestley informed me of your arrival.'

The man's well-modulated manner of speech made it quite
clear to Beresford that both Chadwick and his son had been the
recipients of a good education and, on an impulse, he reached
out and grasped Chadwick firmly by the hand.

'Miss Priestley has been informing me of quite a few things
too, Chadwick,' he told him. 'It seems that we have something
of a problem on our hands.'

'Perhaps we had better go inside, sir,' the man replied carefully and, ushering his visitor into his neat little parlour, he motioned him to take a seat.

'How the devil did this Wentworth manage to get such an upper hand here?' demanded Beresford, as soon as Chadwick had sat down. 'And, more to the point, what on earth possessed my father to appoint him over you?'

'As a matter of fact, he did no such thing!' replied Chadwick, with a sigh. 'Wentworth was originally taken on as head game-keeper, shortly before my dear wife was struck down with an inflammation of the lung and, since Sir Matthew was adamant that I should spend the greater part of my working day with her, he was obliged to hand over a good many of my outside duties to Wentworth. Sadly, my wife did not recover from her illness and...' He paused momentarily and passed his hand across his eyes. 'For several weeks I was somewhat—how shall I put it—distracted.'

Although Beresford gave a sympathetic nod at Chadwick's attempt to conceal his natural distress, his mind was reeling in disbelief at hearing of this new and totally unexpected facet of his father's complex personality.

'I had hardly begun to take up the reins again,' the man went on, 'when I was notified of my son's battle injury and impending arrival. This, of course, necessitated me travelling down to Harwich to collect him. By the time we returned, Sir Matthew had suffered his heart attack and Wentworth was already beginning to make his presence felt and, although I expressed my concern to Miss Priestley, I confess that I was too preoccupied with my son's welfare to do anything about it.'

'Which was perfectly understandable, in the circumstances,' Beresford assured him. 'What can you tell me about my father's death? He had a heart attack, you say?'

Chadwick nodded. 'For some time his doctor had suspected that Sir Matthew suffered from an abnormal pressure of the blood and had been bleeding him regularly during the weeks preceding his death. I understand that he had just returned from his usual morning ride when it occurred. Apparently, Wentworth found him lying in the yard next to his mount but, by the time he had raised the alarm, your poor father had expired!'

The discovery that Chadwick actually seemed to mourn his father's death stirred Beresford's curiosity. 'Do I take it that you were quite happy to be in my father's employ?' he asked.

'After almost twenty years it would be surprising if Sir Matthew and I had not managed to reach some sort of an understanding,' replied Chadwick cautiously. 'And, if I may say so, I am surprised that you should consider it necessary to ask such a question! Those of us who chose to remain in his service for so many years would soon have sought alternative employment had he not been a just employer, I can assure you!'

'I rather seemed to get the impression that certain members of his family were somewhat less than enamoured of him,' returned Beresford drily.

Chadwick eyed him thoughtfully. 'There is some truth in what you say, Mr Beresford,' he admitted. 'Sir Matthew had a very short temper and he was not one to suffer fools gladly. Some might say that he was a hard taskmaster but, over the years, I discovered that it was simply a downright refusal to accept slipshod work or any form of incompetence or ineptitude. However, so long as one performed one's job well, one would eventually earn his respect—Miss Priestley will vouch for that!'

Beresford was silent. Having, for so many years, harboured such strong feelings of anger and resentment towards his father, he now found himself in something of a quandary as to understanding the real nature of the man and, as he was forced to remind himself, with very little likelihood of discovering the truth behind the enigma.

With an effort he drew his attention back to the waiting Chadwick.

'Would I be correct in thinking that you would be willing to be reinstated to your former position?' he asked him.

'Without question, Mr Beresford,' the man was happy to assure him. 'Although I fear that we shall need to address the matter of staff shortage with some urgency if we are to return the estate to any semblance of its former prosperity.'

Beresford nodded. 'I agree, and it is my intention to remedy that problem as quickly as possible. I shall be paying a visit to Ashby market first thing tomorrow morning with the express purpose of hiring more men.'

He stood up and was preparing to take his leave when a sudden thought occurred to him. 'I wonder if your son would be interested in becoming your deputy?' he asked. 'Since he tells me that riding is not a problem for him, I should have thought that he could well prove to be a most valuable assistant to you.'

'How very good of you to consider such an idea, sir!' cried Chadwick, his lined face wreathed in a delighted smile. 'The boy has been growing rather dispirited of late. He has a sharp mind and these months of enforced inactivity have not sat at all easily with him. I am sure that he will be thrilled at this opportunity to demonstrate his worth. He will not let you down, I promise you!'

'Well, do talk it over with him first!' laughed Beresford and, before making for the door, he handed Chadwick the bunch of keys he had confiscated from Wentworth. 'Meanwhile, I suppose I had better go and give our contemptible friend his marching orders!'

When he got back to the stable yard, however, there was still no sign of Wentworth and, after consulting his pocket watch and registering the growing lateness of the hour, Beresford decided to postpone the unpleasant interview until the following morning and went, instead, to his chamber to change for dinner.

Chapter Six

'No, please, Imogen,' moaned Lady Beresford, casting up tear-stained eyes to her niece. 'I simply cannot! Jessica has told me that the man is a bully and a monster! I cannot bring myself to dine with him!' She fell back against the pillows of her chaise longue and closed her eyes.

'Jessica is a very silly girl,' declared Imogen crossly. 'And she knows full well that it was perfectly correct of Mr Beresford to chastise her for her behaviour—she pays absolutely no heed to either Miss Widdecombe or myself.'

Having thought the matter through, she had reached the conclusion that her own continual conflict with Beresford could be put down to a simple clash of two rather strong personalities and, having marked his perfectly acceptable behaviour towards both Nicholas and Miss Widdecombe, she had no reason to believe that he would be anything less than courteous to her aunt.

'Nicky rather admires him,' she ventured. 'And you know how withdrawn *he* usually is around strangers.'

Lady Beresford shook her head and pressed her pale fingers against her brow. 'I believe I feel another of my headaches coming on,' she whimpered.

Breathing deeply, Imogen cast her eyes up to the ceiling.

'Cook is preparing a veritable banquet,' she then offered, re-calling her aunt's constant and peevish complaining about the mundane fare they had all been reduced to eating of late. 'Mr Beresford's friend Mr Seymour apparently sent down to the vil-lage for a huge hamper of supplies—including a haunch of ven-ison, which I know to be your favourite!'

Her aunt's pale green eyes lit up at once. 'Venison, you say?' She considered for a moment, while her restless hands fidgeted with the fringe on her shawl. 'I dare say I could manage a few mouthfuls,' she said eventually. 'Did Cook happen to mention whether she would be serving any of her special desserts?'

Imogen smiled, knowing her aunt's fondness for the myriad of exotic sweets Cook used to send to the table. 'Well, I believe I heard her say something about cherry and almond tartlets,' she replied. 'And, possibly, a crème caramel, if she has time.'

'It *would* be rather ill mannered of me to fail to attend a sec-ond meal when we have guests in the house, would it not, my dear?' murmured Lady Beresford.

'Oh, absolutely, Aunt!' laughed Imogen, as she turned to leave the chamber. 'Shall I send Francine to you?'

'Oh, would you, my dear?' Lady Beresford sat up and pat-ted her head. 'My hair must be in the most frightful mess—do tell her to bring up the curling tongs, Imogen. Oh, goodness me! Which of my gowns do you think I should wear? Black would be most proper, I suppose, although strictly speaking we are no longer in full mourning.'

She rose to her feet and hurried to one of several wardrobes that lined the walls of her chamber and flung open the door.

'Oh, no!' she wailed. 'See how badly creased they all are! I shall look an absolute freak—the man will think me a verita-ble laughing-stock!'

With a resigned sigh, Imogen came back to her aunt's side. 'Tell me which gown you wish to wear and I will iron it for you.'

'But, Imogen, my dear, I cannot possibly allow you to do

such a thing!' protested Lady Beresford. 'That is what I pay Francine for!'

'But Francine will be attending to your toilette,' her niece reminded her, nobly forbearing from mentioning the many occasions during the past year when, unable to pay the ageing mademoiselle her full stipend, she had had to part with several small pieces of her own jewellery in order to persuade the woman to remain at Thornfield. 'I shall be ironing my own gown, so it will be no trouble, I promise you!'

Distractedly rummaging through the many frocks that hung in her wardrobe, Lady Beresford was barely listening. 'Ah, yes—this one!' she said at last, pulling out a soft lavender-coloured creation. Sir Matthew may have been overly harsh in his treatment of some of the members of his family, but he had certainly not been ungenerous in providing them with all the necessary trappings that befitted his own perceived station.

'A splendid choice,' agreed Imogen, hurriedly extracting the gown from her aunt's grasp before she had time to change her mind and, turning on her heel, she made for the door once more. 'I shall call Francine this very instant,' she called over her shoulder as she whisked out of the room.

She ran down the back stairs to the kitchen, from which the most delicious smells were permeating and discovered Mrs Sawbridge, the family's long-time cook, up to her arms in pastry-making, issuing instructions to the room's only other occupant, her son Jake.

Jake Sawbridge was the result of an inappropriate liaison between Amy Sawbridge and the promiscuous son of her previous employer, some twenty years earlier. Sadly, the boy had been born with a limited mental faculty but, because he was an extremely easy-going individual and always eager to please, he had been allowed to remain with his mother ever since Sir Matthew's tender-hearted new bride had been informed of the young woman's plight and had taken it upon herself to hire her as a kitchen maid. Over the years Amy had diligently worked her way up to her present position, earning the courtesy title 'Mrs', as befitted her situation.

Now a stocky, well-developed young man, Jake was as strong as an ox and, as far as Imogen was concerned, he had proved to be more than a godsend, especially since almost all of the original members of the house staff had gradually been forced to up sticks and move on. Added to which, setting aside her unswerving devotion to Lady Beresford, Cook's insistence that her son should remain in her care meant that there had never been any question of either of them leaving Thornfield, regardless of how much money she was owed.

At Imogen's entrance, Jake looked up with his usual vague, wide smile and gestured to the table in front of him. 'Taters, Miss Im,' he said proudly, indicating the pile of vegetables that he had peeled.

'Well done, Jake,' replied Imogen, returning his smile. 'Almost enough to feed an army, I should think!'

The young man grinned at her and nodded appreciatively, before once again applying his full concentration to the task in hand.

'If you're wanting to put the irons on, Miss Imogen, you'll have to use the stove in here,' Mrs Sawbridge pointed out, having seen the garment over Imogen's arm. 'You know we only light the laundry room fire on Mondays, when Bella comes up from the village.'

'Yes, I had realised that, Mrs Sawbridge,' acknowledged Imogen, with a guilty look on her face. 'I will try not to get in your way—but I promised her ladyship that I would iron her gown. I believe I have finally managed to persuade her to come down to dinner and meet Mr Beresford.'

'Her ladyship?' The cook's face cleared. 'You should have said.' She hurriedly wiped her hands on her apron and prodded her son. 'Jake, luv. Go and fetch two flatirons from the laundry room, there's a good lad.'

The young man ambled off to do his mother's bidding while Cook busied herself rearranging the pots on the top of the hob to make room for the irons. 'I'll just clear you a space at the other end of the table and fold a clean sheet over it.'

'That is very good of you, Cook,' said Imogen, laying her aunt's gown over the back of a chair. 'Now I must run upstairs and find Mamselle— I am sorry to say that she will need to heat her ladyship's curling tongs, too.'

''No problem, my pet,' averred Mrs Sawbridge, valiantly re-assessing her cooking times. 'Just you get along and sort out whatever her ladyship needs.'

By the time Imogen had managed to locate her aunt's abigail, tear back down to the kitchen to iron the creases out of the chiffon gown and deliver it to its fretting owner, she was left with very little time to attend to her own toilette. After her earlier confrontations with Beresford, she had intended to take especial care over her appearance that evening, for she was quite determined not to be put at any sort of disadvantage should there be any further difference of opinion between them. However, the unlooked-for delays dealing with her aunt's requests seemed to have caused a slight fraying of her nerves that, added to the considerable effort required to coax her now-dishevelled curls into some semblance of order, resulted in her cheeks being covered in a not-unattractive rosy glow.

With her aunt clinging nervously to her arm, she eventually entered the drawing room where she discovered that Miss Widdecombe and a rather sulky-looking Jessica were ensconced together upon a sofa. Beresford, now immaculately clad in evening dress, the black jacket of which fitted across his broad shoulders without so much as a wrinkle, was positioned in front of the huge bay window in the drawing room, deeply engrossed in conversation with Seymour and her cousin, Nicholas, but, since he had his back to the door, neither he nor either of the other two gentlemen, it seemed, might have registered the ladies' entrance had it not been for Miss Widde-combe's glad cry of welcome.

'Your ladyship! How good of you to join us!'

Beresford spun round to greet his new stepmother but, as soon as his eyes alighted upon Imogen, he found it very diffi-cult to drag his gaze away from the entrancing picture that she presented. With her hair swirled in soft curls about her face and her cheeks, still flushed from her recent exertions, enhancing the lustrous grey of her wide eyes, and the sensuous way that her elegant gown of jonquil satin clung to her shapely curves, she seemed to be having the most disturbing effect upon his senses.

The seconds ticked by while, almost spellbound, he contin-ued to drink in her loveliness until, suddenly, he became aware of the small frown that was beginning to furrow her brow and, perceiving that she was not alone, hurriedly collected his scat-tered wits and strode forward, holding out his hands to her shrinking companion, whom he assumed to be his recently ac-quired stepmother.

'Lady Beresford—forgive my lapse of manners,' he said ruefully, as he lifted her unresisting fingers to his lips. 'I fear that all the accounts work I have been doing today must have addled my brain!'

Although an uncertain half-smile crossed Lady Beresford's lips, there was an unmistakable hint of fear in her eyes and, once again, Beresford silently cursed his deceased father. Striving not to allow himself to be distracted by Imogen's alluring presence nearby, he tucked his stepmother's hand under his arm and pro-ceeded to draw her gently towards the window where he man-aged to perform the necessary introductions with casual poise.

'But I really cannot keep calling you Lady Beresford,' he then said, smiling down at her. 'And "Mama", of course, is to-tally out of the question, since you are clearly no more than a year or so older than myself!'

At this somewhat over-gallant remark, Lady Beresford's expression lightened and she visibly relaxed. 'Lah, Mr Beresford,' she admonished him as she playfully tapped his arm with her fan. 'What a veritable cozener you are!'

'Nonsense, ma'am!' he laughed. 'And pray call me Matt, I beg of you!'

'Then you must call me Blanche,' she insisted.

Imogen's eyes flickered in astonishment at her aunt's sudden volte-face, but, catching sight of Miss Widdecombe's little nod of satisfaction, she realised, almost at once, that their own vexing problem was about to be solved. Should Lady Beresford prove to be sufficiently impressed with Beresford's conduct and happy to allow herself to be guided by him, she and the little governess could be on their way to Kendal much sooner than they had hoped. Allardyce's droning monotone proclaiming that the meal was about to be served broke into her distracted musing. With a start, she realised that David Seymour was at her elbow, requesting that she might do him the courtesy of allowing him to take her into dinner, her aunt having already left the room on Beresford's arm.

When they reached the dining room, she saw that Beresford, apparently dissatisfied with the seating arrangements at the long dining table, which had placed him in his father's seat opposite Lady Beresford at the far end, was instructing the harassed Allardyce to move all the place settings so that they might all sit more closely together.

'For, how are we ever to get to know one another if we are continually obliged to sit at such a distance?' he petitioned his stepmother. 'I shall sit here at your right hand, Blanche, my dear. I am sure that you must have a thousand questions you want to put to me!'

His eyes gleaming with amusement, Seymour favoured Imogen with a conspiratorial grin. He was quite familiar with his friend's considerable expertise at wheedling his way into the good books of members of the opposite sex of a certain age, having witnessed the self-same spectacle on many occasions in the past, when it had proved extremely useful in keeping fond mamas occupied while Seymour spirited their daughters away for a private tête-à-tête.

Somewhat reluctantly, Imogen returned his smile. She had been watching Beresford's performance with a slight feeling of contempt for she, too, recognised it for what it was and, feeling not a little ashamed of her aunt for having been taken in by such shallow artifice, she motioned to Miss Widdecombe to take the seat next to Beresford's while she herself sat next to the governess. Nicholas and his sister had taken their usual seats at their mother's left hand, leaving Seymour to take up the empty place next to a still unnaturally quiet Jessica.

Cook had excelled herself with the number of dishes she had prepared, courtesy of Seymour's timely generosity, the only problem being the considerable delay between the serving of the courses, owing to the lack of staff. For the first time in his life a carefully washed and brushed Jake Sawbridge had been allowed to come up to the dining room with the express purpose of helping to clear away the dishes but he was so overwhelmed at the sight of the ladies of the house in all their finery that, despite frequent proddings from Allardyce, he was unable to do much more than stand and gape at them all. Eventually Imogen, taking pity on the youth, felt obliged to beckon him to her side, whereupon she had a gentle word in his ear, after which he set about his task with considerably more diligence.

Beresford, who had still not fully recovered from the effect that Imogen's appearance had had on him, had glumly observed her deliberate slight to himself in her choice of seating. Nevertheless, he could hardly fail to admire her sensitive handling of the artless young man. Unfortunately, Miss Widdecombe's presence between the two of them precluded him from venturing any favourable comment he might have made. Instead, he directed his remarks to his hostess.

'Your young footman?' he asked, when Jake had left the room. 'He seemed a little—how shall I put it—nervous?'

'Ah, yes—poor Jake,' replied Lady Beresford with a wistful sigh and, unfurling her fan, she proceeded to whisper a brief resumé of Mrs Sawbridge's chequered history from behind its painted vanes. 'He would not normally be allowed upstairs when we have guests but, as you have no doubt discovered for yourself, almost all of our staff have chosen to desert us in our hour of need!'

All at once tears started up in her eyes and the hand that was holding her glass began to shake, causing some of its contents to spill on to the tablecloth.

'Now, ma'am—Blanche, please do not distress yourself!' With one swift movement Beresford had removed the glass from further danger and clasped Lady Beresford's trembling hand in his own. 'It will all be dealt with, I promise you! Tomorrow you shall have a houseful of new servants—as many as you need—you really must not concern yourself about the matter any further!'

His stepmother dabbed at her eyes with her napkin. 'You are too good,' she said, in a tremulous voice. 'How you can find it in you to be so generous to us all, I simply cannot conceive—after the way your father behaved to you!'

'One might say that his neglect was the making of me,' he smiled, patting her hand. 'I have managed to carve out quite a successful career without his help, added to which I have acquired a not insubstantial fortune of my own. Please believe me when I say that I am more than glad to be of assistance to you at this difficult time.'

'It is extraordinary how very unlike him you are!' she said, her voice faltering.

'Just as well he is!' vouched Nicholas staunchly. 'If he were anything like Father, he would be set on criticising us all for not having done better!'

'Nicky! How can you!'

Jessica leapt to her feet and angrily threw down her napkin. She thrust back her chair with such force that it fell to the floor with a resounding crash. 'I simply cannot sit here and listen to you all castigating Papa the way you have been doing ever since *he* arrived! Papa was by no means the tyrant you are all claiming him to have been.'

'Not to you, maybe,' muttered her brother, as he retrieved her chair and returned it to its place. 'We all know how you managed to wind him round your little finger.'

'I did not!' she flung back at him. 'But I do know that he would not have been so easily taken in by this upstart so-called brother of ours as the rest of you seem to have been!'

A trenchant silence filled the room as five pairs of horrified eyes swivelled to observe Beresford's reaction to his sister's outburst and Lady Beresford, her cheeks paling, gripped her hands tightly together as she prepared herself for the full force of his anticipated anger.

For several moments he did not speak, his face an impassive mask. Then, gradually, his eyes softened and the beginnings of a smile hovered on his lips.

'*Touché*, little sister,' he said softly. 'Your loyalty to your father certainly does you credit. However, I do take leave to doubt that even he would have condoned your unseemly behaviour this afternoon and—upstart or not—since I find myself forced to act in his stead as head of this family, I should be very much obliged if you would make up your mind to either leave the room or to sit down and allow the rest of us to enjoy this splendid meal that your excellent cook has taken the trouble to prepare for us.'

Imogen registered Beresford's adroit handling of her wayward cousin with a growing respect and she breathed a sigh of relief as, crimson-faced, Jessica sat down without another word and picked up her fork. She had fully expected the girl to retaliate or, at the very least, flounce out of the room as was her usual reaction to chastisement, but it seemed that Beresford's unruffled response to her accusation had, somehow, brought her to a standstill.

It was perfectly true that Sir Matthew had derived a great deal of satisfaction from the fact that he had sired such an astonishingly beautiful daughter, but the consequence had been that he had spoiled the girl rather dreadfully. As far as he had been concerned, simply to see Jessica's grass-green eyes light up with rapture and to receive her grateful kisses for some new little trinket or other he had purchased had more than helped to alleviate some of the considerable irritation that his shrinking, lacklustre wife and bookish son seemed bent on causing him.

Having sensed that Miss Widdecombe must also feel a certain satisfaction at having witnessed such a remarkable climbdown by her hot-headed young charge, Imogen shot a sideways glance at her neighbour. Unfortunately, the governess had her face averted, her shoulders were gently shaking and she was feverishly dabbing at her lips with her dinner napkin in an attempt to conceal her amusement so, instead of the expected eye-to-eye contact with a fellow conspirator, Imogen found herself gazing straight into Beresford's smiling eyes, the reason for Miss Widdecombe's surreptitious behaviour not having escaped him.

For several seconds it was as though time stood still. Gradually the smile in his eyes faded, only to be replaced by a look of confused bewilderment and Imogen, equally mystified at whatever it was that had passed between them, felt her whole body trembling as she struggled to regain some sort of composure.

Eventually, with a supreme effort, she managed to tear her eyes away from his mesmerising gaze. Glancing nervously round the table, she prayed that the bizarre event had escaped her family's attention and was relieved to find that none of the other guests seemed to have noticed anything amiss, intent as they all were upon enjoying the munificence of the unexpected banquet. She saw that even Jessica's spirits seemed to have been remarkably restored; although that was no doubt due to the assiduous attentions she was being paid by Seymour, who was flirting with her cousin in the most outrageous manner.

Imogen tried to concentrate her attention upon her own meal, but found that she had lost her appetite and, in order not to draw attention to herself, was reduced to toying aimlessly with the food on her plate.

Beresford, desperately trying to focus his attention on the conversations going on around him, picked up his glass, tossed back its contents then signalled to Allardyce to replenish it. He was dismayed to find that he had had no difficulty in recognising the symptoms of this present headiness, having experienced several not dissimilar sensations in the past, but, as he at once realised, any such liaison between himself and his new stepmother's niece was wholly out of the question and he must make every effort to put her out of his mind. He set about trying to convince himself that these disturbing palpitations he was feeling were simply due to the perfectly normal healthy reaction that any red-blooded male would be bound to experience in the company of such a very attractive woman. He reminded himself that the sooner he was able to get down to some sort of active distraction to help him overcome this unwelcome situation, the better. Back home a vigorous game of polo would soon have done the trick and, with that thought now uppermost in his mind, he resolved to take himself off on a head-clearing gallop as soon as the first opportunity presented itself.

He was jolted out of his musings by the sudden awareness that everyone else at the table appeared to have finished their meal. He glanced enquiringly at Lady Beresford, expecting her to rise and motion the ladies out of the room, leaving the men to their port and brandy, as was the usual custom. His step-mother, however, was fidgeting restlessly with her fan and showed no sign of imminent departure. Her former nervous tremor seemed to have returned.

'You do not wish to take the ladies in to tea, ma'am?' he asked encouragingly.

'I await your permission, sir,' she stammered, her eyes widening in alarm. Having been so used to her husband telling her when she might or might not leave the table, she had been waiting for Beresford to direct her movements.

He sighed, immediately grasping the situation, and wondered when, if ever, these new relatives of his would begin to accept that he was *not* Sir Matthew and had no intention of following any of his dead father's somewhat questionable examples.

'And I await your pleasure, my dear Blanche,' he said, rising to his feet. 'It is surely for you to tell me when you are ready to depart—you are mistress of Thornfield and, as far as I am concerned, your wishes will always be given precedence.'

More tears sprang to her eyes as she rose from her seat. 'I thank you, sir,' she faltered, with a weak smile. 'Then, if you will please excuse us.' Raising her head, she signalled to Imogen to accompany her and left the room quickly, offering up a silent prayer of thanksgiving for her perceived deliverance.

Equally relieved that the disquieting meal had finally drawn to an end, Imogen lost no time in following her aunt's example and, without another word, departed with Jessica and the governess close on her heels.

Nicholas, too, rose to leave the room, but Beresford motioned to him to sit down. 'I think you might be allowed to take a small glass of brandy, young man,' he smilingly informed his delighted brother, as Allardyce placed the tantalus at his elbow. 'And now, gentlemen, if we could return to our earlier discussion.'

Chapter Seven

'Well, I still think that he is a perfect beast!' declared Jessica, plumping herself down on the cushioned window-seat overlooking the terrace.

'I seem to recall that you thought he was a perfect angel barely twelve hours since,' remarked Miss Widdecombe drily, as she busied herself with the tea-making things. 'But I dare say that was merely because he had agreed to reinstate your allowance.'

'Had it not been for him, my allowance would never have been stopped in the first place,' retorted Jessica. 'He has no right to treat me like a child.'

'Then may I suggest that you endeavour to stop behaving like one,' the governess advised her, as she took her seat on one of the two sofas in Lady Beresford's little salon.

'But he made me look foolish in front of Wentworth!" wailed the girl, angrily punching one of the cushions.

'If my understanding is correct,' remarked Imogen quietly, 'I believe you managed to accomplish that remarkable achievement all by yourself. And you would do well to remember, Jessica, that Mr Beresford has all but promised to see that you have your début next year. If you insist upon bringing yourself to his attention in this absurd manner, he may well have cause to regret his generosity.'

'*His* generosity!' Jessica jumped up and stamped her foot angrily. 'You know perfectly well that if Papa had lived I should have had the most glorious Season imaginable. Now I shall have to wait almost another whole year and it is just too unbearable!'

'Do pull yourself together, Jessica!' said Miss Widdecombe tartly. 'Six months is hardly a year! It is true that, had your father lived, no doubt a good many things might have happened differently but, since he did not, we have all of us had to make considerable sacrifices. You would also do well to remember that, had it not been for Imogen's selflessness, our lives these past months would have been completely untenable.'

'I do think you ought to heed Miss Widdecombe, Jessica dear,' put in Lady Beresford, leaning back on the squabs of her *chaise-longue* with an uneasy frown. 'We must surely do our utmost to avoid doing anything that might offend Matt until he has decided what to do for the best.'

'But I don't agree that going to live in a poky little house in Bath is for the best!' wailed her daughter. 'I simply cannot understand why you continually refuse even to consider London.'

Wearily Lady Beresford put her hand up to her brow. 'As I have explained to you on so many occasions, Jessica,' she said, 'I cannot cope with the appalling dirt and deafening clamour of the metropolis. I was obliged to spend almost three months there at my own presentation and I found it quite unbearable.' She turned to her niece, hoping for her support. 'You must remember how it was when you were there, Imogen?'

'It was rather noisy at times,' agreed Imogen rather reluctantly, for she had quite enjoyed her one sojourn in the capital some four years earlier.

'Constantly!' moaned her aunt. 'Shrieking street traders from dawn until dusk, carts and carriages clattering by at all hours— I simply could not face having to live there permanently.'

'You would not have dared to say that to Papa,' muttered Jessica mutinously, flinging herself back on to her seat in the bay. 'He would have obliged you to accompany me.'

'That is quite enough, Jessica!' reproached Miss Widdecombe, registering the stricken look on her employer's face. 'It is most unbecoming of you to speak to your mama in that manner!'

'Well, I think it is most unfair! Imogen had the most wonderful time—she used to tell me so herself—and I will never understand why she didn't get away from this dreary little backwater when she had the chance.'

'I was perfectly content to remain here,' replied Imogen, busily refilling her aunt's teacup. 'I am free to occupy myself in whatever way I choose and, more importantly, I can ride for miles over the fields without encountering another soul. Personally, I have never hankered after the social whirl—in fact, I found it all rather shallow and superficial—but I do understand your wanting to experience the whole thing for yourself. You must just strive to be a little more patient.'

Miss Widdecombe nodded. 'And, do not forget, my dear,' she added encouragingly, 'Mr Seymour has offered to escort you both to any local assemblies, should you wish to attend.'

Jessica's face brightened. 'He really is most awfully amusing, isn't he? How he came to have Matthew Beresford for a friend I cannot begin to understand. I wonder what the extent of his fortune is?'

'Oh, honestly, Jess!' laughed Imogen. 'You are quite incorrigible!'

'I don't see why you should say that,' protested her cousin, with a hurt look on her face. 'Papa used to tell me that it was most important to discover the extent of a gentleman's wealth before deciding whether or not to cultivate his friendship.'

Imogen's eyes darkened. 'It was precisely because of that sort of narrow-minded attitude that I was only too happy to quit London. As soon as word of my own fortune got about, it became increasingly impossible to distinguish the bogus from the genuine amongst a decidedly motley collection of so-called "gentlemen", all of whom seemed desperately keen to cultivate my friendship!'

'But then you do have the added advantage of being quite pretty, too,' Jessica deigned to concede.

'Thank you, little coz,' laughed Imogen. 'Be that as it may, however, it certainly did not prevent most of my "devoted" beaux from paying equal court to a number of other heiresses— one or two of whom one might have flatteringly described as "homely"—hardly the sort of behaviour one could regard as complimentary!'

'Well, I shall not be taken in!' avowed Jessica, tossing back her ringlets. 'I have never been in the least bit impressed by the clumsy advances of any of our neighbours' tiresome sons— even Papa used to laugh at their feeble attempts to woo me.'

'I think you may discover that town blades are a little more accomplished in the arts of courtship than Squire Bloxham's boys,' said Imogen with a smile, as she rose to collect her aunt's cup and return it to the tea tray.

Just then the door opened and Beresford entered, followed by his two companions.

A vexed frown appeared on Imogen's brow when she realised that he appeared to be heading, quite intentionally, straight for the very sofa she herself had just vacated, the presence of her green-and-gold paisley wrap over its arm unfortunately making her prior occupancy of the seat perfectly obvious. Conscious that he had his eyes on her, and was clearly expecting her to return to her former place, she turned away from the table with as much nonchalance as she could muster and took up the vacant seat on the opposite sofa, alongside a somewhat perplexed Miss Widdecombe.

A flicker of anxiety entered the little governess's eyes as she glanced from the now stony-faced Beresford and quickly back again to her one-time charge who, she saw, was keenly examining one of the completed pieces of tapestry that she had extracted from the workbox situated between them, as though her life depended upon it. Miss Widdecombe gave a little sigh, adjusted her spectacles and returned her attention to her self-imposed task of repairing the hassock covers from the local church.

Seymour had made an immediate beeline for the window-seat where he proceeded to set about entertaining the delighted Jessica with some of his less risqué anecdotes about his hunting trips in the Himalayas and Nicholas, having strolled over to his mother's *chaise-longue*, pulled up a chair and leaned towards her, smiling his usual lopsided smile, eager to impart what, to him, were very glad tidings.

'Matt has suggested that I should return to Rugby as soon as possible,' he said. 'If I am to get into Cambridge next year, I shall have to work very hard to catch up with my studies and, although Mr Boscombe has been very helpful these last few months, Matt feels that I should do better back with my own school tutors.'

'You must, of course, do whatever your brother thinks best,' said Lady Beresford, with a cautious glance in Beresford's direction. Having had very little to do with her children's education, she did not feel qualified to give any sort of opinion on the matter. In fact, it was entirely due to Miss Widdecombe's generous offer to deal with the sadly worn hassocks that the local vicar had been persuaded to spend a few hours a week helping Nicholas with his Greek and Latin.

'Matt says that he can see no reason why I should not enter the Church if that is what I really desire,' said Nicholas eagerly. 'But I should like your blessing, nevertheless, Mama.'

'How very sweet of you,' she murmured, patting her son's hand in a slightly self-conscious manner. 'I am sure that you will do splendidly in whatever occupation you choose.'

At that, Imogen finally raised her eyes and exchanged a hopeful glance with Miss Widdecombe. It would appear that everything was progressing smoothly towards their imminent departure and, as soon as she was once more in funds, the two of them could leave Thornfield without any further qualms. After just one evening in his company, it seemed that her aunt would be perfectly satisfied to place herself entirely in Beresford's hands and he, from what she had observed, appeared more than capable of dealing with both of her cousins' futures. She could now concentrate her own efforts on carving out a brand-new life for herself.

As she had tried to explain to her young cousin, her own rather less than satisfying experiences on the field of romance had left her with a somewhat cynical attitude towards the opposite sex, as well as having put her off the whole idea of marriage. She was eternally thankful that her parents had left her so well provided for, but, since the mores of society frowned upon the idea of a single, young gentlewoman setting up an establishment on her own, no matter how wealthy she might be, Imogen had welcomed the opportunity to invest in Miss Widdecombe's venture. The excellent reputation that the little school in Kendal had gained would afford her a certain status in the town and, as she herself would not be required to teach, but merely to keep the books in order, she would still have plenty of free time to indulge her interests. She was just reminding herself how ideally suited were the rolling hills of the Lake District for her twin passions of riding and rambling, when the sound of Beresford's voice broke into her reflections.

'Would you care to take a turn on the terrace, Miss Priestley?'

He was holding out his hand to help her to her feet and, other than draw unnecessary attention to herself, she had no alternative but to incline her head and gracefully accept his offer.

He tucked her hand into the crook of his arm and led her out on to the brightly moonlit south-facing terrace. Her rather pointed slight over the matter of the seating had irritated him somewhat and, in spite of his recent decision to keep her at arm's length, he found himself anxious to try to make up whatever ground he had lost earlier.

'I was contemplating a trip to Ashby market tomorrow,' he began, somewhat tentatively, as they strolled along the length of the house. 'Would you be willing to accompany me, I wonder? You will, perhaps, be the better judge of what is required in the matter of household servants.'

Imogen swallowed, feeling rather as she imagined a rabbit caught in a snare might feel. She was well aware that the unusual situation in the household had left him little choice but to solicit her co-operation in the hiring of staff, but the last thing she wanted was to have to spend the whole day in his company although, curiously, she found it impossible to say why. She was not exactly afraid of him, but his very masculine proximity did seem to be causing the most uneasy quivering sensations in the pit of her stomach.

'I believe that will fit in quite well with my own arrangements,' she said, choosing her words with care and keeping her expression as non-committal as she could make it. 'I have been meaning to go in and speak to my lawyer for some time.'

He gave a swift nod before turning to retrace their steps. 'That brings me rather neatly to another matter that has been causing me some concern. I believe I am somewhat indebted to you for "keeping the ship afloat", as it were? I would like to settle my account, if you will allow me.'

'I could not even consider such a thing!' she said, flinging a shocked look at him. 'Please, do not think of mentioning it again!'

'But I flatly refuse to have you so much out of pocket on my behalf, Miss Priestley,' he replied stiffly.

'On *your* behalf, Mr Beresford?'

Imogen came to an abrupt halt and, although she was careful to lower her voice, he quickly registered the warning flashes in her thundercloud eyes. 'Any money I may have spent these last few months has been solely for the benefit of my family—*my* family, may I remind you, sir, and whether or not Lady Beresford may choose to reimburse me remains a matter purely between my aunt and myself!'

She attempted to extract her hand from his hold, but found, to her consternation, that he had chosen to press his arm firmly against his side, preventing her from leaving without an unseemly struggle.

'Try not to make a scene, my dear girl,' he said, then, grasping her imprisoned hand securely with his free one, he proceeded to propel her past the well-lit bay window through which Jessica could be seen laughing helplessly at some gem his dauntless friend was sharing with her.

'How dare you, sir!' Imogen hissed at him through gritted teeth but, heavily conscious of the fact that both Miss Widdecombe and her aunt would think it most odd of her should she unexpectedly return to the salon without Beresford, she was left almost speechless with rage. 'Let go of my hand this instant!'

'Or you will do what?' he grinned, his blue eyes sparkling in sheer devilment as he looked down at her. He was rather enjoying himself, having suddenly discerned that beneath Imogen Priestley's carefully constructed façade of cool detachment lay what looked to be a highly desirable woman capable of the most intense passion, and the unexpected thrill that ran through his body at this fascinating discovery caused him instantly to forget his earlier undertaking to keep well away from her.

Realising that their perambulations had taken them almost to the corner of the house, slightly in its shadow and temporarily out of sight of any possible onlookers, Imogen, quite determined to puncture the man's incredible ego, seized the only opportunity she was likely to get. Wrenching herself away from his grasp, she took a deep breath and rounded on him, her cheeks flushed, her stormy eyes flashing with fury and the creamy orbs of her bosom swelling with righteous indignation, ready to serve her captor with the full rigour of her pent-up anger.

Caught off guard, Beresford was totally overcome by the magnificent spectacle that she presented, and, before Imogen had time to gather her wits, he had swept her forcibly into his arms, clearly intent upon capturing her mouth. His head swam, his whole body filled with desire and all sense of reason momentarily deserted him, but barely had his lips brushed hers, so warm and tantalisingly soft beneath his own, than the sudden awareness of his actions hit him with an icy force. Jerking abruptly to his senses, he thrust her away from him and, with a hoarse imprecation, turned and stumbled blindly to the balustrade, unable to believe that he had committed such unpardonable folly.

Imogen lurched backwards, frantically grappling for some purchase in the knotted stems of the ivy that covered the house wall. Violent tremors were running through her, the world seemed to be spinning in some dizzy vortex as her hands finally made contact with the twisted foliage, preventing her from falling heavily against the cornerstone. Her whole body quivered with a mixture of shock and bewilderment, every vestige of her former rage having vanished, only to be replaced by a feeling of utter disbelief for, in that one brief moment when Beresford's lips had made contact with her own, she had found herself filled with an overwhelming desire to return his embrace.

Before she had time to dwell on that extraordinary discovery, however, Beresford had recovered his senses and, in two swift strides, was back at her side.

'Imogen—Miss Priestley,' he began urgently, holding out his hand in a plea for forgiveness, but she, eyes wide with alarm, recoiled from his touch and made as if to flee.

Increasingly conscious that their prolonged absence might become apparent to the laughing pair seated at the lighted window just a few feet away from them, Beresford did not hesitate. He seized hold of her hand, placed it gently but firmly into the crook of his arm and proceeded to propel her unceremoniously back along the terrace.

'Walk!' he commanded her, his voice husky with concern. 'Walk and smile, for God's sake!'

Still in a daze, Imogen did her utmost to obey him and, although she seemed to have little control over her lower limbs, she somehow managed to keep up with his purposeful stride until they were well within sight of the bay window, at which point he motioned her towards the balustrade opposite, and only when the weight of her body was resting firmly against the parapet did he finally release his hold and step away from her.

Gradually, as her sanity returned, she found sufficient courage to steal a sideways glance at him. His fingers were gripping the edge of the parapet, his face was rigid and his eyes seemed to be focussed on a spot somewhere in the far distance. He was, no doubt, endeavouring to frame some sort of acceptable apology for his unpardonable conduct, thought Imogen scornfully, turning her head away in disdain and racking her brain for a few withering rejoinders with which she could floor him in response to whatever feeble explanation he might choose to offer for his extraordinary behaviour.

At last he spoke and, to her amazement, his tone was perfectly composed as he said, 'Then, if it is convenient, Miss Priestley, may I suggest that we leave at eight o'clock, in order to get the best pickings, as it were?'

Imogen drew in a sharp, indignant breath. Surely the man did not mean to ignore what had just happened? As the minutes ticked by and his silence continued, it became abundantly clear that he had no intention of mentioning the matter at all.

Knowing that she could never bring herself to be the first to refer to the embarrassing incident, she managed to stifle her mounting anger and found herself saying, 'Yes, thank you.

Eight o'clock will be perfectly satisfactory,' and was astonished to find that her voice sounded almost normal. 'Will you instruct Wentworth to have the carriage ready or shall I?'

Beresford was jolted back to reality. A thirty-minute journey in an enclosed carriage with her was absolutely out of the question. He cast about for another solution.

'I, myself, would prefer to ride in, if you have no objection,' he said quickly. 'And indeed, it has occurred to me that your young cousins might care to accompany us—I mean to see about organising the restitution of their allowances and I am certain that Jessica, at least, will find a thousand ways to make immediate use of her unexpected affluence!'

A flicker of a smile touched Imogen's lips. 'No doubt,' she replied coolly, suddenly determined that Beresford's remarkably detached manner in the face of their recent imbroglio would in no way surpass her own. 'Although, may I suggest that the family coach might be more suitable to accommodate all the purchases she is likely to make if she is given free rein!'

Beresford eyed her with a growing respect. He was, of course, perfectly well aware that he had behaved abominably and that he should have offered an immediate apology and explanation for his outrageous conduct. The most disturbing thing was, however, that no matter how hard he strove to understand what had happened, he was unable to come up with any sort of reasonable explanation for his reckless behaviour. The whole incident had astounded him, being, as it was, so completely out of character with the self-possessed way in which he normally comported himself.

Years of having to fend for himself had taught him this remarkable self-discipline—never to rely totally on anyone else's support, never to put himself in the invidious position of being obligated to anyone and, most important of all, never to allow another living creature to catch even a glimpse of the slightly insecure, neglected small boy who still lurked beneath the grown man's urbane composure.

Like Seymour, he had had his share of romantic liaisons in India, even in the face of a persistent shortage of eligible European women. Both men had, somehow, managed to find themselves at the right social gathering, at just the right moment, to avail themselves of whatever opportunities might arise—and there were always the local women, of course, even though the Company frowned upon such liaisons. Nevertheless, throughout all of his amatory adventures, Beresford had never allowed any of them to spiral out of his control and had always been ready to bow out of a situation if it seemed to be getting out of hand. He had almost certainly dented a few hearts along the way, but his own still remained remarkably unbruised. Until today, that was, and, as the realisation of what was happening to him gradually dawned, he discovered that he did not at all care for the terrifying sensation of helplessness that it engendered and determined to rectify the situation.

Glancing down at his silent companion, he was mortified to see that she was shivering slightly and realised that the air had grown much cooler.

'You are getting chilled,' he said and, ignoring her disclaimers, he took her firmly by the arm and led her back into the warmth of the candle-lit salon. Imogen was astonished to find that their prolonged absence had barely been noticed, Lady Beresford having fallen fast asleep on her *chaise-longue*, despite the fact that the remainder of the group was engaged in a rousing game of Newmarket.

At their entrance Jessica looked up with a wide smile.

'Oh, do come and join us, Matt,' she cooed invitingly, clearly having forgiven him for his earlier rebuke. 'Seymour is winning all the hands—I swear he must be cheating!'

'Not so!' protested Seymour, laughing. 'Hand on heart, Miss Beresford!'

'I dare say that he has had a good deal more practice,' returned Beresford drily and, turning to Imogen, he said, 'What do you say, Miss Priestley? Shall we show them how it is done?'

She smiled faintly, but did not meet his eyes. If he wanted to pretend that nothing out of the ordinary had occurred between them, so be it. She was more than happy to forget the whole sorry incident, but then reminded herself that she must be constantly on her guard in his company, for the man was obviously not to be trusted. The sooner she could remove herself from Thornfield and from him, the better!

Chapter Eight

Having slept very badly, if at all, Imogen leapt from her bed as soon as the dawn light began to spread its pearly glow across the sky and hurriedly donned her riding habit, intent upon getting out of the house before any of the others should wake and demand to join her in her early morning ride.

Crossing the stable yard, she glanced nervously about her, all the time expecting Wentworth to make one of his sudden unwelcome appearances. She wondered where he might be hiding himself and peered cautiously into the dim recesses of the tackroom before going in to collect her saddle and bridle. There was no sign of him, but, on entering the stable block, she saw that Midnight, her late uncle's black stallion, was not in his stall and a wave of anger ran through her at the manager's overconfident presumption that he could help himself to whichever horse took his fancy, whenever he chose to do so. It would appear that Beresford's words had had little effect on his audacious conduct as he seemed to be intent upon carrying on just as he had done before Beresford's arrival.

As she guided her mare up the little lane past the farm, she could hear the distant clanking of the pails in the cowshed, along with Ben Chadwick's soft, encouraging murmur, and realised that, as early as it was, he must have already started the milking. She wondered what was going to become of the injured man now that a new master had finally appeared on the scene and hoped that Beresford would be able to find him some occupation more in keeping with the fine education that Chadwick had afforded his son.

Once she was out into the open country, she rode furiously for some miles, giving Portia her head at every available opportunity and taking all her fences at breakneck speed, often with a careless disregard for life or limb, until her natural common sense prevailed and she gradually relaxed her reckless pace to a steady canter before eventually turning the mare's head towards the tranquil seclusion of a little spot she had found some years previously.

Reining in at the top of the little hill, she gazed down at the picturesque view beneath her. It was quite her most favourite place in the area and where she was wont to hide herself whenever she needed to be alone with her thoughts. The sparsely wooded incline in front of her swept gently down to the riverbed below, through which the placid Ancholme curved its way north through the Kelsey Becks before combining with the great Humber itself and flowing out to the North Sea. It was a very peaceful spot, seldom frequented by any but the local rabbit population, and Imogen had spent many a quiet, contemplative hour sitting on the riverbank, watching the graceful swans gliding majestically downstream or laughing at the comical antics of the ducks as they squabbled amongst themselves.

Edging Portia close to a rocky outcrop, which served as a convenient mounting block, she dismounted and, after tethering the mare securely to the low-hanging branch of a nearby tree, removed her hat and gloves and untied her stock, shaking out her hair until it fell in a loose tumble of waves about her shoulders.

Throwing back her head, she filled her lungs with the clean, fresh morning air, revelling in the growing warmth of the sun, before carefully picking her way through the lightly wooded slope that led down to the riverbank. She was aware that she had very little time to spare before she had to return to Thornfield to keep her appointment with Beresford, but was determined to pay just one more (possibly her last) visit to her secluded haunt. Any free time that she might have had was now bound to be spent in helping Chadwick set the books to right, or in training new housemaids, making it very unlikely that she would be given any further opportunity to take herself off on one of her solitary rides before she and Miss Widdecombe departed for Westmorland four weeks hence.

She had almost reached the bottom of the grassy slope when, to her dismay, the nearby sound of a resonant baritone voice raised in song penetrated her hearing. She froze instantly in her tracks, and then cautiously sidestepped behind the trunk of a nearby birch tree, before furtively peeping out around its slender silver girth. The astonishing sight that met her eyes caused a hot rush of blood to her cheeks and she had to clamp her fingers to her mouth in order to stifle the gasp of combined disbelief and admiration that threatened to escape her lips.

On the brink of the riverbank, a mere twenty yards downstream from where she had concealed herself, the totally unclothed figure of a man stood poised, his back towards her and his arms outstretched, evidently about to dive into the cool, limpid waters of the river below him. Awestruck, Imogen was unable to take her eyes off the sheer athletic grace and taut muscular strength of the impressive physique with which she inadvertently found herself confronted.

Then, in a flash, the splendidly bronzed form pierced the water like an arrow, slid underneath the surface and momentarily disappeared, only to resurface several yards further upstream, almost opposite her hiding-place. As the man proceeded to flip languidly over on to his back, Imogen hastily retreated, her cheeks burning in consternation as she recognised the identity of the naked swimmer below. Then, to her horror, her heel caught in the trailing hem of her riding skirt and she tripped and fell forward. Unable to regain her footing on the dew-drenched grass, she slid unceremoniously down the remainder of the slope, landing at its foot in an ungainly sprawl.

Beresford, his eyes closed, floating peacefully in the river's gentle current, immediately snapped to attention at the violent, crashing noise that had so rudely invaded his reverie and, instinctively turning on to his front, he ducked under the surface. Within a few swift strokes he had reached the river's edge where, treading water, he raised his head warily above an overhanging limestone shelf and found himself looking directly into Imogen Priestley's panic-stricken eyes, scarcely five feet away from him.

'Well, I really would not have taken you for a Peeping Tom, Miss Priestley,' he grinned, leaning his forearms on the ledge, his face alight with laughter, as he watched her angry attempts to rise to her feet amidst the confused tangle of skirts and petticoats.

'In the normal way, of course, I would be only too happy to offer to assist you in your difficulty,' he said, with a deep chuckle, and made as if to pull himself out of the water. 'But, perhaps, in the circumstances…?'

Scarlet-faced, Imogen shot him a look of unabated fury.

'Do not dare, sir!' she hissed, as she finally managed to stand up, and dragged her twisted petticoat round with such force that the waist strings snapped and it fell to her ankles in a snowy, billowing heap.

'Hmm—Valenciennes lace—how very charming!' observed Beresford, his smile widening. 'Was it your intention to join me in an early morning dip?'

Now deeply embarrassed, Imogen struggled to extricate herself from the offending garment and, in so doing, fell to her knees once again.

Beresford stopped smiling and his eyes filled with concern. 'Are you hurt?' he asked anxiously.

'I am perfectly fine, thank you,' she said, through gritted teeth, scrambling awkwardly to her feet and angrily swishing her riding-skirt back into place. 'There is nothing I like better than rolling about a muddy riverbank!'

'A strange pastime, if I may say so!' he laughed, his golden tan emphasising the whiteness of his teeth. 'And, would that be along with spying on unsuspecting swimmers or instead of, I wonder?'

'I assure you that I did not realise that there would be anyone else here,' she retorted angrily, bending down to retrieve her crumpled petticoat and gathering it up into an untidy bundle. 'It is normally quite deserted—I cannot imagine how you came upon it so far from Thornfield.'

'Quite by accident, I promise you, Miss Priestley,' said Beresford, smiling up at her as he rested his chin on his folded arms. 'I was following the river, looking for a likely spot to take a dip.'

She flushed, recalling the powerful sensations that had run through her at the unexpected spectacle of his lithe, naked flesh.

'Then I must apologise for interrupting you,' she said, as she hooked the hem of her riding-skirt over her arm and turned to go. 'I will leave you to continue your—activity.'

'If it is all the same to you, ma'am, I believe I would just as soon quit,' he replied, suddenly threshing his legs in the water. 'Small creatures appear to be taking an excessive interest in my lower half! If you were to wait for a few minutes while I dress, perhaps we could, at least, ride back together?'

'You are surely not suggesting that I should remain here while you climb out and collect your garments?' asked Imogen, endeavouring to appear affronted, for she was finding it very difficult to keep her eyes averted from the fascinating sight of the rivulets of water trickling down from the dark, blond tendrils of his wet hair on to his naked bronzed shoulders. And, try as she might, she could hardly help but cast her mind back to the previous evening and, more particularly, to the totally unexpected sensations that had arisen within her when those same muscular arms had pulled her so powerfully into that broad manly chest.

'Well, since you already appear to have seen as much of me as there is to see,' came Beresford's voice, teasingly interrupting her distracted thoughts, 'I was rather hoping that I might persuade you to go and fetch them!'

'Mr Beresford!'

Hurriedly regaining her senses, Imogen's eyes widened in shock. 'I assure you—I did not—that is—I was not...'

But then, as the latter half of his speech registered, her voice suddenly trailed away and a speculative gleam came into her eyes, then, to Beresford's utter astonishment, she started to chuckle, softly at first, but, as her shoulders began to shake with the effort of suppressing her amusement, she finally let out a delicious gurgle and was soon helpless with laughter, tears streaming down her face.

'Miss Priestley?' Beresford was completely bewildered, but, situated as he was, he could do no more than wait and watch in fascinated wonder until, at last, Imogen managed to regain a degree of control.

'I—I do b-beg your pardon, Mr Beresford,' she hiccoughed, wiping her streaming eyes with a fold of her discarded petticoat. 'I was just trying to imagine what Miss Widdecombe would do in a similar situation!'

'My guess is that she would probably run a mile,' said Beresford with another wide smile, finding himself more than slightly curious over Imogen's unexpected change of manner.

Still smiling, Imogen shook her head. 'No,' she averred. 'She would be more likely to whack you soundly over the head with her parasol.' She turned and looked searchingly along the riverbank. 'Now, where did you leave your clothes?'

Blinking in surprise, Beresford gestured to a large clump

of bushes that was situated up in the copse further along the riverbank.

'Just under that big hawthorn up there,' he said. 'But, are you sure that you want to do this, Miss Priestley? If you would just turn your back for a moment, I can be out of the water and collect them myself in two shakes.'

'Oh, I assure you that it is really no trouble at all, Mr Beresford,' she answered sweetly and started towards the spot he had indicated.

His eyes narrowing, he stared after her departing figure. Then, with a vehement oath, as the awful realisation of her intentions suddenly hit him, he twisted frantically in the water and, with furiously powerful strokes, began to cover the short distance downstream.

Imogen, hearing the splash, made a desperate effort to quicken her steps but, encumbered as she was with her petticoat roughly bundled under her arm, having to gather up the trailing hem of her now rather damp and heavy riding skirt with only one hand meant that her progress along the slippery grass was rather slower than she would have wished.

Gasping for breath, she eventually reached the foot of the incline below the spot where Beresford had indicated that his clothes were secreted and began to scramble up the slope which, as she very quickly realised, was much steeper and far more thickly wooded than her own preferred route to the riverside.

Another loud splash told her that Beresford had emerged from the water and was close on her heels. Feverishly she tried to make her way through the tangled undergrowth, unable to discern the simplest way up.

'And now what, Miss Priestley?' came his deep, mocking voice behind her.

Then suddenly, she felt his hand upon her shoulder and froze, rigid with shock. Although her heart seemed to have leapt violently into the region of her throat and she could hardly breathe, she made herself stand absolutely still and waited for what she felt sure would be the ultimate degradation, when her captor would surely spin her round and gleefully force her to face his unclad maleness. Her rash and foolish prank had badly backfired and she must now be prepared to face the consequences. She clenched her fists and closed her eyes, waiting for the inevitable.

To her surprise, however, Beresford merely tightened his grip and proceeded to thrust her forward through a narrow gap in the scrub.

'Just keep your eyes to the front,' he advised her tersely, gritting his teeth and cursing silently as the sharp twigs sprang back and lashed at his unprotected flesh.

Her alarm increasing with every step, Imogen allowed herself to be propelled forwards until she saw, with a mixture of relief and trepidation, that they had finally reached their objective. There, folded into a neat pile and carefully concealed between the roots of a large hawthorn bush, were Beresford's riding clothes.

All at once, a glimmer of hope stirred within her and she cast around for some possible means of exit from the little clearing. They must be very close to the top of the escarpment by now, she surmised, and Beresford would undoubtedly have to unhand her in order to dress himself.

Sadly, it was not to be, for Beresford had been puzzling over that very problem and had found that a ready solution to his dilemma had already presented itself. Due to his having to stay in close proximity with his captive during the climb, he had experienced considerable difficulty in keeping clear of the trailing fabric of her riding habit, but now that they had arrived at their goal, it was but a simple matter to tread firmly on the hem, reach for his breeches and clamber into them.

'I advise you not to turn your head, Miss Priestley,' he said mischievously, as he proceeded to haul his shirt over his head in one swift movement. 'Although, I realise that, in your case, the temptation to do so must be considerable—ah! Too late, I fear! Now I am perfectly respectable and you may feast your eyes upon me for as long as you care to!'

The instant Imogen sensed that he had lifted his foot from the back of her habit, she was off, having spotted a clear opening to her left. Sure enough, it led her straight to the top of the slope and out on to the open common above where, to her amazement, she came upon Midnight tethered to a nearby tree. Biting her lip in guilty recall, she realised that it had not been Wentworth who had made free with Sir Matthew's horse, but Beresford who, of course, was perfectly entitled to do so.

The germ of another wild idea crept into her head but, after giving it some consideration, she shook her head and was reluctantly consigning the rather novel thought to perdition when the fully clad Beresford appeared.

'If you are thinking what I surmise that you are thinking, Miss Priestley,' he drawled, as he pulled on his gloves, 'I beg you not to consider it! Even if you did succeed in sending him on his way, I would have no difficulty in reaching your mare before you, which would mean that you were the one obliged to make your way home on foot, not I—as I suspect was your actual intent!'

She rounded on him, her eyes flashing. 'You, sir,' she ground out, 'are no gentleman!'

'Excuse me, madam!' he snorted indignantly. 'Were I not a gentleman, you might well have found yourself in a pretty pickle back there!'

'I suppose you consider your behaviour last evening to be that of the gentleman, too?' she could not resist taunting him. 'Whilst that sort of behaviour may have been commonplace in the society in which you recently resided, kindly allow me to inform you that to go around forcing your kisses on unsuspecting young ladies in this country is considered totally beyond the pale!'

'Forcing my kisses!' he spluttered, completely taken aback at her accusation. 'I will have you know, Miss High and Mighty, that I have never in my life found it necessary to force my kisses on to any female—either here or abroad!' Clenching his fist, he struggled to control his irritation. 'In the event, I seem to recall that I managed to resist your temptations rather well, so you can hardly count yourself compromised!'

Imogen was outraged. 'I trust that you are not suggesting that your actions were due to any encouragement of mine, sir!' she flung at him.

'No, sadly not,' he countered, unabashed, and a wicked gleam crept into his eyes. 'I fear that I shall have to blame that particular aberration on the harvest moon.'

A rosy blush covered her cheeks. 'You might, at least, have apologised for your shabby conduct,' she murmured reproachfully, although she could not help feeling that she was in considerable danger of losing the moral high ground.

He looked down at her and his heart catapulted. 'True enough,' he conceded. 'And, if you will allow me to do so, I should be very glad to remedy that omission by humbly begging your forgiveness here and now.'

She inclined her head gracefully. 'Since you are prepared to admit that your behaviour was quite outrageous…'

'Oh, come now, Miss Priestley!' he exclaimed, his lips quivering as he held back a smile. 'You are surely not going to tell me that I am the only man who has ever tried to kiss you?'

'I have no intention of telling you anything at all about my affairs, Mr Beresford,' she retorted loftily and, nose in the air, she flung her skirt hem over her arm and proceeded to stalk off in the direction of the spot where her own mount was located.

His eyes crinkling with laughter, Beresford untied Midnight, looped the reins around his hand and, within a few rapid strides, was soon strolling casually at her side.

'Affairs, is it!' he teased. 'Now I am really intrigued! Is the doughty Miss Widdecombe aware of these clandestine liaisons, I wonder?'

Against her will, Imogen found her lips beginning to twitch. 'Are you being deliberately obtuse, Mr Beresford, or does it come naturally?' she asked him, in a deceptively sweet tone of voice.

'Years of practice, I assure you, Miss Priestley,' he replied, with a careless smile, although he was inwardly marvelling at Imogen's speedy return to good humour and, suddenly recalling Nicholas's remark about her disinclination to bear a grudge, he began to feel deeply ashamed of his recent behaviour and wondered how on earth he was going to manage to redeem himself.

Portia's whinny of welcome soon informed them that they had arrived at the linden tree where she was tethered and, after retrieving her hat and gloves, Imogen set about trying to rectify some of the damage done to her appearance by her unfortunate tumble down the hillside, thankful that she had chosen to wear her old brown habit on which the tell-tale muddy patches were less likely to show.

'Here, give me that damned petticoat,' Beresford ordered gruffly and, too deflated to enter into any more verbal fisticuffs with him, she handed over her soiled undergarment. To her astonishment, he then proceeded to smooth it out carefully before folding it into a tight, neat bundle.

'It seems far more likely that I will be able to secrete it back into the house than you will,' he said, affecting complete nonchalance as he stuffed the superfluous garment down the inside front of his jacket. 'And, please do not concern yourself. I am quite sure that I will find some inconspicuous way of returning it to you.'

Although Imogen, meanwhile, had managed to coil up her hair and bundle it under her riding hat, she was agonizingly aware of Beresford's frank perusal as she tied her stock and, finally, drew on her gloves.

'Will I pass muster, do you suppose?' she asked him nervously.

For several seconds he surveyed her in silence, his expression unreadable, then, giving a brisk nod, he turned to untie her mount. 'It will suffice,' he said, a husky catch in his throat and, finding that he needed some sort of instant distraction, he pulled out his pocket-watch and flipped open the lid.

'Good Lord!' he exclaimed, hastily shoving his timepiece back into his pocket and, taking Imogen's raised foot into his cupped hands, he tossed her expertly on to her saddle. 'It is almost half past seven and I instructed Ben Chadwick to have the carriage round at eight!'

'Ben Chadwick?' Imogen gasped in surprise, as she wheeled Portia round and waited for Beresford to mount. 'I doubt if Wentworth will stand for that!'

'Wentworth seems to have gone to earth,' he replied abruptly. 'I was unable to find him anywhere—Ben's our new under-manager, by the way.' He gave her a quick glance. 'We will have to ride like the very devil! Ready?'

In response, she flicked her whip lightly on Portia's flank and took off, but the laughing Beresford was soon hot on her heels and, having discovered that they had barely half an hour to cover the ten-mile journey, there was no further opportunity for conversation. In point of fact, since both horses were perfectly happy to tackle a second invigorating gallop across country, they managed to arrive at Thornfield with several minutes in hand.

Chapter Nine

Upon entering the stable yard, they were confronted with the unexpected sight of a motley collection of individuals gathered at the back door of the house, several of whom Imogen recognised as having been previous members of her late uncle's staff.

One fresh-faced young man hurried over to her and reached out to steady Portia as Imogen unhooked her knee from the pommel and stepped down on to the mounting block.

'Morning, Miss Imogen,' he said awkwardly. His eyes held a somewhat anxious look. 'Heard you was taking people on again—couldn't have me old job back, I suppose?'

'I am afraid that you will have to speak to the new master, Jimmy,' she told him kindly, gesturing towards Beresford.

'But you'll put in a word for me, miss?' he asked hopefully, hovering at her side, as she made her way towards the expectantly waiting throng. 'I never wanted to leave, you know, but me mum needed me wages…'

'I am sure that you have no need to worry, Jimmy.' She smiled. 'Mr Chadwick will give you all the references you require. He always spoke very highly of you.'

'Thanks, miss.' The youth's eyes glowed with gratitude as he stood back to allow her to enter the house through the kitchen door.

Beresford, dismounting near the stable, had watched the little scene with growing interest and, as soon as Imogen had disappeared into the house, he called the lad over to him.

'Jimmy, is it?'

The youth nodded, a wary expression crossing his face.

'What position did you hold in Sir Matthew's employ?'

'I were training for under-groom, sir,' replied Jimmy, nervously straightening his shoulders.

'Excellent! Consider yourself re-employed,' grinned Beresford, and tossed Midnight's reins to him. 'I shall check them both, mind, so make sure you do a thorough job!'

'Right away, sir!'

Carefully leading the sweating stallion into his stall, the delighted youth was soon happily involved in his favourite task. The past few months had not been kind to him and he had gone from one lowly paid job to the next, glad to take whatever was available in order to bring home some sort of wage to his widowed mother.

Beresford strode over to the open office door to be greeted by a beaming Chadwick, who had already set about reorganising the untidy pile of paperwork left on the desk to his own exacting standards.

'Word of your arrival seems to have reached the locals, sir,' he said, with a satisfied smile on his face. 'Quite a few of the old faces, too, if I am not much mistaken.'

Beresford nodded. 'So I hear,' he replied and nodded towards the stable block. 'By the way, I have just reinstated one of your ex-grooms—young lad—name of Jimmy—Miss Priestley seemed to approve of him.'

'Yes? Excellent! That will be Jimmy Fairchild—very good worker. I was sorry to see him go.'

'However, it does look as if our trip to Ashby is going to be somewhat delayed,' observed Beresford, as he surveyed the growing number of hopeful workers in the yard. 'I had better have someone inform Miss Priestley that our plans have changed.'

As it happened, Imogen had already appreciated that the un-expected return of so many previous employees would, of ne-cessity, demand her immediate and wholehearted attention and, as she hurriedly climbed out of her soiled riding-dress and pulled on a dark blue morning gown, she realised that their ar-rival would also provide her with a perfect excuse to decline Beresford's invitation to accompany him to the market.

After her highly unsettling experiences earlier, she was somewhat reluctant to find herself obliged to spend any more time in close company with him although, having had the op-portunity to reflect upon her own, rather shocking performance, she was bound to acknowledge that his adept handling of the situation had actually been quite estimable.

Indeed, as she sat at her dressing table, brushing the tangles out of her hair, she discovered that she was already beginning to revise her previous poor opinion of him and, as she recalled the uncomplaining way in which he had endured his enforced sojourn against the muddy embankment, her lips began to curve in a little smile of appreciation. She was then obliged to admit to herself that, in those rather trying circumstances, Beresford's remarkable stoicism deserved more than a modicum of admi-ration, especially in the light of his offhand allusion to the un-welcome activities of the 'small creatures' beneath the surface.

However, no sooner had that rather emotive image presented itself to her, than other, more enticing, memories began to flood into her consciousness and she found herself flushing with guilty shame as she recalled the disquieting sensations that had invaded her body in that breathtaking moment when she had first caught sight of Matt Beresford's bronzed nakedness poised on the riverbank.

She stared into the looking-glass, aghast at the wicked thoughts that were running through her head, then, taking up her brush again, she swept it vigorously through her hair with renewed determination, reminding her wide-eyed reflection that this preposterous state of affairs simply would not do.

Although she could hardly help being fascinated by his very engaging manner, her natural common sense told her that, as with the majority of men fortunate enough to have been blessed with both handsome face and outstanding physique, he was simply an accomplished flirt and, in that respect, no different from his friend Seymour, who evidently regarded that particular pastime as a way of life. Such a practised charmer as she suspected Beresford was would, no doubt, be well skilled in dealing with relatively unsophisticated females like herself.

Although it was perfectly true that Imogen had been besieged with offers during her one and only visit to the capital, her numerous suitors had comprised, on the one hand, a succession of ageing roués desperate to get their hands on her fortune, and an equally hopeful but rather foolish coterie of young popinjays on the other, not one of whom had impressed her in the slightest.

Even Lady Sydenham, who had taken it upon herself to preside over her god-daughter's coming-out and with whom Imogen had resided during her stay, had expressed sorrow and disappointment at the unusual dearth of suitable and presentable young men that year. However, Imogen had felt bound to remind her sponsor that the country was, after all, at war and the majority of able-bodied men with any real spirit were surely more likely to be overseas involved in the fighting than attending balls and soirées in London.

Moreover, it was not as if she had gone to London with any high expectations of coming face to face with Prince Charming although, as she recalled wistfully, in those days she had been rather more of a romantic dreamer than she was now.

As it happened, she had been introduced to his Royal Highness, the Prince Regent, and had found him to be ugly, gross, and not at all charming. Quite the reverse, in fact, for he had ogled her décolletage quite dreadfully and she had been rather thankful when the presentation line had moved her forward out of his view.

She stabbed the final pin into her hair and gave a little sigh. Barely two days ago she had been looking forward to starting a new life in Kendal and leaving all the vexing problems at Thornfield well behind her and now, it seemed, she found herself presented with a far more difficult and dangerous predicament to overcome.

She was idly wondering whether it would be possible to persuade Mr Widmark, her man of business, to advance her the coming quarter's allowance in order to hasten her flight from Thornfield, when she heard Allardyce knock on her door bringing her the message from Beresford.

'And what am I to do about the press of people at the back door, Miss Priestley?' he wanted to know. 'Mr Beresford has already taken quite a large number of them and is presently dealing with them across the yard, but there are still a good many hoping to regain their positions.'

'I shall be with you almost immediately, Allardyce,' Imogen assured him. 'If you are able to pick out any ex-members of staff who you would be happy to re-engage, you might show them up into the morning room and I will speak to them.'

She spent the remainder of the morning tirelessly interviewing past and prospective employees, stopping only once to partake of the light nuncheon that Miss Widdecombe, having brought up the tray herself, insisted that Imogen must consume without delay.

'If Mr Beresford and Mr Chadwick can see fit to suspend their activities long enough to catch their breaths and take in some sustenance, my girl,' chided the governess, 'then so can you! Eat up, now, we cannot have you fainting all over the new help.'

'Now, that *would* be rather spectacular, Widdy,' agreed Imogen laughing, as she helped herself to a dainty cucumber sandwich from the plate that Miss Widdecombe proffered. 'Have you any idea how they are progressing out there?'

'Quite well, I believe,' the governess replied. 'Nicholas tells me that most of the old farm workers have returned and have been given back their cottages, although what sort of state they will find them in, Heaven only knows! I doubt if anyone has looked at them since they were vacated.'

'I will go down and check them later,' nodded Imogen, wiping her mouth. 'I take it that there has been no further sign of Wentworth?'

'None at all,' confirmed Miss Widdecombe. 'But it would appear that he has removed all of his belongings from the gamekeeper's cottage so, with luck, we have seen the last of the scoundrel. I dare say the Sawbridges will be particularly delighted that he has gone.'

Imogen stood up and took a few turns about the room to stretch her cramped limbs. 'Jake especially, I should think. He was really afraid of him.'

'So Mrs Sawbridge told me,' replied the governess. 'Anyway, it seems that the lad has been out in the stables helping young Jimmy Fairchild most of the morning. I recall a time when it was almost impossible to keep him away from the horses but, sadly, Wentworth soon put a stop to that after your uncle died. Jake would never even venture into the yard if he thought Wentworth was about.'

'That is hardly surprising, when you consider how beastly the man was to the poor lad when he thought no one was looking. I must try to have a word with him when I have finished with this final group of applicants.'

'You really must stop trying to do everything yourself, Imogen!' said Miss Widdecombe tartly. 'You will wear yourself out and then where will we be?'

'And you, dear Widdy, really must stop worrying about me,'

said Imogen with a smile, as she returned to her seat and picked up the lists that Allardyce had given her. 'Just at the moment, I confess that I am rather glad to have such a lot to occupy me.' She did not feel it necessary to add that it prevented her mind from dwelling on other, more disturbing matters.

'If you say so, my dear.'

After casting a doubtful glance in Imogen's direction, Miss Widdecombe picked up the tea tray and left the room. She had not lived in the same house for sixteen years without having learnt to recognise when her former pupil was deeply troubled and, being far wiser than many people gave her credit for, the little governess sincerely hoped that her growing suspicions as to the cause of her young friend's discomposure would prove to be far from the case.

By late afternoon, Imogen had successfully filled most of the vacant posts, the majority of which were taken up again by former members of the household. Several of these, only too eager to return to their previous positions, assured her that they would be more than happy to resume their duties the following day. However, since she had been unable to find a suitable housekeeper, Imogen deemed it advisable to seek out Mrs Sawbridge and instruct the cook on the below-stairs etiquette that she would be obliged to follow until this important post could be filled.

'It seems that Mrs Harvey has left the district and taken up a position elsewhere, Cook,' she informed her. 'Until we find a suitable replacement for her, I fear that I will need you to take charge of the entire female staff. However, I am sure that you will be relieved to hear that both Becky and Janet will be returning to the kitchen tomorrow. So, it is to be hoped that everything in your own domain will be almost back to normal by next week.'

'Don't you worry, miss—reckon it's not beyond me to manage a few housemaids,' Mrs Sawbridge assured her, then urged, 'Now, you sit yourself down and let me make you a nice cup of tea. You look fair worn out and that's a fact.'

Imogen shook her head. 'I would dearly love to do just that, Cook, but I really must go across and inspect the cottages before it gets dark. I need to see if any of them are fit for re-occupation. I did want to have a quick word with Jake, though—is he out in the yard?'

'Still in the stables,' said Mrs Sawbridge, beaming. 'Been there most of the day. Haven't seen him this happy for ages. Keeps telling anyone who cares to listen that the "bad man" has gone away.' She gave a short laugh and brushed away the tears that were threatening to form. 'He were right wicked, that Wentworth, miss. Fair broke Jake's heart when he drowned them kittens.'

'Yes, I remember,' said Imogen, her own eyes clouding over as she recalled the youth's heartrending sobs following Wentworth's unjustified removal of the cat's litter from the stable loft and worse, the man's abominable act of cruelty when, in front of Jake's horrified gaze, he had callously tossed the helpless creatures into the duck pond and had stood by, laughing uproariously as they struggled vainly to save themselves.

She shook her head. 'It is impossible to fathom the depths to which some human beings can sink, Mrs Sawbridge,' she sighed. 'But, hopefully, given time, Jake will be able to put all that behind him and go back to being the happy-go-lucky soul he once was.'

'Amen to that, miss,' replied Mrs Sawbridge fervently. 'Until that fiend came there wasn't a day went by without me blessing the day that her dear ladyship took me on all those years ago, babe and all and, if it weren't for her…' Sniffing, she picked up the corner of her apron and dabbed it to her eyes.

'I know, Mrs Sawbridge.' Imogen gently squeezed the cook's shoulder. 'And I am sure that Lady Beresford will never forget how indispensable both you and Jake have proved to be over the last year. I really do not know what we would have done without you.'

'Ah, no, miss!' protested Cook, although Imogen's words seemed to have cheered her somewhat. 'We all know that it's you that's really kept everything together and it seems to me, now that this Mr Beresford has finally come to take charge, you can give yourself a well-earned rest.'

'We can but hope,' replied Imogen with a weak smile, as she turned to leave the room. 'In the meantime, I still have to go and check those cottages.'

Crossing the now-deserted yard, she could not help wondering if Beresford was still involved in his labours. She cast a curious glance in the direction of the office, but saw that the door was shut fast, making it impossible for her to see whether or not the room was occupied. She was making her way past the stable block when Jake Sawbridge appeared, toting a heavy bale of straw on his shoulders. However, the instant he set eyes upon her, he dropped his bundle and, waving frantically, he hurried over to her and clutched at her arm.

'Bad man's gone, Miss Imo,' he said gleefully. 'Gone right away!'

Imogen laughed as she patted his hand. 'Yes, Jake,' she said. 'Good news for all of us, I think!'

'Made things go dead, he did, Miss Imo. Did bad things.'

'Yes, Jake, I know he did, but he has gone now and you must stop worrying about him,' Imogen told him gently.

He fastened his eyes on her face. 'Don't want Jake to go dead, miss.'

She frowned, puzzling over his words. 'We would never have allowed him to hurt you, Jake. You must know that, surely?'

He blinked several times and looked away. 'Bad man won't come back to get Jake?'

'Get you?' Imogen was at a loss. 'No one is going to "get" you, Jake, I promise you. Now, how would you like to walk down to the cottages with me? I might have need of a big, strong boy like you to help me move some things.'

'Yes. Big, strong Jake help Miss Imo,' he replied vaguely, at the same time casting a longing look back towards the stable door. 'Jake help with horses.'

'Yes, Jake,' said Imogen, guiding him persuasively towards the back lane. 'You can come and see the horses again later.'

Picking up a stick, the youth shambled along beside her, aimlessly swishing at the hedges as he passed. He seemed to be rapt in thought and Imogen found herself wondering, as she had so often done in the past, what actually went on inside his mind and how much of what was happening around him he really understood.

They had almost reached the first set of dwellings when Beresford appeared at the far end of the lane. The unexpected sight of his tall figure ducking out of one of the doorways caused Imogen's heart to lurch severely and an extraordinary mixture of anticipation and apprehension swept over her.

'Ah, Miss Priestley!' he hailed her, as he strode quickly towards them. 'Good wits jump to similar conclusions, it seems. Am I correct in surmising that you, too, have come to cast an eagle eye over these cottages?'

Although her heart was thumping quite dreadfully, she forced herself to return his smile. 'Why, yes, Mr Beresford, you are perfectly correct in that assumption. Do I take it that my presence is superfluous?'

'If by that you mean, "Is the task completed?" then the answer must be "Yes", Miss Priestley,' he said, with a challenging gleam in his eye. 'In any other respect, I doubt if such a thing could be possible!'

As a slight blush coloured her cheeks, Imogen quickly glanced round to determine whether Jake was still within earshot.

Not that the lad would have the slightest idea what Beresford was talking about, of course, but that did not prevent her from feeling somewhat discomfited at Beresford's provocative words.

To her surprise, she found Jake lurking behind her with a highly uneasy expression on his face. It was not difficult to fathom out the cause of his concern. Taking his arm, she drew the reluctant youth forward.

'Come now, Jake,' she said, with an encouraging smile. 'This is the master—you remember—you saw him in the dining room last evening.'

The youth backed away, shaking his head. 'Not master,' he argued. 'Master went dead—Jake saw.'

'New master,' said Imogen patiently. 'He will not hurt you, Jake. He is a nice man, a good man.'

'Oh, praise indeed!' From over her shoulder she heard Beresford's faint murmur and she felt herself flushing again, but, knowing that she could not rise to the bait in front of young Jake, she chose to ignore his remark.

'*New* master, Jake,' she repeated, then sighed as she realised that Jake was no longer listening to her, but was scowling suspiciously at Beresford, his lower lip thrust out in a stubborn pout. Racking her brain for some sort of inspiration, she had a sudden brainwave.

'New master is going to give you a kitten, Jake,' she told him. 'As soon as Tabby has her next litter, master will allow you to choose one of her kittens to keep for yourself. Just think, Jake— a kitty of your very own to take care of!'

Catching sight of the astonished look on Beresford's face, she flicked him a warning frown and gave him a brief nod.

Although he had not the slightest idea of what was going on, Beresford cleared his throat and eventually managed to ask, 'You would like a kitten of your own, Jake?'

Jake's face cleared instantly. 'Kitty for Jake,' he said, with a beaming smile.

'Say "Thank you" to master, Jake,' Imogen reminded him.

'Yes, thank master,' repeated the youth. 'New master, good master.'

Imogen breathed a sigh of relief.

'You may go back to the stable and see the horses now, Jake. Thank you for helping me.'

Her eyes were full of compassion as she watched the youth amble slowly back down the lane then, turning to Beresford, she gave him an apologetic smile. 'I am so sorry about that, Mr Beresford. We normally have no problem with the boy. It is just that he has been in a constant state of excitement since he found out that Wentworth is no longer with us.'

He shook his head, marvelling at her resourcefulness. 'Please do not apologise, Miss Priestley,' he protested. 'You appeared to have the situation well in hand, although I am blessed if I understood all the stuff about kittens—the lad may have as many kittens as he wants, as far as I am concerned.'

Imogen laughed. 'I had to think of something quickly in order to take his mind off you for a moment—he does get a little fixated, sometimes. But do let me explain about the kittens.'

She went on to give him a brief but succinct account of Wentworth's malicious harassment of the youngster, after which Beresford remained silent for several moments. Then, with a slight catch in his voice, he said, 'Like all bullies, the man proved to be an out-and-out coward, of course.'

Imogen nodded. 'He certainly seemed to take a fiendish delight in deliberately badgering Jake, who was unable to retaliate, of course. I did try to remonstrate with him on several occasions, but he chose to ignore me.'

Beresford eyed her thoughtfully, 'You have had a pretty awful time of it really, have you not, Miss Priestley?' And, as he was unlikely to forget, his own less than-chivalrous conduct towards her had hardly improved matters.

Imogen shrugged. 'One does what one has to do, Mr Beresford. Jake has been part of my life for as long as I can remember and it disgusts me that anyone could derive pleasure from tormenting him.'

'My own sentiments exactly,' he replied. 'There is no excuse for that kind of behaviour and you have my word that I will do all I can to make certain that any new hand we take on understands that the lad is not to be taunted or ridiculed.'

'Oh, would you?' Imogen stopped and turned to face him, a soft, warm glow lighting up her eyes. 'I really would be much obliged. We have all grown rather fond of him and, as you have seen, he is such an innocent.'

Looking down at her eager expression, Beresford's heart seemed to skip a number of beats and it occurred to him that, at this moment, there was nothing in the world that he would not do to keep that ardent look on her face. He was then obliged to remind himself of the vow he had made less than twenty-four hours previously and, as he did so, he felt a sudden lowering of spirits, for it was now becoming quite obvious to him that every minute he spent in Imogen's company was going to place him in serious danger of breaking that vow, and it was absolutely imperative that he should not do so. To become involved in a casual affair with Imogen Priestley was totally out of the question and any suggestion of a more lasting attachment, highly compelling though that thought might be, was even more impossible to contemplate.

As far as Beresford was concerned, constant reminders of his own mother's untimely death had persuaded him that no man with a grain of decency would ever invite any lady for whom he had the slightest regard to join him in the stifling heat of the disease-ridden plains of India, although he was well aware that, not only his father, but a good many of his own East India associates had chosen to do just that.

Over the years, it had pained Beresford to register the arrival of wave after wave of hopeful young women who, having been petitioned by equally positive suitors, had happily left their homeland behind, more than eager to begin what they had been given to believe would be a bright new future in the mysterious hinterland of the tropical sub-continent. It had become depressingly obvious to him, however, how very few of these delicate creatures managed to survive the oppressive heat of their first monsoon. Those who did so were then often left with insufficient stamina to withstand their first bout of the debilitating cholera or the endemic malaria that seemed to accompany every rainy season and for which, as yet, there was still no known cure. It had been his unlucky fate to observe that more than half of his colleagues' wives and, almost worse, an appalling number of their children, had eventually succumbed to the rigours of the unforgiving climate, to which fact the overflowing cemeteries of Calcutta could bear testament.

That Beresford had, thus far, chosen to remain unwed could, for the most part, be attributed to his utter determination never to find himself in that unendurable situation which his colleagues had, as far as he was concerned, brought upon themselves. He had always sworn that he would never commit the folly of asking any gently bred female to share his life out in the tropics, no matter how compelling that thought might be, since he had learned that only the toughest and most robust women could hope to survive in such extreme conditions and he, personally, was not prepared to risk another's life on such a selfishly reckless gamble.

Until this particular moment, that is, as he found himself strolling along a leafy English lane in the late afternoon sunshine, alongside the only female who had ever caused him to call into question the rigid philosophy upon which he had based his entire way of living. His admiration for the unflinching steadfastness with which this lovely and intelligent girl had, in the face of the considerable odds stacked against her, struggled to keep the family afloat, was increasing by the minute. Her charm, her undoubted self-assurance, tempered by faultless manners, her delicious sense of humour—all the qualities any man would look for in a wife. How well she would fit into the social life in India, he found himself thinking but, at the self-same moment that this incredible thought entered his mind, an involuntary shudder passed through him. *India!* God, no! Had he not seen more than enough English roses wilt in that oppressive climate? His jaw clenched and he was very much aware that, unless he took immediate steps to counteract this growing regard, his usually steadfast resolve might well be in danger of crumbling away.

Beresford's silent contemplation and his failure to offer any sort of response to Imogen's final remarks about Jake Sawbridge's difficulties caused her to wonder if she had been, perhaps, rather more forthcoming than was proper in the circumstances. The man had already given her the impression that he would have preferred not to have to deal with the vexing problems that his estranged father had bequeathed him, so it was hardly likely that he could be expected to have any real interest in the lives of his father's workforce, other than to see that they carried out the duties for which he was having to pay them.

It occurred to her that what she had taken to be a caring and sympathetic proposal on Beresford's part was, in all probability, merely what he considered to be the most sensible way to avoid possible future difficulties during his enforced visit. In any event, he would, doubtless, be leaving as soon as he had completed his task—by which time, of course, as she was hastily obliged to remind herself, she too would have left Thornfield.

Conscious of the growing silence between them, not to mention Imogen's frequent puzzled glances in his direction, Beresford sought to find a more light-hearted subject upon which they might discourse and one which might take his mind off her tantalising nearness.

'You will, no doubt, be glad to hear that I found most of the cottages to be in a fairly good state of repair,' he eventually managed. 'Some roof tiles need to be replaced on a couple of them, but, apart from the wilderness state of the garden plots, I deem them fit for habitation.'

Her eyes swivelled to his impassive face and, determined to appear as coolly objective as he seemed to be, she replied evenly, 'I imagine that the men will be far too glad to get their jobs back to concern themselves over the state of the gardens. I must confess that I was rather more concerned about the internal living conditions—some of the men will be returning with wives and young families. You inspected the chimneys, I suppose?'

'Well, I did not climb up on to the rooftops, if that is what you are asking!' he faltered, somewhat taken aback by her question.

She pursed her lips. 'You know perfectly well that is not what I meant,' she retorted. 'I was referring to the possibility of sootfalls in the fire grates. We can hardly expect people to move into accommodation that is full of soot!' She came to a halt in the lane and, rounding on him, she demanded. 'You did check them properly, Mr Beresford? Otherwise I shall be obliged to go back and do it myself!'

'Oh, really, Miss Priestley!' he protested, with just the glimmer of a smile appearing on his lips. 'I am beginning to get the impression that you take me for some sort of novice. Please allow me to assure you that I gave each and every cottage a thorough going over and, as I believe I said earlier, I deem them fit for occupation. Satisfied?'

'Well, if you are absolutely certain,' she replied, only slightly mollified. 'Men sometimes do not notice the sort of things that women consider to be important. You forget that I have known most of these men and their families for a good many years— several of them were forced to leave Thornfield with their wages still owing to them. You must see that I cannot help feeling a certain sense of responsibility for their welfare.'

He inclined his head and looked away, determined not to weaken in his resolve. 'Believe me, Miss Priestley, I do understand,' he said quietly. 'But you must persuade yourself that I really am perfectly capable of attending to these matters. Chadwick and I have already dealt with a good many of the servants' outstanding wages and, if it will make you feel any happier, we have also arranged for handcarts to be sent to collect the belongings of those of them who still live in the nearby vicinity.'

A guilty flush spread over Imogen's cheeks. 'You must think me the most awfully high-handed female,' she stammered. 'I really had not meant to interfere but, you see…' Her voice trailed away and she bit her lip in confusion.

'I do see perfectly,' he replied abruptly, as he struggled to maintain his detachment. 'You have carried what has been a quite intolerable burden for far too long.' His voice softened. 'Please allow me to relieve you of that burden, Miss Priestley. If you will forgive my presumption for saying so, it is my belief that the whole business has thoroughly exhausted you.'

Imogen fought back the tears that threatened to overset her studied composure. 'It *has* been a rather tiring day,' she admitted reluctantly. As well as being a far from uneventful one, an insistent voice from within seemed bent on reminding her but, as the memory of that particular scene began, once more, to invade her mind, she hurriedly turned away and said, in the most casual tone she could muster, 'No doubt one of Cook's excellent dinners will do much to revive the pair of us, Mr Beresford. I believe we could both do with some refreshment after our labours.'

They walked back up the lane in silence, he racking his brains to think of acceptable ways in which he might occupy his hours, thereby reducing the necessity of spending too much time in her company, and she, having caught the pensive frown on his face, wondering in what way she could possibly have offended him.

With a little shake of her head, she came to the conclusion that, after the highly unsettling events of the past two days, she would do well to steer clear of the man, who seemed to her to be a complete enigma. However, knowing that it was going to be quite impossible to avoid him completely during her remaining time at Thornfield, Imogen vowed to take whatever steps necessary to ensure that she did not find herself alone with him, for she had made the unwelcome discovery that, after just a short time in his company, very odd things seemed to happen to her wits. So much so, it seemed, that she was rather afraid that she might find herself doing or saying something that she would later regret. The very last thing she wanted was to find herself succumbing to his obviously well-practised overtures, no matter how tempting that thought might be!

Chapter Ten

Although the return of most of the Beresfords' original members of staff did manage to relieve Imogen of the onerous task of training newcomers, the re-allocating of sleeping quarters and the setting in motion of a thorough spring clean of the entire house took up a good deal of her time in the days that followed.

However, she was not entirely displeased to discover that the extra workload she had taken upon herself did at least have the useful effect of reducing the number of occasions upon which she was obliged to cross paths with Beresford.

Having taken note of the fact that he, like herself, was inclined to be an early riser, she now made a point of coming down to the breakfast room only after having made certain that he had already departed. Nevertheless, other than inviting inquisitive questions from both Miss Widdecombe and her aunt, she was, of course, required to join the family for their evening meal. Luckily, the seating arrangement that Beresford had introduced on his first day now seemed to be accepted as the norm and, in view of the fact that she had had the forethought to position the doughty governess between her own seat and his, there seldom arose any necessity for Imogen to exchange more than the briefest of commonplace remarks with him.

Added to which, when the ladies left the table to take tea, it had become the usual practice for the three men to abscond to the billiard room, where they now chose to spend the remainder of their evenings, emerging only to wish the ladies 'goodnight' when they heard them exiting the salon. But, because Imogen was, by that hour, far too weary to involve herself in idle chit-chat with her cousin and her aunt, she was seldom party to this dutiful exchange of greetings, having got into the habit of excusing herself shortly after she had finished her tea.

Not that these relatively early nights were proving at all beneficial to her peace of mind because, no sooner had her head touched the pillow, than her mind was immediately plagued by a series of highly discomfiting images that, no matter how hard she tried, she was quite unable to banish. The consequence of which was that she often rose from her sleep more exhausted than when she had gone to bed.

Beresford, even though his own days were crammed with an equally punishing schedule, was not slow to register the dark shadows that were beginning to appear under Imogen's eyes. Nor did he fail to observe, with growing dismay, the increasing lack of spring in her step and the continually pensive expression on her pale face. Heavily conscious of the fact that she was doing far more than was good for her and, wretchedly aware that his own rather cavalier performance may well have contributed to her present reticence, he determined to take matters into his own hands.

One morning, after a particularly restless night, Imogen arrived at the breakfast table well after the rest of the family had left. Allardyce was already in the process of instructing the maids to clear away but, since she seldom took more than a slice of bread and butter with her coffee, Imogen directed them to carry on with their work while she partook of her simple meal.

She was just patting her lips with her napkin and preparing to set about her own duties, when Jessica burst into the room, followed, at a more stately gait, by Jane Widdecombe.

'Oh, Imo!' the girl gasped, as with a fit of giggles, she collapsed on to one of the dining chairs. 'You will never believe what has happened!'

Imogen's startled eyes flew from the rather unedifying spectacle of her cousin sprawled inelegantly over the dining table, apparently helpless with laughter, to take in the expression on the governess's face. To her astonishment, it was abundantly clear that Miss Widdecombe was doing her level best to contain her own amusement.

Intrigued, she rose at once to her feet. 'For Heaven's sake, Jess,' she exclaimed. 'Do stop that nonsense and tell me what has happened!'

Still hiccoughing, Jessica shook her head, at the same time gesturing to Miss Widdecombe. 'You tell her, Widdy!' she gurgled. 'I simply cannot speak for laughing—it is just too priceless for words!'

Hurriedly biting back the smile that was threatening to form on her own face, the governess eyed her charge with as much disapproval as she could muster. 'Kindly have the goodness to exercise a little restraint, Jessica,' she said blithely then, turning to Imogen, she declared, 'It appears, my dear, that, from henceforth, Lady Beresford is of a mind to take control of all household matters!'

Ignoring her cousin's derisive snort, Imogen stared at Miss Widdecombe. 'I am sorry, Widdy,' she said weakly, as she sank back on to her chair. 'But I do not quite understand. Exactly what do you mean by "take control"?'

Slightly affronted, the governess knitted her brows. 'Excuse me? I was not aware that I spoke in riddles!' Glowering reprovingly at her one-time pupil, she proceeded to elaborate. 'It seems that Mr Beresford's deferential behaviour towards your aunt has impressed her to such a degree that she has allowed him to persuade her to reclaim her rightful position as mistress of the house and to take up the reins of responsibility—she is, even as I speak, engaged in lengthy consultation with Mrs Sawbridge as to the correct procedure to follow!'

Dear God, thought Imogen, in amazement, the man is either a genius or a confidence trickster! She was finding it hard to believe that they were discussing the same woman who, hardly a week ago, had clung so pitifully to her hand in her efforts to avoid meeting the dreaded stepson!

As far back as she could recall, Sir Matthew had never made any secret of the fact that, unlike his first wife, the second Lady Beresford was totally incapable of mastering the intricacies of household management. Unfortunately, this intolerant attitude had not helped his young bride overcome her youthful nervousness. Following a series of minor domestic disasters in the early days of their marriage, he had coldly instructed her that, for the foreseeable future, she must leave such complicated matters in the hands of the expert Mrs Harvey. Having been Sir Matthew's own choice of housekeeper, this formidable female's capabilities were, therefore, unimpeachable.

Finding herself somewhat shaken by Miss Widdecombe's announcement, Imogen hurriedly sat down. 'I cannot pretend that I am not taken aback by your news, Widdy,' she said eventually. 'However, it does occur to me that we all seem to have forgotten that Thornfield is, after all, my aunt's house and she is, of course, entitled to run it in her own way, no matter what any of us might think! At any rate, I have to suppose that it is only right that she should be encouraged to try.' Then, after another thoughtful pause, she added, 'As a matter of fact, I do have to admit that I have long been of the opinion that my Aunt Blanche was perfectly capable of doing anything she put her mind to, if only she were given sufficient encouragement.'

'You may very well be right, my dear,' responded the governess, with a sagacious nod. 'And, fortunately for us, it has not taken Mr Beresford many days to reach a similar conclusion.

It would seem that this young man has a good deal more insight than his father ever had!'

Perhaps a little too much insight for my liking, Imogen thought darkly, rising from her seat. 'I suppose I ought to go and find out if my aunt requires my assistance,' she said, with an uncertain glance at the governess. 'But, Widdy, I really do not want her to think that I am interfering. If she is serious about this, then we really ought to allow her to set about it in her own way.' Then, with a little shake of the head, she added, as much to herself as to anyone else who might care to listen, 'It is hardly as though she can do a great deal of harm, after all. I have already given the staff their orders for the day…'

She stopped, shamefaced, as she realised the implication of her words and her cheeks grew pink. In consternation, she laid her hand on the governess's arm. 'I am so sorry, Widdy. That was an appalling thing for me to say! It is simply that I have been so used to being in charge that I find myself at a bit of a loss to know how to deal with this new development.'

'Pray do not distress yourself, my dear,' said Miss Widdecombe, patting Imogen's hand. 'I understand perfectly. If you want my advice, you will regard this as an excellent opportunity to permit yourself a well-earned rest—or better still, why not take yourself off for a ride? An invigorating gallop in the fresh air will do you the world of good and, who knows, it might even bring back some of the sparkle to your eyes.'

In the normal way, there was nothing in the world that Imogen would have enjoyed better but, knowing that it was more than likely that Beresford was also riding somewhere out on the estate, she was reluctant to act upon Miss Widdecombe's helpful suggestion, for the last thing she wanted at this moment was to run into him. In spite of her resolve to avoid any protracted intercourse with him, she was finding it increasingly difficult to harness her growing fascination with him, to such an extent that she would almost swear that she could feel the hairs on the back of her neck standing up whenever he entered the room. Which disquieting discovery made her all the more determined to keep well away from him.

'I may very well do as you suggest, Widdy,' she smiled, in answer to the governess's words. 'Possibly after lunch. In the meantime, however, I do believe I shall pop across to the stable this very instant and see how Portia is managing without me. I have sorely neglected her these last few days and really ought to pay her a visit.'

Still a little uneasy at what her aunt might have taken it into her head to involve herself in, Imogen made her way across to the kitchens, only to be informed by one of the kitchen maids that both her ladyship and Mrs Sawbridge were taking tea in what had been the housekeeper's sitting room, which was located further along the passage. For a moment, Imogen contemplated joining them but, with a determined shake of the head, she made up her mind that, in this case, discretion would certainly be the better part of valour. Instead, she collected a handful of sugar lumps and, putting them into the skirt pocket of her gingham housedress, strolled across the yard to the stable block, where she was dismayed to discover that, because the stableboys were hard at work mucking out the horses, access to Portia's stall was temporarily denied her.

Feeling slightly thwarted, she was about to return to the house but, after having considered the possible upheaval she might find there, she decided that, since she had already pocketed the lumps of sugar, she might just as well go and sit in the walled garden until the boys had finished their task.

Sir Matthew, always intent upon trying to impress his less affluent neighbours had, in one of his more grandiose gestures, employed the services of the celebrated Humphrey Repton to design this rather extravagant project. Situated directly behind the carriage house, the rear wall of which formed part of its enclosure, the garden was, in fact, a series of little avenues, bordered by either lush carpets of bedding plants, or by many different species of hedgerow. To compensate for the land's natural decline on this side of the property, sets of shallow steps led down from these thoroughfares on to lower terraces of similar design leading, eventually, to a miniature lake, complete with waterside pavilion. On the far side of the lake, a sloping embankment rose up to join the path that ran alongside the garden's rear boundary wall.

As with the rest of the estate, the garden had suffered badly from its long-term neglect and, as Imogen wandered along the pathways, shaking her head in dismay at the now sadly misshapen box hedging, she found herself wondering just how many of the estate's shortcomings Beresford intended to rectify before putting the property up for sale. He was certainly going to have his work cut out in here, she mused and then, having calculated the extent of the enormous task that he had been forced to undertake on behalf of his previously unknown family, she found herself feeling almost sorry for the man.

She walked on, down the steps on to the lower terraces, stopping every so often to take in the abysmal state of the once-glorious rose beds, heavily choked with weeds, the shrivelled stems of the trailing fuchsias and the lavender bushes, whose rampant stems now seemed set on overrunning the path completely.

Eventually, she arrived at the final set of steps that led down to the open area at the bottom of the garden, where the pavilion was situated overlooking the ornamental lake. She was just about to enter the little building when it occurred to her that the neglected stone benches would, in all likelihood, be far too grimy for her to sit on. Reluctantly, she turned away, intending to make her way back up to the garden's gated entrance when she came to an abrupt standstill, having caught sight of the very person that she had been determined to avoid!

Standing with his back to her, no more than five paces away, was Beresford, his hands in his pockets and his shoulders hunched against the furthermost pillar of the pavilion, apparently lost in some private meditation of his own.

Imogen did not hesitate. Spinning on her heel, she picked up her skirts and started to sprint back up the steps, as though all the devils in hell were after her, at the same time wondering if it could just be her imagination that, no matter where she chose to go, the dratted fellow always seemed to have forestalled her.

As luck would have it, Beresford chose that very same moment to curtail his own sojourn and, turning from his contemplation of the placid waterside vista, was just in time to catch sight of her rapidly fleeing form which, since its owner had been the subject of his turbulent thoughts for the past hour or so, he had no difficulty in recognising.

Without pausing to consider his actions, he strode forward to the base of the steps. 'Miss Priestley?' he called sharply.

Her heart pounding, Imogen halted and, squaring her shoulders, she turned to face him.

'Why! Mr Beresford,' she replied, somewhat disingenuously. 'I understood that you were over at the farm.'

Beresford gritted his teeth. He was only too aware that, after all the internal tussles he had been having with his conscience in his attempts to quell his growing regard for her, it had been the action of a fool to curtail her flight. Nevertheless, he was quite certain that she had seen him and was intrigued as to why she should pretend otherwise. However, upon contemplation of the matter, he decided that it might be unwise to pursue it.

Joining her on the pathway, he gave a laconic shrug and said, 'Midnight threw a shoe just after we left. Had to bring him back. One of the lads has gone down to the village to fetch the farrier so I thought I might take a look at this little gem.'

'Such sarcasm does you little credit, Mr Beresford,' she replied, almost defensively. 'These gardens used to be quite lovely.'

Beresford stared down at her in surprise. 'I was not being at all sarcastic, I assure you, Miss Priestley,' he protested. 'I meant what I said—it truly is a little gem—and one that I shall take great pleasure in putting to rights.'

He waved his hand towards the ragged clumps of rhododendron that they were approaching. 'These must be splendid when they are in full bloom—we have them back home, of course...' he paused, then hurriedly corrected himself '...in India, I should say.'

Imogen nodded. 'Yes, I knew that they originated from Asia.' She flicked her eyes in his direction. 'Does your house have a large garden, Mr Beresford?' she asked curiously.

'Nowhere near as large as Thornfield's acres,' he replied, smiling down at her. 'But large enough, I suppose—not that I have a great deal of time to enjoy it, in the usual way.'

'Oh, why is that?'

He gave a little frown, considering his answer. 'I suppose it is because I am seldom at home—in my own bungalow, that is. In my work, I have to travel a great deal and, when I do return, I seem to spend most of my time sitting in other people's houses.'

Her interest roused, she asked, 'Is that by choice or necessity?' Then, conscious that he might think that she was prying into his private affairs, she blushed and added quickly, 'Not that it is any of my business, of course. I just wondered.'

Beresford shook his head. 'It is an interesting question, Miss Priestley,' he said thoughtfully. 'And, I have to say that I have never really given the matter a great deal of thought, but I suppose it must be because it is just a good deal easier to accept invitations than it is to refuse them.'

His forthright answer astounded her.

'But surely, if one chooses to accept one's friends' invitations, one is, occasionally at least, duty bound to reciprocate—or is that not the normal custom in your part of the world?'

For some moments he did not reply and Imogen was afraid that he had taken offence at her, rather personal, remark. She had not intended to delve quite so deeply into his affairs, but was finding herself to be filled with curiosity about his lifestyle. How did he spend his time—was there a special someone awaiting his return—?

As she felt the blood rushing to her cheeks once again, she bit her lip. She took a deep breath and was just about to apologise for having uttered such an impertinent remark when he spoke.

'As a matter of fact, I have, on more than one occasion, attempted to host what you might call a "return match",' he replied, as a self-deprecating smile appeared on his face. 'Unfortunately, it seems to be pretty difficult to run a halfway decent gathering without a competent hostess. Most of my friends do tend to have wives, you see, and, although my house-boys are excellent, of course—without a woman's touch…' He stopped, thinking how very trite these reasons must sound to a female who had run an entire country estate almost single-handedly for over a year. He gave a little grimace. 'In all probability,' he finished quickly, 'it is just that I am too darned idle!'

In spite of herself, Imogen had to laugh. 'Judging by your splendid efforts over the last few days, Mr Beresford, it would be difficult to imagine anyone *less* idle than yourself!'

His face cleared. 'I believe I have had quite a bit of competition in that direction, Miss Priestley,' he said cordially. 'You are hardly what one would call a sluggard yourself. If my observations are correct, you have barely stopped to take a breath since the day I arrived.'

They had reached the top set of steps, which, because the land inclined more abruptly at that point, were slightly steeper than those in the lower terraces and, as a common courtesy, Beresford held out his hand to assist her.

Imogen pretended not to notice. 'That may have been the case previously, Mr Beresford,' she said airily, as she mounted the steps unaided. 'But, as you can see, I have stopped now. Rather unexpectedly, as it happens, I find that I am about to have a good deal of free time on my hands. It seems that my aunt is bent on taking up her given role as mistress of the house.' Casting him a sideways glance from beneath her lashes, she added, drily, 'For which astonishing development, I understand we have you to thank?'

Beresford's fist clenched slightly as his hand dropped to his side and he followed in her wake.

'It was merely a suggestion on my part, Miss Priestley, I assure you,' he replied, in as nonchalant a manner as he was able to muster. He had not failed to register her slight to what had been simply an automatic gesture of good manners on his part. A violent irritation swept through his body and he could not stop himself thinking that having such an independent streak was all very well, but surely there were limits!

Struggling to take command of his feelings, he strode after her, a vexed frown on his face. Then, fixing his eyes on the rigid set of her shoulders, he asked cautiously, 'Do I take it that you disapprove of Lady Beresford's decision?'

While he had not actually expected thanks for having engineered his stepmother's apprehensive incursion into relatively unknown territories, he had to admit that he had hoped that Imogen might be just a little pleased to be relieved of the heavy load that she had carried for so long.

Taking a deep breath, Imogen halted and turned slowly to face him.

'No, really, Mr Beresford! Please do not think that I am not grateful—'

'For God's sake, woman!'

His face like thunder, Beresford cut short her words.

'I do not want your gratitude, dammit!' he growled. 'Any fool could see that you were wearing yourself out! Dear God! Can you not, just for once, let someone else shoulder some of the burden?'

A deep flush covered Imogen's cheeks and, as treacherous tears threatened to overwhelm what was left of her fortitude, her lips started to tremble.

'I did not mean to cause you offence,' she faltered. 'I do realise that you meant well. It just came as something of a surprise.'

Beresford's jaw tightened. It was all he could do to prevent himself gathering her into his arms there and then. Instead, he withdrew his handkerchief from his pocket and handed it to her.

'Please, wipe your eyes,' he said abruptly, and turned his head away for a moment to allow her time to compose herself.

'A sure sign of exhaustion,' he felt constrained to point out, when she had finished dabbing her eyes, although his tone was now much gentler.

'You are probably right,' she agreed, her voice unsteady. She was, in turns, both embarrassed and confused and wanted nothing more than to escape from the scrutiny of his penetrating gaze. 'I—I really ought to get back.'

His lips curved in a little smile. 'May I ask why?' he enquired. 'As I recall, the whole point of the exercise was to restrict your household activities and give you a little more time to follow your own pursuits.'

Horrified at the idea that he had cruelly manipulated her aunt for her benefit alone, Imogen threw up her head and glared at him. 'I do hope that you do not intend to check on my every movement, Mr Beresford!' she ground out, almost defiantly. 'For your information, I was simply going to take a look at Portia. I trust that meets with your approval!'

A wide grin creased his face. 'Good for you, Miss Priestley,' he said appreciatively and, before she could stop him, he had taken her hand and tucked it into the crook of his arm. 'However, since it does appear that we are both on our way to the stables, I fail to see why we should not arrive there at one and the same time.'

Imogen could not reply, for no sooner had she felt the warm

touch of his hand on her skin than her wayward senses descended into complete turmoil and now seemed set on running through the entire gamut of emotional awareness.

Beresford looked down at her rigid expression. 'Come now, Miss Priestley,' he said encouragingly. 'Unless you can bring yourself to summon up at least the vestige of a smile, you will have young Jake thinking that I have committed some unforgivable sin, then I shall have to incur his marked displeasure for at least a week—and, since the stable cat is not yet in kitten, I have no idea how I could ever hope to restore myself to his good graces!'

Despite herself, Imogen felt her lips beginning to twitch. 'I should certainly hate to see all my previous efforts on your behalf go to waste,' she replied lightly. 'Although, if that unlikely event should occur, I fear that I should just have to leave you to fend for yourself.'

He laughed. A deep, warm sound that sent a ripple of pleasure running through her body. 'Welcome back, Miss Priestley!' he congratulated her, as they exited the garden.

Chapter Eleven

The following morning, Imogen found herself indulging in the almost forgotten luxury of idling in her bed. Relaxing dreamily against the plumped-up pillows at her back, she took a sip of the steaming cup of fragrant chocolate that her recently returned maidservant had just brought to her.

'I am so thankful that you were able to come back to Thornfield, Bertha,' she said, with a warm smile, at the same time thinking how very pleasant it was to be cosseted once again. Having spent almost all of her waking hours during the past year endeavouring to attend to everyone else's problems, she had been left with little time to consider her own welfare.

'No more than I am, Miss Imo, I can tell you,' came the older woman's brisk reply, as she cast a critical eye over the contents of her mistress's wardrobe. 'Though what in the world you've been doing to your gowns while I've been gone, I hardly dare hazard a guess!'

Carefully examining the collection of somewhat soiled and bedraggled dresses, she shook her head in dismay.

'Most of them look barely fit for the rag-bag. Nary a one without a rip or a tear somewhere and, if I may say so, this pretty blue jaconet looks as though it must have been slept in!'

I shall have to get them all down to the laundry room, else you'll have nothing fit to wear!'

Imogen's face creased in a wide smile, as she realised just how much she had missed, not only her maid's deft ministrations, but also her down-to-earth strictures.

Sipping at her chocolate, she watched appreciatively as the woman flitted about the bedchamber, competently stowing away the piles of items that Imogen had been forced to leave about the room in her constant haste to be elsewhere.

'Now, drink up, do,' reproved Bertha, handing her a dressing robe. 'Else your water will get cold and I know how you hate washing in cold water!'

Imogen's eyes flicked over to the steaming jug on the marble washstand. She forbore from mentioning the fact that, until Bertha's return, it had been many months since she had enjoyed the luxury of hot water with her morning toilette.

With a resigned sigh, she slowly swung her feet over the side of her bed and padded over to the washstand to begin a second day of unaccustomed idleness.

After rubbing a warm flannel over her hands and face, she slipped into a relatively unsoiled dress of primrose yellow muslin, sat down at her dressing table mirror and delivered herself into her waiting maid's hands.

Once again, to Imogen's never-ending satisfaction, the woman's nimble fingers soon restored perfect order to the long brown hair that, after yet another night of pillow tossing, had managed to knot itself into a tangled mass. Her eyes gleamed with admiration as, with breathtaking competency, Bertha's swept the now-sleek locks up into an elegant chignon of awe-inspiring simplicity and, as she stared at her reflection in the looking-glass, Imogen found herself marvelling over the many extraordinary changes that had taken place during the last few days.

While she had been more than happy to be relieved of the onerous problems that had fallen her lot to deal with since her uncle's death, she was beginning to feel that things did seem to be moving rather more quickly than she had anticipated. Nevertheless, she was bound to concede that Beresford's high-handed tactics did seem to be proving eminently successful, at least insofar as the other members of the household were concerned. Nicholas was clearly blossoming under his new brother's influence and Jessica's behaviour of late had improved almost beyond recognition!

Above all, she knew that she ought to be glad that Beresford had, in some mysterious way, provided Lady Beresford with the much-needed spur that her aunt had long required to bring about this latest dramatic change because, to give him credit, he seemed to have succeeded in doing just that!

No sooner had Amy Sawbridge informed her mistress that the dreaded Mrs Harvey had no intention of returning to Thornfield than Lady Beresford had set to with a, hitherto unrevealed, dogged determination. Within a few short hours, she was revelling in her newfound ability to direct all the maids and footmen to do her bidding. Not content with taking over Imogen's ongoing campaign to rid the house of all traces of dust and grime, she had, in addition, availed herself of the opportunity to remove a good many of Sir Matthew's prized Eastern artefacts for which, over the years, she had developed a deep loathing.

Had she been challenged on the subject, Imogen would have been obliged to admit that she was almost certain that Lady Beresford's sudden enthusiasm for housekeeping might well prove to last only as long as it took to get Beresford to put the property up for sale. Nevertheless, insofar as her own plans were concerned, the very fact that her ladyship seemed perfectly content to allow him to regulate her life did mean that Imogen need have no further qualms about leaving her aunt's future in his very capable hands.

However, as she replayed in her mind the unfortunate confrontation in the garden and, in particular, her own abysmal performance during that encounter, it was not very long before it struck her that Beresford's hands seemed to be so very capable of dealing with any manner of situation that arose that her own presence at Thornfield was fast becoming redundant. She grimaced at her reflection, striving to put away such an uncharitable thought, but was unable to prevent the slight feeling of resentment that the realisation engendered.

'Sorry, Miss Imo,' came the maid's voice, full of apology. 'Am I pulling too hard?'

Imogen jerked back to reality. 'Oh! No! Not at all, Bertha,' she assured the woman. 'I am rather afraid that my mind was wandering.'

She waited until the maid had put the finishing touches to her hairstyle then, with a reluctant smile, she stood up, saying, 'I really ought to spur myself into action, otherwise breakfast will be finished altogether!'

Opening her bedroom door, she just managed to avoid cannoning into Jessica, who was waiting impatiently outside her room.

'Goodness, Jess!' exclaimed Imogen, stepping back in surprise. 'You gave me quite a start. What on earth are you doing skulking about out here?'

Jessica pouted. 'I was not skulking—I was merely waiting for you to appear.'

Warily, Imogen studied the eager expression that had appeared on the girl's face. 'Whatever for? Do you have something you want to tell me?'

'Absolutely!' Her cousin nodded. 'The most exciting thing you could imagine!'

Imogen laughed. Jessica's idea of excitement was far removed from her own. 'Could you not have waited until after I have eaten breakfast?' she asked. 'If I do not get down soon, they will have cleared away.'

'I simply cannot think why you are always so late these

days,' complained her cousin, as she accompanied Imogen down the flight of stairs that led to the first floor. 'Once upon a time you were up and dressed well before the rest of us, but, since Matt arrived, you hardly ever join us at the breakfast table!'

Imogen raised an eyebrow. 'You have certainly changed your tune! I seem to recall that, before your brother arrived, you hardly ever came down to breakfast at all! More often than not, Widdy and I were the only ones at the table.'

'That may be true,' replied Jessica carelessly. 'But since he came, Mama has insisted that we have to be there because he chooses to be—and, of course, it simply would not do to upset her precious stepson!'

Imogen hid a smile. 'Try not to be so disrespectful, Jess,' she chided. 'Your mama has made enormous strides during the past few days and you should be very glad that Mr Beresford has given her a new purpose in life.'

'I suppose you are right,' said Jessica, who was not at all convinced that her mother's renaissance was particularly beneficial as far as she was concerned, since she now found herself at her constant beck and call. 'Anyway,' she continued brightly, 'none of that has anything to do with what I wanted to talk to you about. Do come into the morning room for a few minutes— Amy will always make you a cup of tea later, if you ask her nicely.'

Imogen, having reached the conclusion that further protest would simply be a waste of time, finally capitulated and gave a little nod, whereupon the gleeful Jessica grabbed her by the hand and drew her into the nearby morning room. Settling herself on one of the many sofas positioned about the sunny room, Imogen patted the seat beside her and invited the youngster to join her, doing her best to hide the smile that threatened as she caught sight of the girl's fervent expression.

'Very well, Jess,' she said briskly. 'I think you had better tell me what it is that has caused you to go into such whoops of excitement.'

Hardly able to contain her glee, Jessica's wide green eyes lit up with enthusiasm. 'Oh, Imo,' she breathed. 'The most wonderful thing! The hugest pile of invitations has arrived—Daniel brought them up from the gatehouse before breakfast!'

'Good heavens!' interrupted Imogen, with a frown of disbelief. 'So that is why you've been hanging about in the hall, waiting for the post with such interest! But surely that is not the reason for this somewhat clandestine meeting?'

Jessica's face fell. 'You might show a little more interest, Imo,' she complained. 'Matt caused such a stir when he accompanied us to church on Sunday that I was quite certain that everyone would soon be queuing up to put him on their visiting lists! We have been out of circulation for so long now that I can barely recall the last invitation we received!'

'Silly goose!' her cousin reminded her gently. 'You know perfectly well that it is not usual for people in mourning to be invited to social gatherings. And, we have hardly been in a position to invite anyone here, now have we?'

An aggrieved pout marred Jessica's lovely features. 'Well, it has been my distinct impression that we were being positively ostracised!' she muttered resentfully.

Imogen gave the youngster a sympathetic smile. 'Only by those acquaintances of your papa who hold views similar to those he was always advocating to you, Jess,' she told her bluntly. 'And, since his death, it has seemed that those so-called "friendships" were heavily influenced by our former wealth and position, rather than by any real affection for us as individuals. Our true friends, such as the Holloways and the Bloxhams, have proved themselves not to be the sort who would turn their backs on us simply because we hit a hard patch.'

'But the Bloxham boys are so deadly dull—forever prosing

on about shooting and fishing and other stupid things,' grumbled Jessica. 'And as for Barbara Holloway! She is always spouting about her amazing travels with her godmother—as if anybody could possibly be interested in what she did all those years ago! I swear she only does it to annoy me! She is so behind the times and knows next to nothing about the latest fashions!'

'Perhaps she feels that there are other more important things to do with her time,' replied Imogen, whose own interest in the current mode was also somewhat less than fanatical. 'I, personally, have always enjoyed hearing about her foreign adventures. In any event,' she reminded her cousin, 'she chose not to desert us. Had it not been for regular visits from Barbara and her friends, you would have been sadly at a loss for company these last few months.'

'That is true, I suppose,' conceded Jessica grudgingly, but then her forehead furrowed in a puzzled frown as she asked, 'But, Imogen, I couldn't help noticing that there are invitations from both Lady Holloway and Mrs Bloxham. Surely that goes to show that they are just as pushing as Lady Rathbone and the rest?'

'Have you been peeking at your mama's correspondence again?' asked Imogen, fixing her cousin with a steely glare. 'It is really too bad of you, Jess! I cannot think how many times Widdy has spoken to you about it.'

'Oh, but I made quite sure that no one was looking,' said the girl, undaunted, although she did, at least, have the grace to blush before continuing. 'Anyway, you have not answered my question.'

Imogen sighed. 'Honestly, Jess, you are such a ninny sometimes. It is no more than one would expect, in the circumstances. The news of Beresford's arrival will have travelled very quickly and the fact that all the local busybodies are fighting to make the acquaintance of Sir Matthew's mystery son is hardly going to prevent our friends from being equally keen to get to know him, now is it? If it were up to me, I should make quite sure of accepting their invitations well in advance of anyone else's.'

Now somewhat crestfallen, Jessica wrinkled up her nose in disgust. 'But we have been to their houses loads of times,' she pointed out. 'It would be so much more fun to go to Rathbone Manor! Now that I am past eighteen, I will be allowed to join in the dancing and all the other amusements that I used to be too young to be invited to. I wonder which Mama will choose to accept?'

'It is more than likely that she will say that it is for Mr Beresford to decide,' replied Imogen, then, cautiously glancing at the clock and realising that Beresford must have left the house some time ago, she got to her feet and motioned to her cousin to join her, saying, 'Well, now that you have caused me to miss breakfast altogether, I suppose I shall have to do as you suggested and go and beg Mrs Sawbridge for a cup of tea.'

Jessica jumped up and clutched at her cousin's hand. 'Please say that you will try to persuade Mama to accept at least some of the invitations, Imo,' she begged her.

Imogen shook her head. 'If your mama decides to leave the final decision to Beresford,' she said, with a wry smile, 'I rather think that it is he who will require any persuading that is to be done and, if my memory serves me correctly, Jess, you are far more versed in that particular skill than I could ever hope to be!'

Jessica beamed and inclined her head. 'That is very true. Gentlemen usually do seem to do whatever I ask of them.' Then she hesitated, biting at her lower lip before adding, plaintively, 'Except, I do have to admit that I find Matt rather odd in that respect. He has a very strange habit of fixing his eyes on one and staring at one in the most disconcerting way. Do you know what I mean, Imo?'

Imogen, who had been the recipient of that disconcerting stare on more than one occasion, felt that she knew exactly what her young cousin meant. However, she was in no mood to stay and discuss the matter.

'You will simply have to regard him as something of a challenge!' she declared brightly as, with a smile, she headed for the door.

Chapter Twelve

With his spirits slightly more buoyant than they had been for some days, Beresford, mounted on the now fully shod Midnight, set out to complete his day's tasks. Having pondered, at length, over the unexpected garden encounter, he had eventually persuaded himself that his defences had suffered no lasting harm, although it was true that the sight of Imogen's tears had almost brought him to his knees. Nevertheless, confident that he had prevailed upon her to take a back seat from the domestic chores, thus allowing her aunt free rein in her new domestic role, he felt that he had gone some way to salving his guilty conscience. He reasoned that, having done what he could to lighten her load, he would now be able to put her firmly out of his mind and get on with the job he had come to Thornfield to do.

Today, as with each of the preceding days since his arrival, both he and Seymour had been fully occupied in trying to remedy some of the damage that had resulted from Wentworth's wilful neglect of the property, as well as making themselves known to Thornfield's two tenant farmers, both of whom had rented their smallholdings from Sir Matthew for a good many years.

During his conversations with these two men, it had not taken Beresford long to discover that, not only had Wentworth substantially increased the rents for both of these outlying properties, but he had also failed to enter the amounts as paid, clearly having pocketed the proceeds himself.

'The scoundrel seems to have taken advantage of every opportunity he possibly could to bleed the estate dry,' observed Seymour, after his friend had shared with him this latest example of Wentworth's perfidy. 'It is hard to fathom how he managed to get away with it for so long.'

'There was no one here with any real authority,' Beresford reminded him. 'One elderly manager, who was totally wrapped up in his own affairs, a stripling of a boy, who admits that he knows less than nothing about farm management and three females, only one of whom seems to have had any inkling about what the devil was up to!'

'Pretty astute, that Miss Priestley, would you not agree, Matt?' said Seymour, as he followed Beresford through a narrow gateway. 'Seems to me that she has done amazingly well to keep the whole thing together all this time—not many women would have that sort of pluck.'

'Miss Priestley is certainly rather unusual in that respect,' acknowledged Beresford, 'But hardly a threat to someone like Wentworth.'

'Maybe not, but one of the field hands was telling me earlier that, when it looked as if no one else was going to attend to it, not only did she go out and supervise the spring sowing herself, in order to make certain of some sort of harvest, but—and you do have to admit that this is really incredible—she even managed to persuade one of the local bigwigs to have his bull brought over to service the dairy herd! You really have to admire the girl!'

'You do indeed,' replied Beresford shortly, and spurred his horse into a brisk canter. Having been doing his level best to banish all thoughts of Imogen from his mind, he had no desire to involve himself in a protracted discussion about her finer qualities.

Seymour was quick to follow his friend's example; as soon

as he had drawn level with him once more, he looked at Beresford sympathetically and said, 'You are probably cursing the day that I persuaded you to make this confounded trip. I seem to have landed you with one hell of a mess, don't I?'

'Forget it, old chap,' returned Beresford. 'I hardly care to think what would have happened to them all if we had not come.'

Seymour glanced sideways at him. 'Would I be correct in assuming that you are beginning to get quite attached to this new family of yours?'

Beresford gave a dismissive shrug. 'I have to admit that it is becoming rather difficult not to feel some sort of responsibility towards them,' he replied, with a slight smile. 'It seems to me that they have been served a pretty shabby deal through no fault of their own.'

'Chin up, old chap,' said Seymour encouragingly. 'I grant you that it did all seem pretty bad to start with, but it is by no means hopeless and, between the two of us, we will soon have it all shipshape again. Young Chadwick has already got the men hard at work clearing the ditches and rebuilding the damaged drystones.'

Glad of the change of topic, Beresford nodded. 'By my reckoning we should be able to start cutting on Monday, if the weather holds.' He paused, then added quietly, 'Your support is greatly appreciated, David. You do know that, I hope?'

'Good Lord, man!' returned his friend, with a careless laugh. 'Think no more about it, I beg of you! You have done more than enough for me in the past. Just let us get the job done and then we can both return home with clear consciences.'

For some minutes the two men cantered side by side in silence then, all at once, Beresford reined in and brought Midnight to a halt. Caught off guard, Seymour had gone several yards further up the lane and found himself obliged to wheel swiftly round to join his friend.

'What's up, old man?' he wanted to know.

'Hush—just listen,' said Beresford, and with an arrested look on his face, he raised his hand to shade his eyes as he searched the sky.

On the still summer air came a melodious rolling chirrup. In an instant Beresford had pinpointed the sound and, grinning with delight, he gestured upwards to his perplexed friend. High above them a small brown bird seemed to be hanging suspended in space until, suddenly, with a spiralling swoop it plunged almost vertically to land in the field alongside the lane.

'A skylark!' breathed Beresford, his face wreathed in satisfaction. 'My God, David! I had quite forgotten what an amazing sight that is!'

He swung his horse round to face Seymour. 'Do you never miss living in England?' he asked curiously.

'Occasionally, I suppose,' admitted his friend, with a self-conscious shrug of his shoulders. 'But I have been doing rather well back home of late and, anyway, I have always believed that it don't do to dwell on such things overlong.'

'You are probably right,' said Beresford absently, his eyes fixed intently upon the upward flight of yet another lark as it ascended into the azure sky. 'It just brought back memories of the summers I spent at my tutor's family home in Sussex. Great times we used to have, he and I.'

As Seymour studied his friend's rapt expression, a rather perturbing notion suddenly crept into his mind. Thrusting it to one side and choosing his words with the utmost care, he said, 'I seldom hear you talk about your boyhood, Matt. Sounds fascinating. What are all these things that you've been missing, then?'

Beresford strove to formulate an adequate reply. 'Foolish, inconsequential things mostly,' he said, with a light laugh.

'Such as?'

'Oh, just trivial things, really. Snowdrops, for instance and daffodils—the colours of the autumn leaves—the smell of pine logs at Christmastime—apple-picking...' His voice trailed away and he gave his friend an apologetic smile.

'Just listen to me!' he said, ruefully. 'Rambling on like a veritable mooncalf! Can't think what can have got into me— A-hah! What have we here?'

He had spotted a small, squat building a short distance further up the lane and, glad of the chance to move away from a topic that was becoming far too unsettling for his liking, he said, 'Looks as though it might be one of our local taverns. What say we call in and check out mine host's home brew, David?'

'Excellent idea,' replied Seymour, breathing a little sigh of relief, for his friend's odd behaviour of late had been starting to cause him some concern. 'All this heart-searching is jolly thirst-making, if you ask me!'

The hubbub of easygoing chatter that had filled the taproom ground to a halt as the two men entered. Finding himself under the scrutiny of a dozen or so pairs of curious eyes, Beresford strode purposefully up to the bar and ordered two mugs of the landlord's best.

'Name's Beresford,' he offered laconically, as he tossed a handful of small change on to the counter and cast his eyes around the smoke-filled room, somewhat amused to be the focus of so much interest. 'Any of you gentlemen care to join me?'

Their faces creased with pleasure, most of the local denizens raised their mugs to him, quickly downed their drinks and accepted his offer with alacrity.

'Sam Juggins, at yer service, sir,' said the landlord, with a warm smile as he deftly unhooked a number of pewter tankards from a rack above his head. 'Heard tell ye'd arrived. Dare say ye're going to have yer work cut out, puttin' the ol' place back to rights?'

'Certainly looks like it,' Beresford nodded agreeably. 'You were acquainted with Sir Matthew?'

'He useter pop in every now and then,' answered the landlord, signalling to the fresh-faced, pretty young girl who was sitting quietly in a corner behind the bar to come and assist him. He then proceeded to fill the mugs one by one from a barrel situated under the counter beneath him. As he did so, the girl rose awkwardly to her feet and came round to the front of the bar, from where she began distributing the foaming mugs around the room, which was soon once again echoing the clink of tankards and the sound of lively conversation.

Knocking back a satisfying swig of the refreshing ale, Beresford leaned against the bar counter, idly watching the girl busying herself collecting up the empty mugs and wiping spills from the tables. As she rounded a table and started to walk towards him, her condition became immediately apparent and his eyes widened in disbelief for the girl, who looked to be a good deal younger than his new sister, was clearly in an advanced state of pregnancy.

'Surely she ought not to be carrying those heavy trays in her condition?' muttered Seymour in his ear.

Beresford shot his friend a warning frown, but Seymour's carelessly spoken words had not escaped the innkeeper's sharp ears.

''Fraid the lass don't have a lot of choice, gentlemen,' he grunted drily. 'P'raps, while ye're sortin' out the rest o' yer pa's business, ye might like to deal with the swine what got my Rosie that way!'

Beresford's face blanched and he lowered his tankard from his lips. 'Do I take it that you are implying that one of Sir Matthew's ex-employees is responsible for your daughter's present state?' he demanded.

As his words reached the ears of the nearby locals, an unfriendly murmur began to ripple across the room, the ominous sound of which caused the pregnant girl to put down her tray in dismay. Stretching out a pleading hand towards her father, she begged, 'No, Pa, please don't.'

Her father ignored her plea. 'I weren't speakin' of any ex-

employees,' he returned truculently. 'I were referrin' to yon
Wentworth fellow—him as took over after yer pa passed away!'

Seymour shifted uncomfortably as he watched his colleague
carefully place his unfinished drink on to the bar top and, turning to the truculent innkeeper, he attempted to remonstrate with
the landlord. 'Now, look here, my good man…' he began, but
stopped as Beresford shot a restraining glance in his direction.

Beresford had not failed to observe the growing signs of agitation on the girl's face. 'Mr Wentworth is no longer in my employ,' he informed Juggins, keeping his voice down. 'In point
of fact, he appears to have absconded and, whilst I cannot be
held responsible for the past behaviour of any of my father's
employees, you may take my word that I have every intention
of bringing that particular scoundrel to justice.'

'Not afore time, neither, if ye ask me,' muttered the innkeeper,
only slightly mollified. 'My Rosie were a good girl and—I might
as well tell ye now—she bain't the only one what that varmint
led astray—not by a long chalk!' he ended portentously.

Beresford clamped his lips together. All at once, he was beginning to feel very weary and not a little depressed at the increasing number of problems that were piling up at his door.
Whilst it was not difficult to appreciate Juggins's point of view,
as sympathetic as he was to the man's obvious bitterness, he
was in no mood to discuss the matter further. Signalling Seymour to finish his drink, he quickly downed the last of his own.

'I shall be in touch,' he informed the innkeeper, in as cheerful a tone as he could muster, then, to the man's surprise, he
turned towards the still distraught Rosie and said gently, 'In the
meantime, my dear, if there is anything you need…?'

The girl hurriedly shook her head and lowered her tear-
filled eyes.

'She'll be alright along o' me,' declared Juggins stoutly, taking his daughter's hand in his. 'So long as that fiend gets his
just deserts!'

'I will certainly do my best to see that he does,' Beresford assured him, as he made for the door.

The innkeeper slowly nodded his head. 'If ye're headin' back to Thornfield,' he then offered, in a belated gesture of appeasement, 'ye'll find it quicker to take the shortcut through yon Piper's Woods.' He jerked his head back down the lane. 'Ye'll find a bridleway on the left—it'll bring ye out to the back o' Mr Chadwick's farmhouse—save yersels a good few miles, ye will.'

When the two men had at last exited the inn and mounted their horses, Seymour finally allowed himself to let out a gasp of relief.

'I really thought we were in trouble for a few minutes back there!' he confessed. 'One or two of those men were beginning to look decidedly hostile!'

'Well, you do have to remember that the pair of us are strangers to them,' reasoned Beresford, as he manoeuvred Midnight through the narrow opening that appeared to lead to the described bridle path. 'It is hardly surprising that they would be somewhat partisan!'

After moving down a slight incline, the two riders entered the copse and, although the late afternoon sun was still shining, the dense woodland through which the path meandered managed to obscure most of its available light, due to the many overhanging branches on either side. Consequently, instead of the short enervating canter back to Thornfield that Beresford had envisaged, the men found themselves obliged to ride through the murky, tunnel-like thicket at a rather sedate trot.

'Hope this so-called short cut was not our host's perverse idea of a joke,' muttered Seymour, as his horse followed his friend's mount through the deepening gloom.

Beresford laughed. 'I think you may be crediting him with rather too much—!'

Whatever he was intending to say was left unfinished as the sudden sharp crack of a pistol shot resounded through the trees.

Instinctively, both men ducked low over their saddles, only just avoiding the bullet that whistled across their vision and embedded itself with a splintering crunch in the trunk of an oak tree within inches of Seymour's head.

'Good God, man!' he croaked in dismay. 'We're being shot at!'

'Coming from our right, if I am not mistaken,' replied Beresford pithily, as he vigorously applied his crop to Midnight's rump. 'Get a move on, David! We need to get out of range as quickly as possible!'

As the riders urgently pressed their mounts into a hasty gallop through the dimly lit thicket, two more shots were fired in rapid succession, one of them passing so close to Beresford's ear that he actually felt the air move as it ripped past the back of his neck.

Since it was necessary for them to lie low over the backs of their horses, in addition to keeping their heads well down, the riders might have had some trouble identifying the narrow path in the shadowy half-light had it not been for the surefootedness of Beresford's mount, Midnight. It soon became apparent that the powerful black stallion was well acquainted with the route, his old master probably having traversed it on many previous occasions for, even at full stretch, the receptive creature seemed to have little difficulty navigating his way through the many twists and turns of the gloomy bridleway. Eventually, in one final confident swerve, he brought both riders safely out of the copse to the top of a short incline, below which the welcoming sight of Chadwick's farmhouse lay peacefully bathed in the still-warm rays of the remnants of the afternoon sun.

After reining in to a breathless halt, the two men immediately wheeled their sweating mounts around, intent on searching the dim recesses of the copse for any sign that would help them identify their would-be assailant, but there was neither sight nor sound from within the now still woods. They had clearly outrun their unknown attacker—not that either of them felt that there could be any real doubt as to the man's identity.

In the uneasy silence that followed their headlong dash, the wide-eyed Seymour stared at his friend in disbelief. 'What the devil was that all about?' he gasped.

'Parting shots from our old friend Wentworth, I should imagine,' replied Beresford with a grim smile, as he leaned forward to pat Midnight's sweating neck.

'But how could he have known we were going to be in those woods?'

'Must have been on our tails all day, just waiting for such an opportunity. It would seem that we are not going to get rid of the beggar quite as easily as we thought.'

'He obviously doesn't intend to give up his position without some sort of a fight,' said his friend tersely, his chest still heaving. 'Can't think what he expects to gain from putting a bullet into you, though!'

'Revenge, perhaps?'

Seymour shuddered. 'Thought we had left all that sort of thing behind us when we had to get the troops to put an end to that sepoy uprising last year. Certainly didn't expect to have anyone taking pot shots at me when I came back to England!'

With a pensive frown, Beresford turned the stallion's head towards the farmhouse and, having led the way down the slope, he indicated to his friend the route that would take them out on to Cottage Lane.

'No need to mention any of this when we get back,' he called over his shoulder. 'Wouldn't do to get the ladies in a panic.'

Seymour came up alongside. 'But, surely, Matt, if that madman is set on skulking round the place with a gun,' he asked, in some concern, 'ought they not at least be warned to be on their guard?'

'Hardly think that will be necessary, old chap,' replied Beresford, with a laconic smile. 'It seems perfectly obvious to me that I am the one he's after—I shall just have to unpack my pistols and make a point of being extra careful!'

The rest of the journey was completed in a thoughtful silence, with a frowning Seymour forbearing from pointing out that, since Beresford, presumably, had no idea either where or how Wentworth might choose to carry out any further attempts on his life, guarding against such an attack might prove rather difficult.

Riding back into the stable yard, the men were greeted by a beaming Jimmy Fairchild, who had come running out of the stable block to relieve them both of their now rather weary mounts.

'I certainly get the feeling that the whole atmosphere of the place has improved considerably in the last few days,' observed Beresford, a satisfied grin on his face as he indicated the freshly scrubbed doorsteps and the neatly swept cobblestones in the busy stable yard. 'It has not taken these lads long to knuckle down to their jobs!'

The two men entered the house by way of the office and made their way along the little passage that led into the great hall, which, since its recent regeneration, always managed to bring a smile of pleasure to Beresford's face. Gone were the dusty cobwebs and the dismal hangings that had greeted him on that first day. Now, the twin scents of lavender and beeswax assailed his nostrils every time he walked across its pristine floor tiles. Every visible surface had been lovingly polished and the glasses of the dozen or so oil-lamps that hung on the walls gleamed and glistened. The final rays of the setting sun, now casting their beams through the spotless panes of the tall front windows, were striking every facet of the pear-shaped crystals that dangled from the two huge chandeliers above their heads, sending a myriad of sparkling rainbow-coloured spectrums flickering across the chequerboard tiling.

Blanche Beresford had certainly done justice to his faith in her ability, thought Beresford contentedly for, insofar as he was able to judge, not one particle of dust had been allowed to escape the dedicated offensive that had taken place during the last couple of days.

As the sound of their booted footsteps resounded across the hall, Allardyce, looking a good deal more sprightly than he had done on their early encounters with him, appeared as if from nowhere to relieve them of their outer garments. They had barely had time to divest themselves of these, however, before the library door was flung open and a highly excited Jessica burst out of the room.

'At last!' she exclaimed, grasping hold of Beresford's hand and attempting to drag him towards the library. 'I was beginning to think you would never come back! Do be quick! Mama has the most wonderful surprise for you!'

'Steady on, Jess!' protested Beresford, laughing. 'You can hardly expect me to go into your mama looking like this! Just let me get out of my riding gear and I will be back down in two shakes!'

'Oh, pooh to that!' she said, dismissively. 'I insist that you come this very instant! It has taken us almost all afternoon! Mama is getting quite beside herself and I, for one, simply cannot bear to wait a moment longer!'

Spinning round to confront Seymour, she clasped her hands together, fluttered her long lashes at him and, favouring him with the full benefit of her emerald orbs, she entreated him breathlessly, 'Do make him come. I promise you that it is really most frightfully important!'

Although Seymour was, of late, beginning to find Jessica's mercurial changes of mood somewhat daunting, he still found himself quite unable to resist the captivating power of those lovely eyes and was, temporarily, bereft of coherent speech.

With an effort, he managed to tear his gaze away from their spellbinding influence and, turning to Beresford with a dazed expression on his face, croaked weakly, 'Rather think you had better do as the lady asks, Matt.'

Disgusted at the speed of his friend's submission, Beresford shook his head sorrowfully and, nobly suppressing the urge to chastise his sister for her blatantly coquettish behaviour, held up his hands in resignation and motioned her in the direction of the library.

However, as he walked passed the still-transfixed Seymour, he was unable to resist a discreet murmur in his ear. 'Try not to make a complete ass of yourself, old man!'

At once, Seymour snapped out of his trance and gave his friend an apologetic grin. 'I am doing my best, Matt, I promise you—but it ain't easy!' he stammered, hastening after the pair.

Chapter Thirteen

It was with considerable reluctance that Beresford followed
Jessica into the library. Ever since his first encounter with the
disapproving image of his father that hung above the mantelshelf, he had made a point of avoiding the room and the subsequent tight schedule that he had imposed upon himself had,
unfortunately, prevented him from finding the time to order the
removal of the hated portrait.

The moment he stepped over the threshold, however, he became instantly aware of the undercurrent of anticipation that
pervaded the atmosphere and, as Nicholas and Miss Widdecombe turned towards the door to acknowledge his arrival, he
was quick to register that they both seemed to be looking highly
pleased with themselves.

Keeping his eyes carefully averted from the mantelshelf, he
executed a swift bow to his stepmother and, after apologising
for coming to her in his dusty riding gear, he said, 'Jessica
seemed to think that you wanted to see me on a matter of some
urgency…?'

Lady Beresford, her faded green eyes shining with barely
suppressed excitement, was resplendent in an elegant, if slightly
outmoded, gown of turquoise silk. Looking perfectly at ease,

she was seated in one of the two large leather armchairs beside the fireplace which, he was surprised to note, had been returned to their former positions facing towards the portrait. That his stepmother had chosen to sit in that particular spot astounded Beresford somewhat, given her rather obvious antipathy towards her late husband.

Leaning forward, she gripped his hand eagerly in hers and, although her lips were curved in a wide smile, he could not fail to detect the nervous tremor in her voice.

'Oh, Matt, my dear!' she exclaimed, in earnest tones, 'Do tell me that I have done the right thing! Both Imogen and Miss Widdecombe seemed to think that it would please you...!'

At the mention of Imogen's name Beresford was unable to prevent himself casting swiftly around the room to seek her out and at once located her seated at a table in the embrasure at the far side of the library. Outwardly giving the impression that she was deeply engrossed in the book on her lap, she chose not look up, seeming quite content to carry on with that activity.

Beresford doubted that she could have failed to observe his entrance but, having no time to dwell on that perplexing matter, was obliged to redirect his attention to his stepmother's words.

'Thought that what would please me?' he asked, a questioning frown on his face.

Lady Beresford gestured towards the mantelshelf wall. 'The portrait, dear Matt—please tell me that you approve!'

Beresford clenched his fists and forced his eyes to swivel slowly in the direction she had indicated. His jaw dropped and he drew in a swift breath as he found himself confronted with a far different painting that now hung above the mantelshelf in place of Sir Matthew's portrait.

Surrounded by a frame much smaller and far less grandiose than that which had held his father's likeness, a gentle-faced young woman looked down at him, her lips curved in the sweetest of smiles. Seated on a garden bench surrounded by a mass of colourful flowers, her corn-gold hair fell in a profusion of curls around her shoulders and her wide, bright eyes reflected the summer blue of her simple gown.

As he stared up at what was clearly his mother's image, a hard lump gathered in his throat and Beresford felt his own, identically coloured, eyes beginning to moisten. At last he was able to put a face to the woman who had died giving him life and whose likeness, for as far back as he could remember, had only ever been, at best, the shadowy conjurings of his youthful imagination.

For several minutes he was unable to trust himself to speak, finding the intrusive scrutiny of several pairs of eyes far too daunting for such a deeply personal moment. Reluctantly dragging his gaze away from the portrait and striving to bring his shattered emotions under control, he was obliged to clear his throat several times before he could turn to face his stepmother. 'You found it!' he eventually managed, his voice thick with emotion. 'But you must not think that I expect you to hang my mother's portrait in your house!'

Lady Beresford, full of relief that the scheme had not gone awry, held up her hand and gave a tinkling laugh. 'My dear boy! I can promise you that I no longer have any reason to resent your poor mother,' she assured him. 'As you can see, she was hardly more than a child and looks to be the sweetest-natured creature, far removed from the monstrous image that has festered in my mind all these years.'

Still considerably affected, Beresford fought to control the tremor in his voice 'It was most awfully good of you to go to all this trouble, ma'am,' he replied shakily. 'I really cannot thank you enough.'

'Enough of the "ma'am", if you please, young man!' retorted Lady Beresford, her confidence growing. 'In point of fact, it is really Imogen who deserves your thanks. She went to quite considerable lengths to track down its whereabouts and, let me tell you, she was absolutely covered in dust and cobwebs by the time she eventually located it!'

Beresford looked across the room and found Imogen's tear-filled eyes fixed on his face with a warmth that spoke volumes but, the moment she saw that he was looking in her direction, a deep flush stained her cheeks and she immediately dropped her gaze.

'Then it is clear that I must offer Miss Priestley my personal thanks!' he said and, to her consternation, proceeded to make his way across the room towards her.

'Although, in truth,' he began softly, a warm smile on his face as he looked down at her, 'I doubt that I will be able to find the words that sufficiently express my full gratitude.'

Unable to drag her eyes away from his, Imogen, her heart pounding dreadfully, gave a little shake of her head. 'Oh, no, really, Mr Beresford,' she stammered. 'Do not trouble yourself. I was more than happy to have found the portrait.'

Beresford's smile deepened and, indicating the chair beside her, was just about to ask if he could join her, when he felt an impatient tug at his sleeve.

'Oh, there will be plenty of time for you to chat with Imo later, Matt!'

Jessica, her eagerness barely contained, had stepped between them, preventing any furtherance of their conversation.

'She will not mind in the least!' his half-sister went on, undeterred by Beresford's swift frown. 'Besides which, there are far more important matters to discuss at this moment!'

'Such as?' ground out Beresford, struggling to disguise his fury at the ill-timed interruption. Jessica's lack of good manners and self-centred attitude were beginning to bore him and he was particularly irritated that she had chosen to curtail his attempt to speak to Imogen who, he now bleakly observed, had returned to the contemplation of her book and appeared to have lost interest in the whole proceedings. He grew suddenly weary and was desperate to escape to his own chamber for a moment's calm reflection.

Imogen, too, had been somewhat disappointed that Beresford had been prevented from conveying his thanks for what had been, after all, a not inconsiderable exercise on her part. Although, having caught the fleeting expression of vulnerability that had appeared on his face when confronted with his mother's portrait, she had been much moved and was bound to admit that his reaction had more than made up for any difficulty that she may have encountered during her search of the dusty attics. In fact, the more she thought about it, she was inclined to suspect that his casual air of self-possession was little more than a façade. Given more time, she mused, it might have been something of a challenge to find out what really lay beneath that mask of suave confidence, and she could not help wondering whether her decision to maintain a safe distance between herself and Beresford had been entirely necessary. After all, she reasoned, what possible harm could it do her to indulge in a simple little flirtation?

Nevertheless, her common-sense instincts then warned her that this kind of artless thinking might well lead her into all manner of danger, given that Beresford must surely return to his home in India just as soon he judged that his work here was completed. With a reluctant sigh, she persuaded herself that she would be far better sticking to her original course of action, which was to steer well clear of the man's extraordinarily winning ways!

Jessica, as usual, was far too full of her own concerns to notice Beresford's somewhat terse response to her entreaty. 'Mama needs to know which of the invitations you would like her to accept,' she said as, with practised skill, she clasped her hands together beseechingly and gazed up at him with a soulful expression in her wide, green eyes. 'She will need to send her replies at once if we are to attend any of this Saturday's events!'

Beresford held his breath, wishing that he could think of a way to bring the silly creature down a peg or two; it was all he could do to stop himself giving her the sharp slap that she so deserved. Wisely, he put this thought aside, aware that Lady Beresford did, indeed, seem to be waiting for him to give some sort of pronouncement on what he considered to be the most trivial of matters. Pasting a smile on his face, he then assured her ladyship that he was perfectly happy to accommodate her wishes in regard to whichever of the invitations she chose to accept. Then, deciding that he had heard quite enough of Jessica's silly nonsense for one day, he begged his stepmother to excuse both Seymour and himself, in order that they might change out of their riding clothes and make themselves suitably presentable to join the family for dinner.

Nicholas, who had already been obliged to sit through several versions of his sister's tedious monologues regarding the merits or otherwise of the various invitations his mother had received, also begged to be excused and thankfully left the room with the two older men.

Hardly waiting until the door had closed behind the three of them, Jessica clapped her hands and gave a little squeal of delight. 'I just knew that he would agree!' she giggled excitedly, then demanded of her mother, 'Which shall you choose, Mama? I still think that Lady Rathbone's "Dancing and Cards with Late Supper" sounds absolutely divine! Do let us attend!'

'Do you not think that it might be better to wait until you have acquired some new gowns before attempting anything quite so sophisticated as one of Lady Rathbone's famed soirées?' came Miss Widdecombe's dry tones. 'You will hardly want to be seen in last year's fashion at such a grand gathering, I imagine?'

Jessica's face fell. 'I had not thought of that!' she wailed. 'I could have asked Matt! Now we shall not be able to go anywhere at all until I have had at least one decent evening dress made up!'

'The gowns we already have will serve us perfectly well if your mama chooses to accept the Holloways' invitation,' interposed Imogen, crossing the room to join the group.

'My own sentiments exactly,' replied her aunt, nodding. 'As you were good enough to remind me earlier, my dear, both the Holloways and the Bloxhams have proved very good friends to us these past months.'

'Boring, boring, boring!' pronounced Jessica, stamping her foot in disgust. 'We might just as well stay at home!' And, tossing her silver ringlets to show her utter contempt for her mother's choice, she flounced out of the room in a petulant sulk.

'Perhaps it would teach her some manners if you were to leave her behind on Saturday,' sighed Miss Widdecombe, gathering up her sewing things and preparing to follow her charge. 'I did think that Mr Beresford's calming presence was beginning to have some beneficial effect upon her behaviour, but it appears that my optimism was somewhat premature!'

Lady Beresford's brow puckered in concern. 'I do hope that she is not going to cause him any displeasure,' she said. 'Everything has been going splendidly so far. He has done so much for us and he seems such a very nice young man, do you not think, Imogen?'

'He is certainly very efficient,' conceded Imogen, with a slight flush, all too aware of Miss Widdecombe's raised eyebrows. 'He has managed to achieve some quite remarkable changes since he arrived.'

Not the least of which was her aunt's extraordinary regeneration, she reflected soberly, as she cast her mind over the events of the last few days.

Dinner that evening proved to be a somewhat subdued affair. It was as if they were all beginning to suffer from the after-effects of their recent labours and what little conversation there was bordered on the desultory. Beresford, wrapped in some private world of his own, was, unusually for him, relatively silent and, since Jessica had subsided into one of her petulant moods, Seymour gave up trying to cajole her and concentrated his attention on his meal. Imogen could not avoid heaving a deep sigh of relief when, after what seemed an eternity, the meal finally dragged itself to a close and the ladies were, at last, able to take their leave and retire to Lady Beresford's little salon to await the tea things, leaving the three men to linger over their post-prandial brandy.

Having observed that her aunt had involved herself in conversation with Miss Widdecombe, Imogen went over and sat down on one of the window-seats that overlooked the terrace, which was now bathed in moonlight. She was just about to pick up her book when the salon door opened and Allardyce appeared, carefully pushing the loaded tea trolley in front of him. To her bewilderment, however, no sooner had the manservant exited the room than Beresford and Seymour walked in, closely followed by her cousin Nicholas.

In a certain amount of suppressed excitement, she waited, quite certain that Beresford would choose to come over and sit beside her. Steeling herself not to rise to any of his provocative jibes, she bent her head to her book but, after several minutes had passed with still no sign of him joining her, she peeped up cautiously and was stunned to find that he had elected to sit with Lady Beresford's group at the far side of the room. Seymour, now doing his best to cajole her out of her recent fit of the sulks, had joined Jessica on the other sofa and Nicholas was seated at the pianoforte, idly strumming some tuneless ditty.

A little shiver of disappointment ran through Imogen's body as she dropped her eyes and she found herself wondering why Beresford had chosen not to sit with her and, more curiously, why had the men curtailed their usually quite long, drawn-out, after-dinner drinking and billiards session?

Beresford, doing his best to involve himself in Lady Beresford's protracted description of the Holloway family was, rather morosely, beginning to wonder much the same thing. He had, in fact, been so eager to waylay Imogen—simply to thank her for her earlier efforts in the dusty attics, he hastened to remind himself—that, in spite of Seymour's incredulous protests, he had urged the other two men to finish their drinks quickly, in order to make certain that she did not leave the salon before he had a chance to speak to her. It had not escaped his notice that she seemed to be going out of her way to avoid direct contact with him. However, since he was fully determined to quench any sign of his own growing ardour before it got out of hand, he had been only too grateful that she, for whatever reason, had seen fit to absent herself from his line of vision.

He had started out that morning with his usual resolve, which was to make sure that he and Seymour were occupied well away from the house for the whole day. However, being presented on his return with his dead mother's portrait without warning had had such a profound effect on him and had left his emotions in such a capricious state that he could feel his resolve slipping away. Added to which, he was beginning to find that the intriguing phenomenon of Imogen's rather pointed disregard was causing him to experience the most extraordinary ripples of excitement in the pit of his stomach which, try as he might, he seemed quite unable to master.

He shot a quick glance in her direction and his heart contracted as he took in the graceful tilt of her head, profiled so clearly against the backdrop of the moonlit terrace, her mind apparently still engrossed with the same damned book that had kept her so occupied in the library earlier!

Hardly aware of what he was doing, he rose from his seat, excused himself from Lady Beresford's side and, in four quick strides, had crossed the floor space between himself and Imogen and positioned himself in front of her. But then, having achieved his objective, he found that, for the life of him, he had not the slightest idea of what he was going to say.

'I should have thought that this light was rather too dim to read by,' he managed, somewhat fatuously.

Although Imogen's eyes had been focussed on her book, none of her other senses had been so engaged and, from the moment Beresford had risen from his seat and started towards her, her heart began to thump most erratically and she was filled with a mounting sensation of wild elation that was proving very difficult to control.

She blinked, took a deep breath and raised her eyes slowly. 'It is good of you to express such concern, Mr Beresford. As it happens, however, I had all but finished for this evening.'

Tremblingly conscious of his nearness, she made as if to rise, but he put out his hand to stay her.

'We seem to have had very little opportunity to converse this evening and I have been unable to extend to you my heartfelt thanks for your magnificent efforts in locating my mother's portrait.' He indicated the space next to her. 'May I sit down?' he said.

As if in a trance, Imogen gave a weak nod, but then, feeling his firm, muscular thigh brush against her own as he lowered himself into the restricted space of the window-seat, she quivered and shifted uneasily to one side, pressing herself back against the embrasure.

'It was really of no account,' she faltered. 'I was glad to have been of assistance.'

Smiling, he shook his head. 'Please allow me to contradict you, Miss Priestley. It is of immense account to me, I assure you.'

A light blush stole across her cheeks. 'I beg your pardon,' she stammered, in some confusion. 'I assure you that it was not my intention to suggest your mother's portrait was of no account—I merely…'

She stopped, having caught sight of the roguish gleam in his eyes.

'Unfair, Mr Beresford! You knew perfectly well what I meant,' she declared indignantly.

His lips curved. 'Of course!' he acknowledged, with a wide grin. 'But it seems that I just cannot help myself. You rise to the bait so beautifully.'

Imogen was, momentarily, lost for words. She knew that she ought to stand up and leave immediately, but her legs seemed unwilling to do her bidding. His azure-blue eyes were gazing into hers with such intensity that she found it impossible to drag her own away, but then, as she felt her trembling fingers gripping at the comforting solidness of the book on her lap, she was jerked back to reality.

'I—it is getting rather late,' she murmured breathlessly and, before he had the wits to recognise her intention, she had risen to her feet, saying, 'And, if you will excuse me, I believe I shall retire now.'

Equally shaken by the feelings that had just swept through him, Beresford managed to scramble to his feet. In a last-minute effort to delay her departure, he placed himself squarely in front of her and, his voice a husky undertone, he said desperately, 'I must talk to you. Won't you, please, step outside for just a few moments?'

Imogen was unable to believe that she had heard aright and assumed that this was another of his underhand tactics to cause her to 'rise to the bait', an activity that, to her fury, seemed to cause him great amusement. For the briefest of instants, she was tempted to accede to his request—merely to give him a piece of her mind, she assured herself. However, as her flashing, storm-grey eyes flew up to challenge his, her breath caught in her throat as she read the mute entreaty emanating from within their clouded depths.

'No! Please!' she gasped and, as she raised her hands, as though to ward off some impending onslaught, her book slipped unnoticed from her fingers and hit the floor with a dull thud, causing her aunt and Miss Widdecombe to turn their startled eyes towards the pair.

Beresford's lips twisted briefly, then, with barely a moment's hesitation, he stood aside to allow her to pass.

As if from a great distance, Imogen heard her voice bidding him 'good evening' and, hardly aware of how she managed to do so, crossed the room and made her excuses to the rest of the company.

As the door closed behind her, Beresford slumped back on to the window-seat, a wry grimace on his face as he racked his brains to find some sense in what was happening to him.

Leaning forward, he bent down to pick up Imogen's discarded book and sat, flicking aimlessly through its printed pages when, all of a sudden, one passage seemed to leap right out at him. The writer seemed to be of the opinion that, given both the inclination and sufficient time, even an 'unconquerable passion' *could* be well and truly vanquished. Fascinated, he turned the slim volume over and read the gold embossed title on the spine, *Mansfield Park, vol. III*, by an unnamed author.

A brief smile appeared on his face as he re-read the succinct message. He refused to believe that his particular passion was unconquerable. But, even should it transpire that this rampaging obsession within him was going to be more difficult to suppress than he had originally imagined, surely all he had to do was stand his ground and time would soon put an end to this folly—if a cure was what he truly desired, that was!

'Care for a game, old boy?'

Seymour's voice broke in on Beresford's musings. He had been watching his friend for several minutes and was beginning to suspect that he had a fair idea of what was troubling him. However, he was also conscious of the fact that, no matter how sympathetic he might be regarding Beresford's present dilemma, such matters of the heart were not usually the kind of thing that men chose to discuss with one another. Therefore, because he was well aware that his friend had always been careful to keep his innermost feelings very closely guarded, Seymour knew that his best hope lay in trying to take his mind off his troubles.

Beresford placed Imogen's book carefully down on the window-seat and stood up.

'Good idea, David,' he said briskly. 'And I am inclined to think that another glass or two of my father's rather splendid brandy would probably not go amiss either.'

Chapter Fourteen

Imogen had been tossing and turning for over an hour, with all manner of troublesome thoughts invading her mind. Her inability to sleep was not helped by the fact that, due to her having instructed Bertha to leave the curtains open in order that she might take advantage of the cool night air, she now found that her bedroom was far too bright to encourage restful slumber.

She had already worked her way through the time-honoured methods of counting sheep, mentally reeling off her sixteen and seventeen times tables, both forwards and backwards; had recited as much of Homer's *Iliad* as she could recall, but to no avail. No matter how hard she tried to banish the disturbing images from her mind, they persisted in flooding back into her consciousness and refused to be dismissed. In vain had she tried to focus on some other, totally unrelated topic, only to have the recurring image of Matthew Beresford's face thrusting itself into her head.

In spite of her continued determination to keep him at arm's length, she was mortified to discover that it seemed to be almost impossible to stop thinking about him. The way his eyes crinkled when he smiled—the deep resonance of his voice—his lithe, virile physique—and, perhaps, the most disquieting of all, the heart-stopping memory of that moment on the terrace when he had all but kissed her. And, after seeing that unfathomable look in his eyes earlier, she could not help conjecturing on what might have occurred had she agreed to accompany him out there a second time.

She was perfectly well aware that these thoughts were highly dangerous and she must rid her mind of them immediately. However, this admirable objective might have been easier to achieve had it not been for the rather sad fact that, as each day passed, she was finding herself drawn more and more inexorably towards the man and, had she not known better, she might even have fancied herself in love with him!

She pummelled at her pillow, increasingly vexed at her inability to drive the mortifying images out of her mind. She stared up at the ceiling and, as the light from the full moon filtered through her windows, casting its dazzling beams across the room and bathing it in a radiance that was almost as bright as day, it suddenly occurred to her that, if it were not going to be possible to get any sleep, she might just as well to go down to the library and fetch herself a book.

Thrusting her arms into her night-wrapper, she loosely tied the ribbons at her throat and slid her feet into her slippers. Carefully opening the bedroom door, she tiptoed out on to the landing and stood for a moment or two, her head on one side as she listened intently for any sounds of movement, but, apart from the sonorous ticking of the grandfather clock in the hall below, the house was silent.

She was almost at the head of the stairs when it occurred to her that it might be sensible to arm herself with a candle. Her aunt, as she knew, always left one oil-lamp burning in the hall at night in the unlikely event of someone arriving at the front door, but, should the moon choose to disappear behind a cloud while she was searching for something to read, it was hardly likely that the limited light from this one lamp would reach the inside of the library. However, its flame would certainly provide her with a light for her candle, should she require one.

Collecting the candlestick from her nightstand, she crept down the stairs, pausing every now and then to ascertain that there were no suspicious sounds that might indicate that anyone else was about. To her relief, all seemed well and she managed to reach the library without difficulty.

As she had hoped, the light from the moon was clearly illuminating the bookshelves over on the far side of the room but, as she made her way towards them, it became clear to her that her hurried choice of backless slippers for the little expedition had been far from wise, since the clicking noise that the little heeled mules were making upon the highly polished parquet sounded disconcertingly loud in the otherwise silent room. However, having reached her objective, she soon became immersed in scouring the titles for something that might take her mind off the vexing problems that had been besetting her efforts to sleep.

Beresford, startled out of his reverie, watched in fascination as the wraithlike figure flitted across his vision. Seated in one of the high, winged-back leather armchairs facing his mother's portrait, he had been savouring the silent privacy that the sleeping house afforded him. Glass in hand and brandy decanter at his side, he had been, for some time now, engrossed in thoughts of a deeply troubling nature.

For a second he had almost believed that he was seeing a ghost, but, the moment he caught a glimpse of his unexpected visitor's face and recognised the soft lustrous tresses that, freed from the bonds of their normal confinement, now cascaded over her shoulders in rippling waves, he had no difficulty in recognising the identity of this lovely vision!

Hardly daring to breathe, for fear of startling her, his eyes followed Imogen's every movement until, as she reached up to take a book from a shelf, a jolt of disbelief ran through him when he realised that, positioned as she was, with the moonlight casting its dazzling rays through the thin white muslin of her night-robes, her very shapely form was clearly distinguishable!

He took a swift intake of breath and leant forward to better his view, only to grit his teeth in silent fury as the traitorous leather beneath him gave out an audible creak.

With a gasp of horror, Imogen whirled around and, as her startled eyes located the transfixed Beresford, the brass candlestick slipped from her grasp, falling to the floor with a noisy clang. Clutching her night-robe closely about her and, breathless with alarm, she attempted to run towards the door, only to find her progress hampered by her ill-chosen slippers.

As her heels skidded across the slippery wooden floor, she felt herself lurching forward and would have tumbled headlong, had not Beresford sprung up from his seat and, in one swift movement, caught her to him as she fell.

The perfidious moon chose that very moment to hide its radiant light behind a passing cloud, casting the room into almost total darkness but, as his arms closed about the alluring softness of her scantily clad body, Beresford was lost; no matter how much his reason implored him to heed its danger signals, he seemed to have become incapable of rational thought. As the hot blood pounded through his veins, he pulled her closely to his heaving chest and, careless of any implications, lifted her chin and sought her lips, hungrily savouring their tantalisingly sweet delights. Delights that, hitherto, he had barely been able even to imagine.

Imogen, shaken to the core from the moment she had felt the ravenous, bruising impact of his lips upon hers, was powerless to prevent herself from returning his embraces. Her whole body quivered with an exquisite ecstasy. Time seemed to lose its meaning as she pressed herself eagerly against him.

Beresford's own ardour heightened and his kisses grew yet more fervent, but, as the moon's accusing beams flooded across the library floor once more, the delicious moment of madness was shattered. As though a torrent of ice-cold water had been poured on him from a great height, Beresford gave a violent shudder and instantly released his hold on Imogen. In shocked disbelief, he stared down at her swollen lips and flushed cheeks and, as his incredulous eyes took in her dishevelled appearance, he let out a strangled moan.

'Dear God,' he croaked, as his breath caught in his throat, 'I have run quite mad!'

Conscience-stricken, he put out his hand, as if to take hold of hers, but, suddenly mindful of the dreadful consequences of her reckless behaviour, Imogen, her eyes dark with apprehension, backed fearfully away from him and, turning sharply on her heel, managed to reach the open doorway before Beresford had sufficiently recovered his wits to prevent her escape.

He made as if to follow her; then, as he registered her panic-stricken dash across the hall and her subsequent frantic ascent of the stairs, his mouth twisted briefly and he moved back into the library where he stood, suddenly drained of all feeling, staring up at his mother's portrait. He knew that it had to be his imagination, but it seemed to him that those bright eyes were no longer smiling down at him but now held a sorrowfully accusing gaze.

With a deep groan, he sank into his chair, his hands covering his face as the awful reality of his behaviour continued to assail his consciousness with unremitting intensity. It was impossible for him to fathom how he could have allowed himself to break the unwritten rule that no true gentleman, whatever the provocation, would so far forget himself as to force his attentions upon an innocent female in, what was effectively, his own home! His lips contorted in a grim smile as he was then obliged to remind himself that, since he had chosen to accept the role of head of the household, in the absence of brothers or other suitable male relatives, the defence of Imogen's honour had become his responsibility!

What, in God's name, was he going to do about it? he asked himself miserably. Not only could he not keep away from Imogen Priest-ley, but it had now become demonstrably clear that he appeared to be incapable of rational behaviour whenever she was anywhere near!

Although it was true that he had partaken of an extra glass or two of brandy, he knew that he could scarcely lay the blame for his abysmal behaviour at that door. Try as he might, he was unable to recall a single occasion in his life whereby far greater quantities of alcohol than that which he had consumed this evening had affected his reason to such an extraordinary extent. In any event, he told himself wryly, his head was clear enough to recognise that the situation in which he had presently landed himself was rather different from anything he had ever experienced before. A cynical half-smile hovered at his lips when he eventually reached the conclusion that Imogen Priestley was not only far more intoxicating than his father's vintage cognac but, in addition, a far greater threat to his peace of mind!

Frowning, he reviewed his options, few though they were. Having virtually compromised Imogen's position, he knew that the correct thing to do would be to apologise for his behaviour and ask her to marry him, but, even should she agree to accept such a proposal—which he felt reasonably sure was far from likely—that particular solution, as far as he was concerned, was quite out of the question. So, what other alternatives were available to him? Having already done everything he possibly could to fill every hour of every day with some meaningful activity that would keep him well away from the house, he was at a loss to see what more he could do to remove himself from further temptation, short of staying out all night or moving his belongings into the local inn, that was—which inexplicable act would cause something of an unacceptable stir all round! Having worked so hard to gain his stepmother's trust, he knew that this, too, was hardly an option that was open to him.

There was very little doubt in his mind that, after the way he had behaved, Imogen was duty bound to treat him with the utmost contempt, but since he would be the first to admit that his actions had more than earned him that indignity, he resigned himself to having to endure whatever avengement she might choose to inflict upon him.

He let out a weary sigh but then, realising that there was nothing further to be gained from sitting up all night and dwelling on the matter, he rose to his feet and was just about to leave the room when he came to an abrupt halt. Lying on the floor in front of him was one of Imogen's pink satin slippers, and over at the room's threshold lay its fellow! As he stooped to pick up what he now realised must have been the cause of her precipitous stumble, he felt his heart contract. Then, frowning, he cast his mind back to the series of events that had led to that fall and, with a sudden exclamation, quickly bent down to scour the floor around the bookcase area. After a considerable search, he finally managed to locate the fallen candlestick, which had wedged itself behind one of the legs of the escritoire.

Thrusting these items into his coat pocket, he straightened purposefully and, after throwing a rueful glance in the direction of his mother's likeness, proceeded to make his way to the foot of the staircase.

Imogen, having reached the security of her bedchamber, carefully closed the door behind her and turned the key in the lock.

Collapsing on to the bed, her eyes still wide with shock, she stared unseeingly at the ceiling. How could she have allowed herself to behave in such a wanton, abandoned manner! She was no better than a common harlot! An icy shudder ran through her body as the awareness of what might easily have occurred forced its way into her brain. And, what was even harder to bear, there was no doubt in her mind that, had she not been so foolish as to go down to the library in such an obvious state of undress, Beresford would not have been incited into approaching her in the first place. She could hardly lay the blame for her inexcusable behaviour at his door, since she had patently encouraged his advances and it was clearly her own reckless lack of self-control that had fanned the flame of his ardour and impelled him to act in such a way. As far as Imogen was concerned, this realisation could lead to only one, inescapable, conclusion. The whole humiliating fiasco that had just taken place had been her fault and hers alone! Imogen closed her eyes in despair. What must he have thought of her? After tonight's events, however could she ever bring herself to face him again?

Hot tears welled up in her eyes and trickled down on to her pillow, and, as the dreadful recollection of those last degrading moments exploded into her brain once more, she gave in to her wretchedness. Her shoulders heaving with the racking sobs that engulfed her, she wept profusely, and it was quite some time before she was able to staunch the flood. In time, however, her tears subsided and, totally exhausted, she raised her head from her pillow. After allowing herself one last despondent sniff, she wiped her swollen eyes with the sleeve of her dressing robe. It had eventually sunk into her weary mind that what was done was done and could not be undone; this being so, there was nothing to be gained in lying here repining over the shocking incident, no matter how painful the memory might be.

She swallowed and, taking a deep breath, swung her feet to the floor and walked over to her bedroom door, it having suddenly occurred to her that Bertha would think it most odd should she find it locked against her, when she brought up the hot water in the morning.

She was about to turn the key when, to her utter dismay, she realised that the doorknob was moving, added to which, she was positive that she could hear a faint scratching sound emanating from the other side of the door!

'Imogen?'

A *frisson* of alarm ran through her. It was Beresford. Surely he had not followed her to her bedroom, expecting to gain access? She stepped back and stared at the door panels in horror.

'Open the door, Imogen!' His voice was low and urgent.

'Please go away, Mr Beresford,' she beseeched him. 'I have no wish to talk to you.'

'And I have no wish to make a scene,' came his terse reply. 'If you have any sense, you really will do as I ask!'

Fearfully aware that the door to Miss Widdecombe's room was barely two yards further along the corridor, Imogen hesitated only momentarily before leaning forward to turn the key in its lock. She opened the door fractionally, keeping her shoulder firmly against it, although she knew perfectly well how pointless that action was, since a man of Beresford's size and physical ability would have no difficulty in pushing both it and herself out of the way should he chose to do so.

'Wh-what do you want?' she whispered apprehensively, peering at his impassive face through the narrow gap, wishing at the same time that she had had the forethought to cover herself with a more concealing dressing robe.

However, no sooner had the door opened than Beresford stepped back well away from it, holding out his hands to her. 'I thought you had better have these,' he said dispassionately. 'I judged that it would hardly do for them to be discovered by accident.'

Her puzzled eyes fell on to the slippers and candlestick, causing her cheeks first to blanch and then to flood with colour. 'Oh! Th-thank you,' she managed to stammer, as she thrust out a shaking hand to retrieve her possessions. 'It was good of you to bring them up.'

His lips twisted briefly and he turned to leave, executing a sketchy bow in her direction. 'Goodnight, Miss Priestley,' he said softly. 'Do try to get some sleep, if you can. It wants barely two hours till cockcrow.'

He walked along the corridor and made his way back down the stairs to his own suite of rooms on the floor below. It was no wonder that the poor girl was terrified of him, he thought, his lips tightening in pain as he recalled his unjustifiable molestation of her innocent loveliness. How he was going to disentangle himself from this horrendous farrago, he had no idea! She had made it perfectly clear that she had no intention of giving him any opportunity to apologise for his behaviour. In fact, he conjectured grimly, it was rather more likely that she meant to have nothing further to do with him—and who could blame her? And yet, as he cast his mind back to the scene in the library, he would have been almost prepared to take an oath that Imogen had returned his kiss. Then, with a wry smile, he shook his head, having concluded that such a preposterous idea could be nothing more than wishful thinking on his part.

Without waiting to see if Beresford had actually left, Imogen closed her bedroom door and slumped down on to her bed, her heart still thumping violently. She stared at the telltale objects in her hands, well aware that he had taken the most enormous risk in venturing into this part of the house to return them to her. Had anyone seen him outside the door of her bedchamber, at this time of night, his actions could well have been called into serious question. Even Lady Beresford, who had come to regard her stepson as well nigh faultless, would have found such outrageous behaviour totally beyond the pale.

Why had Beresford taken such pains to protect her reputation at the possible risk of damaging his own? she wondered. Having assumed that he must have regarded her shameless conduct in the library with utter contempt, she could think of no reason why he should place himself in such a hazardous situation—*unless*—! At this point, Imogen stiffened and her eyes grew wide with disbelief as the most shocking thought suddenly entered her head. *Unless* he had been hoping to arrange a repeat performance! A horrified gasp escaped her lips. Had he taken her for some sort of lightskirt? While she was perfectly prepared to take full responsibility for her own part in tonight's deplorable events, the idea that Beresford might choose to regard it as an invitation to embark upon some sort of clandestine liaison filled her with unspeakable rage. Clenching her teeth and straightening her shoulders resolutely, she became more determined than ever not to provide him with any further opportunities in which he might seek to take advantage of her wayward emotions.

In fact, the more her weary mind dwelt upon the tumultuous happenings of the previous week, the more convinced she became that the only explanation as to how Beresford had, with so little effort, managed to captivate everyone in the household must lie in his clever and devious employment of insincere blandishments. Uncomfortably aware that she herself had been dangerously close to succumbing to the man's compelling magnetism, Imogen was quick to realise that she would need to be far more vigilant in the coming days. However, with little more than a week to go until she received her next quarter's allowance, she felt that, providing she kept her wits about her, she would come through unscathed.

Her mind now more settled, she stood up and walked over to the window to stare out across the park, where the dawn mist was already beginning to rise above the treetops. Beresford had been quite correct in pointing out that it was almost daybreak. The early rays of the morning sun were already tinting the horizon with their rosy light and, from the clamour they were making, it seemed that all the birds in the nearby trees must now be in full song, tunefully proclaiming their exultation with the new day.

With an impatient shrug, Imogen wrenched the curtains shut and returned to her bed, resigned to the fact that, in her present frame of mind, she was hardly likely to get any sleep. Nevertheless, she reasoned, thankfully laying her aching head on her pillow, it would be some relief just to close her eyes for a little while.

Chapter Fifteen

She was awakened by the sound of rattling crockery, which seemed to be emanating from the far side of her bedchamber. Struggling to rouse herself from a sleep that had been beset by the most vivid and disturbing of dreams, she wondered who on earth could have entered her room at such an ungodly hour.

'Oops, sorry, Miss Imogen!'

Her eyes flew open as the sound of a well-known voice invaded her consciousness and she sat up with a start, trying to bring some sense into her clouded mind.

'Goodness, Bertha,' she groaned, as she slumped back against her pillows. 'I scarcely expected you to appear at such an early hour.'

'Lor' bless you, Miss Imogen,' laughed Bertha, carefully placing a steaming cup of chocolate on the nightstand. ''Tis almost ten o'clock. You've been sleeping like a baby since…'

Her voice trailed away in confusion as her mistress threw back her bedcovers, leapt out of bed and dashed over to the windows to pull open the heavy brocade curtains.

'Great Heavens, it's broad daylight!' exclaimed Imogen, stepping back in shock as a great shaft of sunlight flooded into the room. Then, as the full impact of the previous night's disastrous happenings leapt into her memory, her body began to shake all over and she collapsed in confusion on a nearby chair.

'But how can I have slept for so long?' she demanded of the bewildered maid. 'Why was I not woken earlier?'

An anxious frown appeared on the woman's face. 'Mrs Saw-bridge said as she'd had orders that no one was to disturb you, miss,' she replied guardedly. 'You must have been very tired. My guess is that you've fair worn yourself out with everything you've been doing these last few months.'

Imogen stood up and began to rip at the ribbons of her night-gown in a frantic effort to untie them. 'But this is really quite extraordinary,' she gasped, as she dragged the garment over her head. 'You know better than most that I am normally the first one to rise every morning. I simply never, ever stay in bed past seven o'clock! Who on earth gave Amy such an order?'

Bertha shook her head. 'I'm sure I can't say, miss,' she said briskly, as she picked up her mistress's discarded nightgown and passed her a dressing-wrap. 'I dare say it must have been her ladyship.'

'I hardly think so,' replied Imogen, as she slipped her arms into the proffered robe and wrapped it around herself. Sinking weakly down on to her bed, she sipped pensively at her chocolate, wondering how on earth she was going to get through the rest of the day and, worse, how was she going to be able to face Beresford at the dinner table that evening?

She was still struggling to find some acceptable way to deal with this wretched predicament when Jessica burst into the room.

'Thank heavens you're awake at last!' she panted, throwing herself on to the foot of Imogen's bed. 'I was beginning to think that you intended to stay here all day!'

'Do be still, Jessica,' Imogen begged her. 'You will cause me to spill my drink if you do not stop all that bouncing.'

Jessica fidgeted impatiently with the tassels on the bed-cover, her keen eyes watching intently as her cousin endeavoured to continue to enjoy what was left of her hot chocolate. Finally, unable to contain her frustration, she leapt to her feet and, before Imogen could prevent her, she had plucked the empty cup and saucer from her hand and deposited them firmly on the nightstand.

'Now, do get up and get dressed, Imogen,' she pleaded. 'We have a million things to do today!'

'Goodness me, Jess!' sighed her cousin. 'If you were so eager for my company, I cannot think why you did not wake me sooner. You know I am not normally a lie-a-bed.'

'I would have done, but Matt gave us strict instructions that you were not to be disturbed,' replied Jessica, carelessly. 'Under any circumstance whatever, he said.'

Imogen stared at her cousin, wide-eyed with dismay. 'M-Matt—Mr Beresford did *what*?' she demanded. 'You are talking nonsense, Jessica. What mischief are you up to now?'

Deeply hurt that Imogen appeared to doubt her words, Jessica's face fell. 'No, honestly, Imo,' she insisted. 'That *is* what he said, I promise you.'

Imogen was bewildered and more than a little concerned. 'But why should he say such a thing?' she demanded of the girl. 'What reason did he give?'

'Well…' said Jessica, and chewed at her finger, trying to recall Beresford's actual words. 'He said something about you needing to rest after yesterday—and then he went on a bit about everything you had done for us all—as if we didn't already know that,' she added, with a disdainful sniff. 'Anyway, I really can't remember every single thing he said, except that he was quite insistent.' She stared at her cousin hopefully. 'I did what he asked, Imo, and I made sure that I waited until Bertha had brought up your water. You must be rested by now, surely?'

Although the thought of Beresford's unexpected solicitude had the effect of making Imogen feel even more anxious than she had done earlier, she managed to assure her young cousin that she was quite rested and that, if she would just be good enough to allow her a few minutes to complete her toilette, she would be happy to join her in the morning room to deal with whatever it was that was causing her such excitement. Which, she supposed privately, would probably turn out to be nothing more than another batch of invitations.

'Oh, but I needed to talk to you straight away, Imo,' objected Jessica, lounging back on the bed. 'I really don't mind waiting while you dress.'

'Well, I am sorry to disappoint you, but it so happens that I do mind,' said Imogen with a weak smile and, taking her young cousin by the hand, she ushered her gently to the door. 'I shall be as quick as I can and then I promise you shall have my undivided attention.'

She was as good as her word and, as soon as Bertha had performed her usual proficient services, her reflection in the mirror assured her that, no matter how dreadful she might feel inside, to the outside world at any rate, she appeared to look perfectly normal.

Thanking the maid, she stood up, and, as she girded her few remaining resources to deal with whatever this latest bee in her young cousin's bonnet should prove to be, she observed, 'I suppose I had better go down and see what Miss Jessica wants.'

'If you want my opinion,' muttered Bertha darkly, 'what that young baggage wants is a right good slap!'

'Hush, Bertha!' chuckled Imogen, putting her finger to her lips. 'She has been behaving like a little angel since Mr Beresford arrived. Do not start tempting Fate, for Heaven's sake!'

'Humph!' the woman replied, as she proceeded to tidy away her mistress's nightclothes.

Still smiling a little at the abigail's droll humour, Imogen was just leaving her bedchamber when Miss Widdecombe appeared at the top of the stairs, carrying a little pile of personal linen.

'Oh, there you are, my dear,' she beamed. 'Jessica said that you had risen.' She looked at her young friend over the top of her spectacles. 'Are you sure that you are fully rested, dear child?' she asked anxiously. 'Mr Beresford was quite specific in his demand that you should not be disturbed.'

'I slept very well, thank you, Widdy,' replied Imogen, as a faint blush stained her cheeks. 'Although I have to confess that I am at a loss to understand what possible right Mr Beresford thinks he has to take it upon himself to issue such a curious order on my behalf.'

'It seems that he thought you looked rather tired, Imogen,' the governess said tartly. 'And, I am bound to point out that it would be hard to find fault with such generosity of spirit. I, too, had noticed that you have been looking a little peaked of late, but I, of course, am in no position to issue such commands.' She looked at Imogen curiously. 'Come, my dear, I fail to see why such kindly concern should have the effect of making you so crotchety.'

'Perhaps it is because I don't care to be constantly reminded how hag-ridden I look,' muttered Imogen. She was irritated that Beresford had, once again, obliged her to feel beholden to him, and concluded that the reason he had issued this order was simply to further some ignoble cause of his own!

Miss Widdecombe laughed. 'Oh, Imogen,' she chided, 'you sound just like Jessica! No one, as far as I am aware, has suggested that you look in the least bit hag-ridden—a little drawn, perhaps, which is hardly surprising after all your efforts recently. Mr Beresford was merely suggesting that not everything needed to have devolved upon your shoulders. My own feelings exactly, I might add!'

Imogen gritted her teeth. 'I suppose you think that I ought to go and express my gratitude for his "kindly concern" over my welfare?' she riposted. 'Dare I hope that our paragon of virtue has already left?'

'Oh, he and Mr Seymour have long gone,' replied Miss Widdecombe, frowning somewhat at her young friend's words. 'They went off with Mr Chadwick more than two hours since and, if I understood them correctly, do not expect to return much before dinnertime—more than enough time for you to have recovered from your childish fit of pique, I should think!'

'I am not in the least bit piqued!' exclaimed Imogen indignantly. 'I merely think it rather odd that he should have taken such an extraordinary decision without first consulting me!'

The governess eyed her intently. 'It seems to me that you are behaving in a very strange manner over a rather minor issue, Imogen. I can only assume that Mr Beresford must have offended you in some other way. Is there anything you wish to tell me, dear child? You must know that I have only your best interests at heart.'

Imogen bit her lip and did not reply, since she was unable to conjure up a sufficiently detached response to Miss Widdecombe's searching question. As it happened, she was spared any further cross-examination because, rather fortuitously, Jessica chose that very moment to burst out of the morning room and was calling up the stairwell in the most ill-mannered way, demanding to know what on earth could be keeping her cousin.

Thankful for Jessica's timely intervention, Imogen made for the stairs, observing, 'I really cannot think how she manages to get herself so wound up about the most trivial matters. I had best go to her before she expires from impatience!'

'Another of her storms in a tea cup, I dare say!' said Miss Widdecombe, forcing a smile.

The smile gradually disappeared, however, as she watched her young friend descend to the floor below and usher Jessica back into the morning room. She had not failed to notice Imogen's unusually introspective demeanour during the past few days and was beginning to surmise that she had a fair idea of what was the root cause.

Heaving a great sigh, she walked slowly along the passage to her own bedchamber, to continue sorting out her belongings, ready for the removal to Kendal. She had not been at all sorry when Imogen had suggested that she might accompany her to Margery Knox's school because, following Sir Matthew Beresford's death, Miss Widdecombe had spent a good deal of time worrying over what the future held for the girl.

While her uncle had been alive, Imogen had been relatively free to please herself as to how she spent her days—within the accepted confines of Sir Matthew's rules, of course. Strict disciplinarian though he had been, Sir Matthew had come to have an, albeit, grudging respect for his niece's shrewd common sense and level-headed practicality and, once she had quit the schoolroom, he had seldom found it necessary to take her to task. In fact, such had been his regard for her that he had eventually formed the opinion that she was quite capable of deciding for herself whether to accept or reject the various offers that he had received for her hand and he had, therefore, desisted from applying undue pressure on her on those occasions.

Since neither his lacklustre wife nor his milksop of a son had afforded him any real company, and even he would have been hard pressed to agree that his daughter was anything more than a distractingly beautiful flibbertigibbet, it had been Imogen's cheerful, undemanding presence around the house that had led him, with ever-increasing frequency, to engage his niece in conversations of a more serious nature. Indeed, towards the end of his life, he had begun to rely quite heavily on her astute judgement on many matters of business.

After Sir Matthew's death, it had not taken Miss Widdecombe very long to realise that it would be quite impossible for Thornfield to continue without a proper master. In fact, both she and Imogen had assumed that, knowing how much Nicholas had always dreaded the possibility of having to run the estate himself one day, his mother would simply put the place up for sale and set up house elsewhere.

Had this turned out to be the case, Imogen would then have been given the ideal opportunity to branch out on her own and, since Miss Widdecombe had already accepted her friend's offer to join her in Westmoreland, the idea of participating in this venture seemed to have appealed to Imogen immensely.

In all likelihood, Lady Beresford would have chosen to do just what the pair of them had anticipated had not the disposition of Sir Matthew's will proved to be far more complicated than anyone could ever have envisaged. As it was, Miss Widdecombe knew that Imogen would never have dreamt of quitting Thornfield and leaving her bewildered aunt to cope with all the problems that were bound to arise.

However, as the days and weeks following Sir Matthew's death had gradually turned into long and difficult months, without any word from the missing heir, Miss Widdecombe had come to realise that it was not in her to depart and leave her young companion to shoulder such a heavy responsibility on her own. She had, therefore, elected to remain until such time as Imogen felt able to leave.

Initially, as far as she had been concerned, Matt Beresford had arrived not a moment too soon, but now, having registered the effect that his presence seemed to be having on Imogen, she was not so sure. In fact, given Imogen's laughingly dismissive attitude towards members of the opposite sex in the past, Miss Widdecombe had to admit that, possibly for the first time in her life, she was at a loss to know how to deal with the situation. She was finding it hard to believe that her clever, sweet-natured Imogen, usually so discerning, might have fallen for the rather obvious charms of her handsome step-cousin.

That the man was handsome, there was no denying, but surely, Miss Widdecombe argued to herself, as she folded her undergarments and placed them neatly into a large wicker trunk, Imogen was well past the age when her head could be turned by mere outward appearances. She sighed and shook her head, reminding herself that Cupid was quite random in where he chose to shoot his arrows, she herself having suffered from one such affliction many years ago.

She sat back on her heels, thoughtfully surveying her handiwork, and found herself wondering if, in the event, she would find herself travelling up to the little school in Kendal without her young companion. For, if it was true that Imogen had fallen in love with Beresford and that he, in turn, happened to return those affections, what better resolution could there be to her dear friend's recent difficulties? Marriage to a man one loved was, surely, a far more attractive prospect than immuring oneself in a small town school somewhere in the back of beyond. Had Miss Widdecombe been given such a choice all those years ago, there was no doubt in her mind as to which option she would have chosen!

Chapter Sixteen

Imogen joined Jessica in the morning room, only to discover that the reason for the girl's current state of enthusiasm was nothing more than the simple matter of her wanting her cousin's help in choosing which of her many gowns she should wear to the Holloways' soirée the following evening.

'So, you have decided to grace the event with your presence?' Imogen smiled as she accompanied Jessica up to her bedroom. Glad of any opportunity to rid her thoughts of the vexing dilemma of what might be the correct attitude to adopt towards Beresford when he returned from his day's activities, she endeavoured to focus her attention on her cousin's less taxing problem. 'What caused you to change your mind?'

Jessica shrugged and tossed her silver ringlets. 'Oh, just something that Clara told me,' she replied carelessly, pushing aside the huge pile of assorted garments that was strewn across her bed in an effort to provide Imogen with a place to sit.

'Clara, the chambermaid?' asked Imogen, in surprise.

Jessica, already in the process of divesting herself of her day gown, nodded. 'Mmm. Apparently, she has a sister who works for the Holloways and she told Clara that Sir Frederick's godson has been staying with them while he is on leave from his unit.'

Imogen laughed. 'Ah! A soldier!'

With a seraphic beam on her face, Jessica nodded. 'And that's not all,' she confided. 'It seems that this Harry has brought several of his military friends with him, too—so I thought it might be well worth my while to go, after all.'

Turning her back, she said, 'Do this up for me, would you please, Imo? I want you to tell me if it is still as becoming as Papa used to say it was.'

Imogen bent down to fasten the hooks at the back of her cousin's green tulle evening gown. 'You really are the limit, you know, Jess,' she said, with a rueful smile. 'I believe my aunt has already sent her reply and, as far as I am aware, you were not included!'

'Oh, that won't matter to Lady Holloway,' replied the girl, pirouetting in front of her pier-glass. 'It's not as if it were places at a dinner table, after all—one or two more cannot make the slightest bit of difference, as far as I can see. As a matter of fact, the whole thing did sound as though it was going to be an immensely boring affair, but now—well, you must see that it is quite a different matter. New people, new faces—who knows what might come of it!'

'New hearts to conquer is what you really mean, I dare say,' chuckled her cousin. 'But you really must be careful, Jess. These young men may prove to be rather more worldly wise than those you have encountered hitherto.'

'That is precisely what I was hoping!' retorted Jessica, with an unrepentant gleam in her eyes. 'A little excitement in my life! It is not as though we ever get any here!'

Rather too much for my liking, thought Imogen, kneeling down to straighten her cousin's hem. She was beginning to wonder whether she would not prefer to return to the days of penury and hard work rather than endure any more of the agonising heartache that she had suffered during the last few hours.

'So, what do you think?' demanded Jessica, spinning round and dropping her a demure curtsy. 'This—or the blue taffeta?'

'You would look absolutely lovely no matter what you wore, as you perfectly well know.' Imogen laughed, rising to her feet and standing back to get a better view. 'However, I do have to say that the green has always been my personal favourite, although…'

A small frown gathered on her brow as she studied her cousin's appearance a little more closely, then her face cleared and her lips curved in a wide smile. 'Goodness me, Jess,' she said. 'You have certainly filled out during these last few months! I am inclined to wonder whether that bodice is not, possibly, just a touch immodest for a girl of your tender years!'

'Nonsense!' declared Jessica, preening herself in the looking glass and admiring the curvature of her generous bosom, a good deal of which was protruding above the gown's neckline. 'According to a recent edition of *La Belle Assemblée*—the one that Sophie Bloxham left behind when she last visited—ladies of fashion show far more than this these days—some of them do not even wear undergarments under their gowns!'

'That may well be so,' replied Imogen drily. 'But you are not a lady of fashion, hardly even a débutante—and I trust that you are not even considering adopting such an extraordinary idea! As to the neckline, it seems to me that a little fichu—just a wisp of chiffon to drape across— Do stop pulling that silly face, Jessica, or I shan't help you at all!'

'Well, you are such a spoilsport, Imo!' grumbled Jessica, with a defiant pout. 'And, anyway, unless you happen to have a chiffon scarf in this particular shade of green—which I don't—I suppose I shall just have to wear the blue taffeta.'

'Well, it is true that any other colour would look rather out of place,' agreed Imogen with a frown, as she considered the various alternatives. Then, having suddenly realised that her cousin's small difficulty had provided her with an ideal excuse to take a trip into town, her face brightened and she said, 'I do believe I have the answer! We would be sure to find exactly what we need in Mr Wilkinson's Emporium in Ashby—he has a splendid haberdashery section.'

Jessica clapped her hands. 'Oh, yes,' she beamed. 'Do let us go! Matt has given me almost a whole year's allowance and I have not had a chance to spend a single penny of it!'

Imogen shot a quick glance at the little gilt clock on Jessica's nightstand. Barely mid-day. More than enough time to get to the market town and back before the family sat down to dinner. Also, and rather more to the point, as far as she was concerned, something constructive with which to occupy her mind, to keep it from dwelling on the awful predicament she had managed to get herself into.

'Hurry and get changed,' she instructed her cousin, after quickly unhooking her. 'I will go and tell Jimmy Fairchild to bring the barouche round to the front door—he can drive us in. He will probably be glad of the opportunity to visit his mother. I believe that she lives quite close to the marketplace.'

Twenty minutes later, they were bowling out of the drive gates and down the hill towards the turnpike.

From his vantage point on a wooded slope alongside the lane, Beresford, sitting astride his horse, saw the open carriage cross his line of vision and, although he could not help but speculate upon Imogen's destination, the moment that the carriage had disappeared around the curve in the road, he forced himself to put her out of his mind and return to the job in hand.

Although the traffic on the main highway into Ashby was quite heavy with the usual assortment of carriages, tradesmen's vehicles and farm wagons, Jimmy Fairchild's competency kept them out of trouble and they reached the market town without incident.

Handing the groom the stabling fee, Imogen told him to take

the equipage to the Crown on the High Street, after which he was free to visit his mother's house, if he so desired, but must be sure to return in time to pick up Miss Jessica and herself, no later than four o'clock. Then, after partaking of a refreshing cup of tea at Mrs Carver's nearby tearooms, along with one of her delicious home-made scones, laced liberally with strawberry jam and cream, the two girls strolled across the road to Mr Wilkinson's Emporium, where they spent the next hour or so engrossed in the Aladdin's cave of merchandise that comprised his fancy goods department.

Eventually, beginning to get a little bored with her cousin's apparent intention of trying on every single hat in the store, Imogen decided that this might be just the opportunity she had been looking for to go and sound out Mr Widmark about the possibility of having the coming quarter's allowance paid to her in advance of the due date, which was still over a week away. She was sure that the sooner she could get away from Thornfield, the more quickly she would be able to put all thoughts of Beresford out of her mind.

Bidding Jessica not to move even an inch from her present position, Imogen left the shop and quickly made her way along the busy High Street, from where a side alley led down to a set of narrow buildings, one of which housed her man of business's chambers.

She hesitated slightly at the entrance to the narrow alley, for she had never been very happy venturing into this part of the town, which consisted mainly of lower-class lodging houses and small commercial enterprises. In the past, she had only ever done so when accompanied by her uncle, whose local business affairs had also been conducted by Mr Widmark. However, not wishing to give any of the shifty-looking characters who were hanging about any outward impression of nervousness, she walked purposefully down the alley, her head held high and her eyes facing firmly to the front.

In spite of several ribald remarks flung in her direction as she passed, she managed to reach Mr Widmark's chambers unaccosted and, breathing a huge sigh of relief, reminded herself that, as soon as she had completed her business, she must ask him for the loan of his clerk to accompany her back to the main thoroughfare.

Mr Widmark was, as always, very pleased to see her, although he was a little concerned that she had chosen to come to see him unaccompanied by a groom or other manservant. Nevertheless, after Imogen had explained the reason for her visit, he was anxious to do whatever he could to carry out her wishes. Having been in regular correspondence with Mr Robbins's Lombard Street office, he was well acquainted with the complexities of his late client's will and keenly aware of the problems they had caused the family.

'But unfortunately, my dear,' he was sorrowfully obliged to inform her, 'I will be unable to order you a banker's draft until Monday morning. Being Friday and already well past thre o'clock, Taylor & Lloyd's will have closed their business for the weekend. As soon as I am able to obtain the draft, I shall, of course, despatch it to you forthwith.' He peered at her over the rims of his spectacles. 'I am afraid that this will involve you in another journey into town, my dear, but, as you are aware, only the signatory may cash such a draft.'

'I am relying on you to do your very best for me, Mr Widmark,' said Imogen, rising to her feet and holding out her hand to him. 'As I have explained, I do need the money rather urgently so, as soon as I receive the banker's draft, you may expect to see me again.'

The lawyer took her hand and smiled. 'Be sure to let me have your forwarding address, Miss Priestley,' he urged her. 'There are still another three years to go before we can have the whole of your capital transferred into your name. I would not care to lose touch with you—I think you will agree that we have had more than enough difficulties tracking down missing heirs to last us several lifetimes!'

'Indeed we have, Mr Widmark,' Imogen replied, although her answering smile was slightly forced. She was about to leave when she remembered her other small predicament. 'Do you think Mr Parks would mind seeing me up to the top of the alley?' she asked. 'I have to admit that I was a little nervous coming down here on my own. I will be sure to bring my groom with me on my next visit.'

Happy to oblige his lovely young client, Mr Widmark called his clerk out to perform the service and Imogen was quickly and safely escorted back up the alley and was soon reunited with her cousin.

It required two of Mr Wilkinson's assistants to carry Jessica's many purchases over to the inn but, fortunately, since Jimmy Fairchild was already waiting by the barouche in readiness for their return, as soon as the parcels were stowed in place, he climbed up on to the box and turned the carriage for home.

Imogen's solitary passage down Sharps Alley had not gone unnoticed. A gimlet-eyed Philip Wentworth, standing at the grime-streaked window of his squalid lodging house, had observed her when she had first appeared at the top of the alley, and, having carefully taken note of the fact that she was unaccompanied, had been waiting to accost her on her return journey.

However, the presence of the elderly, stooping clerk by her side put paid to that idea; after gloomily watching his intended quarry disappear into the crowds at the top of the lane, the frustrated Wentworth threw himself on to his unmade bed and lay scowling at the room's cracked and peeling plasterwork.

By hook or by crook, he swore, he would have his revenge on that arrogant swine Beresford. His turning up so unexpectedly had, in a single stroke, shattered the very comfortable little existence that Wentworth had carved out for himself. Had he been given just a little more notice, he could have ordered things a bit more in his own favour. As it was, he had barely had time to collect his belongings together and, although it was true that he had managed to make off with Sir Matthew's brand new sporting carriage and two of his best carriage horses, he had reluctantly arrived at the conclusion that it might be just a little premature to try to sell them at this juncture. However, what with having to pay Jem Tully the two shillings a week that the blackguard had demanded from him for hiding them in his ramshackle barn, Wentworth realised that, unless he hit upon something pretty quickly, he was soon going to find himself homeless and without a penny left to his name.

Desperate for a drink, he wiped the back of his hand across his parched lips. A far cry from his previous unlimited access to old Beresford's cellar, he thought sourly, but, aware that his slattern of a landlady would soon be at his throat clamouring for next week's lodging money, he decided that it would be foolish to fritter away any more of his rapidly dwindling capital on yet another night of drunken carousing.

He sat up, shaking his head to try to clear away the remnants of the haziness that still seemed to be affecting his ability to think straight, knowing that if he was going to stand any real chance of getting rid of the new owner of Thornfield, he would need to keep a clear head. He was only too aware of the fact that, had he not been suffering from the after-effects of an over-indulgence in Peg Garrity's inferior brandy the other day, there was absolutely no chance that his shots would have missed their mark, since there was little doubt that, when sober, he was a first-class shot.

He was sufficiently confident of his own ability to believe that, if he could just get rid of Beresford, he would be able to move back in to Thornfield and reclaim his former position. With the removal of that single obstacle to his claim, the boy Nicholas would be bound to inherit the estate, as well as all the money that went with it and if he, Wentworth, could carry on from where he had left off, he would be sitting on a veritable gold mine. Old Chadwick was hardly likely to give him any trouble, and as for the rest of them—he gave a snort of derision. He would soon put that cleverboots Priestley female back in her place or tell her to clear off altogether and take that mealy-mouthed old biddy Widdecombe along with her!

Once he had sorted them all out, that would only leave the delectable young Jess to deal with. His lips twisted into a salacious grin as he gloated over the various options concerning that tasty little morsel. He had already evolved his plans for her future some months ago and had merely been waiting until she came into her inheritance to put them into operation. Yet another reason to snuff that interloper out, he thought vindictively. Having had the girl practically eating out of his hand, he had been doubly furious with Beresford's treatment of him. Not that he anticipated it taking him too long to recover any lost ground in that department, he recalled, with a reminiscent leer. If there was one area in which he really excelled, that was it!

Nevertheless, it was clear that he still had to find some workable way to achieve these objectives, for he was damned if he was going to concede defeat yet. He had invested far too much time and effort in the scheme to give up without at least one more attempt.

Feeling under the sagging mattress, he drew out the bundle he had placed there for safekeeping, and, after carefully unwrapping it, set about giving his hunting pistols a thorough clean.

Chapter Seventeen

The entry of the Beresford party into Lady Holloway's large and very grand reception room was met with a good deal of undisguised curiosity on the part of the already assembled guests. Sumptuously attired in bronze silk, her hand proudly poised on her new stepson's arm, Lady Beresford led the way, with Jessica, Imogen and Seymour following close behind, Miss Widdecombe and Nicholas having elected not to attend the evening's gathering.

Clad in his black superfine evening dress, his snowy white silk cravat merely serving to emphasise his tan, Beresford's understated elegance earned him many an envious glance from those members of his sex who had chosen to wear more colourful attire. Added to which, his handsome features and manly form had its usual effect of setting quite a few of the female hearts a-flutter as well as bringing to their mothers' eyes the speculative gleam that, over the years, Beresford had learned to ignore.

Jessica's appearance, too, seemed to be causing a certain amount of comment in at least one part of the room, particularly from some of the young bucks amongst the company. Although she had reluctantly agreed to have her abigail tuck the newly purchased chiffon in becoming swathes around the neckline of her gown, she had, in the intervening period, artfully managed to disarrange a good deal of it, thus revealing far more of herself than had been her cousin's original intention.

Having settled Lady Beresford on a sofa next to some of her old acquaintances and leaving her daughter, Barbara, to see to the needs of the two girls, Lady Holloway led Beresford over to a nearby group consisting of several of the neighbouring landowners and introduced the newcomer. Although he soon found himself drawn into the older men's conversation concerning the quality of the current year's harvest, he was unable to prevent his eyes from frequently straying to seek out Imogen's whereabouts. Moving gracefully around the room, exchanging pleasantries with her old friends, she was clad in the same jonquil satin that she had worn on the first evening of his arrival and, to his eyes, looked even more delectable than she had upon that unforgettable occasion.

Her highly nervous demeanour during the last twenty-four hours had not escaped his notice and, still haunted by the fact that it was his own appalling lack of restraint that was the likely cause of her agitation, he had made no attempt to approach her to offer either apology or explanation for his conduct. Instead, he had concentrated on removing himself from her presence at every available opportunity while, at the same time, racking his brains to find some way out of the ghastly nightmare in which he now found himself embroiled.

All at once his searching gaze fell upon Jessica's décolletage and his face darkened. Who the devil had allowed the girl to appear in such an immodest garment? he wondered angrily; excusing himself from the group, he strode over to where his young sister was holding court to a rather dubious-looking set of individuals.

'A word, if you please, Jessica,' he murmured in her ear and, with a polite nod at her collective swains, he lifted her hand, placed it in the crook of his arm and drew her to the side of the room.

'May I ask what you think you are playing at?' he ground out, his voice low and threatening.

Jessica's colour heightened. 'I'm sure I don't know what you mean,' she protested.

'You know perfectly well to what I am referring,' he snapped back. 'You will go to the ladies' tiring room immediately and adjust your dress. I refuse to allow you to carry on making such a public spectacle of yourself!'

'Oh, Matt! There are other ladies here with necklines far lower than mine,' she protested, flicking her eyelashes up at him in what she hoped was a highly appealing manner. The rigid expression on her brother's face soon convinced her of her error and her lips began to tremble in anticipation of his expected wrath.

Controlling the urge to haul the young baggage straight out of the room himself, Beresford cast about him for some sort of inspiration. His eyes soon fell on Imogen, who chanced to be strolling nearby, immersed in conversation with her friend Barbara Holloway. Two quick steps and he was at their side.

'I do beg your pardon, Miss Holloway,' he said to her startled companion, as he held out his hand to Imogen. 'But I wonder if I might borrow Miss Priestley for a few moments?'

As he took her hand in his, Imogen's eyes flicked frantically about the room as if in search of assistance. Beresford, while perfectly well aware of how her whole body seemed to stiffen at his touch, gave no outward sign of having noticed anything amiss and quickly led her over to the now suitably chastened Jessica, who was engaged in a somewhat futile attempt to cover her exposed cleavage with her unfurled fan.

'Your young cousin seems to be having a little difficulty with her gown,' he pointed out, somewhat unnecessarily. 'If you would be so good as to help her attend to the matter?'

Blinking in astonishment as she took in Jessica's revealing neckline, Imogen could do no more than nod weakly. Having overseen the positioning of the gown's infill before leaving Thornfield, she had not considered it necessary to re-check her cousin's appearance upon their arrival.

'We had better go and find the tiring room, Jess,' she exclaimed in dismay, and, doing her best to shield the girl from the curious gaze of those guests who had witnessed the youngster's débâcle, she led her out of the room and along the hallway, into a spacious parlour that had been set aside for the purpose of allowing the ladies to refresh themselves.

However, the moment she had thrust Jessica inside, she slammed the door behind her and, having checked to see that they were alone in the chamber, she rounded on her cousin.

'What on earth possessed you to do such a thing, Jess?' she demanded angrily. 'I cannot believe that even you would be so idiotish as to imagine that you could get away with it!'

Tears filled Jessica's eyes. 'I didn't think it was so awfully bad, Imo,' she wept. 'None of the gentlemen I was talking to seemed to find my appearance in the least bit out of the ordinary! Beresford was the only one who took any objection to it!'

'You little ninny!' exclaimed Imogen heatedly. 'What man would not want to feast his eyes on a young girl's cleavage, given half a chance? But for you to blatantly parade yourself in polite company in such an obvious manner is outside of enough! I really do not know what we are going to do about you, Jessica Beresford!'

Stung, Jessica wiped away her tears with the back of her hand and tossed her head defiantly. 'Well, you need not think that I am going back in there,' she blurted out. 'I shall stay in here until it is time to go home.'

Imogen sighed. 'You will be the subject of even more censure if you do that,' she gravely advised her cousin. 'Far better to let me fix your dress as it was meant to be and pass the whole incident off as an unfortunate mistake—and trust that most of Lady Holloway's guests were far too engrossed in their own affairs to have noticed anything amiss.'

'A lot of them were staring at me when we left,' replied Jessica mutinously. 'I simply cannot bear to go back.'

'Come now, Jess,' said Imogen, with a sympathetic smile. 'Surely you have more courage than to allow such a trifling matter to overset you? Just hold up your head and behave as if nothing untoward had occurred and, above all, ignore anyone who might seem to be trying to make capital out of it. If I remain at your side, I shall endeavour to ensure that no one attempts to insult you.'

'But Beresford was absolutely furious with me,' Jessica pouted, raising her arms to allow her cousin to readjust the chiffon drapery.

'That may well be,' replied Imogen gently. 'But he is your brother and I would be very surprised if he did not do his best to shield you from spiteful comment.'

Leading the still reluctant girl by the hand, Imogen returned to the reception room. In spite of her own reservations about him, she was heartily glad to see that Beresford appeared to have been waiting by the door for their return. The moment they entered the room, he strode forward to meet them and, after casting a single, brief glance in the direction of his sister's now perfectly respectable neckline, he favoured her with a gentle smile of approval.

'Well done, Jess,' he said, taking her hand and giving it an encouraging squeeze. 'You are just in time to join in the dancing—I hope you will allow me to be your first partner?' Then, after a brief nod in Imogen's direction, he said, in the coolest of voices, 'I must thank you for your assistance, Miss Priestley. You will excuse us?'

Imogen's eyes held a wistful expression as she watched Beresford confidently shepherd his sister into the first set and take up his place opposite her. Although she could not pretend that she would not have enjoyed being in Jessica's shoes at this moment, she was more than relieved that Beresford's recent demeanour seemed to indicate that he had decided to disregard the incident in the library. She made up her mind that, in order to survive the few days that remained until her departure, she would also undertake to do her best to behave in the polite but distant manner that he had adopted.

She glanced about the room, hoping to locate Barbara but, since her friend did not appear to be among the groups of dancers on the floor, she came to the conclusion that she had probably gone out on to the terrace to take the air. Due to the enormous number of candles that Lady Holloway had ordered to be lit, the crowded reception room had grown excessively stuffy and a good many of the guests had already chosen to slip outside to take advantage of the balmy evening breeze.

However, when she stepped out on to the terrace, she was dismayed to see that her friend was strolling in the garden below with none other than Beresford's flirtatious friend David Seymour. The two of them were engaged in a highly animated conversation, which appeared to consist mainly of wildly exaggerated hand gestures and a great deal of laughter.

A pensive frown crossed Imogen's face. She hoped that Barbara was not about to allow herself to succumb to Seymour's mischievous charm which, she felt, could only lead to her friend suffering from a heartache somewhat similar to her own. She determined to find an opportunity to take Barbara to one side in order to warn her that, just as his friend Beresford, Seymour was not in the business of looking for a long-term relationship since, as soon as the men had completed the task they had set themselves, it was a foregone conclusion that they would both be returning to their own well-established lives in East India.

'I was wondering if you would care to take the floor, Miss Priestley?'

Startled out of her preoccupation, Imogen whirled around to find an eager-faced young man standing beside her. Dressed in the green regimentals of a rifle brigade, she judged him to be slightly younger than her own twenty-two years.

'My name is Harry Stevenage,' he said shyly. 'I am Sir Frederick's godson. I realise that we have not yet been introduced but, every time I find someone to do the deed, you seem to have disappeared. This is what you might call "a last-ditch stand"! I do hope you are not offended by such impertinence?'

Imogen found herself smiling at such youthful zeal. The young man certainly had a very disarming manner. 'Not at all, Mr Stevenage,' she replied, holding out her hand. 'I am flattered to think that you have gone to so much trouble.'

His cheeks flooded with colour as he took her hand in his and led her back into the reception room, where couples were now assembling for the next dance.

'Oh, dear! I do believe it is going to be a waltz, Miss Priestley,' he said doubtfully, as the orchestra struck up the musical introduction. 'Perhaps we ought to wait for the next set?'

'Come now, Mr Stevenage,' laughed Imogen. 'I am certain that you must have waltzed on many previous occasions.'

He grimaced. 'Well, yes, but not with—that is—I mean to say…'

Gently propelling him on to the square of floor that Lady Holloway had allotted for the dancing, Imogen placed one hand on his shoulder, and lifted the other, which action obliged the anxious young man to take hold of it whilst placing his other hand at her back.

'Courage, mon brave!' she whispered encouragingly. 'No one will be an expert, you will see. We just have to do our best!'

As it turned out, once he had conquered his nerves, young Stevenage proved to be quite adept at guiding her round the floor. A little stiff to begin with, perhaps, but as soon as he had got into his stride, he seemed bent on enjoying his moment of triumph to the full. Imogen, too, found that the sweeping, ex-hilarating music was having the effect of lightening the som-bre mood that had been hanging over her for the past few days.

Beresford, who had returned his sister to her mother's side and was now on his way to fetch them both a drink, caught sight of the laughing couple as they whirled past him. Hypnotised by the expression of carefree happiness on Imogen's face, he felt his throat tighten and he had to clench his fists very tightly to his sides in order to stop himself from marching across to the pair and ripping her out of the embrace of her insolent young partner who, as far as Beresford was concerned, seemed to be holding her a good deal more closely than was warranted! He scowled, his sharp eyes tracking their every move. What he would not give to be holding her in his arms in such a way, he thought bitterly. Even on a dance floor would be better than nothing. Better than this hollow, aching emptiness that seemed to be pervading his very being.

'Not dancing, old chap?'

He started and turned to find Seymour at his side.

'This always used to be one of your favourites,' said his friend, with a grin. 'None of these lovely young ladies take your fancy?'

'You seem to be rather pleased with yourself, if I may say so,' answered Beresford, trying to match his friend's jaunty mood. 'I was looking for you earlier, but you had disappeared.'

Oh?' replied Seymour, somewhat nonchalantly. 'What did you want with me?'

Beresford nodded towards the sofa where Lady Beresford and Jessica were seated. 'It seems that young Jess kicked up a bit of a storm over a slight lack of modesty.'

Seymour nodded. 'Yes, I have to admit that it didn't escape my notice,' he grinned. 'Thought it was just a touch *outré* for a girl of her age.'

Beresford fixed him with a stony glare.

'We have to make sure that she suffers no harm from her silly prank,' he said bluntly. 'If you could take her up for a couple of dances, as I intend to do myself, I am sure the whole thing will soon blow over.'

'Happy to oblige, old man,' replied his friend. 'A swift repair seems to have been effected, I see.'

'Yes, luckily Miss Priestley was on hand to take care of the situation,' said Beresford, with another quick glance over at the dance floor. 'This number appears to be reaching its conclusion and, since I have been commissioned to fetch some drinks to my stepmother, if you wouldn't mind holding the fort in my stead…?'

'At your service!' saluted Seymour and turned immediately to make his way through the throng to where Lady Beresford sat vigorously fanning herself.

The music drew to a close and, after thanking her exultant partner very prettily, Imogen suggested that he might like to come and be introduced to the other members of her family.

'If you would agree to meet my friends, too,' he replied quickly. 'They will never believe me when I tell them that I have danced with the loveliest girl in the room!'

'Oh, no, Mr Stevenage,' a laughing Imogen contradicted him. 'When you meet my cousin Jessica, you will discover that that is far from the case!'

'I take leave to doubt that, Miss Priestley,' he replied stoutly, as he led her back to her aunt's corner. However, the minute he laid his eyes on Jessica's angelic perfection, he was struck dumb and could scarcely articulate his responses to Lady Beresford's pleasant questioning about his life in the military.

From his deferential manner towards her cousin, it was clear to Imogen that Harry Stevenage had not been present at the time of Jessica's indiscretion and when, after the tongue-tied young subaltern had been doing his level best to apply his mind to the general conversation, three of his fellow officers elected to join the group, begging for introductions, she was pleased to observe that none of the young men gave any impression of having witnessed the unfortunate event. Jessica, finding herself besieged with requests to take the floor, stroll about the room or simply to sit and hold court, soon forgot her fit of the sullens and threw herself wholeheartedly into the process of making the most of her success. On the odd occasion that one of her new conquests chanced to catch any other young buck smirking slyly at her as she passed, a challenging glare in the supposed rival's direction seemed to settle matters quite amicably and the evening passed without further incident.

Beresford, having discovered that his offices to defend his sister's honour were no longer required, would have been perfectly happy to escape to the anteroom, where a good many of the other gentlemen had gathered to indulge in a few rubbers of bridge. Thus far, Imogen's undoubted popularity had relieved him of the obligation of having to petition her for a dance. Nevertheless, he had been unable to prevent his eyes from following her every time a new partner led her out.

Unfortunately, it was not long before Lady Beresford spotted his apparent reluctance to dance, remarking that his hostess would think it very odd in him if he did not favour at least one of the numerous young ladies with a turn about the floor.

'I dare say you think them all to be a lot of silly gooseheads,' she murmured sympathetically from behind her fan. 'And, although I have to confess that I would be inclined to agree with you, I hasten to point out that, even as we speak, Lady Holloway appears to be bearing down upon us with the dreadful Victoria Packham in tow. Quickly, my boy, while you still have the chance—Imogen's set has just finished, I see. She will be more than happy to help you out of a scrape, I am sure.'

Having taken one look at the salmon-clad, moon-faced dumpling determinedly puffing her way across the room towards their corner, Beresford blinked in consternation and, no sooner had Imogen been returned to her seat, than he stepped forward and requested that she do him the honour of granting him the following dance.

Taken aback at his somewhat abrupt manner of asking, Imogen racked her brains to find a suitable excuse that would spare her from the one thing for which she had spent the whole evening alternately hoping and dreading, but it soon became clear that she was to be given no time to prevaricate.

'I pray you to take pity on your cousin without further ado, my dear,' interposed her aunt, under her breath. 'Else he will be obliged to take the floor with Miss Packham—and such a fate I am convinced you would scarcely wish upon your worst enemy!'

Without a word, Imogen rose, laid her hand on Beresford's proffered arm and allowed him to lead her on to the floor. It was only when the musicians struck up the first chord that she realised, to her dismay, that the dance in which they were about to engage was another waltz. At the touch of Beresford's hand on her waist, light though it was, her whole body quivered to such an extent that she was convinced that he could not fail to be aware of her agitation.

However, since his own nerves were strung almost to breaking point, Beresford steeled himself to ignore the trembling beneath his fingertips. Setting his jaw, he made every effort to focus his attention on the compulsive rhythm of the dance. Fortunately for his peace of mind, his concentration was soon fully occupied with the business of avoiding the ignominy of being cannoned into by a series of gentlemen whose adroitness in steering their partners was a good deal less skilful than was his. In no time at all, Imogen was spellbound by the complete mastery of his footwork as, circling and weaving between the other couples with apparent ease, he nimbly shepherded her around the floor.

She was on the verge of complimenting him upon his considerable expertise when, on looking up, she found herself confronted with the sight of his expressionless face. The effect upon her was so lowering that, biting back a gasp of dismay, she was obliged to remind herself that the only reason he was dancing with her was to avoid partnering the unfortunate Miss Packham. That he was finding no enjoyment in the activity was self-evident.

Beresford, instantly aware of her scrutiny, shot a quick glance downwards and was, momentarily, so stunned by the anguish in her eyes that he missed the beat and was obliged to side-step quickly to avoid a collision with another couple. As he deftly guided Imogen out of harm's way, he swore to himself that, from this moment on and to the utmost of his ability, he would make every effort to ensure that she enjoyed every last second of this dance. And, since this was likely to be the one and only chance he was ever going to be given to hold her in his arms again, to hell with the consequences of such folly! Taking a deep breath to steady his nerves, he flexed his shoulders and pulled her more closely towards him, refusing to waste a single heartbeat of the few precious minutes that were left.

Feeling his hold tighten, Imogen experienced a moment's alarm, but, as Beresford swung her gracefully out of yet another reverse turn, she found herself so completely enthralled by his lithe expertise, that she forgot everything but the heady thrill of being so tantalisingly close to him and allowed herself to succumb, once again, to the lilting music and the giddy, whirling rhythm of the dance.

Almost overwhelmed by the intoxicating closeness of Imogen's warm, curvaceous body swaying in perfect time with his own, Beresford suddenly became aware that the music was drawing to a close and, reluctantly returning to reality, allowed himself one last extravagant twirl before finally bringing his partner to a breathless halt. Looking down at her flushed cheeks and shining eyes, there was no doubt in his mind that his efforts had been more than amply rewarded. With supreme effort, he released his hold, bowed his thanks and proceeded to escort her back to her aunt.

Imogen had, until that moment, all but forgotten the awful predicament with which she was still faced. She desperately wanted to tell Beresford how much she had enjoyed dancing with him, but was unable to find suitable words that would adequately express the conflict of emotions that were, even now, still raging deep within her soul. In the event, it was in total silence that she accompanied him across the room until, out of the corner of her eye, she happened to catch sight of the Packham family group in the doorway, in the process of bidding their hostess 'goodnight' and, clearly, preparing to depart.

'I see that there will no longer be any need for me to come to your rescue, Mr Beresford,' she heard herself saying. 'Miss Packham is on the verge of leaving—so, you may rest assured that your toes will be perfectly safe for the remainder of the evening,'

Beresford blanched, as he too was forced to recall his original reason for asking Imogen to dance, and the ache in his heart was so great that he almost wished he could turn back the clock and put himself through the discomfiture of trundling around the floor with the generously proportioned Packham female. *Almost,* but not quite, he sighed to himself, as he handed Imogen into her seat.

No sooner had they settled themselves, however, than Lady Beresford announced that she thought that it was time for their own party to leave. By now, her daughter was beginning to feel rather smug about her considerable success.

'You were perfectly correct, Imo,' she murmured to her cousin, as they took their seats in the large family coach. 'I need not have worried. Hardly anyone seemed to have noticed.'

'Or, perhaps, my dear,' said Beresford drily, rapping on the roof to give the driver the signal to depart, 'those who did so were far too well mannered to comment.'

Lady Beresford leaned forward and enquired, inquisitively. 'To what are you referring? I did not notice any untoward incident.'

'Nothing of moment, Aunt Blanche,' Imogen hurried to reassure her. 'I—I happened to catch my heel in my hem and almost tripped, that was all.'

'How very unfortunate for you, my dear,' commiserated her aunt. 'In such a large company that certainly would have been terribly embarrassing for you. It was indeed lucky that you had the foresight to recover yourself.'

'Quite so,' remarked Beresford, with a grim smile. 'Miss Priestley's remarkable ability to turn even the most awkward situation to advantage has to be greatly admired.'

It was, perhaps, just as well that the absence of light in the carriage prevented him from catching sight of the fulminating look that Imogen cast in his direction at this remark, which had been, as far as he was concerned, merely intended to convey something of his appreciation for her quick thinking, whereas she had, quite wrongly, taken it to be a rather pointed reference to her abandoned behaviour in the library.

So, even after all that had passed between them since that evening, she thought angrily, he is still intent on making capital out of the matter. Clenching her teeth tightly together, she vowed that, no matter how many cheap jibes of that sort he made, she would refuse to rise to his bait.

Chapter Eighteen

During the days that followed, it transpired that Imogen's fears were to prove unfounded since Beresford took great pains to ensure that his activities kept him well away from the house.

On the few occasions that simple courtesy obliged him to engage her in conversation, the colourless tone of her responses did not escape his ears. Nor, indeed, did the slight stiffening of her shoulders and the lowering of her eyes whenever he entered the room go unnoticed by him. As far as he was concerned, the reason for her offhand manner towards him was self-evident and, although his heart was heavy with regret, he could do no more than accept what he felt to be a perfectly just reward for what had been totally unacceptable conduct on his part.

Likewise, Beresford's brusque and clipped overtures soon led Imogen to the unhappy conclusion that, since he had made no attempt to importune her in any way, she had been correct in her original assumption that he must have found her extraordinary behaviour so lacking in modesty that he was unable to bring himself to speak to her with anything more than the expected degree of civility.

In a frenzy of self-reproach, Beresford increased his workload even further. Immediately after cockcrow on Monday morning, he summoned all available hands to begin harvesting the few fields that Imogen had succeeded in planting earlier in the year. Two of these fields were merely meadow grass, which would be needed for winter silage, but there were also two large fields of corn and one of barley. Knowing that it was imperative to finish the cutting and threshing and see that the crops were stored or covered before the weather deteriorated, Beresford elected to oversee most of the work himself.

Unfortunately, on inspection of the tool houses, Ben Chadwick discovered that Wentworth had managed to purloin and, presumably, sell off a good many of Sir Matthew's up-to-the-minute agricultural implements, which meant that all the cutting and threshing now had to be done by the ancient, time-honoured methods of scythe and flail.

By the end of a long and arduous day, one whole field of corn had been cut and tied into sheaves, ready to be carted to the barn for threshing at a later date, and it was a very weary, but reasonably satisfied Beresford who joined the family at the dinner table that night where, with a certain feeling of relief, he found that the conversation was, as on the previous evening, almost entirely monopolised by Jessica's tedious recapitulations of her success at the Holloways' soirée.

Having received several morning callers, one of whom had been Harry Stevenage, bearing an enormous bouquet of flowers, as well as several posies and similar tokens of regard from her other new admirers, the girl was exhibiting an air of self-satisfaction that was beginning to cause her family a certain amount of irritation.

At least twice during the meal, Miss Widdecombe had been obliged to take her charge to task about her uncharitable remarks regarding the fashion sense of some of the other young ladies at the Holloways' gathering and a scowling Nicholas had begged his sister to 'stop going on about the blessed affair!'

'Well, it is hardly my fault that I am so much prettier than all the other girls,' Jessica countered, a decidedly smug expression spreading over her face.

'Beauty is as beauty does!' remarked the governess, with some asperity. 'It depends as much upon how one comports oneself as upon how one looks.'

'I comported myself perfectly well, thank you very much,' returned Jessica pertly, looking across at Imogen with a mischievous glint in her eyes. 'In fact, I believe that it was Imogen who almost tripped on the hem of her gown!'

Unable to believe that she had heard aright and uncomfortably aware of Miss Widdecombe's startled glance in her direction, Imogen drew a deep breath, wondering whether it would be at all sensible of her to challenge her cousin's audacious comment. However, before she could do so, she found herself forestalled by an equally incensed Beresford.

'Enough, Jessica!' he barked out, fixing his sister with a deprecating stare. 'That remark is beyond the bounds of acceptability! Furthermore, I believe that we have all heard quite enough about your wonderful triumph on Saturday evening so, if you cannot manage to think of some more general topic of conversation, may I suggest that you save your breath for eating your dinner!'

Jessica pouted. 'Well, I did want to ask you about attending the Little Season,' she said hopefully. 'Mr Stevenage tells me that he and his friends are going back to London next week and—I just wondered…?'

'Not a chance, my girl!' replied Beresford firmly. 'I have already told you that *if*—and on your present form, that is a big *if*—you are to make your London début, it will certainly not be before next spring, so you may as well put all thoughts about Seasons—whether big or little—right out of your head for the present!'

Jessica's lips quivered and she lowered her eyes but, although she spent a good deal of the remainder of the meal glaring across the table at her brother, not another word passed her lips.

Imogen could hardly help but admire Beresford's swift intervention, although she did not imagine that his desire to change the subject had been for her benefit. On the contrary, it merely served to remind her how very quickly and with what remarkable ease he had managed to manoeuvre himself into his involuntary role as head of the household. Her aunt seemed to have settled into her new position with perfect composure, Nicholas's future was well on the way to being organised to the boy's satisfaction and it was abundantly clear that Beresford had very little difficulty in controlling Jessica's petulant outbursts, which had been far less frequent of late.

Although she was well aware that all of these things ought to have the effect of making her decision to quit Thornfield a good deal easier, Imogen was growing strangely disheartened at the thought of finally saying 'goodbye' to them all. They had, after all, been virtually the only family she had ever known. Only a year ago, the idea of venturing forth on a brand new future had filled her with eager anticipation; yet now, for reasons that were becoming only too clear, she would have given anything to turn back the clock just a few days...

'Imogen?'

As Miss Widdecombe's voice intruded on her muddled thoughts, she looked up with a start to find that the men had risen to their feet and that her aunt and Jessica were already leaving the room. Hurriedly she pushed back her chair and scrambled to her feet.

'Is there something wrong, my dear?' the governess murmured anxiously, as she stood back to allow her young friend to precede her.

Imogen shook her head and, with a brief smile in Nicholas's direction, she murmured apologetically, 'Forgive me for keeping you waiting, gentlemen,' before making her way to the door.

Although Beresford managed to maintain his rigid stance, there was nothing he could do to prevent his eyes from flicking sideways to catch a glimpse of her as she passed beside him, but the instant he caught sight of the tense, apprehensive expression on her too pale face, his breath caught in his throat and it seemed as though a dagger had been thrust deep into his heart. Such was the sense of despair that washed over him that he found it difficult to re-focus his thoughts.

Lowering himself back into his seat, he signalled to Allardyce to fetch the tantalus, and, as soon as the butler had placed the decanters in front of him, he poured himself a generous measure of port, tossed it back in one swift gulp and immediately refilled his glass.

Seymour, who had been regarding his friend's actions with a puzzled frown, reached across the table for the decanter and poured drinks for himself and Nicholas.

'Quite a successful day, all told,' he commented brightly, in order to break the silence. 'Although I do think that we could do with a few more hands.'

Beresford gave a sudden start, blinked rapidly and then, glad of the opportunity to concentrate his mind on the more mundane problem of the harvest, replied hurriedly, 'The lack of decent equipment is not helping, of course. At our present rate, the work is going to take far longer than I expected.'

'You would not consider approaching some of your new acquaintances for assistance?' asked Seymour. ' I understand that most of them have almost finished their own harvesting. I'm sure Miss Priest-ley could persuade Sir Frederick…'

'Absolutely not!' interrupted Beresford decidedly. 'I shall send young Chadwick to Ashby with a wagon first thing in the morning to see if he can drum up some extra men.'

'As you wish,' said Seymour with a careless shrug. 'However, I trust that I don't have to remind you that I am not at all disinclined to rolling up my own sleeves and working in the fields. Like yourself, I tossed a few bales of hay in my youth and I dare say young Nicky here would not be averse to getting his hands dirty.'

Nicholas blanched. 'Papa would never let me anywhere near the fields when the men were cutting—he used to say that I was too much of a liability!'

Beresford raised an eyebrow. 'And do you have any thoughts on the subject?' he enquired pointedly.

'I would be only too glad to help, of course—if you think I would be of any use, that is,' stammered Nicholas. 'I would not want to get in the way, though.'

'It is going to be all hands to the pump on this occasion, my boy.' Beresford smiled. 'Added to which, I am of the firm belief that at least one day on a haywain should form part of every young man's education!'

Glancing over at the wall clock, he stood up and stretched. 'But now, gentlemen—' he yawned '—if we are to get an early start, a swift "goodnight" to the ladies is on the cards and then, I fear, it is time we took to our beds.'

Her ears keenly attuned to listen for the sound of the dining room door opening, Imogen had already gathered up her belongings in readiness for her usual swift exit, but when the three men simply poked their heads into the salon and called their 'goodnights' from the doorway, she relaxed and returned her attention to the lists she had been compiling. With her customary attention to detail, she had worked out a possible travel schedule, settling upon the coming Friday morning as the most favourable time for her departure. However, until she had the promised bank draft safely in her hands, she felt that it would be unwise to mention her intentions to her aunt.

She had, of course, given Jane Widdecombe a brief outline of the result of the meeting with Mr Widmark, but, slightly concerned that her friend, in her understandable excitement at the knowledge that her long-awaited project was finally about to get underway, might inadvertently let slip their secret before her plans were finalised, she found herself reluctant to share with her the full extent of her planning.

Continuing to peruse her lists, she realised that the biggest difficulty, as far as the forthcoming journey was concerned, was going to be the matter of transport. There were still one or two suitable carriages left in the carriage house, despite Wentworth's impertinent selling-off of the cream of Sir Matthew's prized collection, on the pretext of paying the veterinarians' account. However, Imogen baulked at the idea of requesting the loan of one of them from Beresford. Instead, she decided that to hire a chaise and pair from the Wheatsheaf to convey Miss Widdecombe and herself as far as the Doncaster staging post, would suit her purpose better, supposing that she could then purchase two seats on the following morning's stage to Leeds.

She would need to find overnight accommodation, of course and, unless one could book in advance, the coaching inns themselves would probably be fully occupied. Her limited experience of such matters warned her that these busy, noisy places were also likely to be swarming with a motley selection of individuals, any one of whom might be inclined to try to take advantage of two unaccompanied ladies.

She chewed at the end of her pencil, trying to decide how best to overcome this problem and eventually arrived at the conclusion that perhaps the landlord at the Wheatsheaf might be able to recommend a smaller, more genteel inn in the vicinity of the Doncaster staging post. She made a note to remember to ask him when she went down to arrange the carriage hire.

Glancing up from her paperwork, she saw that both her aunt and Jane Widdecombe had risen and were preparing to leave the room, the still rather subdued Jessica having left some time ago. Gathering her papers together, Imogen stood up, ready to join them.

'You have been very distracted this evening, my dear,' remarked the governess, nodding to the sheaf of papers in Imogen's hand. 'I trust that you are not back to checking Mr

Chadwick's figures again? I was under the impression that Mr Beresford had delegated that activity to Mr Seymour.'

'No, it is nothing like that, Widdy,' said her former pupil, as she hurriedly stuffed the papers into her reticule and followed the two ladies out of the room. 'I have just been jotting down a few points that I mean to take up with Mr Widmark when I next visit him, that is all.'

Her intention was to see that the whole endeavour was completely cut and dried, right down to the very last detail, before she announced their imminent departure, by which time it would be too late for anyone to try to persuade her to turn back. No matter how much of a wrench it would be to leave Thornfield and no matter what difficulties she might encounter in the future, she felt that it was imperative that she got away from Matthew Beresford as soon as possible! With her common sense telling her that the next few days were likely to tax her few remaining resources to their very limits, she climbed wearily into bed and sent up a fervent prayer that the hoped-for bank draft would arrive in the morning.

As if in answer to those prayers, Mr Widmark's clerk did, indeed, arrive the following day, bearing the crucial package but, unfortunately, since it was well past noon by the time Allardyce had sought Imogen out, it was far too late for her to attempt the journey to the bank. However, seeing that it was such a pleasant afternoon, she judged that she would have more than enough time to walk down to the Wheatsheaf and sound out the landlord over the, still unresolved, matter of suitable accommodation.

Dismissing Bertha's suggestion of a shawl, she collected a straw bonnet and set out up the lane towards the village, passing the fields of reapers who were hard at work in the afternoon sunshine.

Her mind totally occupied with her plans, she was just making her way past the entrance to one of the hay meadows when she heard Nicholas calling her name. Clambering on to the lower bar of the wide, wooden gate, she craned forward, wondering what on earth her young cousin could be doing here amongst the farmworkers and was astonished to see him perched atop a partly loaded hay wagon, gaily waving his pitchfork at her.

A broad smile lit up her face as she waved back and she found herself thinking that, in spite of his having proclaimed that he feared and detested the idea of being obliged to tread in his father's footsteps the boy, at this moment, looked to be enjoying himself immensely. With Beresford's encouragement, he had blossomed from a shy, repressed and highly nervous adolescent into this cheerful and confident youth.

After giving her cousin a final wave, she was about to step back down into the lane when, against all of her better judgement, she was overwhelmed by a sudden urge to see whether Beresford had also chosen to involve himself in the haymaking. Gripping the top of the gate, she climbed to the next bar and leaned forward, more than half-hoping to catch a glimpse of the cause of all her recent torment. In less than a moment, her searching eyes lit upon Beresford's lithe, splendid physique and she found it quite impossible to tear her gaze away from the magnificent spectacle that he presented.

Stripped to the waist, he was on the far side of the wagon, tossing up bundles of hay for Nicholas to stack. He had his back towards her, but, even at this distance, Imogen could see that his taut, still lightly tanned shoulders were damp with perspiration. As she watched his almost effortless forking up of the piles of hay, Imogen's heart was filled with a wild, inexplicable yearning. Then, almost as though he had sensed her presence, Beresford stiffened and slowly swivelled his head in her direction. The moment he sighted her, his whole face seemed to light up. Involuntarily, he began to raise his hand in a greeting of welcome but then, as if collecting himself, he lowered it hurriedly to his side and resolutely turned away from her. Clamping his lips together, he squared his shoulders and, with a swift intake of breath, gripped the handle of his pitchfork and began, once more, to apply himself to his labours.

As though he had physically attacked her, Imogen reeled backwards and almost lost her balance. Her eyes wide with shock, she stumbled away from the gate, her whirling brain frantically trying to come to terms with his dismissive gesture. Then, in a sudden flash, the plain truth of the matter hit her with such an incredible force that she knew that, no matter how hard she might try to convince herself otherwise, there was little point in trying to deny what, to her utter despair, had now become all too blindingly obvious. This all-consuming, over-powering emotion that had taken hold of her senses and callously scattered them to the four winds was no mere fancy. In spite of all her precautions, she had allowed herself to fall in love with a man who was no longer even bothering to disguise the fact that he regarded her with nothing but contempt!

As the full horror of this awful realisation slowly sank into Imogen's consciousness, she began to tremble to such an extent that, for several minutes, she seemed to be rooted to the spot, unable to control the violent shudders that ran through her. Fighting desperately to return her shattered thoughts to the task she had set out to complete, she eventually managed to will herself to proceed in the direction of the village and, although she knew that she would find it quite impossible to concentrate on the vagaries of coaching timetables, she was miserably aware that it had now become more essential than ever to hasten her departure from Thornfield.

Beresford, unable to maintain his detachment for very long, soon managed to manoeuvre himself into a position that gave him a clear view of the gateway and, although Imogen had her back to him as she walked off down the lane, her dejection seemed almost palpable. For one foolish moment, he was of a mind to toss his pitchfork aside, leap over the gate and rush after her to beg her pardon for his unchivalrous gesture. Instead, he shrugged but, as he turned away, his lips twisted in a wry grimace. Although the idea filled him with distaste, he reflected that, in order to preserve what little sanity he had left, it was far better that she should think him a cad and a coward. The sooner he had completed his tasks here, the sooner she would be able to put his visit out of her mind and get on with her life.

Chapter Nineteen

'I wonder if Mr Beresford will have the Servants' Supper this year,' mused Miss Widdecombe, as she stabbed her needle into the final hassock cover.

'I doubt if he knows anything about it,' replied Imogen, with a slight frown. She had not much enjoyed the custom of the annual thanksgiving that her late uncle had established many years previously, at which he had obliged the family to join him on a dais while he presided over the estate workers' Harvest Supper. 'I could never understand why encouraging the servants to consume such huge quantities of liquor should be considered a good thing to do. As I recall, most of the men were unable to carry out their work for several days afterwards. I often thought that it would have been far more sensible to have given them some more practical reward— I am sure that their wives would have preferred it.'

'That does sound a much better idea,' nodded her aunt, who had been idly listening to the conversation. 'I am fully in favour of rewarding one's servants for their hard work and loyalty, but I did so hate having to sit up there on that platform like some sort of Lady Bountiful! Added to which, I was always perfectly certain that the servants did not feel at all comfortable being watched over while they ate. Perhaps we might put your novel idea to Matt, my dear?'

Jessica intervened, saving Imogen the embarrassment of replying to her aunt. 'Maybe we could have a fête with sideshows, like the Bloxhams have always done?' she suggested brightly. 'Then we can all join in the fun!'

'Oh, I hardly think so,' replied her mother, shaking her head. 'I imagine that that sort of thing has a habit of getting out of hand.'

'Papa would never allow us to stay for more than half an hour, so I can't see how you can say that,' said Jessica mutinously. 'And now that everything is almost back to normal, surely it's time we got back to giving dinner parties or something!'

'I will leave it for your brother to decide when it is time to start entertaining,' returned Lady Beresford firmly. 'These last few days, neither he nor Mr Seymour has stopped to take breath and Nicholas was practically falling asleep over his dinner this evening. It would be quite wrong to deprive them of the few hours' relaxation they get at the end of their day's labour.'

Jessica jumped up and began to rummage through the pile of invitations on her mother's writing desk. 'Does that mean we won't be accepting any more of these invitations?' she wailed.

'Not just at present, dearest,' said her mother. 'But I have engaged for us to attend Mrs Bloxham's ball at the end of the month, which will give us all ample time to have new gowns made up.' She beamed at her daughter. 'Surely that should bring a smile to your face?'

'But that is almost two weeks away,' wailed Jessica. 'And Harry Stevenage and his friends will have gone off to London by then!'

'Perhaps the Bloxhams might be persuaded to drum up one or two soldier godsons for your benefit,' said Imogen, hiding a smile.

Jessica rounded on her cousin. 'You are forever finding fault with me!' she fulminated. 'Just because none of them found you in the least bit interesting!'

At her daughter's unwarranted outburst, Lady Beresford was shocked into a tentative attempt to discipline her. 'For goodness' sake, Jessica!' she cried, with a nervous look towards the door. 'Do have a care! I hate to think what Matt would say if he were to hear you making such wicked remarks!'

Jessica threw herself on to the sofa. 'He would be sure to side with Imo,' she said unrepentantly. 'One cannot help noticing that he always does.' She flicked a mischievous glance in her cousin's direction. 'I dare say he is carrying a secret *tendre* for you!'

Imogen's cheeks turned scarlet. 'You are being very foolish, Jessica,' she reprimanded her. 'It is a pity that you cannot find some more worthwhile way to exercise your mind.'

'Satan finds work,' muttered Miss Widdecombe ominously.

Jessica laughed. 'I was only funning, for Heaven's sake! Anyone can see that you positively dislike the man!'

Conscious of Miss Widdecombe's eyes on her, Imogen bent her head to her book and did not reply. Still shaken by her earlier discovery, she had spent the last few hours in a slight daze, almost incapable of coherent thought. Having barely managed to keep her head long enough to conduct the business with the local innkeeper, she had returned home and retired to her room to wait, in growing trepidation, for the dinner gong.

The meal had been a long, drawn-out agony. Apart from a diffident 'Good evening' upon her arrival in the drawing room, Beresford had not uttered a single word in her direction, for which, she reminded herself, she should be extremely grateful, since his conduct that afternoon had made it almost impossible for her to know how to respond to him.

With the bank draft now safely in her possession, she made up her mind to take herself off to Ashby first thing the following morning, collect her cash and make some last-minute purchases for her journey. With only two days to go, she knew that she ought to begin packing some of her belongings. She was well aware that Miss Widdecombe had been diligently gathering her own things together for quite some time, long before Beresford had arrived upon the scene. Two strapped and bulging hampers had been standing in the corridor outside her door for over a week now and the entire household was well used to the sight of the little governess carrying piles of this and that up to her room to stow safely away in her boxes.

However, Imogen was quick to realise that, without drawing undue attention to her purpose, the getting down of her own travelling trunks from the attics would be quite a difficult matter to arrange. She wondered how she was going to manage to overcome the problem. It was not essential that she take all of her belongings with her, of course. If she could keep her plans secret until Thursday, she could then instruct Bertha to pack up the bulk of her things and have them sent up to Kendal by carrier—but what to do about the necessities?

She raised her head and, as her eyes wandered idly about the room, searching for some sort of inspiration, she heard Miss Widdecombe give a little snort of satisfaction.

'There!' exclaimed the governess, holding up the completed hassock. 'The very last one—I doubt if I shall want to thread another needle as long as I live!'

'A true labour of love.' Imogen smiled, admiring the neat handiwork. 'Well done, Widdy.'

Miss Widdecombe beamed. 'And just in time for Sunday's Harvest Festival,' she said. 'I shall ask Jake to help me carry them down to the church tomorrow—he loves to look at the stained glass windows.'

Picking up her workbasket, she got to her feet. 'If you will all excuse me, I shall take myself off to my room. Now that I have finally finished this work, I can pack away my sewing things. I believe I still have a little room in one of the hampers in the corridor.'

'Packing, packing, packing!' muttered Jessica, in derision,

after the governess had left the room. 'She has been packing for months now. I doubt she will ever leave.'

'Why must you always be so rude, Jessica?' sighed her mother. 'You know perfectly well that, until Mr Robbins has sorted out the difficulties of your father's will, Miss Widdecombe is in no position to attend to her own affairs. She has been of enormous help to us all during this past year.' She glanced apologetically at Imogen. 'As, of course, have you, my dear. Mrs Sawbridge has been telling me about all the sacrifices that you have made. I am dreadfully sorry that I was of so little help to you during those difficult days.'

Tears started into Imogen's eyes and, crossing the room to her aunt's side, she knelt down and embraced her warmly. 'Dearest Aunt Blanche,' she protested, 'you are all the family I have. How could I not share what I had? I beg of you to say no more about it!'

Although she was somewhat taken aback at her niece's unexpected show of affection, Lady Beresford returned the embrace. 'If you insist, my dear,' she replied, as her own eyes misted over. 'But you have my promise that I will never return to those ways. Thanks to Matt, I truly believe that I am a new woman!'

As, to my eternal shame, am I, thought Imogen ruefully, getting to her feet.

Much later, in the solitude of her room, the problem of her packing still unresolved, she became aware of a series of shuffling and rustling sounds outside her door. Highly curious, she opened the door to behold Miss Widdecombe on her knees in the corridor. Surrounded by several piles of books and other bric-a-brac, the governess was in the process of rearranging the contents of one of her hampers.

'Oh, bother!' she groaned. 'Now I have disturbed you. Were you asleep, my dear?'

Imogen shook her head. Sleep had been far from her mind.

'You look to be getting in something of a muddle, Widdy,' she said. 'Can I do anything to help?'

Miss Widdecombe sat back on her heels and passed a weary hand across her brow.

'It was rather foolish of me to have begun this at such a late hour,' she sighed. 'I was sure that there would be room for my workbasket in this hamper, but, no matter how many times I have taken everything out and re-sorted it, I always seem to have something left over!'

'Leave it to me,' said Imogen firmly, bending down to help the older woman to her feet. 'You have done quite enough for today. I shall have it done in no time at all, I promise you.'

The governess looked doubtful. 'Are you sure, my dear—it is a dreadful imposition!'

'Nonsense!' replied Imogen cheerfully. 'Take yourself off to bed. It will take me less than two shakes of a lamb's tail!'

Finally persuading her friend to admit defeat, Imogen ushered her into her room and, having watched the governess climb thankfully into her bed, she closed the door, thoughtfully surveying the untidy heap in front of her. A rather daring idea had crept into her mind. As quietly as she could, she began carrying the piles of books and other assorted objects into her own room, stowing them carefully behind the frilled valances that hung around the framework of her feather bed, hoping that Bertha would not take it into her head to toss the mattress before the weekend. Then, selecting just a few of her gowns, those that she considered would be most suitable to begin her new life, she placed them in the bottom of the hamper. Less than an hour later, she had gathered most of her essentials together and, reasoning that the bulk of her belongings would be delivered shortly after she had arrived at her destination, she then covered the items that she had packed with a deep layer of Miss Widdecombe's treasured possessions and quickly strapped the hamper's lid into place. Should the governess choose to undo the straps to check her handiwork, all she would see was a selection of her own belongings.

When she finally climbed into bed, Imogen reasoned that any other small items, including her *toilette* accessories, could easily be packed into an overnight valise at the last minute and, secure in the knowledge that she now had one less problem with which to deal, she closed her eyes and endeavoured, once again, to forget the one that was causing her the greatest heartache.

The following morning, she dressed quickly, urging Bertha to style her hair in the simplest and quickest way possible, and, after checking that she had the bank draft safely in her reticule, she collected her pelisse and a simple poke bonnet and hurried down the stairs, hoping against hope that she would not be waylaid. She was well aware that both her aunt and Miss Widdecombe would consider it rather odd of her to have gone off in so surreptitious a manner, without giving either one of them so much as a hint as to her intention but, confident that she would be able to conjure up some suitable reason for her sudden absence before she returned home, she dismissed the problem from her mind. The most important thing at the moment, as far as she was concerned, was to collect her two hundred and fifty guineas. Only when she had this money safely in her possession could she begin to put her plans into action.

Casting one or two nervous glances around the yard before she stepped out of the back door, she sped quickly across to the stables, where she instructed Jimmy Fairchild to harness Connie to the gig. Having decided to drive herself into town, she considered that it would not be necessary to have a groom accompany her, since this trip would not entail a walk down Sharps Alley to visit Mr Widmark's chambers.

Less than fifteen minutes later, she was bowling down the lane alongside the hayfields where the reapers were already hard at work. Flicking the reins to urge the pony to quicken her pace, she neatly manoeuvred the little carriage around a sharp bend in the lane, only to find that, just a short distance ahead of her, her passage was being hindered by a slow-moving vehicle. She had no difficulty in recognising the wagon as being one of the farm's largest and could see that Ben Chadwick was its driver. However, realising that the lane was far too narrow at this point to attempt to overtake the cumbersome obstruction, she was forced to gather in her reins to check the horse.

As she found herself having to slow Connie down to what became, eventually, little more than a walking pace, her irritation increased and, craning her head to the right to peer at the road ahead of the wagon, she judged that, in just a few more yards, there might be sufficient clearance to feather her way past the hindrance.

Both Beresford and his fellow workers, labouring in a nearby field, heard the high-pitched, grating rasp as the gig's nearside hub scraped against the metal rim of the wagon's larger wheel. Barely two seconds later, a resounding crash split through the still morning air, followed by the ominous sounds of cracking and splintering wood. As of one accord, the reapers downed their tools and rushed to the gate, intent upon catching some glimpse of the mishap.

Having been working on the farthest side of the field, Beresford was almost the last to arrive at the scene. He pushed his way through the huddle of curious spectators but could not, at first, make out from where the noise had emanated. Directly in front of the gate stood the now stationary farm wagon from which a clearly shocked Ben Chadwick was in the process of scrambling awkwardly down from the driving seat and, although Beresford could hear the shrill, panic-stricken neighing of the horse that was threshing about in the undergrowth opposite, he could see no sign of any other vehicle.

Vaulting over the gate, he made his way round the back of the wagon where, to his utter horror, he was confronted with the sight of an ashen-faced Imogen, valiantly attempting to extract herself from the fractured remains of the gig, which had landed on its side in the ditch on the far side of the road.

Smothering an oath, Beresford knelt down and, flinging his arms around her waist, lifted her bodily out of the wreckage and lowered her tenderly on to the grass verge.

Frantically pushing his hands aside, her eyes wide with shock, she attempted to rise.

'Connie!' she gasped. 'Somebody must release her!'

'Lie still, I beg of you!' he commanded her roughly, as he fought to hold her down. 'Chadwick is dealing with the mare—are you hurt?'

As the sound of the horse's terrified squeals subsided, Imogen's taut body relaxed but then, as the full horror of the appalling incident began to dawn upon her, she started to shiver violently, hot tears welled up into her eyes and slid, unchecked, down her cheeks.

Beresford groaned. 'Please stop crying, Imogen—just tell me where you are hurt.' He was beside himself with anxiety.

Blinking away the tears, Imogen raised her hand to her brow.

'I—I m-must have hit my head,' she gulped weakly. 'And I—I think I f-fell on to a sharp rock—m-my knee feels very sore....'

With shaking hands, Beresford undid the ribbons of her bonnet and, after tossing it to one side, began to run his fingers gently over her head.

By this time, a distraught Nicholas had arrived on the scene. Taking one look at his cousin's prostrate figure, he cast himself down on his knees beside her, begging Beresford to tell him how badly she was hurt.

Shaking his head, Beresford frowned and sat back on his heels. 'Just one slight contusion on her temple, thank the Lord—she says that her knee hurts—but I can hardly...!'

'Nor I,' returned the youngster at once, as a vivid blush stained his cheeks.

'If one of you would be good enough to help me to my feet,' came Imogen's faint but exasperated voice, 'I believe I am perfectly capable of attending to my own bruises, thank you very much.'

'Ought she be allowed to get up in her condition, do you think?' Nicholas asked Beresford in alarm.

'She might well be concussed,' interposed Seymour, who had just joined the group. 'You have to lie still, if you're concussed—one of my bearers was once—'

'For pity's sake, gentlemen!'

As her initial shock gradually abated, Imogen's irritation increased. 'I would have you know that I am far from deaf!' she exclaimed crossly, as she attempted to raise herself up on her forearm. 'And I would really appreciate it if you would all kindly stop discussing me as though I were and help me to my feet.'

Realising her intention, Beresford let out a muttered curse, scrambled to his feet and, gripping the tops of her arms, hoisted her gently upright, bracing her still shaking form against him until the trembling ceased.

'Do you think you can stand without help?' he asked brusquely, fighting back the desire to wrap his arms tightly around her and never let her go.

Resolutely stiffening her shoulders, Imogen gave a desultory nod and pushed herself away from his hold.

'I have a slight headache, that is all,' she faltered, as she struggled to maintain her balance. 'I have to find my reticule.'

Beresford's face darkened. His heartfelt relief that she had survived the accident, apparently unscathed, was slowly being replaced by an uncontrollable fury. Her foolish action had caused him untold agony, and all she could think about was her blessed purse!

'Damn your purse, woman!' he thundered. 'What in the

blazes were you about? Only a half-wit would attempt to over-take on this narrow lane!'

Taken off guard, the explosive force of his anger hit her like a ton of bricks.

'I—I was in a hurry,' she stammered, backing away from him nervously. 'I thought that I would have enough room.'

He passed a weary hand across his brow. 'For God's sake, Imogen! You damned nearly killed yourself!'

His voice was thick with emotion, but Imogen's head was now beginning to ache to such an extent that she was no longer able to take in his words, let alone register the altered tone of his voice.

'I must find my reticule,' she repeated abruptly and, al-though it required a considerable effort to turn to inspect the result of her negligent actions, she forced herself to look at the appalling wreckage in the ditch below.

When the gig's nearside hub had caught the metal rim of the other vehicle's wheel, she had struggled frantically to prevent the little carriage from capsizing into the ditch. It was some-thing of a miracle that, as the awful inevitability of the situa-tion hit home, she had mustered sufficient presence of mind to leap out of the left-hand side of the carriage just before it smashed into the ground. Surveying the shattered remains of the little carriage, she realised how close she had come to death, or, at the very least, serious injury.

His wrath mounting, Beresford reached forward and, grab-bing her by the arm, spun her around to face him.

'Leave it be, Imogen! Let me get you home—you are in shock. You really need to lie down.'

'No! Please!' she cried, wrenching herself out of his grasp. 'You do not understand! I have to find my reticule!'

Clenching his jaw, Beresford signalled to Chadwick who, having cut the traces from the pony, had been standing nearby, doing his best to pacify the frightened beast.

'Get one of the men to climb down and see if he can locate Miss Priestley's reticule, Ben,' he instructed him. 'And then, as soon as you are feeling up to it, I suggest you carry on with your own task. We really need those men and we have already wasted far too much time this morning.'

'I am truly sorry for all the trouble I have caused,' said Imogen bleakly, as she watched Chadwick tying Connie to the wagon before limping off to do his employer's bidding.

Steeling himself to ignore her crestfallen expression, Beresford turned to Nicholas and asked him if he would mind taking the pony back to the stables, adding, 'Sanders will know how to deal with the poor creature—and get him to hitch up a curricle and send it down, would you? We need to get your cousin home as quickly as possible.'

As the boy hurried off to carry out his brother's request, the farm worker who had been searching in the splintered remains of the gig for Imogen's reticule, climbed triumphantly out of the ditch, waving the missing object in his hand.

'Good man,' said Beresford, relieving him of his find. Passing the damp but undamaged bag over to Imogen, he asked curiously, 'What have you got in there that is so important? The Crown Jewels?'

'Just some papers that I have to get to the bank,' she returned nervously, clutching the reticule tightly. The last thing she wanted, at this moment, was to have him question her about her reasons for driving so carelessly.

As he studied her closed expression, he found himself marvelling at the ease with which she had recovered from her recent brush with death. Her cheeks were still ashen, it was true, and the bruise at her temple was beginning to take on a faint, bluish tint, but, all in all, she was clearly made of sterner stuff than he had previously imagined.

'These papers,' he said bluntly. 'Are they really that urgent? Will tomorrow suffice?'

'I suppose it will have to,' she replied dispiritedly as she turned away from him. 'Although, I hardly imagine that you will be willing to trust me with another of your carriages!'

'I was not aware that they were my carriages,' he returned mildly. 'As far as I am concerned, Thornfield is still Nicky's property and I dare say you will have no trouble persuading him to let you take another one out. Although it does occur to me that—if this morning's effort is anything to go by—you could clearly do with a few more lessons in the art of safe driving!'

'How dare you, sir!' she gasped. 'You are quite insufferable!'

At her pointed words, the repellent memory of his recent conduct suddenly flashed into Beresford's mind and, for several minutes, he found himself unable to utter another word. Then, 'So it would appear,' he acknowledged abruptly, causing the nearby Seymour to stare at him in disbelief.

Aware of a growing tension between his friend and Imogen, it was with some relief that he heard the sound of a rapidly approaching vehicle.

'Quick work on Nicky's part,' he said cheerfully, as the curricle came into sight. 'I imagine that you are pretty anxious to get on, Matt. Would you like me to escort Miss Priestley back to the house?'

'Thank you, David, but that will not be necessary,' replied Beresford, who, after finally pulling himself together, had decided to take matters into his own hands. 'I understand that Miss Priestley's journey into Ashby was rather urgent. Therefore, if she will allow me, I intend to escort her into town myself!'

Turning to the startled Imogen, he gave her a quick bow, saying, 'If you will excuse me for just one moment, Miss Priestley. I must go and retrieve my jacket from the haywain, after which I shall be more than happy to see that you accomplish your mission.'

Before Imogen had recovered in time to formulate any

words of protest, he had crossed the road, hauled himself over the hayfield's gate and disappeared from her sight.

Seeing her troubled expression, Seymour made up his mind to act. 'Pardon me if I am jumping to the wrong conclusion, Miss Priestley,' he said suddenly. 'But it seems to me that Matt has offended you in some way. If there is anything that I can do to put matters right…?'

Somewhat disconcerted at Seymour's intervention, Imogen frowned and shook her head.

'You are mistaken, Mr Seymour,' she returned coolly. 'Mr Beresford is merely angry that this accident has interfered with his work.'

'I hardly think so,' returned Seymour abruptly, casting an anxious glance over to the hayfield where he perceived that Beresford, hurriedly thrusting his arms into his jacket as he walked, had already reached the gate.

'He does care, you know,' he blurted out, his apprehensive eyes still on the approaching Beresford. 'But I know him of old. He will never be prepared to admit his feelings, not unless—'

Unfortunately, before Seymour was able to finish his portentous words, Beresford, still carefully adjusting his stock, had joined them.

'Ready, Miss Priestley?' he asked briskly, holding out his hand to help the, now totally confused, Imogen climb into the waiting carriage.

'I will leave you in charge, then, David,' he called down to his friend, motioning to the groom to let go of the horse's heads. 'I doubt if Ben will manage to get back with any new hands before I return.'

'No problem, old chap,' replied Seymour, flicking his worried eyes up at Imogen who, having taken her seat beside Beresford in a numbed silence, was staring down at him with an expression of stunned incredulity. 'I'll deal with it.'

Wearing a distracted frown, Seymour stood gazing after the

curricle until it was well out of sight, fearful that his impetuous remark might have done his friend's cause more harm than good.

'Better get back to work, then?' came Nicholas's voice at his elbow.

'Mmm, yes, I suppose so,' replied Seymour vaguely, then, with a little shake of his head, he gesticulated towards the clutter in the ditch, adding, 'But first I had better send out a couple of the men to clear up this unholy mess!'

Chapter Twenty

'Are you perfectly sure that you are up to this journey?' asked Beresford in concern, as he registered Imogen's pensive expression. 'I really should have insisted upon your going back to Thornfield. This trip was not a good idea. I am of a mind to get hold of a doctor as soon as we arrive'

'No, no,' she exclaimed hastily. 'Truly, here is no need for that—I promise you that I will be fine. It was very good of you to take the time—I am really sorry to have been the cause of so much trouble to you.'

His mouth twisted in an ironic smile. 'Why do I get the feeling that you are going to cause me a good deal more trouble before we are done, Miss Priestley?' he said drily.

'I—I beg your pardon?'

First Seymour and now Beresford! Was it her imagination, wondered Imogen in confusion, or had everyone suddenly taken to talking in riddles? She was beginning to think that the bang on the head she had suffered must have affected her wits more than she had realised.

Having reached the main road, Beresford was soon to discover that the traffic was a good deal heavier than he had anticipated, obliging him to keep most of his attention on the road.

However, after he had skilfully manoeuvred the curricle past a heavily loaded brewer's dray, he managed to cast a quick glance in Imogen's direction. He was finding her continued silence somewhat unnerving and it worried him that she might have been more badly injured than she had been prepared to admit.

'Does your head still pain you?' he asked anxiously.

Imogen who, after carefully considering Seymour's puzzling words, had been endeavouring to summon up the courage to broach the subject of her inexplicable behaviour in the library, reached up and tentatively touched the swelling at her temple.

'I have had worse,' she replied impassively.

There was another prolonged silence then, 'Mr Beresford,' she began tentatively. 'The other evening—that is—I feel that you may have…'

'Not now, Miss Priestley, I beg of you!'

As Imogen's unexpected words registered, the violence of the jolt that shot through Beresford had such a profound effect upon his wits that he was temporarily distracted from his activity and, almost before he was aware of what was happening, he suddenly found himself having to pull hard on his nearside rein to avoid a collision with an oncoming landau, thereby suffering the jeering, caustic comment of its driver.

He took a swift intake of breath and, gritting his teeth, tried to concentrate on the task in hand, but his mind was now a jumble of confusion. The very fact that Imogen had brought herself to mention the distasteful matter at all was evidence enough of her outrage at his appalling behaviour. No doubt she had been summoning up the courage to take him to task ever since he had forced his attentions upon her, his apparent reluctance to apologise on that first occasion clearly having led her to believe that he was in the habit of treating unprotected females in that cavalier fashion.

Pursing his lips, he made up his mind to have an end to it

all right there and then. Spotting an opening in the traffic ahead, he swung the carriage hard over on to the grass verge and, pulling the horses to a halt, turned to face her.

'Miss Priestley,' he began awkwardly, reaching out to grasp one of her hands.

'What are you doing, Mr Beresford?' she gasped, in astonishment. 'We cannot stop here—people are staring at us! Do move on, I beg of you!'

'Can you not be still for just one moment, Miss Priestley?' he glowered. 'I am trying to propose to you, for God's sake!'

Imogen froze. 'W-what did you say?' she faltered, now more certain than ever that her brain must have been damaged by the blow on the head.

'You will have to marry me, Imogen,' he countered abruptly. 'That evening—I—I cannot put it out of my mind. However, since I am well aware that you found my conduct totally unforgivable, I realise that there is little point in trying to apologise but, having compromised you so dreadfully, you must see that I have no alternative but to try and redeem the situation. You must marry me!'

'Unless this is another one of your fatuous attempts to provoke me, Mr Beresford,' exclaimed Imogen indignantly, vainly trying to disengage her hand from his hold, 'I must suppose that you have completely lost your mind.'

'That much is true, in any event,' he agreed sardonically. 'However, to the point—may I take it that you are prepared to agree to my request?'

At first, Imogen could not believe that she had heard aright; then, as the full impact of his words finally sank in, there arose in her breast such a fury that she seemed to have lost the power to think clearly. After having made his dislike of her so patently obvious, had he really imagined that she would be prepared to marry him simply to assuage his guilty conscience! The man was outrageous!

Forcing herself to turn to look at him, she took a deep breath and, in deceptively dulcet tones, she said, 'Do let me see if I understand this correctly, Mr Beresford. You believe that you have to marry me because you feel that you have compromised me?'

'Yes, but—' he began hurriedly. Having arrived at the conclusion that any declaration of love was likely to be met with a withering response, he had purposefully refrained from making any mention of his true regard for her. He was now beginning to have the rather uncomfortable feeling that he had phrased his request very badly.

'And then, I suppose,' she continued, ignoring his attempt to interrupt her flow, 'as soon as you have organised everyone else's life to your satisfaction, you will, no doubt, expect me to accompany you back to your splendid bungalow in East India?'

'I must admit that I had not really thought that far ahead,' he felt himself obliged to admit. 'But in the circumstances—'

'How very generous of you!' she cut in. 'To be prepared to sacrifice your entire lifestyle for what was, after all, a rather insignificant occurrence is, truly, a most magnanimous gesture on your part!'

As a dull flush covered Beresford's cheeks, a *frisson* of alarm swept through him.

'No, no, Imogen!' he protested, in dismay. 'You have obviously mistaken my meaning!'

'Not at all, sir,' she replied sweetly. 'I believe your words speak for themselves.'

Beresford's brow creased in a perplexed frown. He was desperately trying to make sense of Imogen's strangely detached manner, but her expression was enigmatic. Clearing his throat, he endeavoured to rephrase his question in what he hoped would be a more acceptable form.

'I would esteem it a great honour if you would agree to be my wife.'

'Whilst I truly appreciate your having made such a generous offer, Mr Beresford,' she said, finally managing to extract her hand from his grasp, 'I regret that I must decline!'

'But you cannot!' he gasped in astonishment. 'I have compromised you and I am honour-bound to offer you my protection.'

Imogen shrugged. 'And I have rejected your offer,' she said flatly. 'Therefore, as far as I am concerned, the subject is closed. And now, if you have no objection, perhaps we could continue our journey!'

Even though he had steeled himself to expect some sort of resistance from her, Imogen's indifferent dismissal of his proposition had the effect of rendering Beresford almost speechless. Although he had been under no illusions with regard to her perfectly understandable antipathy towards him, he had not realised that she held him in such contempt.

'May I be permitted to know the reason for your refusal?' he managed at last.

'But, of course,' she replied in cool, even tones. 'In the first place, I fail to see exactly how you think you have discredited me. The bare facts of the matter are that you embraced me and I, rather foolishly, returned your embrace. At the very least, I hold myself equally to blame for what occurred, but since, as far as I am aware, our—actions—were not witnessed by any third party, it seems to me that it would be far more sensible, on both our parts, to simply forget that the unfortunate incident ever took place!'

The bewildered Beresford, blanching at her stark, unemotional description of the momentous event that had been causing him untold wretchedness for the past few days, tried, again without success, to read her expression.

'And you are prepared to do that?' he asked, his brow puckering in doubt.

'Of course. It would hardly be in my interests to do otherwise.'

Realising that she had boxed him into a corner, Beresford

was persuaded that there was little point in arguing the matter. All at once, a weird mixture of relief, coupled with an extraordinary sense of desolation, swept over him, and, for several moments, he was at something of a loss to know exactly how to combat this feeling. He had to admit that he had been half-hoping, against all reason or logic, that Imogen would agree to marry him but, at the same time, the possibility that she might have felt constrained to accept his offer, simply in order to extricate herself from the awful predicament in which he had placed her, was profoundly demoralising. Being painfully aware that the overwhelming passion that had lately been playing havoc with his common sense was now far too powerful to be satisfied by mere acquiescence on her part, the thought that she might have been prepared to come to him as an unwilling partner filled him with deep distaste.

As he gradually became aware of Imogen's impatient fidgeting beside him, and recalled her request that they should continue the journey into Ashby, he forced himself to return his attention to the heavy stream of passing traffic. Leaning down, he released the brake lever at his side, flicked the reins to urge the horses forward and although his heart was no longer in it, did his best to concentrate his attention on steering the curricle back on to the busy highway.

At last, the carriage moved on and Imogen tried desperately to relax. Her mind was in such a whirl that it was starting to make her head ache quite badly. How she had ever contrived to drum up sufficient resources to carry off that farcical masquerade, without giving herself away, she would never know. But, the moment that she had realised that Beresford meant her to take his proposal seriously, she had become fiercely determined not to allow him to browbeat her into a preposterous sham of a marriage for which neither of them had the slightest inclination. Resolutely shying away from the fact that that particular fantasy had been the subject of many of her recent dreams, she clutched her reticule firmly in her hands, endeavouring to take comfort from the satisfying feel of the folded parchment bank draft within.

She would collect her money and, if they could manage to get back to Thornfield before it was too late, she would go straight down the Wheatsheaf and finalise her arrangements with Mr Dawes.

'Which bank?'

Beresford's brisk question cut into her thoughts; hurriedly collecting her wits, she directed him towards Taylor & Lloyd's imposing frontage where, having signalled to a passing urchin to hold the horses' heads, he leapt down from his seat and walked round to her side of the carriage to hand her down.

'Do endeavour to conduct your business as swiftly as possible,' he urged her, carefully avoiding her eyes. 'I do not care to keep the horses standing for too long in this traffic.'

Having assured him that she would be as quick as she could, Imogen proved to be as good as her word and, barely ten minutes later, emerged from the bank's chambers carrying a rather cumbersome-looking package that was, clearly, too large to fit into her reticule.

As soon as she appeared, Beresford stepped forward and offered to relieve her of her burden but, to his surprise, she shook her head adamantly and only just managed to hang on to the hefty parcel while he assisted her back up onto her seat.

'So it *is* the Crown Jewels!' he said, making an effort to inject a little light-heartedness into the conversation. 'I trust we do not get waylaid by some rascally highwayman on our journey home!'

At these words, Imogen clutched her packet more closely to her and glanced nervously along the crowded thoroughfare.

Beresford allowed himself a tiny smile. 'Have no fear, Miss Priest-ley,' he drawled, as he swung himself up into the driving seat. 'I have my trusty pistol here in my pocket!'

As Beresford neatly edged the curricle into the heart of the traffic, Philip Wentworth, carefully concealed behind one of the bank's Corinthian marble columns, watched in gleeful satisfaction as the vehicle progressed rapidly down the busy street, eventually vanishing from sight.

It seemed that Fate had played right into his hands. What a bit of luck he had spotted the Priestley girl coming out of the bank. This could be the very chance he had been waiting for! A baleful grin split his face as he hurried down Sharps Alley to his lodging house to collect his weapons. Then, pushing his way through the crowds of shoppers, he hailed a passing cab to take him the short distance to Tully's smallholding, confident that he would have no difficulty in obtaining a horse from the money-grabbing Jem.

With his extensive knowledge of the surrounding countryside, Wentworth estimated that he would be able to cut across the fields, nip through Piper's Woods and reach Thornfield long before his quarry had arrived. This time, he determined, as he leaned back against the squabs of the hack and patted his pocket, he would not miss.

Chapter Twenty-One

On the return journey to Thornfield, since his thoughts were still heavily occupied with the problem of alleviating the awkward tension that continued to exist between himself and Imogen, Beresford was considerably relieved to discover that the press of traffic on the highway had, more or less, abated. After threading his way through a jumble of assorted vehicles, he spotted an open stretch in the road ahead and, manoeuvring the curricle past a slow-moving cart, he relaxed his tight control of the ribbons, thereby allowing his horses to have their heads.

Casting a quick sideways glance at his passenger, he cleared his throat and began, 'In view of our earlier conversation, Miss Priestley, may I suggest that, for the remainder of my time at Thornfield, we endeavour to conjure up some semblance of—amicability—between the two of us. I cannot help feeling that the—how shall I put it?—tension that has existed between us recently cannot have escaped the notice of one or two of the other members of the household. What do you say, Miss Priestley? Since we have resolved to forget our—differences—what say we cry quits and move on?'

At Beresford's words, a faint blush stained Imogen's cheeks. Safe in the knowledge that she was about to move on with her life far more quickly than he could possibly imagine, she was quick to realise that his suggestion had a great deal to commend it, especially when she recalled the shattering effect of his earlier disdain. Added to which, the discomfiting memory of Miss Widdecombe's anxious probing, not to mention Seymour's odd remark, soon made her realise that the awkwardness that existed between herself and Beresford had not gone totally unremarked, even by her addlepated cousin Jessica!

Therefore, praying that she did, indeed, have only one more day in which she would be obliged to conform to his suggestion, she inclined her head graciously and answered. 'I am perfectly willing to make the effort, if you are.'

Beresford smothered a laugh. 'Oh, come now, Miss Priestley!' he cajoled her. 'You will have to do a great deal better than that, if you are to pass Miss Widdecombe's scrutiny!'

Imogen managed a brief smile. 'I am afraid that I have not had much practice in the art of subterfuge.'

Beresford raised an eyebrow. 'Unlike myself, you imply?'

She turned her startled face towards him. 'Oh, no, Mr Beresford!' she replied hastily. 'It was not my intention to suggest—!'

Then, having registered the gleam of amusement in his eyes, she paused and gave a rueful chuckle. 'I never fail to rise to it, do I?'

'But you do it so charmingly,' he assured her, with a wry grin. 'Although, in this instance, you were not far off the mark. As it happens, in my line of work, one might say that subterfuge is a somewhat essential tool for the job.'

In spite of herself, Imogen's curiosity was roused. 'How do you mean?'

With a little frown, he considered her question. 'Well, as far as I am concerned,' he replied, 'the chief occupation of any diplomat is to avoid unnecessary confrontation. For instance, it would hardly do for a representative of his Majesty's government to cross swords with a prince of the Raj, now would it?

However, ever since the Company lost its monopoly, one or two of the local leaders have, occasionally, proved to be less than co-operative and I have frequently found myself having to simulate an air of good-natured bonhomie in less than favourable circumstances, in order to preserve the status quo. Would you not count that a form of subterfuge?'

Imogen nodded uncertainly. 'One supposes that your work must be rather dangerous at times,' she ventured. 'I have read that there are still several tribes in East India who are determined to drive the British out of their annexed territories.'

Beresford was silent for a moment or two, then, 'There is always a certain amount of unrest to deal with,' he returned noncommittally. 'I, myself, am fortunate in that I have never encountered any truly open hostility. In fact, I count at least two of the neighbouring princes among my good friends.'

At this, Imogen was unable to resist a gentle dig at Beresford's expense. 'Also among those whom you seldom entertain in your own home, I take it?'

Letting out a roar of laughter, he shot her a glance of approval. *'Touché*, Miss Priestley! It shames me to confess that, although I have frequently taken advantage of both of their highnesses' lavish hospitality, I have refrained from returning the compliment. Although, in my own defence, I do have to say that it would prove quite problematical to entertain these particular gentlemen, since one would also have to find space for their, not inconsiderable, entourages, including bodyguards! I fear they would consider my little bungalow to be far beneath their exalted standing.'

Quick to recognise that Beresford's self-deprecation was his way of attempting to lessen the conflict between them, Imogen's lips began to curve in a smile of appreciation. He had certainly managed to make her feel a good deal more at ease in his company; her headache had all but disappeared and, given that she could find some way of ignoring the dull ache within her heart, she was beginning to feel that she would have no great difficulty in getting through the next twenty-four hours.

Registering her smile, Beresford heaved an inward sigh of relief and, setting out to lift her spirits even higher, he began to regale her with some of the more humorous aspects of his life in the sub-continent. Having trained himself, from a very early age, to keep his feelings to himself, he was well versed in the art of maintaining the proverbial 'stiff upper lip', as a result of which, he soon succeeded in concentrating his mind on the more productive business of keeping Imogen amused with a steady flow of inconsequential persiflage.

By the time that they reached the turning that led up to the Thornfield estate, a good deal of light-hearted banter had passed between the two of them, with each of them sadly conscious of all the earlier opportunities that had been missed in which they might have discovered this easy-going camaraderie.

Seymour, who had been for some time on the alert for his friend's return, watched with interest as the carriage passed the hayfield, then, greatly relieved that Beresford appeared to have resolved the troublesome issue that had been making him behave so out of character for the last few days, he returned to his occupation of overseeing the new hands.

'As soon as I have deposited you safely, Miss Priestley,' Beresford announced, swinging the curricle through the archway into the stable yard, 'I need to get straight back to work, but, first, I want you to promise me that you will have your maid attend to those bruises.'

Imogen looked at him gratefully. 'If it will put your mind at rest,' she replied, 'I will certainly do as you ask, although I have to say that, apart from some slight discomfort, I really feel perfectly fine.'

With a satisfied nod, Beresford brought the carriage to a halt, tossed the reins to a waiting groom and, having jumped neatly from his perch, held out his hand to relieve her of her package.

For a moment, Imogen hesitated but, having caught a glimpse of the challenging gleam in Beresford's eyes, she gave an apologetic smile, passed the parcel down to him and allowed him to assist her to the ground.

'And be sure to take good care of the "Crown Jewels",' he grinned, as he handed her back the bulky parcel. Then, congratulating himself on having got through the entire encounter without once losing his head, he gave her a casual wave and turned to leave. Now that they had managed to get on a more friendly footing, he was thinking, he would do his level best to allow things to proceed at their own natural pace. And, what then? came an uneasy question from within. He shook his head, firmly telling himself that there was no point in crossing that particular bridge until he had arrived at it.

Reaching the corner of the stable block, he swung his head over his shoulder, in order to satisfy himself that Imogen had left the yard, but saw, to his surprise, that she did not appear to have moved from the spot on which he had deposited her and, in fact, seemed to be intent upon watching his movements. The temptation to find out why she had not returned to the house was too great. He turned on his heel and was about to make his way back to her, when his attention was diverted by a sudden flash that seemed to have emanated from the opposite side of the yard in the region of the carriage-house.

Putting up his hand to shade his eyes from the bright noonday sun, he focussed on the edge of the building, where he soon established that the intermittent flashing was being caused by the sun's rays striking some sort of bright metal. Almost instantaneously, he perceived that the metal was, in fact, the well-polished barrel of a pistol and that its owner was, at this very moment, sidling slowly around the edge of the carriage-house, pointing the weapon directly at him! Instinctively, he jerked to one side, to remove himself from the angle of fire, but his adversary merely grinned and continued to move relentlessly forward.

Philip Wentworth, who had been standing flattened up against the side of the carriage-house wall for some little time, had been waiting for such an opportunity. Having watched the grooms unhitch the horses from the curricle and lead them back into their stalls to attend to their needs, he had figured that the coast would then be quite clear enough for him to carry out his objective. The fact that Imogen was still in the stable yard was, certainly, something of a drawback but, since he was fully determined to put a period to Beresford's life there and then, he dismissed her presence, promising himself that he would find the means to deal with that insignificant problem later.

Even though Beresford, not having any real protection near at hand, was quick to grasp that he was now completely at Wentworth's mercy, his whole attention was concentrated upon Imogen who, to his mounting horror, was moving forward to meet him and, in doing so, was placing herself directly in Wentworth's line of fire!

With not a moment's hesitation, Beresford dived headlong across the distance that divided Imogen and himself and, as the gun exploded, thrust her roughly to the ground, covering her body with his own. The bullet whistled harmlessly over their heads, noisily embedding itself in the water butt that was situated on the corner of the stable block—at the very spot where, less than five seconds earlier, Beresford had been standing!

Providentially, for the pair of them, the sound of running footsteps coming from inside the stable soon had the violently cursing Wentworth turning on his heel and making for the horse that he had concealed behind a nearby hedgerow.

In an instant, Beresford had scrambled to his feet and, after unceremoniously dragging Imogen upright, he quickly thrust his hand into his pocket and whipped out his own pistol.

'Not a word!' he instructed her tersely. 'Leave it to me.'

Imogen, having had the wind knocked out of her by the force of Beresford's hefty form landing on top of her, was powerless to utter a single sound and could do little more than gaze up at him in a stunned silence.

Almost immediately Sanders, the head groom, with two or three stable lads on his heels, came hurrying out of the building to investigate the explosion.

'Thought I heard a shot, sir,' he panted, then, hearing the sound of running water, he turned his head towards the water barrel, the contents of which were now pouring in a steady stream through the neat round hole in one of its oaken staves.

'Regrettably, yes,' owned Beresford, in a rueful voice. 'I am afraid that I accidentally discharged my pistol. Sorry to have alarmed you—can the damage be repaired, do you think?'

'No problem, sir,' said Sanders, motioning to one of his minions to find a bung of some sort. 'Just as long as nobody was hurt.'

'Absolutely, Sanders!' replied Beresford, bending down to retrieve Imogen's scattered belongings, then, tucking her unresisting hand into the crook of his arm, he ushered her gently but firmly in the direction of the back door.

Once inside the passageway, she withdrew her hand and swung round to confront him. 'W-was that…?'

'Wentworth,' he supplied, with a brief nod. 'Allow me to apologise for my precipitate actions, but I am afraid that I was given very little choice in the matter.'

She stared at him, round eyed. 'But you saved my life!' she gasped. 'You might easily have been killed!'

Beresford's lips twisted. 'I believe that was the man's intention,' he said flatly. 'However, I would appreciate it if you did not mention the matter to the rest of the household. It would be a great pity to disturb Lady Beresford's still fragile equilibrium at this early stage, would it not?'

'Yes, of course,' she answered hurriedly. 'I do agree, but surely there is something we can do about him? Inform the constable or the magistrate?'

'Better to leave it with me, Imo—Miss Priestley,' he advised her and, lifting his hand, he brushed away a piece of straw that had caught on the veiling of her bonnet.

'I trust that I did not damage you in any way?' he said softly. 'You have been very brave. Two near misses in one day are more than enough for anyone to cope with, I should imagine, and I am very much afraid that this second encounter with death will have earned you a fresh set of bruises!'

'Bruises I can cope with,' she replied, with a tremulous smile, as she started to make her way along the passage, but then, as a sudden thought occurred to her, she stopped and turned towards him. 'How is it that you do not seem particularly surprised that Wentworth attempted to kill you?'

'Well, he always seemed a pretty desperate sort of cove to me,' he answered half-heartedly. 'And, after everything I have learned about him, nothing that he does would surprise me.'

She frowned; then, all of a sudden, her eyes widened and she stared at him accusingly. 'He has done it before, hasn't he? That is—tried to kill you, I mean!' she amended hastily. 'Why have you not said anything? We must inform the authorities immediately and have him taken in charge!'

'And have the whole house in a state of panic? I hardly think so!'

Shaking his head vehemently, Beresford leaned forward and grasped her by the hand. 'Please, Miss Priestley,' he urged her. 'I admit that Wentworth caught me off guard today, but I will not allow him to do so again, you have my word. I fully intend to see that the scoundrel gets his just deserts. You must trust me in this.'

For the briefest of instants, their eyes locked, but, as a warning quiver rippled through him, Beresford instantly released her hand and, turning towards the door, said briskly, 'It would, however, be preferable if you were to remain within the confines of the house and garden for the rest of day, if you have no objection.'

Although it meant postponing her trip into Kirton Priors, Imogen was disinclined to argue with him, telling herself that her business with the innkeeper could just as easily be dealt with the following morning.

'But you are not going back to the hayfield now, surely?' she pressed him urgently. 'Wentworth could still be lying in wait somewhere!'

He shook his head. 'I doubt it,' he replied. 'He will be long gone by now. He is far too wily a customer to attempt another such attack now that he knows I am aware of his presence.'

'You will be careful?' stammered Imogen. 'I—that is, we—would not want to see you hurt on our account.'

As he gazed down into her anxious face, Beresford found himself thinking how very strange it was that it should have taken such a frightening incident to bring them to this rather pleasant state of truce.

'Your concern is much appreciated, Miss Priestley,' he assured her softly, as he stepped out of the house.

Watching him stride purposefully across the yard and down the lane, Imogen's heart was full. She was miserably aware of the fact that she could never stop loving Beresford, no matter how hard she tried and, that being the case, she had no choice but to leave Thornfield as soon as possible. With a reluctant sigh, she turned away and tried to console herself with the thought that, after today's momentous events, it did at least look as though they could part on reasonably friendly terms.

Quickly brushing herself down and straightening her bonnet, she made her way into the hall, where she immediately found herself surrounded by the rest of the family, who had been anxiously awaiting her return.

'Oh, my dear!' exclaimed Lady Beresford, flinging her arms around her niece. 'You might have been killed!'

For one startled moment, Imogen thought that her aunt was alluding to the recent incident in the stable yard. However, Jessica's incoherent gabble of words soon reassured her that they were all, in fact, referring to the earlier mishap with the carriage.

'Nicholas rushed back and told us all about it,' she was saying, her eyes shining with barely suppressed excitement. 'He said that the gig had smashed into absolute smithereens and that Matt had to climb down into the ditch to drag your unconscious body out of the wreckage!'

'Do stop talking nonsense, Jessica,' Miss Widdecombe reprimanded her sharply. 'Your brother said no such thing!'

'I should hope not,' said Imogen faintly, staring at her cousin in consternation. 'Although it is perfectly true that Mr Beresford did, indeed, help me out of the ditch.'

'What a truly frightening experience for you, my dear,' gasped Lady Beresford and, taking her niece's arm, she ushered her into the library and begged her to provide them with a more complete version of Nicholas's hurried and somewhat garbled account.

'It was certainly a rather unpleasant one,' Imogen was obliged to admit, and, although at that moment she would far rather have been given the chance to escape to the sanctuary of her own room to contemplate the happy circumstance of her newly developed relationship with Beresford, she knew that it would be quite impossible to leave until she had provided her listeners with a full and accurate description of her mishap.

'And you suffered no hurt?' asked the governess, in amazement, when she had finally reached the end of her narration.

'Well, I believe I have a slight bruise here,' replied Imogen, pushing back her bonnet to reveal the swelling on her forehead. 'As to any other damage, I suppose I shall have to wait until I get out of these rather dusty garments before I can investigate properly.'

'Oh, my dear!' exclaimed her aunt, reeling back in dismay at the sight of the ugly contusion. 'How very selfish of us to have badgered you with questions before giving you the chance to have your wounds dressed!' And, rising quickly to her feet, she gave the bell-pull a sharp tug, saying, 'You must go at once and soak your bruises in a nice hot bath—I shall have Allardyce see to it upon the instant.'

More than happy to obey her aunt's command, Imogen gathered up her belongings and retired to her room, only to find herself having to undergo a further cross-questioning from her maidservant. However, since Bertha's strictures were also coupled with a generous helping of affectionate cosseting, Imogen was not at all unwilling to deliver herself into the woman's competent hands and, barely fifteen minutes later, after a succession of maids had trooped into her bedroom carrying large jugs of hot water, she found herself indulging in the luxury of the promised bath.

Closing her eyes, she lay back in the soft, scented water and allowed Bertha to minister to her bruises, which, she was surprised to be informed, were rather more plentiful and widespread than she had supposed.

'It looks as though it is going to be long sleeves for you, for the next week or so, my girl,' muttered the maid, shaking her head in dismay at the unsightly patches of discolouration on Imogen's arms and shoulders. 'I can treat them with hamamelis, of course, but as for *this*!' Gesturing at the lump on her mistress's forehead, she demanded to know why Imogen had not come straight home and have her deal with it at once. 'For it is clearly, far too late to apply any sort of compress now,' she sniffed disapprovingly.

Nevertheless, having liberally applied the witch hazel to the worst of Imogen's bruises, Bertha then insisted that she should lie down and rest until it was time to dress for dinner, a proposition with which, at this point in the proceedings, Imogen found herself more than willing to comply.

Relaxing against the soft pillows, she watched drowsily through half-closed eyes as the maidservant then spent several minutes quietly ferreting through her collection of evening gowns.

At last, having hit upon a dress that met her requirements, Bertha selected an organza stole of the same oyster colour, cast a satisfied glance at her now peacefully sleeping mistress, then hurried out of the room to redesign the sleeves of the garment.

Chapter Twenty-Two

The elegant swathes of chiffon that covered Imogen's arms that evening merely increased Beresford's disquiet. Unfortunately, since it appeared that he was to be given no opportunity to engage her in conversation, he was unable to ascertain the extent of the damage she had sustained from the day's dramatic events. To his intense annoyance, his stepmother chose to monopolise his company for almost the entire evening, repeatedly plying him with tedious questions about the morning's mishap and, although he was doing his best to keep his mind on Lady Beresford's protracted description of how very shocked she had been to hear of her niece's accident, he was unable to stop his eyes from continually straying over to the sofa where Imogen was sitting.

'Although I do have to say,' Lady Beresford was presently reprimanding him, 'I am rather cross with you for not bringing the poor child straight home! Gallivanting about the countryside after such a terrifying experience cannot have done her any good at all!'

As her aunt's words reached her ears, Imogen looked up and caught Beresford's eye. 'I did have some rather important business to deal with, Aunt Blanche,' she intervened hastily. 'I am afraid that it was I who persuaded Mr Beresford to take me into Ashby.'

Lady Beresford frowned. 'I cannot imagine what business could be so pressing as to cause you to have taken such a foolish risk, Imogen.'

Since Beresford had spent some time conjecturing over that very matter, it was with considerable interest that he waited for her niece's reply.

Imogen, however, had no intention of satisfying anyone's curiosity. 'I am very sorry to have caused you so much worry, Aunt,' she said meekly. 'It will not happen again, I promise you.'

'I should hope not, my dear!' returned her aunt, fanning herself vigorously. 'I swear that I nearly had a seizure when Nicholas informed us!'

As his stepmother launched into yet another dreary recital of how very anxious she and Miss Widdecombe had both been while they waited for Imogen's return, Beresford, sighing inwardly, realised that his patience was about to be tested to its very limit and concentrated on murmuring the occasional sympathetic platitude.

Imogen, conscious of his frequent glances in her direction, would have welcomed the chance to have a few quiet words alone with him, since she was very anxious to know whether he had made any provision to protect himself from further attack. The idea that Wentworth might be skulking around in the nearby vicinity, waiting to pounce on him at any given moment, filled her with an indescribable horror. As if having to bid Matt Beresford the most casual of goodbyes and never set eyes on him again were not punishment enough for her folly at having allowed herself to fall in love with him, the thought of him lying dead in a field somewhere was too dreadful to contemplate. She urgently needed to be assured that he had done everything in his power to ensure his own safety.

However, it seemed that neither Imogen nor Beresford was

to be granted an opportunity to have their anxiety assuaged that evening, since Lady Beresford shortly took it upon herself to usher her niece off to bed, even insisting upon accompanying her up to her room to make sure that she had everything that she needed.

After fussing over her for a good many minutes, offering various needless suggestions to the stoical Bertha, Lady Beresford finally bade her niece an affectionate 'goodnight', leaving Imogen suffering more than a few guilty pangs of remorse about keeping her aunt in the dark over her planned departure. In fact, her conscience began to trouble her to such an extent that, as soon as she heard the sound of Miss Widdecombe's footsteps outside her door, she made up her mind to take the governess into her confidence and solicit her advice.

On being informed that they were to start for Kendal first thing on Friday morning, however, the governess was somewhat perturbed that Imogen had thought it necessary to be so secretive and, after listening in silence to her young friend's hurried description of the arrangements that she had made, regarded her with a puzzled frown.

'I must confess that I still do not understand the need for all this havey-cavey concealment,' she said, slowly shaking her head.

'It is simply that I did not want everyone to make a great to-do about our going,' Imogen endeavoured to explain. 'You know how my aunt is.'

'I know how she *was*,' riposted Miss Widdecombe forcibly. 'But I hardly need point out that the Lady Beresford of today is a somewhat different creature from the Lady Beresford of two weeks ago. Besides which, it seems to me that you will provoke a far greater fuss when you eventually decide to confront her with this! Also, does it not occur to you that Mr Beresford will think it very odd of us to leave before your uncle's will has been determined?'

At the mention of Beresford's name, Imogen felt herself flinch, causing her to wonder whether her preoccupation with getting away from him had not, perhaps, brought about a certain loss of perspective. However, whilst she realised that there was a great deal of sense in what the governess had said, she was determined not to allow her friend to shake her resolve.

'Unlike my aunt, Widdy, I am in the fortunate position of not having to concern myself with Mr Beresford's approval,' she reminded Miss Widdecombe, but then, as she stared down at the worried look on the governess's face, her eyes suddenly filled with alarm. 'Surely you cannot have changed your mind about joining Miss Knox!'

'Of course I have not changed my mind!' rejoined Miss Widdecombe tartly. 'I am merely concerned that you should have felt the need to adopt such a surreptitious course of action and, whilst you may not care to hear this, my dear, I do have to confess that I am beginning to think that there is good deal more behind this rather odd behaviour of yours than you are prepared to admit!'

'Wh-whatever can you mean, Widdy?' stammered Imogen, as a deep flush spread across her cheeks.

Pursing her lips, the governess fixed her perceptive eyes on her former pupil's face and said slowly, 'As I hope you are aware, Imogen, I would not normally dream of interfering in matters of a personal nature—'

As Imogen let out a gasp of protest and tried to prevent Miss Widdecombe from continuing with whatever allegation she was about to make, the governess held up her hand and begged, 'Please allow me to finish, dear child, and do believe that I have only your best interests at heart!'

With a weak nod of defeat, Imogen subsided back into her chair, dreading the governess's next words. Surely, her feelings for Beresford had not become so transparent that everyone in the household was now aware of them?

'Correct me if I am wrong, Imogen,' continued Miss Widdecombe, 'but I do believe that Mr Beresford is, somehow, at the bottom of all this!'

Imogen stared at the governess, her eyes wide with trepidation.

'You really must not blame yourself, my dear,' said Miss Widdecombe drily. 'Despite having dismissed several potential suitors, you have never really come across anyone quite like Beresford so, in my humble opinion, it is hardly surprising that you find yourself bowled over by his looks and his charm—both of which, I am bound to concede, are quite considerable. However, I am given to understand that such infatuations seldom last very long and I cannot help thinking that it would be a great pity if you were to allow these passing sentiments to colour your normal good judgement.'

As Imogen listened to the governess's very matter-of-fact dismissal of the powerful emotion that raged within her heart, she was unable to prevent a wry smile from appearing on her face.

'You seem very certain that it is merely an infatuation—how can you be so sure?' she countered.

Miss Widdecombe shrugged. 'I am afraid that whatever it is makes very little difference if the feeling is not mutual, my dear,' she replied, a sad smile touching her lips.

At these words, Imogen shot a questioning glance at her friend, being quite unable to picture the normally undemonstrative little governess ever doing anything so uncontrolled as losing her head over a mere male!

'You sound as though you are speaking from experience, Widdy,' she ventured.

'I am bound to confess that there was just the one time when I fancied myself in love,' replied the governess, with a little sigh. 'However, since my sentiments were not returned, it all came to nothing—and, at any rate,' she continued, in her usual brisk fashion, 'that was all a very long time ago, my dear, but I can

assure you that the feeling does eventually pass. One simply has
to learn to come to terms with it.'

For several moments, as she digested the governess's words,
Imogen said nothing, then, 'What would you have me do,
Widdy?' she asked quietly.

Miss Widdecombe could not fail to register the despair that
was etched upon Imogen's face. It seemed clear to her that
Beresford must have had an even more profound effect upon
her friend than she had originally supposed and then, as the
painful recollection of her own past heartache suddenly forced
its way into her thoughts, she began to wonder whether it might
not be better, after all, to accede to Imogen's suggestion that
they quit Thornfield sooner rather than later.

'Well, my dear,' she replied, eventually making up her mind,
'if you are really set on leaving on Friday morning, I do think
that you must lose no time in letting Lady Beresford know your
intentions. In fact, I believe that you should go and inform her
of your arrangements this very minute!'

With a reluctant nod, Imogen stood up and prepared to leave
but, on reaching the door, she hesitated, then, turning back to
face the governess, said tentatively, 'Would you be willing to
accompany me, Widdy? So much has happened today that I am
not altogether certain that I could find the resources to cope if
Aunt Blanche should suddenly decide to lapse into one of her
nervous declines.'

'Of course, my dear,' said Miss Widdecombe, getting to her
feet. 'If you think it will help. I believe that your aunt is still
downstairs, so we may yet catch her before she retires for the
night.'

Imogen halted and slowly removed her hand from the
doorknob.

'I—is *he*—that is—Mr Beresford with her, do you happen
to know?'

'He was in the salon when I left,' the governess replied carefully, having noted Imogen's pensive expression. 'But, my dear, if you can just summon up the courage, I promise that you will feel a great deal better if you can—how shall I put it—"kill both birds with the one stone"—should you be given the opportunity.'

Unfortunately, from Imogen's point of view at least, it seemed that she was to be given very little choice in the matter; no sooner had she and Miss Widdecombe reached the foot of the staircase than both Beresford and her aunt exited from the salon, with Beresford clearly in the process of bidding his stepmother 'goodnight'.

'Good gracious, my dear,' exclaimed Lady Beresford, starting forward in alarm as her eyes lit upon her niece. 'Is there something amiss? I had thought you fast asleep by this hour!'

'No, no, aunt. There is nothing wrong,' Imogen hastened to reassure her. 'But there is a rather urgent matter that I need to inform you about immediately,' and, taking hold of her aunt's arm, she guided her back into the salon, with Miss Widdecombe quickly following in their wake.

Beresford, although highly intrigued as to the subject of the 'urgent matter' that had brought Imogen downstairs, decided that it was probably a private affair and was about to turn away and leave the three ladies to their discussion, when he heard Miss Widdecombe summoning him to join them.

'I believe this matter concerns you, too, Mr Beresford,' she announced, as she took her seat on the sofa beside the now visibly nervous Imogen. 'But I must allow Miss Priestley to tell you the good news herself.'

'Good news?' queried Lady Beresford, puckering her brow. Then, leaning forward to stare, firstly at her niece and then at the governess, her face cleared and she began to nod her head. 'Ah, yes! I do believe I understand,' she said softly. 'You have decided that it is time to go!'

'Go?' demanded the bewildered Beresford. 'Who is going where?'

'I am—that is—we are,' Imogen blurted out hurriedly. 'Miss Widdecombe and myself, I mean—we are to leave for Kendal on Friday!'

'On Friday!' came her aunt's and Beresford's voices in stunned unison.

Having finally brought herself to say the words, Imogen suddenly felt as though an enormous weight had been lifted from her shoulders and a new confidence began to flow through her veins.

'First thing on Friday morning,' she said firmly, lifting her chin. 'I will be arranging for a chaise to collect us at eight o'clock.'

'But, why this sudden rush?' demanded her clearly perplexed aunt. 'Surely you will need far more time to organise such a long journey?'

For one moment, Imogen was at something of a loss. Uncomfortably aware that Beresford's stunned eyes were riveted upon her, she was very reluctant to confess that she had been secretly plotting her escape for several days now. Luckily, Miss Widdecombe seemed to sense her young friend's dilemma and took it upon herself to come to the rescue.

'Miss Priestley and I have just come to the conclusion that, if we wanted to reach Kendal before the start of the new school term, we really ought to be on our way at once,' she explained. 'I understand that the entire journey is to take us several days…'

'Four, to be precise,' put in Imogen, smiling gratefully at the governess. 'Which, I believe, will allow us just enough time to settle ourselves in to our new home before the girls arrive.'

Beresford, whose head was still reeling from the shock of Imogen's initial revelation, had barely managed to recover his senses in time to digest this latest information.

'What school?' he implored his stepmother. 'What girls? Will you kindly explain to me what you are all talking about?'

'Oh, dear!' gasped Lady Beresford. 'I am so sorry, Matt! It totally slipped my mind that you were not party to Imogen's scheme to join Miss Widdecombe in her friend's school in Westmorland. The matter was all agreed some time ago but, as things turned out, they have both felt obliged to shelve their plans until the legalities over your—that is—Sir Matthew's will had been properly validated.'

Beresford swivelled round to stare at Imogen. 'You intend to leave Thornfield to teach in a country school?' he asked in disbelief.

'I shall not be teaching,' she returned defensively. 'My role will be more of an—administrative one.'

'Miss Priestley has very kindly offered to deal with the accounting side of the business,' supplied Miss Widdecombe helpfully.

His shocked eyes still fixed on Imogen's expressionless face, Beresford found himself totally at a loss to know how to deal with the situation. He was well aware that it was not in his power to prevent Imogen from leaving, but, had he just been given a little more notice of her intentions...!

'But Sir Matthew's will has still not been ratified,' he pointed out despairingly. 'Surely it would be wiser to wait until we have all heard what the lawyers have decided?'

'My uncle's will has absolutely no bearing on this matter, as far as I am concerned,' replied Imogen, steeling herself to return his stormy gaze. 'I have adequate funds to cover both Miss Widdecombe's and my own expenses for quite some time.'

Beresford's face drained. That mysterious parcel! That was why she had been in such a tearing hurry to get to Ashby! And he had been the damned fool who had volunteered to drive her to the bank to collect the very means that had enabled her to put her preposterous scheme into action! An icy chill swept over him and, from somewhere deep within him, he could hear a voice shrieking out in protest, *'No! No! You cannot leave! You must not!'*, but no sound came from his lips.

Instead, reluctantly concluding that further argument would

be futile, he gave a careless shrug and said dispassionately, 'You are, of course, at liberty to leave whenever you choose.'

Nevertheless, having registered the stricken expression that had appeared on Imogen's face, he was unable to control the awful trembling that ran through his body and he was suddenly overcome by a desperate need to get out of the room, anywhere away from that wounded look! Turning to offer his stepmother a brief salute, he asked to be excused, adding, 'I believe that Mr Seymour has been waiting for me to join him for some little time now,' before departing with as much speed as decency would allow.

Her lips still trembling at his curt, dismissive manner, Imogen's eyes followed him as he left the room. Had she expected anything less from him? she wondered. He had made his opinion of her perfectly clear and, although he had offered to make the effort to act towards her in a relatively friendly manner, that was hardly likely to include falling on his knees and begging her to stay! As that rather incongruous notion presented itself to her, a self-mocking smile threatened to form on her lips. Then, as the sound of Lady Beresford's voice began to intrude into her turbulent thoughts, she banished the risible image from her mind and forced herself to concentrate on her aunt's words.

''Well, my dears,' she was saying, 'if you really mean to leave on Friday, it will require a great deal of organisation to get Imogen's things ready in time. I suggest that we all go to our beds and get a good night's rest so that we can make an early start in the morning!'

Impulsively, Imogen reached forward and gave her aunt a little hug. 'I must admit that I was rather concerned that you would try to prevent me from leaving, Aunt Blanche,' she confided. 'I ought to have given you more warning, I know, but—'

'But you were afraid that I would have one of my silly turns!' laughed Lady Beresford, as she returned her niece's embrace. 'As I told you before, my dear, I have put those days behind me, and, whilst I shall be very sorry to see you go, I do not anticipate that it will be the last I shall see of you! As soon as I have a place of my own, I shall expect you to come and visit me frequently. Now, off to bed with you! We have a very busy day ahead of us!'

Chapter Twenty-Three

'I simply cannot imagine where the foolish child can have got to!'

The hired chaise, with trunks strapped both fore and aft, had been made ready to depart some time ago; the horses were getting restive and the yellow-jacketed post-boy (who looked to be well over sixty years of age) was doing his level best to calm the fidgeting pair.

Imogen, who, along with the rest of the family, had been standing at the foot of the flight of steps that led up to the front door, waiting for the absent Jessica to make an appearance, was getting more and more agitated by the minute. Painfully conscious of Beresford's presence nearby, she was finding that it required every ounce of willpower to stop herself from turning her head to take one final look at him.

The past twenty-four hours had flown by in such a whirl of activity that, with the exception of a short, tearful interlude in the early hours of the morning, she had barely had a moment to herself, let alone time to dwell on the fact that Beresford had scarcely uttered a civil word to her since his hurtful remark on Wednesday evening. Which—as if she really needed it!—was more than ample evidence of his total indifference to her and why she should now be doubly glad that she was about to put a distance of more than one hundred and fifty miles between them! However, since none of this sensible rationalisation seemed to be having the slightest effect in alleviating the un-bearable ache within her heart, she just had to hope that Widdy's prognostication that this dreadful feeling of hopeless despair would eventually fade would prove to be correct.

'We really oughter get goin', miss!' came the post-boy's apologetic voice at her elbow. 'Them pair's as fresh as a daisy and don't want to be kept standin' fer much longer!'

Miss Widdecombe, who had been patiently standing by the door of the chaise, waiting for Imogen to finish saying her farewells to the family, approached the steps.

'Surely Jessica cannot be so put out about your leaving that she would go to these lengths to avoid having to bid you good-bye?' she asked, a worried frown furrowing her brow.

Imogen bit her lip. 'She did react rather badly when I first told her,' she admitted. 'Although, I have to admit that I thought that that was simply because she was envious that I was about to do something that she could not be party to.'

The governess nodded. 'That was my impression, too,' she sighed. 'Mrs Sawbridge informed me that she saw Jessica mooching about in the garden all afternoon! But, as I recall, she seemed perfectly happy last evening.'

'It may be that she believes that her failure to make an ap-pearance will prevent our leaving,' said Imogen thoughtfully. 'Well, she is about to discover that not everyone is prepared to march to her tune! I refuse to allow her pettishness to delay us any longer! Come, Widdy!'

Then, straightening her shoulders, she gave a quick nod to the post-boy and, turning to Lady Beresford, enveloped her in a swift hug, saying, 'I am sorry, Aunt, but we really must be on our way now. Do tell Jess that I am very disappointed that she could not bring herself to come down and see us off.'

After her tearful aunt promised that she would pass on her message, Imogen gave Nicholas a friendly wave, reminded him again not to forget to write to her, then, without a further backward glance, allowed the post-boy to help her into the carriage, and took her place next to the already seated Miss Widdecombe.

His fists clenched tightly at his sides, a stony-faced Beresford watched in disbelieving silence as the post-boy mounted the nearside horse and gave it the signal to move off. The laden carriage lumbered unsteadily out of the *porte-cochère*, trundled slowly down the drive, then, gathering speed, swung through the gates and gradually disappeared from view.

For several moments, he found himself unable to think clearly. It was impossible to comprehend that Imogen had really gone—that he would never see her again—that he had actually let her leave without telling her how much he loved her. Not that she would have had the slightest interest in any such declaration, he thought bitterly, since it was perfectly clear that it was *him* from whom she been so set on escaping!

His jaw rigid, he turned away from the heart-wrenching spectacle of the empty driveway in front of him and began to make his way towards the rear of the house, ready to start the day's activities, only too conscious of the fact that, without the invisible spur of Imogen's captivating presence, his initial enthusiasm for the project seemed to have vanished completely. As his shoulders slumped at the thought of the long, depressing days ahead of him, coupled with the mountain of work still to be done on the estate, it suddenly came to him that this must have been exactly how his father had felt when he lost the love of *his life!* He was even beginning to have some understanding of why the grief-stricken Sir Matthew had banished all thoughts of his firstborn son from his memory and had eventually turned into the embittered, overbearing cynic who had still refused to acknowledge the boy's existence all those years ago.

Beresford was still pondering over this rather lowering notion when Allardyce's voice broke in on his troubled thoughts.

'Daniel has just brought this letter up from the village, sir. It is marked *urgent*, so I thought I had better bring it to you straight away.'

Breaking open the seal of the communication that the butler had handed him, Beresford skimmed through the long-winded legal verbosity that was typical of the legal profession and endeavoured to grasp some gist of the letter's contents. When he finally reached the end of the three-page missive, the colour drained from his face and the violent imprecation that left his lips was delivered with such an explosive force that Seymour, who had been standing at the corner of the building, waiting for his friend to join him, hurried to Beresford's side to discover the reason for his fury.

'Those damned law lords—they have decided that I am the rightful heir!'

His face like a thundercloud, Beresford thrust the letter under Seymour's nose. 'See for yourself—the whole damned lot belongs to me and there is not a thing I can do about it! How, in God's name, do they expect me to run this place from Calcutta?'

'I thought the plan was to get it back on its feet and then put it up for sale?'

'That was when I was under the impression that it belonged to Nicky,' said Beresford, shaking his head. 'I knew that he wanted shot of the responsibility and I intended to put the money into some sort of trust fund for him. Now, I hardly know what to do—I suppose I had better go and inform Blanche of their lordships' decision.'

'There's nothing to stop you selling up and handing over the proceeds to Nicky, I imagine?' ventured Seymour. 'On the other hand, of course, you could simply stay here and run the place yourself!'

'What are you saying?' Beresford glared at his friend. 'How can I stay here?'

'Well, it's hardly beyond the realms of possibility, is it, old man?' reasoned Seymour. 'My guess is that you've grown pretty fond of the place—not to mention one or two of its inhabitants,' he added with a sideways grin. 'Means you can go after the lovely Imo and bring her back and marry her—she ain't going to die of some tropical fever here, now is she?'

A dark flush covered Beresford's face. 'What the devil are you talking about?'

Seymour shrugged. 'Well, you've never made any secret of the fact that you weren't prepared to take a wife only to have her fade away in the heat of the monsoon and it's clear that you are stuck on the girl, so here's your chance. Go for it, I say!'

'I can't,' said Beresford, with a vehement shake of the head. 'You don't understand.'

'I can't believe that you're really prepared to let her go—just like that!' gasped Seymour, staring at his friend in astonishment.

Somewhat reluctant to embark upon a discussion of his innermost feelings, Beresford began to walk away from his friend. 'It's all far too complicated to explain, David,' he said with a weary sigh. 'Even if I had the energy—which I don't—so, leave it, I beg you!'

'Well, if you really think that I am prepared to stand by and watch you make a pig's ear of your life,' returned Seymour hotly, striding after him, 'you clearly do not know me very well! Why the devil can't you just admit you're in love with the girl and go after her, man?'

With a muttered curse, Beresford halted, then, spinning round to confront Seymour, he growled, 'Very well, David— if you really must know—I have already asked Miss Priestley to marry me and she turned me down!'

'Turned you down!' repeated Seymour, astounded. 'But, why? The girl is nutty about you!'

Beresford gave a wry smile. 'Couldn't be further from the truth, I'm afraid, old man!'

For several minutes, Seymour was lost for words.

'Are you sure about that, Matt?' he asked uncertainly, as he followed his friend through the archway into the stable yard. 'I could have sworn that all the signs were—'

'Signs? What signs? What, in God's name, are you rattling on about, David?'

Seymour shrugged. 'Well, the way she was forever looking at you, for a start—and how she was always pretty quick to drop her eyes if she thought you might be looking at her—God's truth, Matt, you've had no shortage of affairs—surely you ain't got through them all with your brains disengaged!'

Beresford came to an abrupt halt and a dangerous glint appeared in his eyes.

'Have you quite finished?' he ground out, angrily. 'I told you to let it be, David—kindly do me the honour of respecting my wishes.'

Seymour eyed his friend sardonically. 'Well, all I can say, Matt, is that you're a bloody fool—but, if that's the way you mean to play it, so be it! I wash my hands of you!' In a high dudgeon, he stalked across the yard, flung open the office door and disappeared inside, violently slamming the door behind him.

Beresford stared after him in dismay. Was this what he was going to be reduced to? he thought sourly. A miserable, foul-tempered despot, just like his father before him? Shuddering at the thought, his eyes travelled disconsolately down the length of the empty driveway, the memory of Imogen's white, set face still painfully fresh in his mind. He could not believe that he had actually let her go, without a word of protest. Was it possible that his friend could have seen what he, despite all his yearning, had missed?

Clenching a fist, he slammed it into the open palm of his other hand, knowing that he could not live the rest of his life in such uncertainty. He had to know the truth! Spinning on his heel, he was just about to head for the stables, fully determined to go after Imogen and beg her to return, when a white-faced Nicholas came tearing out of the back door.

'You had better come at once, Matt!' he burst out, skidding to a halt at Beresford's side. 'It's Jake—he's locked himself inside the laundry room and won't come out—he's in a fearful state, Matt—you must come and deal with it!'

Momentarily baffled, Beresford stared down at his agitated brother. 'Has somebody upset the lad?' he demanded. 'I gave all the new hands strict instructions not to—'

'I really can't tell,' interrupted Nicholas. 'I haven't been able to get a sensible word out of him—he's ranting on about Jessica and wicked men and goodness only knows what!'

'Wicked men?' repeated Beresford, instantly alerted. 'Are you sure he didn't say "bad man"?'

Nicholas hesitated. 'Well, I thought he said "wicked", but I really can't be sure…'

By this time, however, Beresford was already halfway down the passage that led to the kitchen, off which the laundry room was situated. Once inside the kitchen, he was confronted with a noisy unintelligible babble and saw, to his horror, that every one of the dozen or so assorted members of staff who had crammed themselves into the room seemed equally determined to prove that he or she could prevail upon Jake to open the locked door.

Thrusting his way angrily through the jostling crowd, Beresford eventually managed to reach the laundry room door and, turning sharply on his heel, curtly ordered everyone to leave the room immediately. However, having spotted that an exceedingly tearful Amy Sawbridge had risen from her seat at the kitchen table, seemingly intent upon obeying his command, he quickly held up his hand to restrain her.

'Not you, Amy,' he said gently. 'I think I may need your help.'

'I really don't know what happened, sir,' she sobbed. 'I sent him down to the farm, as usual, to get a jug of milk and—barely five minutes later—he flew into the kitchen as if all the devils in hell were chasing after him—dashed straight inside the laundry room and locked both doors against me!'

'How long has he been in there, Amy?'

''Bout an hour—as far as I can judge, sir. It was just before Miss Imogen took off. Oh, if only she were still here, sir,' she wailed. 'She always knew how to calm the poor lad down…'

If only! echoed Beresford silently, then, rigidly putting that thought away from him, he patted the cook's shoulder and said, 'I will do what I can, Amy. Try not to worry.' Then, aware that his words seemed to have had little effect in stemming her noisy weeping, he cast around for something to distract her. 'Tell you what, Amy,' he exclaimed bracingly. 'Why don't you make us a nice hot cup of tea—I am sure Jake will need something to revive him if we can persuade him to come out and join us!'

This practical suggestion seemed to calm the woman. Resolutely wiping her face on the hem of her apron—although Beresford could still hear her snivelling quietly to herself—she set about complying with his request. He, meanwhile, approached the laundry room door.

'Hello, Jake,' he called, in rallying tones. 'It's master here. I need to talk to you. Could you come out and see me for just a moment?'

'Not coming out—bad man coming!' came Jake's quivering tones.

'Then how would it be if I come in there with you, Jake?' asked Beresford brightly.

There was a moment's silence, then the metallic rattle of a key being inserted into in the lock could be heard. Slowly the door opened, just a crack at first, then a few inches more and then, without warning, Jake thrust out a hand, grabbed hold of Beresford's arm and dragged him quickly and none too gently into the laundry room, shoved him to one side, then relocked the door, carefully pocketing the key.

Momentarily taken aback at the boy's latent strength, the startled Beresford was beginning to wonder whether he had bitten off more than he could chew; then, as he watched Jake lower himself to the floor and place his back against the door, he allowed himself to relax and, pulling up a nearby stool, sat down and gave the youth a friendly smile.

'Tell me, Jake, he said gently. 'Tell master what happened.'

'Bad man come back,' muttered the distressed youth, agitatedly rocking from side to side. 'Bad man makes things go dead. Bad man get Jake.'

'No, no, he won't, Jake,' soothed Beresford. 'Master will look after you. Tell master where you saw bad man, Jake.'

Jerking his head towards the window, the lad mumbled, 'Farm', then, his eyes suddenly brightening, he added, 'Castor and Pollux.'

Mystified, Beresford put his hand to his brow. 'Castor and Pollux?'

The youth gave a satisfied nod. 'Castor and Pollux and Miss Jess!'

Beresford stiffened. 'Miss Jess and bad man, too, Jake?' he asked carefully.

The lad's eyes darkened and he shifted uneasily. 'In master's best carriage,' he stammered.

'My carriage?' asked Beresford, now totally confused. Had Jessica gone off in one of the carriages and been waylaid by Wentworth? he wondered in concern, but Jake was shaking his head.

'Old master's carriage,' he supplied. 'Bad man take it away. Took Castor and Pollux!'

Beresford's face cleared as he realised that Jake must be referring to Sir Matthew's two matched greys, which Wentworth had purloined on the day of his departure, and the carriage…?

'Nice red carriage, Jake?' he offered tentatively, suddenly recalling Chadwick's description of his father's missing curricle.

'Nice red carriage,' repeated the lad, then shuddered. 'Bad man saw Jake!'

'Did he hurt you, Jake?'

Jake shook his head. 'Bad man laughed. Miss Jess cross.'

'Did Miss Jess get into the red carriage, Jake?' asked Beresford, as a sudden sickening thought came to him.

'Yes,' replied Jake. 'Bad man chase Jake!'

Very slowly, so as not to frighten the lad, Beresford rose to his feet and held out his hand. 'Up you get, Jake,' he said. 'Time for a nice cup of tea, I think. Bad man has gone now.'

Long gone and far away, by now, if I am any judge, he conjectured dismally.

Jake put out his hand and allowed Beresford to haul him to his feet, then, diving into his pocket, he brought forth the door key and silently handed it to his master, who quickly unlocked the door.

Propelling him into the kitchen, Beresford instructed the youth's grateful mother to give him something to eat, and under no circumstances to allow anyone else in the household to question him.

Hurrying across to the office, he beckoned the now somewhat remorseful Seymour into the stable yard, where, in a few concise sentences, he gave him his own, pieced together, version of the little bits of information he had managed to extract from Jake.

'I will have to go after them, David,' he told him. 'But it needs to kept from the rest of the household—Jessica's reputation is at stake here—possibly her life, and it won't do to get them all up in arms before I know exactly what the scoundrel is about!' He gave a wry grimace. 'Sorry, I lost my temper, David,' he said, awkwardly. 'I know you are the best of friends—would you be willing to accompany me?'

'Try going without me!' Seymour grinned. 'But first, a quick dash upstairs for our weapons, I think!'

'Been carrying mine for days,' returned his friend, nonchalantly patting his jacket pocket. Turning towards the stable, he called over his shoulder, 'Don't be long—I'll get the horses saddled.'

Ten minutes later they were galloping down the lane towards the main highway. Upon reaching the junction, however, Beresford reined in, uncertain whether to proceed to the left or to the right.

'East or west, I wonder?' He groaned. 'We have no way of knowing the fellow's intentions!'

'I can't think that he would want to hurt the girl,' said Seymour. 'What would be the point? Besides which, it does seem that she went with him willingly—perhaps he is after a ransom of some sort?'

'From what we have learned about his previous activities, I doubt if he means to return Jessica to us—unsullied—as it were!' Beresford ground out savagely. 'But we can't afford to waste time standing here speculating—we have to decide.'

'Wait!'

Pointing his crop a little distance up the road, Seymour indicated a carriage that appeared to have broken down, its driver sitting on the grass verge alongside his fractured vehicle, with his two horses peacefully grazing nearby.

'That chap looks to have been there for some time—possibly he remembers seeing the carriage go by.'

On approaching the man, who was waiting for his groom to return with a replacement pole, they were able to ascertain that he had indeed seen the very curricle that Beresford described, it having passed by him almost an hour ago.

'In a bit of a hurry, too, it seemed to me,' he offered. 'Runaways, were they? Off to the border, I'll be bound!'

'Gretna Green!' groaned Beresford, clapping his hand to his forehead. So that was what the bounder was about!

Then, kicking his heels, he wheeled his horse around and called over his shoulder, 'To the Great North Road it is then, David! We will make more enquiries when we get to Doncaster—at the pace he is travelling, I doubt if his horses will last above twenty-five miles!'

Chapter Twenty-Four

$\mathcal{A}$s the yellow bounder rolled out of the gates and away from Thornfield, Imogen sat rigid in her seat, the hot tears coursing down her cheeks and, although she kept her head averted from Miss Widdecombe, her elderly companion was fully aware of the girl's distress.

After Imogen had confessed her feelings for Beresford, the governess had made a point of paying particular attention to his attitude towards her friend. Upon careful consideration, she would have been prepared to swear that the man was not as indifferent to Imogen as he seemed to be doing his best to appear. However, when it became clear that Beresford had no intention of trying to prevent Imogen from leaving, Miss Widdecombe began to wonder if she had, perhaps, been mistaken in her observations and began to ferret in the dark recesses of her mind, trying to recall something of her own past heartache. Eventually, having reached the conclusion that there were no words of comfort that would help to alleviate her young friend's suffering, she decided to remain silent and keep her counsel for some more propitious moment.

Unable to rid her mind of the stony expression on Beresford's face when he had bidden her goodbye, Imogen was certain that the image of that cold, unrelenting look in his eyes would remain with her for ever. She still could not understand why, having learned that she was about to leave, he had, at first, seemed to be violently opposed to her going but then, totally out of the blue, had rebuffed her with such a cold-hearted snub. It could hardly have been because he was sorry to see her go, she reasoned, for, after that embarrassing interlude in the library and the resultant awkwardness between them, which had finally culminated in a reluctant proposal of marriage from him, one would have supposed that he would have been glad to have found himself let off the hook. Although it was true that he made considerable effort to retrieve the situation, his undoubted skill in this department was hardly surprising since, in his line of work, he must be well used to extracting himself from awkward predicaments.

In spite of all this, she could not help remembering that there had been moments when she could have sworn that she had sensed—what? Concern? A slight warmth? Some sort of regard, perhaps? She shook her head, but although she was unable to pinpoint the exact sensation, she knew that she was hardly likely to forget the breathless agitation that it had engendered within her.

She heaved a trembling sigh, telling herself that it would do little good to repine over what could never be, then, delving into her reticule for a handkerchief, she surreptitiously (or so she imagined) dabbed at her wet cheeks, hoping to remove any telltale signs of woe.

Miss Widdecombe, who had been affecting a keen interest in the passing scenery, had, at the same time, been registering the reflection of Imogen's movements in the carriage's window and judged that now might be a suitable time to engage her young companion in conversation.

'One ought to have guessed that Jessica would take it upon herself to try to spoil our departure,' she said spiritedly. 'She has no thought in her head for anyone else's need but her own.

I trust that she will be suitable chastened, when she discovers that her ploy to prevent your leaving was unsuccessful.'

Imogen inclined her head in agreement, adding thoughtfully, 'Although it does seem rather odd that she should have gone to so much trouble to create such a scene and then not capitalise from it. Had we been prepared to wait just a little while longer, she would probably have made some sort of sudden, dramatic appearance, fairly confident of the fact that we would all be so relieved to see her that no one would bother to chastise her— grabbing the limelight at the same time, of course!'

Gratified to see that Imogen seemed to be making some effort to put her woes behind her, the governess let out a little snort of laughter.

'She will be mortified when she finds that we have left— it would hardly surprise me to learn that she is, even as we speak, sitting at her desk, penning a letter to express her remorse—and which, as we shall soon discover, will be spelled out in her usual haphazard fashion!'

A wistful smile played on Imogen's lips as she tried to picture the scene. Leaving Thornfield had caused her far more pain than she had anticipated. She had been so obsessed with getting away from Beresford that, apart from her aunt and Nicholas, she had been left with barely any time to take her leave of the other long-standing members of the household. She had felt particularly guilty about Bertha who, she knew, had been totally overcome on being informed that her newly regained position was, once again, in jeopardy and, although Imogen had begged her aunt to keep the abigail on, she had to suppose that it would be merely a matter of time before the house changed hands, leaving every one of the servants fearing for their jobs. On top of all this, there was Portia, who had been her mount for these past five years. Leaving her behind had been, almost, the most terrible wrench of all, but, even had Imogen been able to arrange to have the mare transported up to Kendal, she knew that, given her present state of finances, finding suitable stabling and care was likely to have proved to be far more costly than she could reasonably afford.

All of a sudden, she was jerked out of her reverie, as the carriage started to rock violently and, for one frightful moment, both ladies seemed in imminent danger of being catapulted off their seats on to the floor. To their relief, the danger quickly passed, the carriage halted and the postilion came hurrying back to determine that his passengers had suffered no harm.

'Had to swing over to make room for a horseman coming through,' he told them, in an aggrieved explanation of his swerve. 'Practically on top of my nearside wheel, the hotheaded idiot was!'

After Imogen had assured the boy that she and her companion were unhurt, he remounted, clicked his tongue to set the horses in motion once more and the journey proceeded without further incident.

Beresford, having recognised the hired chaise the moment he spotted it on the road ahead, was almost overcome by a very powerful urge to ride up to it, wrench open the door and challenge Imogen on the spot. It was with considerable reluctance that he forced himself to drag his mind back to the rather more pressing issue of his young sister's safety and, knowing that he had very little choice in the matter, he was obliged to grit his teeth and press on.

Nevertheless, he was quite unable to resist the temptation to take a quick peek inside, in the hope of catching a glimpse of Imogen as he passed, but, at the very last minute, having remembered that she was seated on the carriage's nearside, he recklessly swung his mount through a barely visible gap in the traffic, gained the side of the road and, charging up the grassy verge, finally drew level with the chaise.

Unfortunately, when he cast his eyes towards the window,

he saw that Imogen's head was turned towards her companion and all he got for his foolish and rather dangerous manoeuvre was an angry curse from the postilion when he squeezed past the swaying vehicle.

'Damned stupid thing to do!' exclaimed his friend in astonishment, when he at last caught up with him. 'Trying to kill yourself, are you?'

'Idiotic, I know,' said Beresford, somewhat shamefacedly. 'It was Imogen's chaise, you see.'

'So I was aware, but I doubt if she would enjoy the spectacle of seeing you spread-eagled under its wheels!' returned the irate Scymour; then, having observed his friend's gloomy expression, he bit back any further condemnation, reminding Beresford instead that Imogen was also making for Doncaster.

'Just let's track this beggar down and get Jessica away from him, then you will have all the time in the world to make your peace with Miss Priestley!'

For the next half-hour, the two riders concentrated their efforts on threading their way through the increasing volume of traffic on the highway that led into the town. Gradually, as the open countryside on either side of them started to give way to, firstly, a straggle, and then a considerable proliferation of buildings of all shapes and sizes, Beresford urged his friend to keep his eyes peeled for a livery stable or an inn at which Wentworth might be holed up.

After enquiring at several such establishments without success, they were both beginning to feel slightly disheartened at the mammoth task they had taken on until, at last, upon riding in to the stable yard of a neat little inn that was set back some distance from the teeming highway, it would seem that their dogged perseverance had not been in vain. There, in front of them, stood the very carriage for which they had been searching! Leaping from their horses, they entered the taproom from the rear of the building and sought out the proprietor of the inn, who turned out to be a very large, apple-cheeked woman who, bustling from behind the bar, introduced herself as Molly Corbett.

'All my rooms are taken, I'm afraid, if it's accommodation you're seeking,' she said sorrowfully. 'But you could try the Queen's Head further up the road.'

After assuring the landlady that they were not looking for rooms, Beresford casually mentioned the scarlet curricle out in the yard and enquired whether the owner might happen to be one of her guests.

'Oh, yes,' she beamed. 'Fancy little rig that, isn't it—quite a few of my customers have been admiring it—young couple came in, not fifteen minutes since—poor little wifey had fainted with the heat, it seems. Luckily, I still had the one room vacant, so I helped him to get her to bed straight away. Gentleman asked for brandy for her and I were that worried about the poor wee lass that I took up the bottle myself. In a regular state she was, threshing about all over the place! Her husband soon got her to calm down, though.'

'Is the "gentleman" still upstairs, do you know?' enquired Beresford through clenched teeth. He was wondering how the devil he was going to get Jessica out of Wentworth's clutches without revealing her identity and ruining her reputation. 'Would it be possible to have a word with him, do you suppose?'

'About his curricle, you mean?' returned Mrs Corbett doubtfully. 'Shouldn't think he would want to be disturbed at the moment, not with—'

The rest of her sentence remained unfinished, however, as, all at once, the air was rent with a piercing scream, followed by the sound of breaking glass.

Thrusting the landlady to one side, Beresford leapt for the door into the inn's hallway, found the staircase and charged up the stairs with Seymour in hot pursuit.

They had no difficulty in discerning from which room the noise had come, since they could hear Wentworth's angry bellowing quite clearly. At a signal from Beresford, both men took two steps back and then hurled themselves at the door, parting it from its hinges. Staggering into the room, they were confronted with a complete shambles. Broken objects were strewn everywhere, the curtains had been ripped from their rail and a large pier glass lay shattered on the floor. Although it was evident that Jessica had put up a determined resistance, Wentworth had, in the end, overcome her and, his face suffused with rage, was even now, under their very eyes, attempting to pin the terrified girl down on to the bed.

In two strides, Beresford reached the struggling pair and, grabbing the man's collar, hauled him violently to his feet and served him a forceful uppercut to his jaw. Instantly, Wentworth keeled over and crumpled to the floor, but Beresford, ignoring his pleas for mercy, dragged him upright by his cravat and proceeded to hammer his fist into the man's face.

'That's for Jake!' he ground out, as he delivered yet another ferocious blow. 'And that's for young Rosie Juggins!'

His anger was such that, had not Seymour pulled him away from his almost unconscious victim, he might well have killed the man there and then!

'Hold hard, Matt,' his friend urged him. 'Mrs Corbett has sent someone to fetch the constable—best leave him to the law, man! Time to give some thought to your sister!'

His chest heaving, Beresford forced himself to turn away from the bruised and battered heap at his feet and concentrate his attention on Jessica who, despite Seymour's desperate attempts to persuade her to leave the room with him, was still cowering on the bed, too terrified to move.

Lowering himself to her side, Beresford drew the shuddering girl into his arms and gently stroked her disordered curls away from her tear-streaked face.

'It's all right, sweetheart,' he crooned softly. 'You are safe now—the fiend cannot hurt you any more.'

'Oh, Matt, Matt!' she sobbed into his chest. 'I have been so foolish. He told me that he would take me to London.'

Beresford was still struggling to find the words to ask his sister the one question that was causing him the greatest disquiet when the landlady, accompanied by the parish constable and two of his henchmen, hurried into the room.

'I've explained to the constable as best I can, sir,' heaved Mrs Corbett who, having run up and down the stairs several times during the fracas, was red in the face and gasping for breath. 'The other gentleman told me how that man took the young lady off—if only I'd realised that she was trying to tell me something!'

Beresford stood up. 'I would appreciate it if you could take my sister to another room while I talk to the constable, Mrs Corbett,' he said. 'Perhaps you could mix her a drink of brandy and hot water to calm her nerves?'

As Jessica grabbed at his hand and cast an anxious glance up at him, Beresford bent down and murmured gently, 'It will be all right, Jess. I promise you—go with Mrs Corbett—she will look after you. I will be with you directly—as soon as I've dealt with this matter.'

With Seymour's assistance, the motherly landlady helped the weeping girl to her feet and led her to the doorway, saying, 'I will take her down to the small parlour in the front, sir—no one is allowed in there without my permission.'

In a few succinct words, Beresford managed to supply the constable with sufficient information for him to agree to have his henchmen take Wentworth off to the local jailhouse but, just as they were about to haul the defeated man out of the room, Beresford put up a hand.

'Might I have a word, before you remove him?' he asked the constable. 'There are one or two questions I wish to put to him.'

Shrugging, the officer of the law told him to 'help himself' and, after beckoning the chary-eyed Wentworth back into the room, he walked to the door and began a muttered conversation with his colleagues.

Staring at the bloodied-face wretch now standing before him, Beresford demanded that Wentworth explain himself.

'For, as I am sure you realise,' he pointed out grimly, 'the crimes of attempted murder and abduction carry the death sentence. I suppose you thought that, by compromising my sister, Sir Matthew's fortune would be within your reach—which, I must presume, was your ultimate goal?'

'Anything that she got would be mine by rights, if she was my wife,' came the man's surly reply. 'And, if you hadn't stuck your oar in, she would have been only too glad to marry me by now, I can tell you!'

Beresford clenched his fists and it was all he could to keep from throttling the craven brute.

'And Nicholas?' he grated.

At Wentworth's careless shrug, a spurt of fury leapt into Beresford's eyes.

'If Nicholas's demise was also part of your master plan,' he said, in an icy monotone, 'then I am more than delighted to be the one to inform you that he has not, in fact, succeeded his father—*I* have! Thus, Thornfield becomes *my* property and, as with the rest of my possessions, will, at my death, pass to *my* estate, which does not, at present, benefit any of my father's second family. So, even had you succeeded in getting my sister to the border—apart from a paltry ransom, perhaps—your vile scheme would have availed you nothing!'

Having satisfied himself that he and Seymour had arrived just in time to prevent Wentworth from deflowering Jessica, Beresford indicated that he had finished with his prisoner. Before the officer left the room, however, he told him that, in order to preserve his sister's good name, he would be withdrawing the charge of abduction. Being a family man himself, the constable was inclined to agree with this decision, pointing out that the twin charges of attempted murder and fraudulent extortion were more than enough to secure Wentworth's transportation to some far-flung penal colony.

Following the constable down the stairs, Beresford made his way into the little front parlour of the inn, where he found that the erstwhile Mrs Corbett had managed to persuade Jessica to calm down sufficiently for him to set about gently extracting her version of events.

Frequently interrupted by further bouts of weeping, interspersed with hiccoughing sobs, Jessica confessed her sorry tale. It seemed that she had come upon Wentworth when she had been sulking in the orchard the previous evening and, having listened to the catalogue of grievances that she poured out to him, the man had beguiled her into coming away with him.

'He promised to take me to London,' she whimpered. 'He said that he had an aunt living in Knightsbridge who knew all the best people and she would have no trouble introducing me into society. I didn't want to wait until next year!'

Holding back the reprimand that threatened to spring to his lips, Beresford asked quietly, 'But surely you were aware that the man had made off with a good deal of your father's property?'

Jessica shook her head. 'I didn't know that,' she said plaintively. 'He told me you had put him off for flirting with me in the stable yard!'

'I take it that you arranged to abscond with him before your cousin left this morning?'

Jessica dissolved into tears once more. 'He told me we were going to London,' she wailed, 'but, when we got on to the turnpike, I knew at once that we were going in the wrong direction. I begged and begged him to stop and put me down, but he just told me to stop snivelling and whipped the horses to go even faster!'

'And then he brought you to this inn?'

She nodded. 'He refused to stop, even when I told him that I felt sick and needed a drink of water. I was getting so frightened that I must have fainted and the next thing I knew I was lying on the bed in that room. I tried to tell the landlady what was happening, but he was pinching me so very badly—look!' Holding out her arm, she displayed the painful evidence of Wentworth's vicious assault.

Beresford winced. 'Although, if the state of the room is anything to go by, I would say that you did put up a pretty good fight,' he pointed out encouragingly.

Jessica responded with a watery smile. 'When he told me that he meant to marry me, I sort of lost my temper,' she confessed. 'I jumped off the bed and starting throwing things at him. I tried to make as much noise as I possibly could—I knew it was my only hope,' she finished wretchedly.

Beresford gathered her up into his arms and kissed her brow. 'It was very foolish of you to put your trust in such a man, Jess,' he admonished her gently. 'I hope that this will teach you to be a little less headstrong in the future. You will have your Season, I promise you, but not until you learn to conduct yourself in a more ladylike manner!'

'More like Imo, you mean?' she replied, fresh tears filling her emerald eyes. 'And I didn't even say a proper goodbye to her!'

No more did I, thought Beresford dully, as he soothed away his sister's tears and settled her back in her chair.

The hired chaise rolled into the forecourt of the Crown and Anchor just as the constable, ably assisted by his two henchmen, was bundling the now deflated Wentworth into a closed wagon, but the chaise's occupants, being far too concerned with trying to establish the quality of their prospective accommodation, did not witness the event.

'Here we are then, ladies,' said the post-boy cheerfully, letting down the carriage step. 'If ye'd care to go inside and make yourselves known to Mrs Corbett, I'll get your stuff unloaded. Dare say the missus'll have arranged for a handcart to take your hampers up to the Queen's Head, ready to be put on the morning stage.'

Pressing a florin into his hand, Imogen thanked the man for his services and, with Miss Widdecombe in tow, made her way into the small, square hallway of the inn, off which was a staircase that led, she presumed, up to the bedrooms.

Alongside the staircase was a passageway that led down to one closed door and there were two further doors on their right, both of which were also closed. However, since she could just make out the sound of glasses clinking, coupled with the quiet murmur of voices issuing from behind the further of the two doors, she took that to be the taproom. They were just about to knock on the remaining door when it opened and an exceedingly large, but reassuringly cheerful-looking woman came bustling forth.

'I saw your chaise arriving, my dears,' she declared brightly. 'May I take it that you are the Misses Priestley and Widdecombe?'

'*Imogen!*'

From inside the room there came a strangled gasp and Beresford, his expression a mixture of jubilation and disbelief, suddenly appeared behind the landlady. Hurriedly thrusting himself through the restricted gap between Mrs Corbett's ample hips and the door jamb, he came to a stumbling halt in front of Imogen, unable to tear his eyes away from her incredulous gaze.

'Good Heavens! Mr Beresford!' proclaimed Miss Widdecombe. 'How on earth did you manage to find us so quickly?'

Somewhat puzzled as to what the governess could possibly mean by this remark, simultaneous frowns puckered both Imogen's and Beresford's brows.

Mrs Corbett, confused as to this new turn of events, stepped forward. 'These ladies are acquaintances of yours, sir?' she enquired.

Grasping the unresisting Imogen's arm, Beresford nodded and began to propel her into the room. 'Miss Priestley is my young sister's cousin,' he explained briefly. 'She will know how to deal with the matter.'

'Oh, Imogen!'

Jessica hurled herself at her cousin and the exuberance of her greeting would have sent Imogen to the floor had not Beresford steadied the pair.

'Jess?' faltered Imogen, as she hastily extracted herself from his hold. 'How do you come to be here?'

As Jessica's desperate tale unfolded for the second time, Imogen could only stare at the girl in blank horror.

'I know I have been very foolish,' finished her cousin shamefacedly. 'If it had not been for Matt…!'

'Yes, indeed,' replied Imogen fervently. 'We must all be very thankful that he got here in time to prevent—' Then, catching Beresford's eyes on her, she blushed and did not finish her sentence.

Miss Widdecombe, however, had no such reservations and, fixing Jessica with an admonitory frown, she exclaimed, 'I hope you realise that, had not your brother arrived when he did, my girl, you would have found yourself compromised beyond redemption and where would all your fancy plans have been then, do you suppose?'

As Jessica's face crumpled once more, Imogen shook her head and protested, 'Pray do not be so hard on the child, Widdy! She will have learned her lesson, I am sure!'

'I sincerely hope so,' sniffed the governess then, looking up at Beresford, she said pointedly, 'I take it that you will be taking Jessica straight back to Thornfield?'

'That was my intention,' he replied, his eyes still on Imogen.

Having formulated a neat little scheme in her mind, Miss Widdecombe nodded. 'It occurs to me that Jessica will feel far more comfortable in a closed carriage than travelling back in her father's curricle,' she said. 'I imagine that our hired chaise will still be in the yard, and, if it would be of any help to you, I would be happy to accompany her back home. Perhaps your friend Mr Seymour might escort us?'

Neither Beresford nor Seymour had any difficulty latching on to the governess's ultimate aim, but Imogen, unsure of her role in Miss Widdecombe's proposed scheme, shook her head, saying, 'No, Widdy. I should be the one to take Jessica home.'

Holding his breath, Beresford looked at Miss Widdecombe in mute appeal, but it seemed that she had already prepared herself for Imogen's resistance.

'I do not think I would care to remain here on my own for such a long time, my dear,' she said apologetically. 'You would not be back before nightfall. I do believe that it would be far better if I were to accompany Jessica and you were to travel back in the curricle with Mr Beresford.'

'Excellent idea!' chorused Seymour and Beresford in unison.

'But what about our own plans, Widdy?' asked the bewildered Imogen.

'Oh, come, my dear,' reproved the governess. 'Surely your cousin's welfare is more important at the moment—another couple of days will make very little difference to us!'

Imogen, who was beginning to get the feeling that she was, somehow or other, being dragooned, was unable to conjure up any acceptable reason why she should not accede to Miss Widdecombe's suggestion.

'If you are willing to delay your plans for a day or two,' ventured Beresford, in desperation, 'I would deem it an absolute privilege to provide you with a more comfortable means of travel than a public stage—with the addition of a couple of outriders to take care of any little difficulties that you might encounter on your journey.'

Smiling expressively, Miss Widdecombe nodded. 'I would be perfectly happy to settle for that,' she said.

Outgunned and outnumbered, Imogen knew that she had no choice but to bow to the majority decision.

Less than an hour later, however, after they had all partaken of a light luncheon and she found herself standing out in the stable yard waving farewell to the chaise's latest occupants, a little ripple of apprehension ran through her as she realised that she was, once again, alone with the man that she had gone to so much trouble to get away from.

'Perhaps we might go back into the parlour for a few minutes, Miss Priestley,' he said, offering her his arm.

'Oh, I hardly think so,' she stammered. 'I see that the ostler is already hitching up the curricle—we really ought not to keep the horses standing.'

His patience near breaking point, Beresford drew a deep breath and took a step towards her.

'To hell with the horses!' he said softly and, before Imogen knew what he was about, he had shot out his hand, grabbed her by the wrist and was attempting to pull her over to the inn's rear entrance.

Imogen tried to free herself from his grasp. 'Let me go, Mr Beresford!' she demanded indignantly.

As a slow smile crossed his face, he shook his head. 'What you ask is quite impossible, Miss Priestley— I am afraid I find that I cannot let you go—not now—not ever, in fact!'

'I beg you to release me, Mr Beresford,' implored Imogen, heavily conscious of the curious glances of the many bystanders. 'Everyone is staring at us!'

'Let them stare,' he said recklessly. 'The whole world may watch and listen, for all I care—I love you, Imogen—come back to Thornfield with me!'

Her face flamed. 'W-what are you saying, Mr Beresford— is this another of your poor attempts at humour?'

His lips twisted. 'Don't fight me any more, Imogen—I love you so much and I believe that you love me, too.'

'You love me?' whispered Imogen, convinced that any minute now she would wake up in her bed at Thornfield to discover that everything that had happened that morning had been some unfathomable dream. 'How can you love me?'

'How can I not?' he groaned. 'Your very presence has had the effect of turning my whole world upside down. Your rejection of me has driven me to the point of madness. Without you, nothing in my life makes any sense.'

Trembling, she raised her eyes to his, desperately wanting to believe his words.

The heartfelt yearning within his eyes almost took her breath away. It was as though she could see into his very soul. All at once, a wild joy seemed to overtake her reason. It was true! He loved her, he truly loved her!

'Marry me, Imogen—please! Marry me and help me put Thornfield back into shape.'

'Because you believe you compromised me?'

Even though her heart was in her throat, she found that she could not resist the provocative challenge.

He sighed. 'I thought we had agreed to put that particular episode behind us,' he said resignedly, 'but, if it will make you see sense, I am perfectly prepared to make sure that you are well and truly compromised right here and now in front of this entire congregation.'

Then, before she was aware of his intentions, he had pulled her into his arms and fastened his lips upon hers. No sooner did she feel the shuddering heat of the passion of his fervent embrace, than all resistance fell away and, to the astonishment and amusement of the assembled onlookers, she wrapped her arms around his neck and pressed herself to him with such wild abandon that it took every ounce of Beresford's self-control to remember where they were.

Forcing himself to draw back from her kiss, he disengaged her hands from his neck and, holding her slightly away from him, gazed down into her shining eyes.

'Tell me that you love me, Imogen,' he said urgently. 'Promise me that you will never leave me!'

For a moment, she was unable to speak, so completely intoxicated by the depth of his ardour was she, but then, as her silence continued, an anxious, searching look appeared in his eyes. Suddenly she was filled with exhilaration. Her fears were unfounded! All the uncertain torment that she had suffered vanished away in a cloud of euphoria.

'I love you with all my heart, Matt Beresford,' she answered unsteadily. 'I believe I have loved you ever since I first set eyes on you.'

Overcome with emotion, Beresford crushed her to his chest and, oblivious of the ripple of applause coming from the delighted spectators, bent his head and hungrily sought her lips once more.

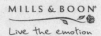

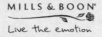

MILLS & BOON®

Live the emotion

Historical
romance™

TEXAS GOLD
by Carolyn Davidson

Faith McDowell had run from her marriage and made
her home on a Texas ranch – but Max McDowell wanted
her back. It had taken him three years to find her,
and he wasn't going home without her – it was a matter
of principle. Until he realised he was more in love
with the woman Faith had become than he ever could
have imagined…

HIS DUTY, HER DESTINY
by Juliet Landon

Sir Fergus Melrose would honour his betrothal – but
first he must claim his betrothed! His task wouldn't be
easy. Lady Nicola Coldyngham was no longer the young
lass who had worshipped his every move, and nor was
she willing to give up her heart. Her defiance became
his challenge – a challenge he was unable to resist…

On sale 3rd March 2006

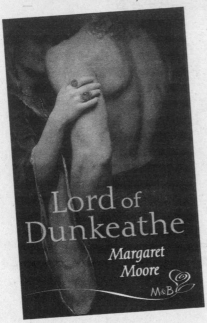

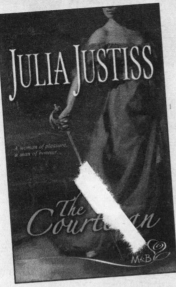

FREE

2 BOOKS AND A SURPRISE GIFT!

We would like to take this opportunity to thank you for reading this Mills & Boon® book by offering you the chance to take TWO more specially selected titles from the Historical Romance™ series absolutely FREE! We're also making this offer to introduce you to the benefits of the Reader Service™—

- ★ **FREE home delivery**
- ★ **FREE gifts and competitions**
- ★ **FREE monthly Newsletter**
- ★ **Books available before they're in the shops**
- ★ **Exclusive Reader Service offers**

Accepting these FREE books and gift places you under no obligation to buy; you may cancel at any time, even after receiving your free shipment. Simply complete your details below and return the entire page to the address below. You don't even need a stamp!

YES! Please send me 2 free Historical Romance books and a surprise gift. I understand that unless you hear from me, I will receive 4 superb new titles every month for just £3.65 each, postage and packing free. I am under no obligation to purchase any books and may cancel my subscription at any time. The free books and gift will be mine to keep in any case.

H6ZEE

Ms/Mrs/Miss/Mr..Initials ....
BLOCK CAPITALS PLEASE

Surname ....

Address ....

....

....Postcode ....

Send this whole page to:
The Reader Service, FREEPOST CN81, Croydon, CR9 3WZ